Undressed

Vicki Lewis Thompson

Suzanne Forster

Alison Kent

Undressed

HARLEQUIN®

TORONTO • NEW YORK • LONDON
AMSTERDAM • PARIS • SYDNEY • HAMBURG
STOCKHOLM • ATHENS • TOKYO • MILAN • MADRID
PRAGUE • WARSAW • BUDAPEST • AUCKLAND

ISBN 0-373-83679-1

UNDRESSED

www.eHarlequin.com

Printed in U.S.A.

CONTENTS

ILLICIT DREAMS

Vicki Lewis Thompson

Prologue

May

HUNTER JORDAN was getting some…again.

Lindsay peered at the lighted dial of her alarm clock. Sheesh. He'd had highly orgasmic sex less than an hour ago. At least that's what Lindsay had concluded from the breathless cries of his girlfriend and his own groan of satisfaction. Now they were starting over. What was with the man?

Or more to the point, *who* was with the man? A very lucky woman, that's who. A blond 38D of a woman, as she'd once seen with her own eyes. Meanwhile Lindsay, a 32B who hadn't had sex—orgasmic or otherwise—since she'd moved here last year, was forced to listen to the steady thump-thump-thump of Hunter's headboard hitting the wall that separated their apartments.

Well, okay, she wasn't exactly forced to listen. She could go into her living room, turn up Sting on the stereo and drown them out, which she'd done during their first go-round. Sort of. Towards the end she'd snuck back into her bedroom to catch the grand finale, pathetic creature that she was. Judging from the way his girlfriend had reacted during their six-month-long relationship, Hunter orchestrated really terrific finales.

Lindsay had to take her kicks where she could find them.

Apparently Hunter was about to create another big fat O for Silicon Sally. She knew because the moaning had commenced. No man had ever made Lindsay moan like that. Well, unless she counted the time that idiot Sherman had mashed her head up against the headboard, repeatedly, and nearly given her a concussion before he realized she was crying for help and not begging him to thrust harder.

Hunter would never make that kind of miscalculation. Anybody could tell he understood women from the way he'd photographed them for this month's swimsuit issue of *Instant Replay*. Lindsay was pretty sure his girlfriend was the one in the purple bikini on the cover. It was hard to tell since she tended not to parade outside Hunter's apartment in a string bikini, but her chest measurements were about right and her face had the high-cheekbone look of a professional model.

Oh, yeah, Hunter understood women, at least according to the cries of feminine pleasure coming through the wall. They escalated in pitch and reached a stirring crescendo. Lindsay was damned stirred, herself. She waited for Hunter to add his deep groans to the mix, but instead the girlfriend started gasping once again, running her words together—*yesohyesohyes*—in a clear indication that Hunter was going for a multi.

Lindsay flung the covers aside and got out of bed, heading for the living room and her stereo. Banging her fist on the wall wasn't an option. She'd been listening to this symphony two or three times a week for six months now, and banging on the wall at this point would let Hunter know she'd been playing voyeur.

She should just buy a vibrator and be done with it, but going down that road was admitting she really wasn't going to have sex with a guy for a very long time. As a perennial optimist, Lindsay kept hoping that wasn't true.

Stomping into the living room, she flipped on her CD player and jacked up the sound, operating by the light from a street lamp outside the window. Then she decided to eat a banana for the oral satisfaction. God, she needed a boyfriend. Hell, she needed a *date*.

Unfortunately, last year's decision to stop catching guys on the rebound had seriously narrowed the field. Her best friend Shauna said it was her nurturing Cancer personality at work. Whatever the reason, she had a real gift for attracting men who'd been recently dumped. Then, after she'd healed their broken hearts, the schmucks moved on. Apparently they didn't like being reminded that once upon a time they'd been extremely vulnerable.

She bit into the banana. Damned poor substitute. Increasingly, the world of men seemed to be divided into the recently dumped and the already involved. Shauna had somehow stumbled upon that rare species, the unattached and unwounded male, and was now engaged to him. Watching Shauna walk around with the satisfied expression of a woman who could have sex whenever she wanted didn't help Lindsay's frustration level any.

As her maid of honor, Lindsay also was required to spend time with Shauna in Divine Events, the wedding shop from hell. Oh, it would be a fabulous place if a girl happened to be having good sex, or even the prospect of good sex. They had this red leather book of sexual fantasies in the reception area, and the pages were meant to be torn out, according to Shauna, who had done her share of tearing. But then Shauna had a guy to act out those fantasies with.

Then there was Lindsay's private torture of living next door to a sex god with bedroom-brown eyes and a body built for loving. Hunter had been part of the already-involved category when he'd moved in, and he was still in that category, damn it. Lindsay couldn't imagine anybody dumping Hunter. He had that killer combo—bad-boy charisma and good-guy charm.

She'd observed the bad-boy charisma from afar, but she'd seen the good-guy charm up close, in the apartment's laundry room. After meeting there by chance one Saturday morning, she and Hunter had discovered they had so much fun talking while the clothes washed that they'd made a habit of it ever since. Therefore she could never, ever let him know that she could hear him having sex through their shared apartment wall. Too embarrassing.

And man-oh-man, did he have sex. Even over Sting at mega-decibels, Lindsay could hear the wild cries, both bass and treble this time, as Hunter and his chesty girlfriend shared their climactic moment. No doubt about it, Lindsay had to get a vibrator...or a genuine, testosterone-laden, certified-to-make-you-come, ready and extremely willing man.

Chapter One

July

AS HE DID every weeknight, Hunter took the "L" from the *Instant Replay* offices in downtown Chicago to his apartment building. Crammed in with other commuters, he tried to keep cool, but it wasn't easy. The furnace outside set at ninety-five degrees was trying to melt the train, plus, as usual, he was thinking about Lindsay Scott.

He wondered if she'd be home from the bank where she worked, wondered if this was the night he should go over and ask for a cup of sugar, or the current *TV Guide,* or a stamp or a couple of fresh batteries for his remote. Those were the best excuses he'd come up with, and they were all lame. Meanwhile, he was burning up with frustration.

The problem had started when they'd accidentally met in the laundry room. Ever since they'd decided to wash clothes together on Saturday mornings, he'd been having lust-filled dreams about Lindsay. The first time it had happened, he'd thought it was because Pamela was away on a shoot and he was horny.

But then Pamela had come back from Arizona and they'd returned to their routine of wonderful sex. Yet the dreams about Lindsay hadn't stopped. In fact, they'd become more graphic. In his dream, she'd prance into the laundry room in her normal Saturday style, her brown hair caught up in a ponytail or in one of those butterfly clips, her freckled face without makeup, her shirttails tied at her waist and her ragged cutoffs brushing her smooth thighs.

She'd see him there and pause. Her blue eyes would darken with lust. And they'd do it on top of the washing machine.

Thoughts of Lindsay had started invading his daytime activities, too. The night he'd fantasized about Lindsay while having sex with Pamela, he'd known he had to face the situation like a man. And it wasn't Pamela's fault, so he'd hated like hell to hurt the woman who'd been a terrific bed partner for more than six months.

He'd tried to stroke her ego during the breakup dinner. She'd demanded to know if there was another woman, and he'd told a half truth when he'd said no. After all, he'd only cheated on Pamela in his dreams. Before meeting Lindsay, Hunter had thought maybe Pamela would wind up being his happily-ever-after. Eventually. When he was ready for that kind of thing.

Obviously he wasn't ready to be anybody's husband, though, if he could be distracted so easily while having outstanding sex with a woman he liked. Still, he had to find out where this obsession with Lindsay would take him. Unfortunately, Lindsay knew he'd been involved with Pamela. And although he'd broken off with her three weeks ago, he couldn't appear at Lindsay's door with, "Hi, my girlfriend's been out of the picture for three weeks, so let's have sex!"

The time just wasn't right for him to be so forward as to ask Lindsay out. Not yet. And he couldn't use the laundry room as the venue for escalating the relationship. No, he'd leave that setup alone, because it was so tied in with his fantasy that he didn't trust himself to stay in control. He'd considered switching banks, just so he'd have an excuse to visit hers and have her wait on him at the teller window. But that was way too obvious.

Better to find some reason to knock on her door in the evening, and see how she reacted to that. Sooner or later he'd come up with an excuse that didn't sound stupid. Then he'd have to return whatever he'd borrowed, and maybe he'd bring her a pizza as a thank-you. He'd take it slow. Eventually he'd mention that he'd broken up with Pamela, but he'd have to make that reference casual.

If he played this wrong, Lindsay might think he was some callous jerk who discarded one woman and moved quickly onto the next. God, he hoped he wasn't that kind of person. On the surface, he seemed to be acting that way. Well, he'd just have to take the relationship with Lindsay at a snail's pace to prove that he wasn't that shallow.

The walk from the "L" station to the apartment house was filled with the kind of ugly heat and humidity mix that made him wonder how his grandparents had lived in Chicago without central air. They'd owned a brick house not far from here, and as a kid he hadn't noticed the temperature at grandma and grandpa's, probably because he'd spent his time running through the sprinkler or eating homemade peach ice cream. Apparently at the age of thirty-two he'd become a wuss about the weather.

He was still feeling hot and sweaty when he started down the hall toward his fourth-floor apartment. That thermostat was going down to *freeze,* baby. And a shower was definitely in his future. He wondered if Lindsay liked peach ice cream.

Then he noticed activity in front of her door, and suddenly he had no worries about the heat wave. She was talking with a delivery guy who had boxes stacked on a dolly. After a quick assessment of the labels, Hunter decided it was an unassembled entertainment center. A light clicked on in his brain.

"Hey, Lindsay," he called out as he passed. Boy, didn't she look sweet and summery in that white eyelet dress. Maybe he should change banks, no matter how obvious that was. With a teller like Lindsay it was a wonder any guy ever used the ATM.

She glanced up from the delivery slip she'd been signing. "Hey, Hunter."

"Looks like a weekend project."

"Yeah, I decided to be a grown-up and buy something to hold my stuff besides the old blocks and boards." She laughed and tucked her hair behind her ear. She'd left it down today, another tempting change from how she wore it on Saturdays.

"Good luck with it." Hunter decided she looked very much like a grown-up in her heels and nylons. Yowza.

"Thanks, Hunter."

Despite wanting to linger, he forced himself to keep walking toward his apartment door. Then he turned, as if his earlier brainstorm had just come to him. "Listen, putting those things together can be tricky. If you need another pair of hands, I'd be glad to help you." *Another pair of very eager hands.* Oh, jeez. No matter how he tried to beat his libido into submission, it wouldn't behave.

The delivery guy had already started wheeling the boxes into the apartment, but Lindsay poked her head back out to acknowledge his offer. "That's very generous of you. Do you happen to have a screwdriver?"

"Yeah. Sure." Somewhere. He hoped he hadn't made a tactical error. He was a magician with a camera but only barely adequate with hand tools. Well, knock-down furniture came with directions, even if they were usually written by folks with dicey English skills. He'd manage.

"Then I might call on you," Lindsay said.

"Anytime." Hunter waited until he was inside his apartment with the door shut before pumping his fist in triumph. *Yes!*

AN HOUR LATER, Lindsay sat on her living room floor surrounded by packets of nuts and screws, various lengths and widths of pressed wood laminated to look like cherry, her Swiss Army knife and a completely incomprehensible set of instructions. The knife was there for its many screwdriver options, but she had yet to screw anything.

Although she'd never assembled furniture in her life, she'd gambled on her above-average intelligence to get her through. Bad bet. Actually, the entertainment center had been a gamble on more than one front. Such a piece of furniture implied that she'd be staying home to be entertained. But for the past couple of months, she'd focused her attention on going out for that purpose. And she was sick of it.

Yes, she'd deliberately avoided her apartment at night so she wouldn't have to listen to Hunter get it on with his main squeeze. But she'd also tried, really tried, to find a guy of her own. Shauna had chipped in with fix-ups. Her girlfriends at the bank had lined up brothers, cousins, clients. Even the owners of Divine Events had offered a couple of possibilities. They'd obviously noticed how Lindsay eyed their red leather book with longing, noticed how much she wished she had a reason to tear out a page.

None of that concentrated effort had paid off by delivering a guy even a tenth as appealing as Hunter. She'd bought the entertainment center after deciding she'd rather stay home and listen to Hunter having sex in the next apartment than waste her time looking for a Hunter clone. There was only one Hunter Jordan, and he was taken. Sometimes life was like that.

Unfortunately, the first part of her plan, an entertainment center to hold the DVD player and enhanced sound system arriving tomorrow, seemed doomed to sit forever on the launching pad. Throwing the directions across the room, she adjusted one of the butterfly clips holding her hair off her neck and wondered what to do next. If she'd thought Hunter was serious about his offer, she might consider going over there and asking for his help.

Well, damn it, why not ask him? He'd said "anytime," and maybe he'd taken woodworking in high school. It wasn't like she'd planned this caper to lure him over to her apartment. Hopping to her feet, she went into her kitchen and checked to see if she had any beer in the refrigerator.

Good deal. She still had three cans. In her limited experience, when you asked a guy to do a guy thing for you, you needed to have some beer around. She was beginning to feel excited about the prospect of enlisting Hunter and she opened her door to head over to his place.

No sooner had she opened the door than she slammed it shut. His girlfriend was coming down the hall. Damn it to hell.

With a sigh of resignation she walked into her tiny kitchen, opened the refrigerator and took out one of her three beers. This turn of events called for a swig of something stronger than soda. She'd been gone so much she hadn't heard their bedroom symphony in a long time. She didn't want to hear it now, either.

Unfortunately she'd disconnected the speaker wires on her stereo in preparation for putting everything in the entertainment center. She couldn't even use Sting to get her out of this episode. At least one thing was certain—Hunter hadn't meant it when he'd said he'd help her "anytime." He should have added "anytime I'm not having sex with Silicon Sally."

As Lindsay debated whether to tackle the instructions again or put on her shoes and go to the deli for a sandwich, she heard Hunter's girlfriend yelling. Except she wasn't yelling in the way she usually did when she was with Hunter. This sounded a lot more like fighting than fooling around.

Fighting? Thoroughly ashamed of herself, Lindsay ran to the kitchen and grabbed a glass from the cupboard. She didn't know why a glass to the wall worked to make the sound clearer, but for some reason it did. No one would ever know that she'd used a glass a few times back in her pathetic days, when she'd been having vicarious sex with Hunter.

Whoops. Looks like she'd finally admitted to herself what she'd done in the first months of being his neighbor. Putting herself in his girlfriend's place. Ah, self-knowledge could be painful.

She wasn't hearing sexual things tonight, however. Tonight his girlfriend was furious. Lindsay balanced the glass against the bedroom wall, pressed her ear against the bottom and sipped her beer while she listened.

"You thought I cared about you?" the girlfriend bellowed. She had good lungs, that one. "It was about two things—sex and your connections at the magazine. Those are the only reasons I stayed!"

Hunter was harder to hear because he wasn't shouting. Lindsay thought he said something like "I always cared for you," or maybe it was "I'll always care for you." She hoped it was the first and not the second, because this sounded like a really serious fight. If so, she wanted Hunter to walk away with his heart in one piece.

Then she had to admit the chances of that weren't too good. He'd acted as if he really liked this woman, and here she was telling him that he'd been nothing more than a convenient stud service and a good business connection. What a witch.

But if Hunter ended up with a broken heart, then he'd move from the category of already involved to the category of recently dumped, and Lindsay had sworn off that category. Yes, but this was *Hunter* she was talking about. Maybe for him, the star of her forbidden fantasies, she could make an exception. *No,* damn it. No exceptions. She'd been down that road too many times.

"And I'll tell you something else," proclaimed Hunter's soon-to-be-ex. "It was average sex! On a scale of ten, I'd rate it a five-minus!"

"Ouch." Lindsay's heart ached for Hunter. He was sure to be wounded after this tirade. But if what they'd been doing didn't rate any more than a five-minus, she should win an Oscar.

"Have a nice life!" yelled the woman.

When Hunter's apartment door slammed, Lindsay jumped. It was over. Hunter, the guy she'd never expected to be dumped, had been horribly dumped. She couldn't imagine why. Maybe *Instant Replay* wouldn't promise the model she'd be on the cover of the next swimsuit issue and she'd thought it was Hunter's fault. Or maybe she was just plain crazy.

But poor Hunter. The apartment next door was silent now, and she pictured him slumped in a chair, staring at the wall as he questioned his self-worth and his sexual prowess. Lindsay had listened to plenty of guys tell her how unmanned they'd felt after being dumped. Hunter had been totally emasculated. What guy could handle hearing that he wasn't good in bed? None.

She couldn't stand it. Nobody should have to be alone at a moment like this. She would pretend she hadn't heard them fighting and ask him to help her put the entertainment center together. Demonstrating his manly skill with a screwdriver might bolster his sense of self. He needed a friend, and she would be that friend. It wouldn't go beyond friendship, though. She'd made a resolution, and she was sticking to it.

HUNTER SIGHED and ran a hand through his still-damp hair. Pamela had caught him in the shower, and he'd answered the door in a towel. Yeah, he'd hoped it might be Lindsay asking him to help her with the entertainment center. He was guilty of thinking that the caught-in-the-shower routine might make an impression on her that he could capitalize on later.

He'd probably had a smile on his face when he'd come to the door, too. That's what he got for not checking the peephole first. Pamela's opening move had been to smile back and reach for the knot holding the towel around his hips. When he'd stopped her, all hell had broken loose.

Well, damn. He'd hoped she'd just go away, but apparently she hadn't believed that he didn't want her back in his bed. He doubted very many men, if any, had turned down sex with Pamela. He was a little surprised that he had. Fully clothed, Pamela had the kind of body that made guys forget about being politically correct. Pamela inspired a full-out ogle. Naked, she was centerfold material.

She was also incredibly self-absorbed. At first he'd been turned on by her willingness to flaunt her body in front of him. She loved to masturbate, and she'd been perfectly happy to let him watch. He'd never met a woman so uninhibited. He had to admit the sex had been amazing.

Funny, but she'd just flung at him the same words he could have said to her. For him, it had been all about the sex. In a way, he owed her, because she'd opened his eyes to inventive games men and women could play in the bedroom. But with Pamela, once they'd moved beyond mutual sexual pleasure, there was nothing left.

So maybe that was the source of his obsession with Lindsay. He longed to take the anything-goes mentality he'd learned from Pamela and apply it to someone he could talk to afterward. Or he had longed to do that, before Pamela had graded him. Five-minus. Damn. He told himself that she'd said that because she was hurt. But she'd had a lot of experience, and maybe he was below average in her book.

Hell, how did a guy ever know what a woman thought of his technique in the sack? Faking was easy for a woman. Now he wondered if all that time she'd been pretending to have multiple orgasms to guarantee that she'd have a good shot at another swimsuit edition cover. He'd sure thought she was really coming, and he'd felt contractions, but maybe a woman with good muscles could fake the contractions, too. He didn't know what to believe.

Standing here wasn't accomplishing anything, though, so he might as well get dressed and figure out what to do about dinner. Lindsay probably had her entertainment center put together by now, so even that supposedly golden opportunity had likely fizzled. With another long sigh, he started back to his bedroom, his hand loosening the knot of the towel.

The doorbell chimed before he could reach the bedroom. As he retraced his steps, he reminded himself of the lesson he'd learned the hard way this afternoon. From now on, he was never, ever opening his front door without looking through the peephole.

Wonder of wonders, Lindsay stood on the other side in a drool-worthy halter top and those cutoffs she liked to wear. She was barefoot. Hunter had never seen her toes because she wore running shoes down to the laundry room. He noticed that her toenails were a bright coral. Sexy.

He opened the door, although by now his hair was too dry for him to look as if he'd just stepped out of the shower. In fact, he might look dorky, as if he was a nudist who couldn't wait to get home and get naked.

Sure enough, Lindsay's smile faltered as her gaze swept downward. "Uh, I didn't mean to disturb you."

"You didn't. I was in the shower, and then...then I was checking out the Cubs game." *Weak, extremely weak.*

For some reason she seemed to buy it, even though his TV screen was dark. "Oh. Did you, um, want to watch the game?"

"Nah. They're losing."

"Ah. All righty, then." Her smile returned. "Did you mean it when you said you'd help me with the entertainment center? Because I'm in terrible trouble over there. I can't make heads or tails of the instructions."

Shaky confidence or not, he'd be a fool to turn down a chance like this. "I'd be glad to help you. Let me get dressed, and I'll be right over."

"Super. I have beer."

"Beer?"

She paused, looking flustered. "You know, to drink after you help me." She peered at him. "Maybe you don't drink beer."

"I do drink beer." He thought the opportunity was expanding exponentially. "Maybe we can order a pizza, too, once we get the entertainment center built."

"Perfect!" She beamed at him. "Then I'll see you soon."

"Five minutes."

"Great." She started back to her apartment. Then she turned back. "And bring your screwdriver. That's where I'm really gonna need a hand. I don't know how you'll feel about helping once you find out how many screws are involved."

He had no idea how he kept a straight face. "I think I can handle it."

Apparently what she'd said finally registered, because she turned red. "I mean, it looks pretty complicated."

"I knew that's what you meant." He bit the inside of his cheek to keep himself from laughing.

"Bye." Turning, she dashed back inside her apartment.

Hunter closed his door and grinned. How refreshing. A woman who could still blush. Now if he actually managed to help her with the entertainment center, he'd be making progress. And down the line, way down the line, maybe he'd discover what it was like to make love to Lindsay Scott...well, after he'd recovered from Pamela's grading system. Then again, a woman who could blush might not notice that he was only a five-minus.

Chapter Two

OMIGOD, OMIGOD, OMIGOD. Lindsay leaned against her closed door in shock. She'd seen Hunter practically naked. She knew the pattern of his chest hair—little swirls over his pecs and a furry line down to his belly button. She knew the color of his nipples—dark rose. She knew where he had the cutest little mole—to the left of that impressive six-pack.

And under his white towel, he'd been wearing...absolutely nothing. How she'd ever held a normal conversation without drooling right onto his bare feet was a miracle. But she hadn't held a normal conversation. She'd invited him to bring his tool so they could screw.

She put her shaking hands to her still-hot cheeks. How could she have said such a thing? She never slipped up like that. But then she'd never been confronted with the sight of her love god draped in a towel, either. And the big question, the positively *huge* question, was how in heaven's name had that nutcase of a girlfriend walked out on Hunter? Hunter wearing a towel, no less!

Whoever that insane woman was, she must have stopped taking her meds. No mentally healthy female would stand there looking at Hunter in a towel and proceed to break up with him. Incomprehensible. Unless...unless Hunter had a very small…no, not likely. Even though Lindsay hadn't actually seen what was under that towel, God wouldn't create an Adonis like Hunter and give him a tiny tool. No way.

It wouldn't matter to her, of course. Small, large or in-between was of no consequence, because she wouldn't be having anything to do with that part of his anatomy. She only wanted to cheer him up after he'd been slam-dunked by the vicious ex-girlfriend. Even if he was under-endowed—which Lindsay doubted, and it made no difference *anyway*—he didn't deserve that sort of goodbye speech featuring a grade of five-minus.

Sherman, now there was a five-minus for you. Maybe even a three-minus, considering the way her head had hurt for two days. There was no way Hunter, with a body like that and a smile like that and big brown eyes like that, could be in the same league with Sherman. Lindsay trusted her instincts there.

She was still leaning against the door when Hunter tapped on it, which made her jump about two feet in the air. She glanced at the clock on her living room wall and, sure enough, she'd been sagging against the door, recovering, for five minutes. Hunter was here.

Opening the door, she held onto the knob and cocked one hip, trying to fake total relaxation, as if she hadn't just seen him almost naked. "Hi, there." *I see you're dressed now. Damned shame.*

"Hi."

As she stared at his Cubs T-shirt and khaki shorts, she seemed to develop X-ray vision. His clothes miraculously vanished except for his briefs, or boxers or whatever covered his package. She had no mental picture for that area. Nor would she ever have. Nope. Not ever.

"I found my screwdriver." He held it up, all fourteen inches of it.

"Wow." She stood back and let him into the apartment. "Now that's a screwdriver." She wondered if men bought big screwdrivers as some kind of compensation device. Not that it mattered, of course. Not to her. She wasn't in the market for a guy on the rebound, whether he was packing a big screwdriver or a small screwdriver.

"It's probably too big for this job, though," he said. "It was the only one I could find. I think I used this on the car."

"I wouldn't know if it'll work or not." She gestured toward the mess on the floor. "Obviously, I couldn't even figure out how the parts fit together, let alone which screws go in which holes." And that sounded decidedly sexual. She hadn't meant it to. Really, she hadn't. She would not look at the fly of his shorts. Would not.

Hunter glanced at the scattered pieces and tapped the blade of the screwdriver against his palm. "Did it come with directions?"

Yes, and I'll bet I could come, too, if you directed me to a bed. She had to stop this. Everything reminded her of sex. "You mean the ones I threw under my sofa bed?" Now why had she told him it was a sofa bed? Did he care? Did she need to bring the word *bed* into the conversation? *No.* But she was obsessed with the topic of sex right now. She stepped around two boards and picked up the printed booklet lying on the floor.

He cleared his throat. "Those sofa beds are great for company. That looks like a good one."

And he qualified as company, so there you go. "I got it for when my folks visit." That was better. Talking about her very conservative parents ought to straighten her up. "But I let them have my bed and I sleep out here. It's amazingly comfortable. Nice and firm." Or maybe she couldn't be straightened up, not with a man like Hunter on the premises.

He eyed the blue plaid cushions. "It looks like it would be comfortable."

"Almost like a real bed." *Want to test it out?*

"And when you get this entertainment center put together," he gestured toward the scattered pieces with the enormous screwdriver, "you'll be all set to watch movies or listen to music in bed."

"Sure will." Oh, baby. She wanted to pull that bed out right now, and let the entertainment center remain in pieces forever. She'd lay money that Hunter was a lot more entertaining than anything she'd stack on those shelves. And she was convinced, despite what his girlfriend had said, that his big ol' tool could do the job just right.

"Then I guess we should get it together." He put out his hand. "Let me take a look at those directions."

As Lindsay gave him the booklet, she reminded herself that her goal was to make him feel better by letting him help her construct the entertainment center. It was not in her job description to mend his ego by having sex with him on the sofa bed and telling him that he was so not a five-minus. She wasn't even supposed to know that he'd been graded and then sent to Dumpsville.

But she did know, and as she sat on the sofa bed next to him watching him earnestly study the directions, she thought about the cushy mattress folded right underneath them. Hunter looked like such a good guy, such a sweet guy. She could imagine his girlfriend's words running through the back of his mind, even now. They were terrible words, and Lindsay wondered if putting together an entertainment center would be enough comfort.

AN HOUR LATER, Hunter gazed at the wobbly structure he'd leaned up against the wall so it wouldn't fall over. Several pieces hadn't made it into the design. They lay accusingly on the carpet, looking significant. He studied the directions again, wondering where he'd gone wrong.

"Beer?" Lindsay walked out of the kitchen with an icy can in each hand.

She hadn't been much help on the construction, but he'd loved every minute of her hovering over him while he tried to figure out the combination to this entertainment center. "I thought that was for after we finished."

She grinned at him as she handed him the open beer. "That's not finished?"

"Does it look finished to you?" He took a swig of the cold beer.

"Well...." She squinted at the assembly, which had begun to lean to the left. "It's still a little unstable, I guess." Then she brightened. "Maybe once we put the TV on it, that will make it stand better."

"You put the TV on it, and it'll be goodbye TV, hello Dumpster. This baby needs more work before you put anything on it."

"If you say so. But I think we should take a break." She flopped down on the sofa bed and took a long swallow of her beer.

"I guess you're right." He joined her, careful not to get too close. She was awfully damned appealing. They sat there for a while, just drinking their beer and surveying the entertainment center.

"You know, it doesn't look so bad," she said finally.

"The more beer you drink, the better it'll look."

"Good idea." She took another sip. "You hungry?"

"Yeah, as a matter of fact." This was fun, exactly how he'd pictured hanging out with Lindsay. No pressure. Easy companionship. They'd muddled through the construction of her furniture without getting into a fight. She didn't seem the least upset that he wasn't a maestro with the screwdriver.

"Then let's have a pizza delivered," she said. "Is veggie okay?"

"I can go with veggie. I figure it's a painless way to get healthy stuff into your diet."

"Exactly." She popped up, grabbed her cordless phone from the wall next to the kitchen and phoned in their order.

While she did that, he slid off the sofa and sat on the floor next to the extra pieces of wood. Then he picked up the directions again.

"I don't care if we have boards left over." Lindsay sat down next to him and leaned against the sofa bed, stretching her tanned legs in front of her while she continued to sip her beer. "I could use them for shelves under my bathroom vanity."

"But we're not supposed to have boards left over. That's why it's unstable." He leaned back next to her so their shoulders touched, just barely. Cozy. Not too cozy. Just nice. Man, did she have terrific legs. Once more they sat in easy silence, sipping their beer.

"It needs more support," Hunter said at last. The beer was making him very mellow, and he remembered he hadn't had much to eat for lunch, so the alcohol was probably hitting him faster than it normally would.

"Well, I think we should just screw it to the wall and call it good," Lindsay said.

Instantly, cozy went to hot. He now had a picture of Lindsay up against the wall, her raggedy shorts down around her ankles. He tried to put the image out of his mind. "The super would go apeshit if we did that. Besides, you couldn't take it with you when you move." Now there was a depressing thought, Lindsay moving.

"I'm not moving." Her shoulder nudged his and her silky thigh brushed his leg. "Let's screw it to the wall."

He liked the subtle body contact, but he wished she'd quit saying that. He was having a tough time erasing the idea of her bare tush up against the plaster, her legs wrapped around his hips and her halter top untied. "We'd have to find the studs first."

"I know where one is."

He glanced at her, wondering if she meant what he thought she did. "Yeah?" He sounded a little raspy.

"Yeah." She pushed herself to her feet and smiled at him.

If she held out her hand and asked him into the bedroom, he wondered if he could resist.

But she didn't. Carrying her beer can with her, she sashayed over to the wall and knocked on a section of it. "There's a stud right there. I used to have a picture there but I took it down yesterday. The nail hit solid wood when it went in."

"Oh." He didn't know whether to be glad she wasn't coming on to him or sorry. Wait a minute. She didn't know that he'd broken up with his girlfriend. If she started coming on to him, that would be a bad thing. That would mean she was trying to break them up. That wouldn't be nice.

"So here's how we can do it." She stood in front of the lopsided entertainment center and pushed it into position with both hands, which made her cute little bottom stick out. "We nail a board to the back, and use those long screws we have left over to lock this baby right up against the wall. What do you think?"

He thought she was way too sexy, and he could feel an erection coming on. "I think we need to unscrew the top board and put in another shelf. That's what we're missing, is that extra shelf."

"That's too much work. Let's use the stud and a nice long screw." She gazed at him, a challenge in her blue eyes.

He couldn't shake the idea that she was coming on to him. He was debating whether to ask her point-blank whether she was or not when the doorbell rang.

"Pizza's here." She let go of the entertainment center, which sagged even more to the left.

Saved by the pizza. He didn't really want to confront this issue, did he? If she said no, she wasn't coming on to him, he'd feel like an idiot. If she said yes, then he'd have to think less of her for trying to steal another woman's boyfriend. He wasn't another woman's boyfriend anymore, but Lindsay didn't know that.

Setting down his empty beer can, he got to his feet and reached in his back pocket for his wallet. "Let me get it."

"Absolutely not. You're helping me with my entertainment center, so this is my treat." She grabbed her purse from a hook by the door.

"Considering the way that entertainment center is listing to the left, I should be buying."

"Nope." She opened the door, took the pizza box from a kid in a red shirt and thrust a couple of bills at him. "Thanks. Keep the change."

"Okay," Hunter said as she closed the door, "you win. But next time, it's on me."

"Fine." She approached with the pizza box, paper napkins tucked in the side flap. "We could sit in the kitchen, but I'd rather stay out here and study our work in progress."

"Sounds good to me. Want me to get us each another beer?"

She frowned. "Oh. Now that's a wee bit of a problem. I'm out."

"It's absolutely no problem. I have some in my fridge. Be right back."

"I'll leave the door open."

"Just like in *Friends*," he said with a grin.

"I know! And *Seinfeld* was like that too. Nobody in those shows ever locked a door. Or knocked, for that matter."

"Want me to knock?"

"No." She laughed. "I'll know it's you, silly. Just go get us some more beer. This project requires more beer."

"I agree." Smiling to himself, he hurried down the short stretch of hall to his door, unlocked it and walked quickly into his kitchen. He couldn't remember the last time he'd had so much fun. This was great, cruising back and forth between his apartment and hers, ordering pizza, sharing their stashes of beer.

He still had to wonder about that *use a stud and a nice long screw* remark, but maybe that was the beer talking. One beer had made him feel pretty damned loose, and she weighed a lot less than he did. The alcohol could have affected her even more, especially if she hadn't had much to eat today, either.

Grabbing a six-pack from the bottom shelf of his refrigerator, he closed the door. For one brief moment he wondered if he should take all six cans over there. If one beer encouraged Lindsay to make suggestive remarks, he wondered what three would accomplish.

He shouldn't want to find out. After all, he'd promised himself this would be a slow, careful campaign. It would take place over weeks, not hours. Getting Lindsay plowed wasn't part of the program.

Ah hell, he doubted they'd drink more than one more apiece, but it was simpler to take the whole thing than to pry a couple out. Then again, if he took the whole six-pack, and matters got out of control, sexually speaking…would he really turn down an opportunity like that?

Being a realist, he had to admit he might not. Under these circumstances, when a woman was throwing out comments about studs and long screws, a guy might be wise to put a couple of condoms in his pocket. He didn't expect to use them—he certainly didn't *plan* to use them.

Come to think of it, taking them along might jinx the possibility of sex, just like carrying an umbrella always kept it from raining.

Well, that settled it. He'd take two condoms as a sure-fire way to keep from having sex with Lindsay.

THE PIZZA soaked up some of the beer in Lindsay's system, which was a good thing. After the half can she'd had before inviting Hunter over and the full can she'd had before the pizza arrived, she was feeling way too frisky and way too willing to bend her rule about avoiding guys on the rebound. Earlier, she'd flirted outrageously with him, but after a couple of warm, cheesy slices of most excellent pizza, she'd regained control of her urges.

"So you're happy with this apartment, then?" Hunter asked, finishing off his fourth slice of pizza.

"Uh, sure." She realized she'd been watching him eat with a little too much rapt attention, but he had such a nice mouth, and watching those even, white teeth bite into the pizza gave her a thrill. "On good days I can walk to work, and on hot days like today, or in the winter, I take the bus." And she lived next door to Hunter, which was really the only perk she cared about.

"I like it, too. It's a good place. Quiet." Hunter drained his beer.

"Pretty quiet." Oops. She should have just agreed with him. "I mean, yes, it's quiet." *Mostly.*

He glanced at her. "What do you mean by *pretty quiet*? Am I making too much—"

"You look like you could use another beer." She jumped up and grabbed the empty can from his hand.

"Well, I—"

"I'm going to have one, too." She quickly swallowed the last of hers. Good grief. The last thing he needed to think about was the wild lovemaking he'd enjoyed with his girlfriend, the she-devil who had just dropped him like a bad habit.

"Are you sure you want another beer?" he called after her.

"Absolutely." She took their empties and escaped into the kitchen. Once there she knocked her forehead softly against the front of the refrigerator. She shouldn't be allowed to drink and talk.

Pretty quiet, indeed. Her tongue was getting looser and looser. She would not drink this beer she was getting out, only pretend to drink it. One more beer and no telling what she'd say. Or do.

As she walked back into the room, she decided to maneuver a change of subject. After handing him his beer, she remained standing, her attention on the entertainment center. "I have a new idea. I can prop my easy chair up against the side that's leaning. In fact, if you'll hold my beer, I'll move the chair."

He waved a hand in protest. "Don't go moving the chair over there yet. That will look dumb." He patted the floor next to him. "C'mon and sit down and we'll talk about other options."

"I think the chair's a great option." But she sat down next to him, anyway, because she really didn't want to drag it over there right this minute. It was a very heavy chair.

"Propping the chair against the entertainment center is not a great option, even if it looked good, which it won't," he said. "Because then you won't be able to see the TV from the chair. Sometime you might have people over and need that chair for watching TV."

"Maybe."

"After we finish this beer, we'll take the top shelf off and put in the middle one. That'll fix the problem."

"Okay." Now she'd done it. He expected her to finish

the whole can because she'd made a big deal about wanting it.

"Listen, Lindsay, I've been thinking about something. My apartment's on the end, so you're the only neighbor I could hear, and I don't get any noise from your apartment. From the way you bolted when we started discussing this, I have to believe I'm the one who's been making too much noise. Have I?"

She took a gulp of her beer and thought about what a rotten liar she was. "Oh, not really."

"Have I been disturbing you?"

"Nope, not at all."

"I think I have. Your face is kind of red, like you're embarrassed about something." ·

She wondered if there was biofeedback training to stop blushing. "Listen, you really haven't bothered me. The thing is, I'm usually here by myself, so naturally you wouldn't hear me." *Yikes, girl, after jamming one foot in your mouth, now you have both of them in there.* "What I meant to say is—"

"Hold it. I'm getting a picture here." He scanned the room. "Your apartment floor plan is flip-flopped from mine, which means that your bedroom...oh, good lord."

She couldn't look at him. Instead she took another healthy swallow of her beer and stared at the sagging entertainment center.

Hunter cleared his throat. "Lindsay, please tell me you can't hear every single thing that goes on in my bedroom."

"Not...really clearly." *Except when I put a glass to the wall.*

He groaned and sank back against the sofa bed. "You heard it all. God, now I'm the one who's embarrassed. If I hadn't had two-plus beers, I'd probably be so embarrassed I'd have to leave right now. But instead I'll just stay here and ask if there's any way in hell you can forget all about what you heard."

Not a snowball's chance in hell. She pressed the cool aluminum can to her hot cheek. "It's no big deal. I think we're too uptight about such things, anyway. I mean, back in frontier days, families had to live in one big room, and don't you suppose that—"

"Lindsay." He put down his beer, caught her chin and turned her to face him. "I'm sorrier than I can say, and I promise you this—you won't be hearing that anymore."

She looked into his brown eyes, so filled with regret, and she felt like the biggest jerk in the world for reminding him that his girlfriend had walked out on him only hours ago. "She's an idiot."

He smiled gently and stroked his thumb over her chin. "No, she's not," he said softly. "She just—"

"With the way she was moaning, there's no way you're a five-minus!" Then she squeezed her eyes shut. "I didn't mean to say that. I'm sorry, Hunter. I could have gone all night without saying th—"

His mouth covered hers, slicing off her apology.

Considering how she'd bungled things, she thought she'd better put down her beer and kiss him back. It was the neighborly thing to do.

Chapter Three

HUNTER WOULDN'T HAVE KISSED Lindsay if she'd kept her eyes open. But when she squeezed them shut as she rattled off her apology, he couldn't resist. And the minute he kissed her, the condoms started burning a hole in his pocket.

She tasted of pizza and beer, a combo he loved on their own. Add in the plumpness of her lips, the warm slide of her tongue against his, the little whimper that made him immediately hard, and he was ready to unwrap a raincoat.

No. He wouldn't do that, even though she was winding her arms around his neck and opening her mouth for some serious tongue play. The bare skin of her back was so smooth, so warm. He wanted to get closer, just a little bit closer. Mouth-to-mouth was good, but he wanted more body contact. Body contact was okay if they kept their clothes on.

If he moved his legs this way, and she moved her legs that way...she followed his lead, shifting her weight, aligning her torso with his. Oh, excellent. Chest to chest. With only her halter top and his T-shirt in the way, he could feel her nipples poking against him—a very encouraging sign.

She was as much into this kiss as he was. If her nipples were hard, then he could be reasonably sure other things were happening in that compact little body of hers. Things he'd fantasized about for weeks.

He moaned without meaning to. She wiggled closer. That little wiggle gave him a breast rub that nearly knocked him out. There was something to be said for firm, high breasts that stayed put, bra or no bra.

Although he made his living taking photos of women with extravagant measurements, this was what he really liked—classic proportions, a size that fit his palm when he cupped her breast, when he massaged it, feeling the fullness under his fingers, exactly as he was doing right now....

Whoops. He hadn't meant to do that, either, but she whimpered again when he stroked his thumb over her nipple, so he could hardly stop, could he? And the kiss was getting hotter and wetter by the minute. Lots of heavy breathing going on here. Damn, it felt great to stroke her like this.

Before he could control the urge, he'd pulled at the ties holding the halter top around her neck. It was a mistake to untie them, and he knew it was a mistake, but she broke their intense lip-lock long enough to murmur "yes." That word was enough to make him abandon all thoughts of backpedaling. He was committed to at least this much of a make-out session.

He couldn't have retied that halter, anyway, not with the way he was shaking. The only thing to do was pull that material down and out of the way so he could bring both hands into the equation. Mmm. Perfection. His mouth had been very busy enjoying her mouth, but now his hunger shifted. Breasts that felt this good would taste even better.

He lifted his mouth from hers and dragged in some air. "L-Lindsay..." Damn, he was so worked up he was stuttering. "I want—"

"Me, too, oh, me, too." And with that she shifted her

body yet again, pulling him down with her. They knocked over both beer cans.

He didn't care, but it was her carpet. "Lindsay—"

"Leave them." She was panting, which made her chest heave and those perfect breasts quiver. "Just—"

"You bet." Her tight nipples claimed all his attention. And she was incredibly responsive. Every flick of his tongue made her gasp. When he finally settled down to some intense oral stimulation, she dug her fingers into his scalp and arched right up off the floor, moaning his name.

Good thing she did that, because for a moment there he couldn't remember his name. Her cry reminded him of who he was, and what he didn't intend to do tonight. Unfortunately his penis had a whole different take on the matter. Through no conscious decision of his own, he found himself wedged between her thighs.

Worse yet, she'd begun rocking her hips against him. A continuation of that move would have predictable results, and if he was going to come, he damn sure wasn't going to do it like that. With a groan he forced himself to relinquish her breasts and rise to his hands and knees. He wobbled there, breathing hard, and looked down upon his fantasy woman.

They weren't on top of the washing machine, but otherwise all the elements were in place. Her blue eyes had darkened with lust, exactly as he'd imagined they would, and her hair was coming loose from its butterfly clip. Her halter top was pulled down and her round, sweet breasts glistened from all that contact with his mouth.

The only part left was to strip away her panties and cut-offs. He tried to remember why that was a bad idea. Funny, but right now it seemed like a very *good* idea. She looked ready. He was definitely ready.

She struggled for breath. "Why...why did you stop? Is

it because I'm not very…" Her hands went to her breasts in the first self-conscious move she'd made since he'd kissed her.

"No!" He sank back on his heels so he could grasp her hands and gently ease them away, leaving her breasts bare again. "I love to look at you, touch you, taste you. You're wonderful, everything I want."

She searched his expression, as if she didn't believe him.

He could imagine what this was about. She was comparing her endowments with Pamela's. He could tell her that Pamela's generous breasts had never turned him on like this, but he didn't want Pamela's name to be part of what they were sharing. "I stopped because I want you too much. I'm losing control. I didn't intend—"

"Me, either." The anxiety cleared from her eyes, and the lust came back in a rush. Freeing her hand from his grasp, she reached down and unfastened the metal button at the waistband of her cutoffs. "But now, if we don't finish this, I think I'll go crazy."

He swallowed. "Lindsay, are you sure?"

"Yes." She pulled down the zipper. "And while I'm slipping into something more comfortable, like my birthday suit, you can go next door and get condoms. I'm sure you have some over there."

"I, um, don't have to go next door."

Her eyebrows lifted.

"I thought…" Boy, did this sound stupid, but at the time it had made perfect sense. "When I went to get the beer, I—"

"You planned this?" Some of the light went out of her eyes.

"No! I didn't, I swear! I thought by putting a couple of condoms in my pocket, I'd guarantee that we wouldn't have sex. You know, how whenever you take an umbrella, it never rains."

The light returned to her eyes and the corners of her mouth tilted up. "Well, guess what?"

His chest was so tight with anticipation that he could barely breathe. "What?"

"It's raining."

LINDSAY HAD TRIED to behave herself. She'd really tried. But the minute Hunter had kissed her, she'd sensed his desperation. He needed to make love to someone tonight to validate his sexual ability and wipe out the self-doubt caused by his ex and her grading system. When confronted by that kind of need, especially coming from a babelicious guy like Hunter, Lindsay couldn't turn away.

Not to mention that pumping up his sexual confidence would be no hardship. So far, on a scale of ten, she'd rank him a fifty-eight. Fifty-eight and moving up. She wasn't kidding about needing to finish this. *Right now.*

Then there was the other persuader, too. Once he'd worked himself in between her thighs, once she'd felt the impressive bulge representing his package, she was ready to take him on sight unseen.

She'd had a moment of angst when he'd called a halt, though. After all, she didn't have the D-cup banquet Hunter was used to. But the look in his brown eyes when he'd reassured her had been more than convincing. He was still looking at her that way, not taking his eyes off her except for the split second required to yank his T-shirt over his head.

She managed to pull off her halter top, but then the view of Hunter getting naked sidetracked her. She'd been afraid she'd never see that glorious chest again, and here it was, available for touching, kissing, full body contact. Her mouth began to water.

Then he took the condom packets out of his pocket, which reminded her that time was a-wasting. She lifted her hips from the floor and was about to shove her panties and cutoffs down when he stood, unzipped his shorts and got rid of both shorts and briefs in one smooth move.

The sight of his very large, very erect penis immobilized her completely. Slowly she sank back to the carpet, her gaze riveted to that top-of-the-line sexual equipment. No way could a presentation like that result in a five-minus. No way.

"Is something wrong?" His voice was thick, a perfect complement to the part of him that had totally captured her imagination.

"Everything's right," she murmured as a fresh rush of moisture dampened her panties even more. "Extremely right."

"Lindsay, don't think you have to build me up because of that…that comment Pamela made about me."

So that was her name. Pamela. "Was the woman blind?"

His smile was a little off-center. "Size isn't everything. And I—"

"It's a damned fine start!" Galvanized into action, she shimmied out of her now soaked panties and cutoffs.

He caught his breath. "So beautiful," he said softly as he sank back down to his knees and positioned himself exactly where he'd been before. Only this time, nothing was between them… nothing at all.

Making no move to pick up one of the condom packets, he stayed right where he was and looked his fill, his gaze hungry. That surprised her. This was a man used to swimsuit models, after all. The way he was looking at her, she'd think that he hadn't had sex in a year.

She was the one who hadn't had sex in a year. She could imagine the starving expression on *her* face.

Bracing his hands on either side of her shoulders, he leaned down and kissed her. The restrained passion in that gentle kiss made her tremble. His whole body was taut with sexual energy, and yet he kissed her lightly, brushing his lips over hers as if the moment of truth was hours away instead of seconds. She hoped it was seconds.

"I want you," she whispered. "I really, really want you."

"Good." His warm breath tickled her skin as he kissed her jaw and the hollow of her throat. "Because I really, really want you, too."

She believed him because his wounded ego craved a willing partner tonight. But she didn't dare kid herself that he wanted *her* specifically. She'd made that mistake before, only to have her pride trampled after discovering she'd been the Band-Aid for a broken heart and nothing more.

Having sex with Hunter tonight wasn't wise, but she couldn't resist him, not when he needed her so much. And not when she'd gone so many months without the feel of a man's lips on her body. And certainly not when he kissed her and his slightly bristly cheeks rubbed against her skin, a sensation that was extremely sexy and reminded her this was a bona fide stud braced above her.

He started making little circles with his tongue as he moved lower. She read the signal, and the thought of what he intended to do nearly made her climax. But this was a big step to take, considering they'd never been naked together before. Maybe they needed to work up to a maneuver like that.

"Hunter?" Her voice sounded as if she'd recently run a marathon.

He paused, his tongue dipping lightly into her navel. "Yes, Lindsay?"

"Are you planning to, um, keep going in that direction?"

"Uh-huh."

"I'm…I'm not sure you know me well enough yet."

Laughter trembled in his voice. "I will in a minute." He drew circles with his tongue on her tummy.

Her heart beat so fast she felt dizzy. "You don't think we should start...with the basics?"

"Nah. That's for those five-minus guys." With that he closed in on his target.

And Lindsay lost her mind. He had the mouth of a devil, and he used it without hesitation. She'd had no idea oral sex could feel so encompassing, as if he'd made contact with every single one of her pleasure points.

She moaned, she cried out, she even laughed in delirious abandon as he made her come once, then again, then a third time. She bubbled and fizzed like a bottle of champagne opened on a roller coaster.

Then, while she was still gasping from the last orgasm, he slid back up her damp body and gave her a come-flavored kiss. She savored the erotic taste with long, lazy swipes of her tongue over his. She'd never felt so saturated in sex in her life.

"You're amazing," he murmured against her mouth.

"And you..." She kept her eyes closed as she nibbled his full lower lip. "I rate you about six thousand and eight."

He chuckled. "That's all? Not six thousand and nine?"

"Wouldn't want you to get a big head." She felt the press of his erection against her tummy and reached down to wrap her fingers around it. "I see that one part of you is already swelling out of control."

"Careful." He nuzzled her ear, his breath warm. "After the way you just reacted, I'm right on the edge."

"Then slap a body suit on this bad boy and settle in." She let out a little giggle. Then, exploring him with a light touch, she found herself getting excited all over again. "I'm so ready for you." So this was what sex could be like. Who knew?

"Thanks for the invitation. I accept." He shifted his weight and reached for one of the packets lying beside them on the rug.

She opened her eyes. "You would have waited to be invited?" Such chivalry in connection with sex was totally foreign to her.

He smiled as he propped himself on his elbows and tore open the packet. "It's better that way. You might have needed some recovery time."

"And you would have waited for me, even though you're ready to go off like a rocket?"

"Sure." He reached down and rolled the condom on one-handed.

One-handed. This was obviously a man who didn't fumble. "Tell me, have you ever banged a woman's head against the headboard accidentally when you were thrusting?"

He looked at her as if she'd suddenly started speaking in Greek. "No."

"Didn't think so." Bingo. Even if she only had him for tonight, she now had a whole new yardstick for future lovers. She spread her thighs and beckoned to him. "Come here, you patient man. Let Lindsay make you feel really good."

SO MAYBE he wasn't a five-minus. Despite the red haze of lust clouding his brain, Hunter took a moment to congratulate himself on his first move with Lindsay. She hadn't been faking those cries, not considering the way she'd flailed around and gasped for breath. He'd made her a happy woman, three times over.

Still, he could blow it by rushing this next phase. Poised between her thighs, eager to bury his penis in her silken heat, he forced himself to slow down. That wasn't easy with her clutching his butt cheeks in both hands and urging him forward.

Resisting, he smiled at her and shook his head. "Not so fast. I don't want to hurt you."

"Don't worry about a thing." She gave him a gentle

massage. "Your treatment a while ago left me more than ready."

Between her massage and his intense anticipation, he was having trouble keeping cool, but he needed to remember she was small-boned. She might have to get adjusted to him. "Let's see." He eased the latex-covered tip just inside and moaned softly. She was very wet. He clenched his jaw and fought the urge to shove deep.

Her eyes widened. "You *are* big."

He struggled for breath. Not coming immediately was going to be a major challenge. He'd thought about this, dreamed about this for so long, and the reality was threatening to overwhelm him. "That's...why we're... not rushing."

"Slow is one thing." Her breathing quickened as she continued to knead his bottom. "You've come to a dead stop."

"I'm letting you adjust."

"I'm adjusted. I want more."

"Okay." He slid in another inch and almost climaxed. Looking into her eyes, all he could think about was the laundry-room scene he'd replayed a million times in his head. Her expression in his fantasy had been exactly like this—intense, focused and so hot for him she looked ready to explode.

Her breasts quivered with her rapid breath. "I didn't think...I'd come again..."

"I did." He levered himself forward a little more.

"Hunter, I do believe...you've found my...G spot."

"Then let's work it." He hoped he could manage this without losing control. Instead of pushing any deeper, he adjusted his angle and began to stroke back and forth. It was torture for him as he tried to hold back, but judging from the way she was panting, it was heaven for her.

"Ah, yes...right there...oh, my...oh, yes, *yes,* YES!" She arched toward him just as he eased in.

Without warning, he was up to the hilt as her contractions milked his penis. He came quickly, loudly, explosively. For the next moment he was blind, deaf and dumb to everything but the incredible pleasure centered in his groin, the shuddering beauty of each spasm that seemed perfectly matched to hers.

Gradually the room stopped spinning and the ringing in his ears let up. He found himself still balanced on his outstretched arms. In his semiconscious state, he could easily have collapsed onto her, but she was too small to take his full weight. He opened his eyes and discovered hers were squeezed shut as she gasped for air.

Then he glanced down to where, sure enough, they were locked together tight. He should pull out, in case he was hurting her. But this felt so good. "Are you...okay?" He prayed she'd say yes and let him stay a little while.

She kept her eyes closed tight. "I...am...spectacular."

He sighed in relief.

"I'm waiting...for the room to stop spinning."

"I understand. Can I do anything?"

"Yes."

He would do anything, anything she asked, especially if she'd let him come back inside again soon. Very soon. He could already feel the urge returning. "What?"

"I want your ex's phone number."

"Her *phone number?* Why?"

"So I can tell her..." She opened her eyes and grinned at him. "...that she's a freaking idiot!"

He laughed. Sex with Lindsay wasn't really about repairing his ego, but if she wanted to pass out a few compliments, he wouldn't mind. Now the rest of him was as happy as his penis. "Thanks for that." He levered himself away from her. "I need to use your bathroom."

"Sure."

When he returned, she was sitting up, her back braced

against the sofa, but she hadn't put on any clothes. He appreciated that, considering that he was walking around her apartment naked. He sat down next to her and took her hand in his. Although he wasn't ready to call it a night, she might be. "This has turned into quite an evening," he said.

She smiled at him and nestled closer. "You could say that."

Her warmth reached out to him, teasing his penis back to life. "But we haven't finished the entertainment center."

"No. We sort of *became* the entertainment center."

"Yeah, we did, didn't we?" He hesitated. She could certainly see that he wasn't ready to call it quits, but he should give her a chance to do that if she was tired. "You, um, might be ready to have me go home, though."

"Funny, but you don't look ready to go home."

"But maybe I should, anyway."

"Why, so you can stock up on condoms?"

He grinned at her. "Ah, Lindsay, I like how you think."

"Listen, if you need to go home, get some sleep, whatever, that's fine with me, but—"

"Actually, I had a different idea."

Her blue eyes took on an interested gleam. "Such as?"

"I was thinking we might do some laundry."

Chapter Four

"LAUNDRY?" Lindsay tried to control her disappointment, but she couldn't imagine a more boring interlude to follow what had been such a mind-blowing experience. "Why, are you out of socks?"

Hunter swallowed. "It's not about the laundry."

"But you just said—"

"It's about this fantasy I haven't been able to get out of my head. But, hey, it's probably a dumb idea, and I suppose we could get arrested if anybody caught us."

She stared at him as heat flooded through her. Whatever he was leading up to, it was getting him excited. The evidence was right there within her reach. Maybe laundry wasn't such a boring subject, after all. "You've had a fantasy about the laundry room?"

"The laundry room…and you."

This just got better and better. "What sort of fantasy?"

His brown eyes began to smolder and his grip on her hand tightened. "You come into the laundry room, dressed in your halter top and cutoffs, and I…I take off your clothes, and we…we do it on top of the machine."

"You've actually imagined that happening?" And she thought he hadn't noticed her except as a laundry buddy.

"Yeah. Are you shocked?"

"Flattered." Her nipples became rock-hard. "In this fantasy, is the machine going?"

"I don't know. Is it?"

"Yes. It's vibrating."

"Okay." His erect penis twitched. "The washer's going."

"I know just the spot. The two older washers in the corner do the most shaking." She felt like a bungee jumper at the edge of a steep drop. "Let's do this, Hunter. Let's actually do this."

"You don't have to convince me." He stood and pulled her up with him. "Assuming I can zip my pants, I'll meet you down there in five minutes." He let go of her hand and started putting on his clothes. "Whoever gets there first can start those machines."

She grabbed up her own clothes, but she was quivering so much she decided to dress after he left. Or maybe she'd wear a different set, to make the fantasy more interesting. After all, he'd already removed these particular cutoffs.

Then she had another thought. "What if someone else is in the laundry room?"

"At this hour on a Friday night? I don't think so." He somehow got his shorts fastened over the considerable bulge in his briefs.

"Is there a lock on the door down there?"

He pulled his T-shirt over his head before meeting her gaze. "No."

"So we take our chances that somebody will come along?"

He paused in the act of stepping into his deck shoes. "Lindsay, you don't have to do this."

"Are you kidding? I absolutely have to do this. Now get going."

"All right, but if you change your mind—"

"I won't."

"Then I'd be a fool to pass up the chance." He shoved his feet into his shoes and started for the door.

"Oh, one more thing. Are we actually washing clothes?"

He turned back to her. "We might as well."

"Then bring extra condoms. No telling what we'll think of once we're down there and have to stay awhile."

He groaned. "At this rate, I'll be so hard I won't be able to walk down the stairs."

"But you'll manage it, won't you?" she asked hopefully.

His gaze was hotter than the cotton setting on the dryer. "I'll manage it. See you soon."

Once he was out the door, she dashed into her bedroom, her heart racing as she yanked open drawers and rummaged around, putting together her outfit. This event called for her low-riding cutoffs, her black lace panties and her red silk halter top.

She hurried getting dressed so she wouldn't have any time to think of what she was doing. A quick redo of her hair, a touch of lip gloss, and she was ready. Thank goodness her laundry ritual was set, because otherwise she'd have forgotten her key and her change purse for sure.

She was headed for her door, a wicker basketful of clothes propped against her hip, when her phone rang. Thinking it might be Hunter with some last-minute fantasy instructions, she snatched up the receiver with a breathless hello.

"I'll bet you're struggling with that entertainment center," Shauna said. "I should have volunteered Tim to come over and put it together. Why don't you leave it until tomorrow when he can help, and come have a drink with us? We're going down to Rush Street to hear some jazz."

"Um, thanks, but I'm...on my way to do laundry."

"Laundry? At this hour? I thought you always did laundry on Saturday morning with what's-his-name, your sexy neighbor. Hunter, the swimsuit photographer."

Lindsay was so bad at making up stuff. "We, uh, decided to do it now."

"Oh, you did? On a Friday night? That's a major date night. I thought he had a girlfriend with very big—"

"They sort of broke up."

"Really? How long ago?"

Lindsay knew what was coming, and she rushed to fend it off. "I know what you're going to say, but you don't have to worry, because I'm totally in control of this situation." Now there was a big, hairy lie.

"He just broke up with her, didn't he? Oh, Lindsay, tell me you're not going to mend his broken heart. Tell me you're not going down that road again, after all you've been through. I know we haven't come up with anybody decent yet, but sooner or later we will. In the meantime, please don't pick up a guy on the rebound. Please don't."

"I won't." One night of crazed lust didn't make for a relationship, she told herself. She'd swear off Hunter tomorrow. After they had laundry-room sex.

"Well, I suppose it can't be too romantic between you guys, if you're spending your Friday night washing clothes. So you can let him pour out his woes during the spin cycle if you have to, but don't get involved, okay?"

"I won't get involved. I'm not that dumb. I realize he'll go back to swimsuit models once he's over this breakup." Maybe even the same swimsuit model. Some of her dumpees had made up with their old girlfriends after gaining confidence from her nurturing care.

"That's exactly right. And don't you forget it."

"I won't. Bye, Shauna."

"Before you hang up, tell me if you need Tim to come over tomorrow and finish up your entertainment center. He'll be glad to do it."

Lindsay glanced at the sagging structure that she and Hunter had labored over. She really didn't want Tim to see it and start laughing at their efforts. "That's okay. It's about done. But thanks, anyway."

"Call if you change your mind. Bye."

Lindsay put down the phone and stood still for a moment debating whether she should go down without her laundry and tell Hunter this fantasy wouldn't be happening tonight. Maybe she shouldn't get in any deeper with him, knowing that she was only filling a temporary need.

But, damn it, then she'd be cutting short her one night of abandoned sex with him. Surely she could allow herself this one night. The mistake would be in letting things progress beyond that. She absolutely would not become his interim girlfriend, a temporary replacement for his swimsuit model. If she did that, she'd leave herself open to being discarded once he was over being dumped, exactly as Shauna predicted.

Just for tonight, she would salve Hunter's bruised ego and enjoy the thrill of sex with the man of her dreams. After listening to him through the wall for six months, she certainly deserved that much of a reward.

HUNTER HADN'T WORN his watch, but he was pretty sure more than ten minutes had gone by already. He had his whites in one washer and his darks in the other, and both were agitating like crazy. Still Lindsay hadn't shown up. Well, he'd been afraid this night was too good to be true.

Damned shame. The laundry room had been deserted when he'd arrived, as he'd expected for a Friday night. On the way down here he'd tamed his runaway erection, but once he'd put money into the two machines, added soap and clothes and closed them up, he'd started imagining what was about to happen on top of those white enameled lids. Now his penis strained against his briefs again.

But Lindsay wasn't here. She'd probably had a chance to think of what he'd suggested and come to her senses.

A year ago he never would have thought of something like this, but Pamela had put all kinds of wild ideas into his head. She'd coaxed him into doing it in an elevator and out on the beach next to the lake. He'd discovered the thrill of sexual adventure, and now he wanted to share it with Lindsay.

Instead he might have convinced her that he was some sort of weirdo. She'd seemed excited about the idea while he was there, but she'd still been pumped up with adrenaline from their previous session. When that faded, she might have decided against taking this kind of risk. That could mean he'd screwed things up between them, which was extremely depressing to contemplate.

Then he heard footsteps coming toward the laundry room, and his heartbeat kicked up a notch. But wait...Lindsay didn't walk with a loud clump, clump, clump. Her footsteps were quick and light. These sounded like they were being made by at least a size fourteen.

Sure enough, a guy who looked as if he could play for the Bears came through the doorway carrying a laundry bag over his shoulder. A very big laundry bag. "Hi, bro!" He grinned at Hunter. "Looks like neither one of us scored a date tonight, huh?"

"Well, I—"

"Hey, don't think less of yourself. Women these days...they got *attitude,* man." The guy swung his bag to the floor with a thud. "Half the time they'd rather go out with their girlfriends and drink those fancy martinis than hang with a guy, you know? Anyway, once the Cubs game was over, I wasn't sleepy so I decided to get this done." He opened the bag and started throwing clothes in the nearest washer. Then he moved to the next, and the next, filling up all of the remaining three.

Hunter watched him with a sense of doom. Even if Lindsay showed up, which she might not, the laundry-room fantasy would have to be scuttled unless he could think of some way to get rid of this dateless dude. Maybe Dateless would put his clothes in and leave. That would provide at least twenty minutes of privacy.

Dateless glanced up. "You don't look like you brought anything to do, man."

If you only knew.

"Me, I always bring my games." He reached into the depths of his laundry bag and pulled out a Palm Pilot. "We can both play, if you want."

"Thanks." Hunter grasped at the first thing that came to him. "But you know what? It seems dumb for both of us to stay down here. Why don't you—"

"Hey, want me to mind your clothes for you? I'd be glad to do that. I don't really have anything else to occupy my time tonight. Come on back in an hour or so, and I'll bet most of it will be dry. Just leave me some money for the dryer."

"I was thinking the other way around," Hunter said. "That if you want me to take care of yours, I could do that."

Dateless shrugged. "Like I said, I'm not sleepy and I don't have anything else going on right now." He brightened. "I just downloaded this new game. We could have, like, a tournament while we wait for the clothes."

Hunter wondered if he should agree to the tournament. Lindsay didn't seem to be coming, after all, and his clothes were churning away in the washing machine. Funny how an evening could go from outstanding to disastrous in no time. He'd almost decided to play that tournament when Lindsay walked into the laundry room.

She'd changed to a different pair of cutoffs and halter top, which explained her delay in getting down here. He'd also bet she'd put on new, exciting underwear. Women thought about things like that. Hunter wanted to bang his fists on the washing machine in frustration.

Lindsay paused in the doorway, her expression confused.

"Hi, Lindsay." Hunter couldn't let on that this meeting was more than coincidence. He didn't want Dateless getting any ideas that the rendezvous had been planned. "Guess you decided to wash clothes tonight, too."

"I thought about it." She glanced at Hunter before sweeping her gaze around the laundry room at all the machines humming away. "But it looks like all the machines are taken. I'll come back."

"No, wait!" Dateless said. "This guy's machines were already going when I got here. Look, they're almost to the rinse cycle. Those two machines will be freed up in a jiffy." He seemed desperate not to let this other source of Friday-night company get away. "So you two know each other?"

"We're neighbors," Hunter said.

"Oh, that's cool." Dateless smiled. "I'm Paul. From the second floor. Listen, Lindsay, put your clothes right over there on the folding counter, and you can play in the tournament with Hunter and me until his clothes are done."

Lindsay backed up a step and threw another glance at Hunter. "That's okay. Thanks for the offer, but I have tons of stuff to do upstairs."

Hunter felt like howling in agony. *The opportunity had been right in his grasp.* Now it was gone, and he wasn't sure where he stood with Lindsay. He'd laid everything on the line, probably way too fast. If they'd been able to enact this fantasy, they might have taken off from there, but this roadblock might change everything.

He didn't know what to say, what he could say, with Dateless Paul hanging on their every word. "Sorry about that," he murmured.

She gave him a small smile. "Maybe it's just as well."

He didn't need an interpreter to figure that one out. She was relieved to have the fun and games canceled. He'd made the exact mistake he'd vowed not to make with her—moving so quickly after his breakup that she doubted his sincerity. How ironic. He'd never been more sincere in his life.

After Lindsay walked out of the laundry room, Paul cleared his throat. "Your neighbor, huh?"

"Yeah." Hunter continued to stare at the empty doorway.

"Ever date her?"

"No." *He'd skipped that part and headed straight for the sex. What a class act he was.*

"Boy, I would have by now, that's for sure. I would have asked for her phone number, except with you two knowing each other, I wasn't sure if I'd be trespassing or something."

Hunter glanced up at Paul, who had to be at least seven feet tall. "Actually, I'm not dating her, but I plan to."

Paul smiled. "I thought so, from the way you were looking at her. She's a little skittish, though, huh?"

"I'll work through it." He hoped he could work through it. He was very afraid that he'd blown his chance to create something wonderful with Lindsay.

"Well, good luck. Just because I'm not getting any doesn't mean you shouldn't. Wanna play this game?"

Hunter sighed. Sometimes life just sucked. "Sure."

LINDSAY CARRIED her laundry back upstairs and tried to tell herself that she'd dodged a bullet. Having Paul show up to spoil the party had been like having a seven-foot-tall guardian angel swoop down to save her. Eventually, like maybe in about fifty years, she might forget the sex she'd had with Hunter in her living room. But she would never have forgotten laundry-room sex.

For Hunter, though, it would have been different. He'd been very recently dumped, so laundry-room sex for him would have been about repairing his ego. One wild session in the laundry room might have done the trick, especially with the way Lindsay had been rating him off the charts. Then he would have had no more need for her, while she'd be desperate for more of him.

Well, she was already desperate for more of him. So that proved that laundry-room sex, added to living-room-floor sex, would have made her life one big ball of misery when Hunter decided he'd rebounded and was ready for more swimsuit models. Yeah, Paul had done her a gigantic favor by getting the urge to wash his duds tonight. Really.

After letting herself back in the apartment, she plopped the laundry basket on the floor. No sense in putting it away, because she still had to do laundry this weekend. She wouldn't be doing it tomorrow morning, though. Saturday-morning laundry encounters with Hunter were over, so she'd find another time slot and shake up her routine.

Unsure what to do next, she sat down on the floor beside the laundry basket. For the moment she couldn't make herself go into the living room, where the overturned beer cans and partly assembled entertainment unit would remind her of glories that would never be again.

Oh, Hunter might want to get it on some more. After all, his fantasy had gone unfulfilled. But Lindsay had promised herself not to drag out the connection beyond tonight, and she would keep that promise.

A soft knock sounded at her door. "Lindsay?" Hunter called softly. "Are you still awake?"

The urge to leap up and fling open the door nearly overpowered her. No, she must not. She wouldn't respect herself in the morning.

He tapped again. "Lindsay?"

Her resolve was slipping. She couldn't get up and move away from the door because he might hear that. But listening to his voice was torture. She grabbed some laundry in each hand and held the bunched clothing against her ears, blocking out the sound of his voice. Then she closed her eyes and pictured all the guys who had come crawling to her, their hearts broken, only to say goodbye once the pain was gone.

After many long moments, she took the wad of laundry away from one ear. Silence. Hunter had left.

With a deep sigh, she tossed the laundry back in the basket and stood. Considering how gorgeous Hunter was, and considering his job as a photographer of swimsuit models, she would give him about two weeks before he replaced Silicon Sally with one of her big-busted friends. Although that thought gave Lindsay physical pain, she had to face reality. Once he started dating someone else, her decision to cut off their interaction would be vindicated. The next two weeks promised to be a living hell.

Chapter Five

AS THE DAYS PASSED, Hunter looked for some sign, any sign, that Lindsay thought kindly of him. But if they happened to pass in the hall, her smile was automatic and fake, the kind of polite smile that you gave to strangers on the street. There was no welcome in her eyes whatsoever.

He was sure that she thought he was slime. He didn't know how to correct the picture, because he *was* slime. Instead of following his game plan of several casual dates leading up to more intense dates and finally culminating in the sleepover date, he'd jumped straight to "hide the salami." He had the restraint of a bunny rabbit.

But he still might have saved the situation if he hadn't suggested the laundry-room sex. They could have stayed right up there in her apartment and enjoyed themselves some more, but no, he'd brought up his fantasy. Dumb, dumb, dumb.

After she'd left the laundry room on that fateful night, he'd thought maybe if he talked to her before she cooled off completely, he'd be able to explain himself. But she hadn't answered her door. She'd already cooled off by that time, apparently. Yep, he was slime.

And the worst of it was, he thought this woman might be the one, his soul mate, his forever-and-ever girl. There she was living right next door, and he'd messed up his chance to create a relationship by suggesting kinky sex. Plus he had no idea whatsoever how to repair the damage.

She'd changed her laundry time. He found that out right away, because the next morning he'd gone down there on the chance that she'd be washing her clothes at ten, the way she always had. No Lindsay.

Desperate and pathetic man that he was, he started checking the laundry room at various times on Saturday and Sunday. The first weekend after their disaster he'd had no luck. He'd wondered if she'd resorted to trundling her clothes to the Laundromat three blocks away.

The second weekend, though, he hit pay dirt. He poked his head in on Sunday afternoon and, sure enough, there she was, sitting on the laundry room's only folding chair reading a book while her clothes whirled in the dryer.

He walked in. "Hi."

She glanced up and, for a second, there was a spark in her eyes. Then she doused it. "Hi, Hunter. How have you been?"

He wondered what she'd say if he told her the truth, that he had trouble sleeping, and when he did, he dreamed of her constantly. She'd probably think it was a line to get her back into bed. She might not believe that he was so tortured over her that he hadn't been concentrating at work and had screwed up a couple of shoots in the past week alone.

So he told her he'd been fine. "How about you? How've you been?"

"Just great." She smiled that fakey smile again. "Couldn't be better."

"Good." He nodded, wondering how in hell to proceed. "That's good." He glanced at her clothes tumbling in the dryer. The silence was broken only by the thumps and clicks her stuff made as it hit the metal drum.

"Entertainment center working out okay?" he asked, knowing he was treading on dangerous ground mentioning that.

"Sure is."

He sincerely doubted that, unless she'd called in a carpenter to shore the thing up. "It holds everything?"

"Yep."

"Good." Somehow he had to prolong this conversation, because the sight of her was like water to a man dying of thirst. Her halter top was new, but her cutoffs might be the same ones she'd stripped off for him, or else the second pair she'd worn down to the laundry room. He thought they were the original pair that had got left in a heap on her living-room floor.

"You don't have a laundry basket." Apparently she was tired of his dumb questions. "What brings you down to the basement?"

"You." He had no better answer. "I can understand if you'd want to avoid me, but—"

"Hunter, we can hardly pretend nothing happened and go on like before."

He studied her no-nonsense expression and wondered if that's the one she used when one of her customers was overdrawn at the bank. He was way overdrawn at this bank. "I know," he admitted. "But I really miss the talks we used to have every week while the clothes were washing."

"And the fantasies you were having at the same time?"

He groaned. "I should never have suggested we follow up on that. All the problems started because I suggested it."

"As I said at the time, maybe it was for the best." Her expression didn't soften.

"Look, is there any chance that we can be friends?"

Her gaze flickered slightly. "So that we can do what?"

Start over. "Well, we can—"

"Sharing laundry day is not happening. And that was

pretty much the extent of our friendship. Unless you want to grocery shop together, or we both adopt dogs that we need to walk, I'm not sure what activities we can do as friends."

He rubbed the back of his neck while he gazed at her. She was tougher than he'd thought. When he'd made love to her, he could have sworn that she'd enjoyed every second, like him. She'd been carried away by the moment the same way he had. But there was no getting carried away now.

The more he thought about how she'd reacted that night, the more he wondered if she shouldn't take some of the blame for moving too fast. She'd tempted him, hadn't she? Yes, come to think of it, she definitely had tempted him.

If she thought he was a jerk for making love to her so quickly after his breakup, why hadn't she said so in the beginning? Why get all high and mighty now that it was too late? Getting mad at her felt good, so he allowed himself to do that.

"I guess you're right." He let his irritation show. "Once the cat's out of the bag, or the genie's out of the bottle, there's no shoving it back in, is there?"

"Not really." She looked a little less sure of herself, though.

"I mean, the river moves on, you know? If you stand in one place, it's a different river going past all the time, right?" He had no idea what that image was supposed to mean, exactly, but it sounded sort of indignant and philosophical at the same time, like he was above any petty concerns like whether he'd ever get to touch her again.

"I guess so."

"Then I'll see you around, Lindsay." He stalked out of the laundry room, wishing the entire time she'd call him back. But she didn't. From all indications, she was glad to get rid of him.

FOUR DAYS AFTER the laundry-room confrontation, Lindsay met Shauna in front of the glass-and-brass entrance doors of Divine Events. They were using their lunch hours to choose favors for the reception. Lindsay was glad they'd set up the appointment, because she needed to talk to Shauna.

Lindsay had ended up having to ask Tim to redo her entertainment center, after all. That had been the Sunday right after the fateful Friday night and, while Tim had been hard at work in the living room, Shauna had dragged Lindsay into the kitchen and pried most of the story out of her, even the near miss with laundry-room sex.

Shauna had praised Lindsay for her fortitude in ending the affair before it could go any further. She'd been just as certain as Lindsay that Hunter only needed a boost to his ego, and then he'd move on like all the other guys. They both knew Lindsay had a talent for healing broken hearts that caused her to be taken advantage of.

Lindsay had managed to hang onto her resolution to keep far away from Hunter, but this past Sunday's encounter had shaken her resolve. She needed to find out what Shauna thought about this latest turn of events. Lindsay didn't feel even slightly objective about it.

But Shauna's job as a paralegal had kept her very busy so far this week, and between that and spending her evenings with Tim, she hadn't had available gal-pal time. Although this noon meeting would be short and rushed, Lindsay hoped for a moment to talk.

Shauna's blond hair was twisted into a casual arrangement on top of her head, and she'd taken off the short jacket that matched her blue linen dress. "Whew, can you believe the temperature?" She tucked her sunglasses in her shoulder bag. "I'm melting."

"It's hot." The continued heat wave hadn't helped Lindsay's mood. Sexual frustration, indecision and humid heat made for a miserable existence. She grabbed the brass door handle. "Let's get inside and bask in the AC."

"I'm right behind you."

The blissfully cool lobby scented with a gigantic vase of flowers should have soothed Lindsay's frayed nerves. The flower vase sat on a large round table in the center of the room, and the multicolored arrangement was spectacular. Unfortunately, right in front of the vase lay that damned red leather book of sexual fantasies, taunting her. She wondered if any of the fantasies included laundry-room sex.

"Hi, Shauna, Lindsay," called Livia Divine from the top of a wrought-iron spiral staircase. All the offices and consultation rooms were on the second level. "Give me a sec to straighten out a pesky detail, and I'll be right with you."

"Okay, but don't forget we're both on our lunch break," Shauna called back.

"I won't. In fact, I have some hors d'oeuvres for you to munch on while we talk. I told Gia I'd have you taste them and make a decision on that today, too. I only need a couple of minutes to deal with a small crisis involving some mismatched tablecloths, and don't panic, because it's not your event." With that, she hurried back into her office.

Lindsay admired how well the three cousins who ran the business interwove their capabilities. Livia Divine handled all visuals, from decorations to gowns, while Cecily Divine took care of entertainment and Gia Divine was the caterer. If Lindsay ever had a wedding, which at this point was in serious doubt, she would definitely plan it through Divine Events.

"I sure hope she makes it quick." Shauna walked over to a love seat and sat down. "Work is crazy, and I probably shouldn't even be taking lunch." She opened her purse and started searching through it. "I hope I remembered to bring the list of things I wanted to ask Livia."

Lindsay sat beside her. "Yeah, I know you've been busy, which is why I haven't called you."

Shauna must have picked up something from her tone, because she stopped searching for her list and met Lindsay's gaze. "What's up?"

"He doesn't have a new girlfriend yet."

Shauna didn't have to ask who Lindsay was talking about. "So what? It hasn't been that long."

"More than two weeks. I thought a guy with his contacts would have been dating again within two weeks."

Shauna considered that. "He could be dating. You don't know that he's not dating."

"Yes, I do. He's not dating."

"How do you know that for sure?" Shauna laughed. "Did you sneak over there and bug his apartment?"

"I live right next door. If he was seeing somebody, I'd catch a glimpse of her sooner or later." Although Shauna was her best friend, Lindsay hadn't told her about all the nights she'd eavesdropped on Hunter's nighttime activities. And she would *never* admit to putting a glass against the wall, not even under extreme torture. "But that's not all. He's been trying to find out when I do laundry. And Sunday he came down to the basement while I was there to talk to me."

Shauna's eyebrows lifted. "And? What did he say?"

"That he missed our laundry-room chats, and he shouldn't have asked me to help him enact his fantasy."

Shauna nodded. "And you said...?"

"That we couldn't go back to the way things had been before."

"Excellent. Keep away from that bad boy. He's rebounding, and you're in the line of fire."

Lindsay stared at the huge bouquet of flowers, a riot of reds, purples, pinks and whites. She'd expected that response from Shauna. "But don't you think if he hasn't started dating again, and he's still wishing we could be friends, and he followed me to the laundry room, that—"

"No, I do not. Look at me, girl." Shauna caught Lindsay's chin and forced her to meet her gaze. "I'm the one who's been around to pick up the pieces, remember?"

"Yes, but this time maybe it's diff—"

"Lindsay, Lindsay, Lindsay. You're a caring, nurturing person. A guy pulls a hangdog expression and you're ready to cuddle him and make it better. Hunter might need that now, but once he's over the breakup, you *know* what he'll do. You've seen him at his most vulnerable. A guy can't handle that. He has to split. We've talked about this a gazillion times."

Lindsay sighed. "I'm sure you're right."

"I am right. I'm only thinking of you, honeybunch. Once I get through this rough patch at work, we'll go out trolling again. Your dream guy is out there. We just haven't found him yet."

Yes, I have.

Livia appeared at the top of the wrought-iron stairs. "Come on up, you guys. Let's pig out on Gia's concoctions while we choose some wedding favors!"

THIRTY MINUTES LATER, chock-full of pâté, minced olives, smoked salmon and various kinds of cheese, Lindsay descended the spiral staircase with Shauna. On the way out the door, she glanced longingly at the red leather book sitting in front of the flower vase.

Although she'd tried to keep her attention on wedding favors and hors d'oeuvres, she'd spent most of the time in Livia's office thinking about Hunter. He'd come looking for her on Sunday. Considering his recent breakup, taking a chance on another rejection had required a lot of courage. And, sure enough, she'd rejected him.

He'd reacted with anger, as any man with an ounce

of pride would have. She couldn't expect him to approach her again. According to Shauna, that was a good thing, but Lindsay couldn't accept the finality of it. She'd dreamed about Hunter for six months, and then she'd experienced the most wonderful sex of her life with him.

If that night had been nothing but first aid for his wounded ego, then why hadn't he found another woman to pick up the slack? Two weeks later, which was a long time for a highly sexed guy like Hunter, he still wanted to spend time with her. That wasn't rebound behavior, and she was the expert on that. The guys she'd nursed through broken hearts had clung to her like Velcro for the first two or three weeks after they'd been dumped, as if they needed constant reassurance that they were worthy of attention. She'd seen Hunter a single time over the past two weeks.

Maybe Hunter's ego was in better shape than she'd thought. If so, then she'd blown the chance of a lifetime by brushing him off when he'd come looking for her on Sunday. Making up for that would require something spectacular.

On the sidewalk outside Divine Events, Shauna gave her a hug. "Next week we'll have a girls' night out," she said. "I feel terrible for ignoring you when you're going through this Hunter thing." She looked into Lindsay's eyes before she put on her sunglasses. "Be strong. If you find yourself weakening, call me on my cell and I'll talk you down."

Lindsay smiled. "You sound like I'm addicted to rebound guys."

"For a while there, it was beginning to look that way, but it's been a whole year since you got involved with someone like that. Stay away from Hunter and you're home free."

"Right." Lindsay put on her sunglasses, so Shauna couldn't read the doubts in her eyes. "See you next week."

"Tuesday night," Shauna said. "Let's make it then. We'll start with the usual spot and branch out from there."

"Okay, Tuesday night." The thought of hitting jazz clubs looking for available single men next Tuesday night sounded awful. She simply wasn't interested.

With a wave, Shauna headed down the street toward the law office where she worked.

Lindsay's bus stop was in the opposite direction. She had exactly enough time to make the next bus, which would get her back to the bank before her lunch break was over. She hesitated, battling her indecision.

She knew herself, and if she walked away from Divine Events now, she wouldn't come back until Shauna scheduled another appointment, which could be three or four weeks away. In three or four weeks her opportunity would have disappeared. It was now or never.

Her heart pounded as she grabbed the brass door handle and walked back inside. No one was in the reception area. She had the red book all to herself. She ran two fingers over the supple leather. There was no title embossed on it.

From Shauna's description, she already knew the book was actually a large paperback the size and thickness of one of her bank training manuals. The leather cover was there for propriety's sake, to disguise the racy title from casual observers. She opened it now and read the title page. *Sexcapades: Secret Games and Wild Adventures for Uninhibited Lovers.*

Hunter would love this. If she had the courage to act out one of the suggestions in this book, he would…what? Be her slave forever? Maybe not. That was a lot to ask for. But after hearing about his laundry-room fantasy she knew that sexual games would definitely get his attention. Did she want that?

She heard a sound from upstairs. Flipping open the book, she grabbed one of the perforated pages and ripped it out. The sound echoed in the reception area. She stuffed the page quickly into her purse and headed for the door. Although she had torn out a page, that didn't mean she had to follow through. She could throw it away when she got home.

"Lindsay? Did you need to see me?" Livia called out to her from the second floor.

Lindsay turned and glanced up the stairs, feeling guilty as a bank robber, certain she was blushing as red as the book on the table. "I, um, forgot something."

Livia smiled. "That happens a lot around here."

"I took a page out of the book," she confessed in one breath. She'd never make a decent thief.

"You're welcome to do that. We leave it on the table so that people can help themselves. When it gets too thin, we bring out a new one."

"Still, it's supposed to be for Divine Events clients, and technically I'm not a client."

Livia smile widened. "Then I'd better warn you about something."

"What?"

"That book has the power to turn you into a client."

Chapter Six

WHILE SHE WAS at work, Lindsay didn't dare look at the fantasy she'd torn out, and the afternoon of standing at the teller's window smiling at customers dragged by. Maybe she should have torn out several so that she'd have a choice. This one might be way beyond her comfort zone.

Wait a minute—had she really decided to tempt Hunter with a sexual fantasy? Had she gone from merely considering it as a far-fetched possibility to actually planning the seduction? She'd better find out what sort of adventure she'd chosen before she made that decision. Shauna had said some of the concepts in the book were over the top.

She was so caught up in thinking about her *Sexcapades* page that she almost missed seeing Hunter standing in line waiting for a teller. This wasn't his bank, so there could only be one reason why he was here—to see her. That became crystal clear after he let someone go ahead of him when it was his turn and Lindsay was still busy with Mrs. Detweiler.

He looked wonderful—cool and crisp in a white polo shirt and khaki slacks. She'd actually held this beautiful man in her arms. Then she'd turned away the chance to do it again. She was as crazy as his ex.

Or maybe not. Seeing Hunter ignited a sexual response

in her, but that wasn't the only thing going on. Her heart ached with the kind of longing that suggested she'd moved beyond mere lust. Maybe she'd gone beyond mere lust weeks ago. Shauna had told her that she suspected Lindsay was falling in love with Hunter, thus Shauna's fiercely protective stance.

Hunter posed a danger, no doubt about it. And yet he didn't look dangerous standing there. He looked dear, sweet and sexier than should be legal. Most important of all, he'd come to the bank to see her.

Poor Mrs. Detweiler must have thought she was on drugs. A simple deposit of the white-haired woman's Social Security check turned into a three-act play as Lindsay entered the wrong amount twice, dropped the deposit slip on the floor and tore it in half when she pulled it out from under a corner of the counter.

"This isn't like you, Lindsay," Mrs. Detweiler said. "And you look flushed, too. You'd better go for a checkup."

"I'm fine, Mrs. Detweiler." Lindsay finally managed to hand the older woman her deposit slip while she tried to ignore Hunter gesturing yet another person ahead of him in line. "It's been one of those days."

"All the same, it wouldn't hurt to see a doctor. Dealing with people all day, you could have picked up anything, anything at all."

"I suppose that's true."

"Young people today don't take care of themselves. You don't get enough sleep, for one thing."

Lindsay certainly fit in that category. She found it tough to sleep while yearning for Hunter.

"So will you promise to make an appointment for yourself?" Mrs. Detweiler asked.

"Yes, yes, I will. And thank you, Mrs. Detweiler." When Lindsay forced herself to smile, her face felt stiffer than cardboard. Despite that, she wanted to appear as cool and collected as Hunter looked standing there in line. Instead a fire raged inside her and sweat trickled down her back.

"You're welcome. See you next month." Mrs. Detweiler tucked her deposit slip into her purse and left.

Hunter walked toward her window and Lindsay swallowed. "Hello."

"Hello." He slid a check across the granite counter. "I need to cash this."

"Certainly." Her pulse racing, her response on autopilot, Lindsay took the check, which was from *Instant Replay*. When she flipped it over, she saw that he'd forgotten to sign it. Maybe he wasn't as composed as he looked. "You need to endorse this." She pushed a pen toward him along with the check, willing her hands not to shake.

"Oh, right." He scribbled his name across the short end of the check. "I, um, I'm going out of town on assignment."

"Out of town?" The question came out in a squeak of protest. Damn. She cleared her throat. "I, uh, mean...I didn't know you were going somewhere." That could have an impact on several things, including the fantasy she had hidden in her purse in the back room.

She glanced at the address on the front of his check and noticed the *Instant Replay* offices were on Michigan Avenue not far from Divine Events. Lucky she hadn't run into him after tearing out the page. No telling how she might have reacted.

"The editor just told me yesterday. There's a women's tennis program down in Florida that's turning out some awesome players. I'll take a day to shoot some of the stars, and then I'm flying down to Nassau to do a photo spread on snorkeling."

"Sounds like a fairly extensive trip."

"Ten days."

Ten days. If she had to spend ten days stewing in her

knowledge of how she felt about him and debating whether to use the fantasy, she'd be ready for the funny farm by the time he got back. She opened her cash drawer. "How did you want this?"

"All hundreds, I guess. No, wait, better give me at least two hundred of it in tens and twenties."

She nodded and concentrated on the money as she counted it out for him. If she'd screwed up Mrs. Detweiler's deposit, she was certainly capable of short-changing Hunter.

When she finished laying the bills on the counter, he scooped them up and stuffed them in his wallet. "Thanks."

"When are you leaving?" She tried her best to make the question sound like idle curiosity.

From the way his head came up and the intensity of his expression, she'd failed. "I'm taking the red-eye out tomorrow night. Why?" He waited expectantly.

She had no idea what to say. "I...wondered if you... wanted me to...water your plants." *Or give you a going away party you'll never forget?*

"Thanks, but I don't have any plants. Although now that you mention it, I could use a favor." He fished in his pocket and came up with a small key. "I'd appreciate it if you'd take in my mail."

Her hopes, raised by his cashing a check here when he could have cashed it at his own bank, died. He needed someone to take in his mail, and he'd thought of a way to cash his check and get the mail question out of the way in one trip.

"I can do that." She took the mailbox key and tucked it in the pocket of her jacket.

"Thanks. I'll see you when I get back, then."

"Have a safe trip." Now wasn't that a boring exchange? He would never guess from this conversation that earlier today she'd ripped a page out of a book full of wild sexual adventures and that she'd been planning to use the page to seduce *him*. Obviously he'd put his laundry-room fantasies behind him and now he only saw her as a convenient neighbor who'd take in his mail. Meanwhile she'd fallen hard for the boy next door. What a depressing turn of events.

HUNTER LEFT the bank and headed for his favorite corner bar and an early dinner. He ordered a beer and a sandwich. Then he ordered another beer, and another. Watching sports he didn't care about and talking with people he barely knew, he proceeded to get thoroughly smashed.

If he'd had some idea that Lindsay would be sorry to see him leave on this trip, or that she'd suggest they might have dinner together before he went, he'd been dreaming. The mail thing had been his feeble, pathetic excuse to see her again and tell her he was going. He didn't need her to take in his mail. For years he'd had an arrangement with the post office and they held his mail any time he went out of town. All he had to do was notify them.

Now he'd roped Lindsay into collecting his mail, and she would, because she was polite and considerate. She was a helpful person. She'd looked incredible in that turquoise silk suit, although the jacket had hidden her curves. She'd look good wearing a green garbage bag. She was a goddess. And he was a sex-crazed lunatic who wasn't worthy of standing in front of her teller window.

Finally he grew tired of the bar and poured himself into a cab. Back in his apartment, he stumbled around getting ready for bed. Then he tried to be a little quieter. Now that he knew how easily Lindsay could hear him, he didn't want to add to his sins by waking her up.

Yes, he did. He wanted to pound on that wall and beg

her to let him come over and make love to her until he had
to fly out tomorrow night. He could imagine how she'd
react if he started banging on the wall and shouting her
name. She'd probably call the cops.

With a heavy sigh, he lay on the bed under the cooling
breeze of the AC. It didn't help cool his blood a damn bit.
The bed began to revolve, and he grimaced. He'd have a
beauty of a hangover at work tomorrow. Fortunately all
he had to do was handle a backlog of picture editing he'd
been putting off for weeks. He always liked to tie up loose
ends before he took off on an assignment.

But there was one loose end he wouldn't be able to do
anything about. When he got back, Lindsay would be
even farther away, even though she continued to live
right next door. He turned over and pounded the pillow
in despair.

LINDSAY WAS SITTING UP in bed, the fantasy sheet on her
lap, her thoughts scrambled, when she heard Hunter come
home. She automatically listened to discover whether he
was alone. Judging from the way he was banging around
without talking, he was most definitely alone, and he was
either upset, drunk or both.

She'd had some time to think after Hunter had left the
bank. He'd never asked her to take in his mail in the many
months they'd been neighbors, and she knew for a fact
he'd gone out of town on assignments before, because he
used to tell her when he wouldn't be showing up to do
laundry.

Because of all the traveling, he would have set up a system with the post office a long time ago. It was only log-
ical. That meant the visit to her bank and the mail request
had been another attempt to make contact, to break
through the barrier she'd thrown up.

She didn't know if it was sexual desire or something

more that was driving him. Shauna would say that he was still in rebound mode, and for some reason he was stubbornly counting on her to get him through. Maybe so, but Lindsay had a gut feeling that something else was going on.

Shauna would kill her for even considering that Hunter's attraction to her might be the real deal and not his reaction to being dumped. But Shauna didn't know the whole story, and because of Lindsay's history, she had reason to be skeptical. Lindsay didn't want that history to cause her to make a terrible mistake of a different kind from that which Shauna feared.

Hunter had approached her again, and that was huge. After being rejected by his ex, he'd risked more rejection by coming to the bank today. Sure enough, she'd offered him no encouragement. If he was banging around his apartment because he was upset, she might be the reason.

She could go over there, knock on his door and find out. But if he'd spent the night drinking his cares away, the encounter might not be all she could hope for. Besides, that wouldn't have even the slightest touch of fantasy, and if she and Hunter had a future, she wanted that future to be filled with the kind of sexual excitement they both loved.

Glancing at the page from *Sexcapades* lying in her lap, she took a deep breath. Attempting this sexual fantasy would take courage even if she were completely sure of the man in question. With Hunter, she was sure of nothing. She might embarrass herself and go down in bitter defeat.

But then again, she might win the day. She had very few hours in which to make a decision. Overriding Shauna's warnings that echoed in her head, she read the fantasy one more time.

HUNTER DRAGGED HIMSELF through the next morning with the help of coffee and aspirin. Fortunately nobody at the office needed him for anything, or maybe they sensed he was a bear with a wounded paw. In any case, the rest of the staff left him alone in his little windowless cubicle to work as best he could. By lunchtime he actually felt like eating something and accepted the invitation from some work buddies to go with them to get a sandwich.

His outlook improved considerably after that, and when four o'clock rolled around, he was beginning to think he might live. As he clicked through more digital shots on his computer, he thought about the approaching trip. He'd get some sleep on the plane that night, and by tomorrow he should be in shape to shoot the tennis stars.

The tennis pro running the program had specifically requested him, and Hunter had a good idea why. The pro apparently wanted to put some glamour into his program, and Hunter was known for his ability to take pictures with a certain mystique about them.

Because he'd always had that ability, he'd never questioned it. But after discovering a wilder brand of sex with Pamela's help, he'd concluded that he had a hedonistic streak. Pamela had brought it up to a conscious level, but it had been there all along, running underneath everything he did and influencing the way he photographed women.

He'd spent a good part of the day editing previous work, and when he flipped through his shots, he could see it. He used light to bring out the curve of a breast, the pout of a lower lip, the tilt of a pelvis. He loved the possibilities suggested by the female form. That devotion was the basis of his career.

It was a big part of his attraction to Lindsay, too. She had a classic body, and he was just the guy to appreciate that. He wished they had the closeness that would allow him to photograph her in the nude. With digital photography, it could be a totally private project, produced only for his creative satisfaction.

Yes, Lindsay beckoned to the artist in him, but there was another link, too. As Pamela had recognized the pleasure seeker in him, he recognized the pleasure seeker in Lindsay. She hadn't balked at his laundry-room suggestion. Instinctively he'd known she could be sexually daring.

But she was so much more than that. She was his cheerful companion during their Saturday-morning suds-and-duds fests. She was his spunky neighbor who thought she could put together an entertainment center with a Swiss Army knife. And she was also the caring woman who hadn't wanted him to be alone after getting a sexual rating of five-minus.

No doubt about it, he was hooked on Lindsay Scott. But he couldn't do a damned thing about it. The friendship route was closed to him now, and he'd burned the sexual route to ashes in one ill-advised night.

Maybe while he was on this assignment he'd come up with a way around the difficulties. Maybe ten days without seeing him would make her miss him enough that they could patch things up. Maybe—

"Hunter?"

He glanced up from the screen and blinked. Lindsay stood in his office wearing a trench coat. In July. In the middle of the hottest summer in recent memory. She looked like a moll in a gangster movie.

He swallowed. "Hi. Aren't you...supposed to be at the bank?" *Wearing normal summer clothes?*

"I left a little early." Her cheeks were flushed, probably from wearing the coat outside. Even in the air-conditioned building that coat had to be uncomfortable.

A possibility whispered through his mind, but he dismissed it. Such things didn't really happen. "So what brings you down to Michigan Avenue?"

She cleared her throat. "I, uh, thought that after all that

work helping me put the entertainment center together, you might like to come over and see a movie."

He forgot to breathe. She was issuing an invitation, but he couldn't figure out exactly what kind. And, hell, he was leaving town at midnight. "You mean when I get back from this assignment?"

"I mean before you leave."

Oh, no. She wanted to make up. In the most time-honored way. But he couldn't figure out the trench coat, unless... Surely she wouldn't have some skimpy outfit on under it. Pamela might try something like that, but not Lindsay. At least not this early in the game.

Yet he couldn't imagine why else she'd wear the coat. As his body started heating up, he cursed the magazine for sending him on assignment and wondered how much it would cost him to delay his flight until tomorrow. "I don't have a lot of time."

Uncertainty flickered in her eyes. "Then maybe it's not a good idea. You probably have to pack, and—"

"I'm a fast packer." He'd get on the plane without a suitcase and improvise when he arrived if it meant quality time with Lindsay. "I didn't say I couldn't see a movie tonight. I was only warning you that I have to catch a plane."

"So you would like to do the movie thing?"

He looked directly into her eyes. "Very much."

"Would you like to help me pick it out? There's a video place not far from here, and then we could ride the 'L' home together."

Something was going on. He wasn't sure what, but he had a feeling he was going to like it a lot. "Sure. Let me close up shop here."

"Take your time." She loosened the belt of her trench coat.

He stared at the belt, wondering... No, his imagination was getting the best of him. "Have a seat, if you want."

"I'd rather look around your office. You have some great pictures on the walls. Although I have to say it's a little warm in here." Then she opened her coat.

He gasped. Under the coat she wore stockings, a black lace garter belt...and nothing else.

Chapter Seven

"WHOOPS." Lindsay pulled her coat together and retied the belt. She was *way* out of her comfort zone. Her heart pounded and her palms were slippery with sweat, but Hunter's expression was worth it all.

He looked as if someone had set off a strobe light two inches from his face. "Wh-what…are you…" His voice trailed off, as if he'd forgotten how to string words together.

She smiled and wandered over to the pictures lining the wall near his desk, so he'd get a look at her four-inch heels and the seam going up the back of her stockings. "You're very talented, Hunter. I particularly like this one." She reached up and pointed to a framed photo of a couple silhouetted on a beach at sunset. Her coat rose to mid-thigh.

"Let's get the hell out of here." Hunter sounded like a man with a bad cold.

She glanced over her shoulder. "To the video store?"

His breathing was labored. "Forget the video store. I'll call a cab."

"Oh, no, Hunter." She turned and prowled back to his desk. She was loving this, absolutely loving it. Excitement rushed through her, making her wet and achy. One look at Hunter's lap told her of his condition.

She perched on the edge of his desk and let her coat fall

away from one silk-covered thigh. "You wouldn't want to ruin my fantasy, now would you?"

A muscle in his jaw twitched as he stared at her smooth thigh. When he glanced up, his eyes were nearly all pupil, no iris. "Lindsay, you're *naked*."

"I know. Isn't it amazing?"

"It sure as hell is. And I'm—"

"Going crazy, I hope." She leaned toward him. "You and I know what's happening, but no one else will."

"That's what you think. Don't forget, I don't have a trench coat."

She laughed and gazed deliberately at his crotch. "So you have a slightly *bigger* challenge, so to speak. But you're not running nearly the same risk, so don't complain to me."

He quivered. "I can't believe you're doing this."

"But I am." She slid off the desk and walked deliberately toward the door of his office. "Next stop, the video store."

"Wait!"

"Sorry, I have to get a move on. You said something about needing to catch a plane." As she left his office, she heard his soft curse and the sound of rapidly clicking keys on his computer.

Then he was beside her, his camera bag slung over one shoulder. "Okay, let's go."

"Glad you could make it." She smiled at his curious co-workers as she and Hunter headed down the hall and through the *Instant Replay* reception area. She was prepared to stroll, but Hunter took her elbow and propelled her as fast as her four-inch heels would allow. "In a hurry?" she asked.

"You have no idea." He called out a few quick good-byes along the way before hustling her out into the hall and shoving her into the first available elevator.

When the elevator turned out to be empty, she flashed him again, quickly opening her coat and then closing it just as fast.

He groaned.

"It's all part of the fantasy." She retied the belt as the elevator stopped to take on more passengers. Desire was so thick in the small enclosure she wondered if the two businessmen who got on would sense it.

They both eyed her with interest, glanced at the grip Hunter had on her elbow and looked away, as if understanding a territorial signal.

Out on the street, people were too busy with their own concerns to pay much attention to a woman wearing a trench coat in July. The sun had disappeared behind the tall buildings, so she no longer needed sunglasses. She left them in her coat pocket.

On the way to Hunter's office she'd worn them for disguise more than anything. She'd been self-conscious about appearing in public like this, but now with Hunter striding along beside her in a state of sexual arousal, she didn't care what anyone else might think. She didn't imagine he'd easily forget escorting a nearly naked woman down Michigan Avenue. The memory should carry him way beyond the ten days he'd be gone.

"What changed?" he asked as they dodged pedestrians on their rapid course toward the video store. He concentrated on keeping them moving and didn't look at her.

"What do you mean?"

"Yesterday you wouldn't give me the time of day. Today you seem determined to turn me inside out." He steered her around a pair of teenagers wearing earphones. "What changed?"

"I had a chance to think about you asking me to get your mail. Did you really have to do that?"

"No."

Warmth flooded through her. What a great feeling to know that Hunter had actively pursued her. "That's what I thought." Or at least what she'd hoped.

"But why—oh, never mind why. I'm not going to louse this up with questions. Here's the video place." He held the door open for her. "Do I have to even ask what section you're going to look through?"

She paused to smile at him. "Probably not. Follow me."

"Don't worry. I'm right behind you."

She located the adult video section and sauntered toward it. She could almost feel Hunter's hot breath on her neck as he followed her. At four-thirty in the afternoon the store was almost empty of customers. She and Hunter were the only ones in the adult aisle, which played right into her hands. Slowly she scanned the shelves.

"I suppose this is going to take a while." Although he was obviously trying to appear blasé, the tremor in his voice betrayed him.

"Naturally." She tapped her finger against her mouth. "Maybe this one." She stretched to the top shelf for a video titled *Caution: Hot When Turned On.* "This could be a sign posted on a clothes dryer, don't you think?"

"I can't think."

"Brain fried?"

"Uh-huh."

"Poor baby." She handed him the video. "Hold this."

"Can we take this one and leave?"

"No." She glanced around to make sure they were still alone. "I just wanted you to hold it so I could do this." She pulled the lapels of her coat apart and gave him a quick peek at her breasts.

"Lindsay!"

She covered up again and batted her eyelashes at him. "Goodness, but you're jumpy."

He lowered his voice. "I'm about to jump *you*, right

here in the aisle. How would you like that, if I backed you up against a shelf and did you, right here and now? I could be inside you in three seconds."

A shiver, part excitement, part apprehension, ran from the base of her spine to her neck, making the tiny hairs stand on end. "You wouldn't do that."

"An hour ago I would have agreed with you." His eyes glittered. "But you're pushing me. No telling what I might do if you push far enough."

"That sounds like a threat." She ran her tongue over her lips. The *Sexcapades* book hadn't anticipated a man out of control. As the seducer, she was supposed to have him at her mercy, ready to obey her command, following her around like a puppy. At the moment, Hunter looked more like a full-grown Doberman.

"I don't make threats." He held up the video. "You might want to get this one."

She backed up a step. "The video store part was supposed to take longer."

"Who says?" He advanced, the video in his hand. "Did somebody script this fantasy?"

She wasn't prepared to tell him about the *Sexcapades* book, at least not yet. "Uh, well—"

"Never mind. I don't care where you got the idea, but I strongly suggest you rent this video while I go outside and hail us a cab."

"But the 'L' would take longer and build the excitement."

"A trainload of commuters would get quite a show if we take the 'L'."

"It's also cheaper than a cab."

"As if I care at a moment like this." He handed her the video. "See you outside in five minutes."

HUNTER CHARGED for the front door of the video store, afraid if he stood in that aisle another nanosecond he would grab Lindsay and shove her coat open. No woman, not even a wild one like Pamela, had driven him past reason. But as he'd watched Lindsay sashaying along beside the shelves of adult videos, he'd felt reason slipping away and animal instinct taking over.

He stood outside on the sidewalk gulping in the sultry air. His blood pumped frantically, and he had to use his camera case to disguise his erection. Lindsay had no idea the power she had, and she'd used it with reckless abandon. Her stunt was incredible overkill. If she'd suggested dinner yesterday, he would have been her slave. Instead she'd appeared today wearing only a trench coat.

A cab. He was out here to get a cab. With tremendous effort, he shoved the picture of Lindsay flashing him out of his fevered brain long enough to whistle for a taxi. Fortunately one swerved to the curb exactly as Lindsay came out of the store, a small bag in one hand. The video. As if they'd need to watch it.

He used some care getting her into the cab, because he didn't want that trench coat to shift and expose anything illegal. Then he climbed in after her and gave the cabbie the address. As the taxi veered back into traffic, Hunter gripped his camera bag with both hands. Now he had to ride through the streets of downtown Chicago at rush hour with a naked woman next to him.

Lindsay pulled the video out of the bag. "Have you seen this one?"

Hunter gritted his teeth. "No."

"Me, either. That's good, that it'll be a new movie for both of us." She sounded as if she were discussing the latest James Bond flick.

Condoms. He wondered if she'd thought of that, because they wouldn't get beyond the front entryway of her apartment, and he wasn't packing any. Hadn't thought there was a reason to. Hadn't counted on a naked Lindsay waltzing into his office this afternoon.

He cleared his throat. "Do you, uh, have the necessary, uh…" He was afraid the cabbie might be listening. After all, he'd picked them up outside of a video store and one of them was wearing a trench coat in July. He might think Lindsay was a hooker. "I mean, I'm not prepared for…"

She lowered her voice to a silky, seductive level. "I'm prepared. Extremely prepared."

He didn't dare look at her. Instead he faced forward, his back straight and his fingers clutching the camera bag in a death grip. "Good."

She leaned closer and whispered in his ear. "It will be. Very."

"Watch it." His erection strained against his briefs. "We're only halfway home."

"I'm surprised at you," she said softly. "You've had so much experience, that I thought you'd be more calm about this."

"Experience?" Nothing had prepared him for an event like this.

"I'm only judging from what went on in your apartment for six months. From what I heard through the wall, I would assume that you've had lots of—"

"Lindsay."

"What?"

"Don't talk."

"That bad, huh?" She sounded pleased with herself.

"That bad." He wasn't ashamed to admit it. He prayed for an opening in traffic as their journey turned into an endless taxi ride. Every sway of the cab and every jolt when the driver hit the brakes tortured his aching penis. He focused on baseball stats, counted up his frequent flyer miles, silently recited his Social Security number a dozen times and tried to remember the phone numbers of all the people he knew.

Finally. The cab pulled up in front of the apartment building and by some miracle Hunter remembered to pay the guy. Somehow he stumbled up the four flights of stairs without grabbing Lindsay on one of the landings. She seemed to be having a high old time, giggling at his haste. Yeah, well, he'd see how she felt in a few minutes, when he ripped off that trench coat and... No, he'd better not think of that until they were inside her door.

He was glad that she was fast with the key, and he nearly pushed her through the door once she opened it.

"Okay." He plopped the camera bag on the floor. "Forget the video." He turned to her. "I want..." He halted. She still had on that maddening trench coat, but now she was holding her laundry basket.

Her eyes glowed with blue flame and her chest heaved as she struggled for breath. Her calmness seemed to have disappeared. "As you might have noticed, I have...nothing to wear. I need to wash...a few things. Do you mind?"

And he'd thought this couldn't get more intense. He took a shaky breath. "You're gonna kill me, you know that?"

"Yes, but you'll die a happy man." She reached into the basket and tossed him a condom.

His reflexes must not have been totally shot, because he caught it and put it in his pocket.

"Come on, Hunter." She gave him a long once-over. "Let's combine fantasies."

He nodded, his brain spinning, his body straining with almost unbearable tension. Once again, he followed her, this time down to the basement. If somebody was in there washing clothes, he'd throw them out. He didn't care what the consequences would be.

Instead, the door to the laundry room was closed, and a sign was tacked on it that read Laundry Room Temporarily Closed Due to Electrical Problems.

"Damn it!" Hunter's frustration reached the boiling

point. No way could he make it back up those stairs without some kind of relief. No way.

Lindsay laughed, turned the knob and walked inside. "Like my sign?"

Her sign. Hunter dashed inside the laundry room and slammed the door shut. "I love your sign. Lindsay, we don't have to start the washers. We can just do it right here. On the floor. Anywhere. Let me take off that damned coat." He reached for her.

"Nope." She danced out of reach. "These clothes are going in those two old washers."

"I don't care about the fantasy! I need—"

"Hands off." She laughed again, the sound bubbling with excitement as she threw clothes into the washers. "We're doing this, Hunter. Don't chicken out on me now."

That brought him up short, even if didn't do anything for his condition. Pamela used to warn him not to chicken out, and he'd moved beyond his normal limits because of her taunts. He wasn't about to backtrack now just because Lindsay happened to be the hottest woman he'd ever known. No, by damn, he'd prove he was up to the challenge.

So he stood, his fists clenched, all of him clenched, while Lindsay put in soap, *fabric softener,* for God's sake, and money to start the machine.

After eons had gone by, she glanced over her shoulder again. "Hunter, would you please take my coat?"

Oh, yes, he most certainly would. Hands trembling, he reached for the collar and drew the coat down, down, until it cleared her arms. Then he tossed it across the top of the two machines.

Slowly she rotated on those impossibly high heels. "This is it."

And he knew he had to take the time to burn this picture into his mind—Lindsay standing before him, her gaze hot, her breasts lifted, her hips circled with a black lace garter belt. And below that, her downy triangle of curls guided him to everything he desired in the world at this moment.

"You're magnificent," he said, his voice a low growl of appreciation.

"Just call me Laundry-Room Girl."

"I call you amazing." He couldn't wait any longer. Grasping her waist, he lifted her up onto the nearest machine. And didn't that put her in the perfect position for him to drive her crazy for a change? Before she could react, he was on his knees, his shoulders slipping under her silk-clad thighs.

Her gasp as he zeroed in on his target was more than enough reward, but he had more rewards in mind. Loving her this way tested his endurance even more, but finally he had a chance to level the playing field and make her as wild as he was.

"Oh, Hunter...the vibration is...oh...oh, *my.*"

About damn time, he thought. She'd been in control way too long. Her heels dug into his back as he took her higher and higher.

Gasping and crying out his name, she came in a rush of moisture that made him dizzy with triumph. He eased slowly away from her, stood on shaky legs and reached for the zipper of his fly. Then he took out the condom. He could barely manage the necessary movements as he trembled with the need to be inside her, sliding back and forth in that slick, warm chamber.

He gazed at her flushed, responsive body. His voice was thick with unreleased tension. "Lie down."

With a moan of surrender, she turned and lay back, bending her knees. Her upper body rested on one washer and her hips on the other. Hunter had just enough room to climb up between her thighs. "Scoot...scoot up."

She was breathing as hard as he was. "My head will be off the edge."

He grinned at her, feeling wilder and more reckless than at any time in his sexual life. "This is insane."

"Yeah, it is."

He grabbed the control panel at the back of the washer and slipped his other hand under her head. "Scoot up. I'll hold your head."

She did, which put her in range of his very stiff penis. "Now lift your hips."

Clutching the control panel in imitation of his move, she lifted her hips. "Like that?"

"Like that." And he pushed deep inside her. He closed his eyes, his head swimming with pleasure.

"Good?"

"You have no idea." He opened his eyes and gazed down at her. At this moment she owned him, body and soul.

She smiled at him. "Better do me quick before I collapse."

"Trust me, this won't take long." He began a rapid, yet controlled rhythm, and the agitating machines beneath him sent vibrations up through his knees to his groin, creating an unreal sensation that would bring him to a climax in no time at all.

"Mmm." She gripped his bottom with her free hand.

He slowed, forced his body back a few notches, and looked into her eyes. "Gonna come again, Laundry-Room Girl?"

"Could be." She rotated her hips. "Maybe I can hang out in this position longer than I thought."

"Then you set the pace." Somehow he'd hold back the climax shouldering its way toward the front of the line. "Tell me what you want."

"Slower. A little deeper."

He shifted and thrust home, once, twice, three times.

"Like that." She began to pant as he maintained a steady pace. "Oh, yes, like that."

Each time he pushed into her, his heart opened a little wider. They belonged together. Forever.

"There…that's it…yes, *yes!*" She arched against him as spasms rippled through her.

That tipped him over the edge and, with a groan of pure satisfaction, he let go, erupting in a burst that took his breath away. As he shuddered against her, he lost what remained of his heart. She had all of him, to do with whatever she wanted.

Chapter Eight

LINDSAY FELT like a million bucks. Her *Sexcapades* fantasy had worked even better than she'd imagined it would, and Hunter seemed totally blown away by her sense of sexual adventure. But they both agreed that they'd had enough risky business for one night and decided to continue what was left of the evening upstairs, in an actual bed. They took out her soggy clothes—sweatshirts and all her old jeans—and tossed them in the dryer.

Then they crept upstairs and into her apartment, where they ate whatever food they could scrounge from her refrigerator. After that they made love until Hunter finally ran out of time.

"I don't want to leave," he said as he pulled on his clothes so he could go back to his apartment and pack. "I feel like canceling the trip."

"Don't do that." She dressed quickly in cutoffs and a T-shirt. "Too many people are counting on you. The time will go by fast." She didn't believe that, but it was the sort of thing lovers said to each other when they had to part.

"It will drag by, and you know it." He paused to gaze at her. "Lindsay, we need to talk. About us, about—"

She put a finger to his lips. "We will. When you get

back. Tonight has been wild and crazy. Let it all settle in your mind a bit. Then we'll talk."

"You do realize this is serious, what we have going on."

She nodded, happier than she'd ever been in her life. "Yes." But she wanted him to go away for ten days and come back just as sure as he was now. Then she could fully trust the words that came out of his mouth. Right now, they could be a product of all those excellent climaxes.

"Just so you realize that." He kissed her quickly. "My flight home leaves Nassau in the morning, so I'll be back here at a civilized time—before you get off work. Then we'll talk."

"Fine." She could imagine what kind of homecoming that would be. They might have to use his apartment so they wouldn't alarm the neighbors next to her.

"Come over and talk to me while I throw a few things in my suitcase, okay?"

"Sure." She followed him out of the bedroom.

Before he reached her front door, he turned back. "Would you give me a picture to take with me? Have you got one I can have?"

Now there was a very good sign. Hunter wanted to carry her picture with him on this trip. "I think I have one around here. Let me take a look, and I'll bring it over in a couple of minutes. You go get started on your packing."

"Okay." He kissed her again. "See you in a minute. I'll leave the door open."

She grinned. "Like in *Friends*."

"Yeah. Like that." With a smile, he left.

Once he was gone, she returned to her bedroom and rummaged through the photo box where she kept her snapshots. Finding one she wanted to give him turned out to be harder than she'd thought. He was a professional photographer, and he'd dated extremely photogenic women. All she had was a box of candid pictures, most of them including family and friends. In each of them she looked ordinary.

Finally she settled on one that Shauna had taken during a weekend trip to Wisconsin last fall. Lindsay was standing in a pile of autumn leaves, laughing. She didn't look like a model, but at least she looked happy.

Leaving the box open on her bed, she took the picture and headed over to Hunter's apartment. Opening his door without knocking felt very good, as if they definitely had something solid going on. She wanted to believe that.

The minute she stepped inside the door, she heard Hunter's voice coming from the bedroom. Apparently he was on the phone.

"I think it's great that you'll be down there, too," he said.

Lindsay's instincts went on alert. She paused, shamelessly eavesdropping on the conversation. It wasn't like she hadn't done that for months with Hunter.

"Of course we're still on speaking terms, Pamela. I don't hold grudges. You should know that. Yeah, it'll be good to see you, too. Well, I gotta finish packing. See you in Nassau. Bye."

He would be seeing his ex in the Bahamas, photographing her for the snorkeling feature, no doubt. He'd said he was looking forward to it. They'd be together in a place known for romance, the perfect place to make up.

And, as always, Lindsay was the rebound girl, set up to take the fall. It was the umpteenth rerun of a very bad movie, and she'd seen it way too many times.

Ice water running through her veins, she backed quietly toward the door. Then she opened it silently and closed it with a bang. Stuffing the picture she'd brought in the pocket of her cutoffs, she called out to Hunter. "Anybody home?"

"Hey!" Hunter came out of the bedroom, his suitcase in one hand. "I wondered what had happened to you. Did you find a picture for me?"

Lindsay shook her head. "Nothing good."

"Oh, for heaven's sake." Hunter put down the suitcase and came over to pull her into his arms. "I'll bet you have tons of pictures. You just didn't like any of them."

She wondered how she could continue to smile and talk when her heart had been through the shredder. Somehow she managed it. "You caught me. I'm as photogenic as a hedgehog."

"Bullshit." He framed her face in both hands. "When I come back, I want to take about a million pictures of you."

"And risk breaking that expensive camera?"

"Silly woman. You'll be gorgeous." He leaned down and feathered a kiss over her lips. "Stunning."

She fought the tears, but a couple dribbled out and slipped over his fingers.

"Aw, Lindsay, don't cry." He kissed her closed eyelids. "I'll call you while I'm gone."

"That's okay." She sounded choked up, but he probably thought it was because he was leaving. She blinked away the tears. Time to get strong. "You don't have to do that."

"I know I don't *have* to, but I want to."

"I'll bet you don't even know my number."

He looked surprised. "That's a fact. Amazing. Tell it to me."

She recited her phone number, never believing for a minute that he'd remember it.

"Got it." He gazed into her eyes. "I'm going to miss you something terrible, Laundry-Room Girl."

She didn't think so, but he might think he would miss her, at least until he made up with Pamela. "I'll miss you, too," she said.

"I have to go."

"I know."

"Take care of yourself while I'm gone. When I get back, we'll talk."

She nodded. Yes, they probably would. He'd have to tell her that he was back with Pamela, but he'd always cherish the fact that Lindsay had been there when he needed someone. Lindsay had heard it all many times.

Hunter kissed her again, and then, too quickly, they were walking out the door of his apartment. He dropped one last kiss on her lips, squeezed her hand and walked down the hall. At the stairwell he turned and waved. She waved back. And then he was gone.

If this had been the first time she'd ever fallen for a guy after his breakup, she might have been able to convince herself that he wouldn't get back with Pamela during their stay in the Bahamas. She might have been able to explain his conversation on the phone as Hunter merely being polite to someone he still had to work with. Unfortunately, this wasn't the first time. But, by damn, it would be the last.

TEN DAYS LATER, Hunter took a cab from the airport to the apartment. He was going crazy from lack of contact with Lindsay. The trip had been a disaster, with tropical storms screwing up all the plans. Worse yet, the storms had made communication with Chicago dicey. Between the weather and the way it had compressed the shooting schedule, he'd either been without a phone connection or out of time to make the call.

Twice he'd had a brief moment to call when Lindsay was at work, but he didn't have that number. The 800 number for the bank got him a series of voice-mail prompts that ended somewhere in Nebraska, and he'd hung up in frustration. He hoped she'd figured out that the storms had created problems with the phones, because he hated promising to call and not following through.

Lindsay was at work right now, and he considered asking the cabbie to drop him there. But when he saw Lindsay again, he didn't want a teller's cage separating them. He wanted to be able to kiss her senseless, take off every stitch of her clothes and make love until dawn.

What a nightmare of a trip. The storms had messed up the schedule for shooting, and he had virtually nothing to show for all the time spent. On top of that, Pamela had been determined to rekindle the flame. Apparently she'd pulled some strings to get the snorkel layout job because she thought in that tropical setting she'd convince him they were meant for each other.

He was meant for Lindsay, and he'd finally had to tell Pamela that in so many words, to get her to back off. She hadn't been much fun on location after that. The makeup artist had started referring to her as Tropical Storm Pamela.

It was all behind him now, though. He had about thirty minutes before Lindsay came home, time enough to shower and decide how to commemorate this important reunion. He'd bought a single red rose at the airport, and he wanted to think of some clever way to leave it by her door.

The perfect plan didn't come to him until he was standing under the shower in his apartment. After drying off and dressing in shorts and a T-shirt, he emptied the contents of his suitcase into his laundry basket, put the rose on top of it, and placed the basket in front of Lindsay's door. That should send the message he had in mind.

Then he left his door slightly ajar and paced the length of his apartment, too wired to sit down. He hoped she remembered when he was coming back. If she didn't remember, that was a bad sign. If she'd gone out with friends after work, or stopped to run any errands, he didn't know how he'd stand the wait. He'd thought about her constantly for ten days, and at last the long drought was over.

LINDSAY HAD CONSIDERED going to a movie after work in order to delay getting back to the apartment. Hunter was due home this afternoon and, coward that she was, she wanted to put off the inevitable conversation with him. But she needed to show a little backbone to keep her self-respect, so she climbed aboard the bus and headed home, prepared to face the music.

He hadn't called, and although she could blame that on the tropical storms in the Caribbean, she didn't think that was the real reason. It couldn't have knocked out every single opportunity. No, the explanation was clear enough. He'd been too busy with Pamela.

She'd started looking for another apartment, knowing that she wouldn't be able to stay next door to Hunter while he renewed his love affair with Pamela. He might be more careful now that he knew how easily sound penetrated the common wall, but he couldn't possibly be *that* careful. The walls were too thin, and so were her defenses.

For ten days she'd suffered in private, unwilling to hear what Shauna would say if she found out. Shauna had been through enough with her on this score, anyway. So close to her wedding, she didn't need to deal with another stupid sob story, one that was all Lindsay's fault.

With a sense of doom, she climbed the stairs to the fourth floor. Hunter was an honorable and humane man, so he'd want to get this over with fast. He'd be waiting for her. She felt that in her bones.

She spotted the laundry basket the minute she started down the hall, and her stomach lurched. Maybe he was trying to be lighthearted so they could laugh about this. But she didn't feel lighthearted. She felt as if she'd swallowed a helping of hot rocks.

She paused to look down at the laundry basket. *A red*

rose? Maybe that was his idea of a sympathy gift. Her stomach churned.

"Hi."

She glanced up to see him leaning in the doorway of his apartment. He looked so damned good, this man who belonged to someone else. He was smiling tenderly at her, probably because he knew that he was about to lower the boom.

Gulping, she forced herself to say something polite. "Nice trip?"

His smile faded. "Oh, hell. You're upset because I didn't call." He pushed away from the door frame and started toward her. "It was crazy down there, and I—"

"Don't, Hunter." She'd thought she could bear up under the speech, but it turned out she couldn't. "Don't make excuses."

"You're right. I should have found some way. I should have sent a damned telegram. I'm sorry, Lindsay."

"Me, too." She stared at him, her heart like lead. "But that's the way it goes, right? Thanks for the rose." She turned away and fumbled with her key.

"Wait!" He grabbed her arm. "Are you serious? Are you going to let the fact that I couldn't get to a phone ruin everything between us?"

She glanced up at him, determined not to cry. "You mean ruin our friendship? Because I can't do the friendship thing anymore, Hunter. Not after—"

"Friendship?" He grasped her other arm, knocking her purse to the floor as he spun her to face him. "Yeah, that's part of it, but I had some other words in mind. Like *lover.*"

Had she been wrong? Her icy heart began to thaw. Could she possibly have been *wrong?* Her chest tightened as she looked into his eyes, and she had to swallow before she could speak. "You didn't make up with Pamela?"

His jaw dropped.

"I heard you talking with her on the phone before you left." Oh, dear God. Maybe, maybe, she'd been wrong. "So I thought, when you didn't call, that—"

With a groan he pulled her close, his mouth seeking hers, his kiss hungry and insistent. Hope bloomed in her. This wasn't the kiss of a man who'd been enjoying the charms of another woman for the past few days. It was the kiss of a man who'd missed her as desperately as she'd missed him. She'd been *wrong. Totally wrong!* She'd never been so happy about being wrong in her life.

Eventually he lifted his lips from hers, but not before he'd erased every doubt she'd had. "Does that answer your question?"

Tears of joy welled in her eyes as she held him tight and looked into his warm gaze. "I'm so sorry for doubting you." She cleared the huskiness from her voice. "So very sorry."

"You should be." His grin was slow and sexy. "And you can apologize for the rest of the night, in all sorts of interesting ways. It'll probably take many creative fantasies before I'll forgive you."

"Okay." Desire curled in her tummy. She would love making amends.

He shook his head. "I still can't believe you would think such things after what went on between us before I left."

"I know, but you have no idea how many times I've been dumped by a guy on the rebound, so when I heard you talking to your ex, I just assumed—"

"Rebound?" He blinked. "What rebound?"

She realized that guys didn't always understand the finer points of relationships, so she didn't mind explaining. "Pamela dumped you that night we first made love, so that makes me the one you picked up on the rebound. I can see now that I'm more than that, but in the beginning you were definitely on the rebound."

"Was I, now?" Hunter started laughing as he maneuvered her toward the open door of his apartment. "This is what you get for eavesdropping, Laundry-Room Girl. Pamela didn't dump me. I dumped her about three weeks prior to that night. What you heard was Pamela having a hissy fit after I said I wasn't interested in getting back together."

Lindsay's head buzzed. "*You* dumped *her?*"

"Yeah." Hunter kicked the door shut. "Want to know who I dumped her for?"

Lindsay stared at him, completely dazzled. "*Me?*"

"You. Now let's get naked. I can't propose when I'm in this highly aroused condition."

"P-propose?" Lindsay didn't think her heart could hold any more happiness, but here came another bucketful.

"Right." He undid the buttons of her dress. "Because the other words I'd like to use in connection with you are…my darling…and—" He hesitated, looking unsure. "And my wife," he murmured.

"Oh, Hunter." She started quivering.

"But let's do this first." He shoved her dress to the floor. "Then later on I'll get down on one knee and everything, I promise. You'll have the whole deal, except for the ring, which I think we should pick out together, assuming you say yes, which you might not. But don't think about your answer now. Think about getting out of your clothes."

The quivering became worse. He was reducing her to jelly, both mentally and physically. She could barely breathe. "Yes."

"Good." He unfastened the catch on her bra. "I'm glad you're going along with the getting naked program, because otherwise I'd—"

"I mean, yes, I'll marry you."

He went completely still as he looked into her eyes. Hope battled uncertainty in his expression. "Really?"

"Really. I love you to pieces, Hunter."

He swallowed. "I'd hoped...but I wasn't...we haven't been involved for very..."

"Oh, I've been involved with you for months." She smiled, tears blurring her vision. "You just didn't know it."

"Same here." He sighed and cupped her face in both hands. "Lindsay Scott, I love you to pieces. I love you more with every day that goes by."

She'd never heard more beautiful words. Her throat closed as gratitude swept through her. Dreams really did come true.

He stroked his thumbs over her cheeks. "Can you imagine how much more we'll love each other in fifty years?"

"It boggles my mind." Fifty years with Hunter. She'd buy her own copy of *Sexcapades,* that was for sure. "Do you think they'll have washing machines in fifty years?"

He laughed. "I don't know, but whatever they invent, as long as it vibrates I'm sure we'll be able to adapt." He tugged her toward his bedroom. "But on this occasion, I plan to give you a screaming orgasm the old-fashioned way. Fortunately, I have it on good authority that my next-door neighbor isn't home to hear us."

Lindsay started unfastening the button at the waistband of his shorts. "Are you sure about that?"

He stopped and gazed at her. "Actually, she is home," he said softly as he pulled her down to the bed. "Home at last."

UNFINISHED BUSINESS

Suzanne Forster

This one's for Ann, my dear friend,
my sounding board and my shelter in the storm.

Your support means more to me
than I could ever tell you.

Chapter One

Every woman is a pussycat doll, even if only in her own mind. Find that doll, wind her up and let her go.

101 Ways To Make Your Man Beg

"SO I'M OLD-FASHIONED," Melissa Sanders admitted as she lifted her Rum Mocambo cocktail to her lips. "So I'm waiting for marriage. So shoot me!"

A jet of cold water hit Melissa right between the eyes.

"Hey, I was only kidding!" she cried. Blinded, she felt around the table for a napkin while her three girlfriends dissolved in peals of laughter. She managed a good-natured smile through the water dripping off her nose.

But once her vision had cleared, Melissa fixed her old friend Kathy Crawford with a bemused look. She'd noticed Kath digging through her overstuffed tote, but hadn't expected her to whip out the squirt gun she kept there for self-defense. "What's with the water-gun assault?"

Kath's grin challenged her. "I say marry the guy, if you must," she said. "Whatever it takes, you have *got* to have sex with that beautiful man, Melissa. You lost the bet."

"If you can find him," Melissa said, "I'll do the honors right here on this table. Would that make you *bad* girls happy?"

"Yes," they all chirped at once.

"Well, shame on you." Melissa pretended to be busy blotting rum from her much too demure cotton sundress. The girls had been giving her grief all evening about her sex life. She didn't have one, and they'd decided to make that their cause. They were trying to hook her up, and to that end, they'd approached almost every man in the restaurant, begging him to marry her for "just one night."

Melissa was used to their antics by now. The four of them had been friends since childhood and were currently in Cancún on their annual escape-from-civilization trip. But Melissa had not been prepared when one of the guys, a simply gorgeous waiter named Antonio, had dropped to one knee and proposed to her on the spot. She was mortified, but she was also a little tipsy—and okay, pleased. Mostly to show the girls, she'd accepted his proposal—and Antonio had seemed pleased, too. Obviously, he'd heard she wouldn't sleep with anyone she wasn't married to, and he loved a good challenge. It was even possible he'd been talked into the idea by her friends. But the way he'd lingered over kissing the back of her hand had made Melissa's stomach float like a cork on the Gulf of Mexico. Was that his tongue she'd felt? It could have been velvet.

Fortunately for Melissa, Antonio had returned her hand and disappeared with a bow of his sexy dark head. He'd probably thought it was a good joke, but Melissa was still trying to scoop herself off the floor. Now she knew how it felt to be an ice-cream sundae, melting under a puddle of hot fudge.

He'd surprised her almost as much the first time they'd met. The girls knew nothing about that, but Antonio had come to her aid three mornings ago while she'd been walking barefoot on the beach. She'd been gazing out to sea, perhaps a little wistfully, and had seen a stranger coming her way. He'd worn a billowing white shirt and a butcher's apron tightly knotted around his waist, and he'd looked like a man on a mission. She'd had no idea the mission was her until he'd reached her and told her there'd been a shark report. The sensual grate of his voice still resonated in her mind....

"The water's treacherous," he warned. "Don't go in, not even to wade."

He was treacherous, she realized, caught in the riptide of his inexplicable concern for her safety. That mouth, those incandescent black eyes. Just looking at him could pull you under. She would probably be safer with the sharks.

"Thank you," she said, realizing he had her by the hand and was guiding her farther from the water.

"What were you looking for out there?" he asked.

Something about him pulled the truth out of her. With a fleeting smile, she said, "My life."

A look came over him that made her catch her breath. Her mind couldn't process what she saw except to call it a glimpse of naked male power. The desire to protect, and something else too quick and electric to catch. She dug her toes into the sand for traction. He released her hand, and she didn't want him to go, but she had no reason to stop him. After all, he'd simply come there to warn her. She might have thought she'd dreamed him up, except that he was better than any of her fantasies.

"Don't look too long," he said. "You might miss it."

The next morning they'd met again, and she'd asked him what he'd meant. He'd just smiled and said she had pretty feet. She should always go barefoot.

"Melissa, are you daydreaming again?"

Melissa looked up to three sets of eyes fixed intently on her. "Still mopping up, thanks to Kath." She finished blotting her face, sipped what little was left of her drink, and held it up, signaling the waiter that she wanted another one.

The waiter who was not Antonio.

The charming waterfront restaurant had rapidly filled up. Saturday-night guests spilled out onto a tile patio, draped in crimson bougainvillea, where the girls were sequestered on a lovely, airy deck. The patio overlooked a placid blue-water inlet, and they'd planned to have dinner here after their cocktails, but, as far as the ladies were concerned, there only seemed to be one thing on the menu for Melissa: stud service.

"You heard me say yes," she told the girls with a hint of cockiness, then looked around to make sure Antonio was really gone. "You were all witnesses. If he hadn't chickened out, I might have married him. Hey, for one night? Why not?"

Her friends made scoffing sounds, and Melissa pretended to be hurt. "You doubt me? You think I wouldn't do something that impetuous? I'm not capable of sluttiness?"

Kath stood and raised her drink. "To the vestal virgin," she said, "who won't even kiss a guy unless he's wearing a condom."

The other two chimed in, and as much as Melissa wanted to protest, she couldn't. They all knew her, and Kath best of all. They'd grown up together and gone to the same schools, although Melissa had missed a year because of a childhood illness. That was probably why the girls mother henned her a bit and sometimes made her feel like the runt of the litter. They didn't want her to miss out on life.

She and Kath had always told each other everything and still did. Melissa had been through every one of Kath's romantic relationships. She knew her friend had slept with exactly five different men in her twenty-eight years, including a one-night stand. And Kath knew that Melissa hadn't.

Well, there had been one, but that was different. Melissa had thought she was going to marry Roger "Dodger" Boswell, and he'd agreed to wait. But once they were officially engaged, he'd argued that they might not be sexually compatible. He'd finally persuaded her, and it had been a disaster. Melissa had been nervous, and nothing had worked. He'd dumped her the next day, and of course, she'd blamed herself. But wouldn't the right guy have waited? Or at least been understanding?

She'd stubbornly clung to that notion, but there'd been no right guy since, and no sex either. Could a celibate woman burst like clogged plumbing?

The other girls had raised their glasses, too, but Melissa didn't want recognition for her lackluster love life, thank you.

"At least give me the benefit of the doubt." She pouted. "I *could* be a slut."

"Of course you could!" Pat Stafford raised her glass high. Pat was the beauty of the group, a slender blond cheerleader in their high-school days, and still much too lovely to live, in Melissa's opinion.

"You're already a diva of sluttiness by journalistic standards," Kath assured her. "How about all those steamy articles you write for *Women Only* magazine?"

Melissa winced at the reference to her secret life as the author of articles for women about how to be sexually fulfilled. Okay, a couple of them were pretty racy, but everything she wrote was straight out of her own unfulfilled fantasy life. Some women faked orgasms. She faked sex altogether. She probably would have run like a scared rabbit if Antonio had been serious. And she was tired of running, tired of feeling like a fraud.

Of course, he *wasn't* serious. This was all a crazy joke, but she rather liked the idea that he'd been willing to go to such extremes just for one night with her. In fact, it had always been one of her favorite fantasies. She'd always wondered what it would be like to have a powerful man willing to do anything for the chance to satisfy his lustful desires for her. And Antonio *was* powerful, in his way. She was pretty sure he had a few lustful desires, too. Otherwise, why did her mind go weak at the mere thought? And what was that other warm sensation? Were her panties damp?

Renee Tyler, the foursome's ponytailed tomboy, broke in with a bright idea. "Forget men. Let's go score ourselves some chocolate. It's better than sex anyway."

Four glasses shot into the air. "Hear, hear!"

Fortunately, Melissa's glass happened to be empty. Another drink and she would have been on her nose. As it was, she couldn't seem to find the silk shawl she'd worn, and the onshore breezes were getting chilly as the sun went down.

"I can taste the Peanut Butter Cup cheesecake now," Renee gushed. "*Vamanos, señoritas.*"

"One sec." Melissa crouched to look under the table. Where could the shawl have gone?

"Melissa," Kath whispered, nudging her.

"What is it?" Melissa felt around the cool tile floor with her hand. It was dark under the table, and silk was so slippery.

"Look who's here! *Pssssst, Melisssssa.*"

Someone squealed and Melissa thumped her head against the underside of the table, nearly knocking herself cold. A moment later, as she peeked over the top, she saw that the waiter had come back. Not the waiter with her drink. Antonio. He'd changed into a white tuxedo shirt and black slacks, and he'd brought another man with him, one who looked suspiciously like...a priest?

Antonio smiled at her, and she considered going back under the table. But the girls were watching her every move.

"Hello, Melissa." Antonio pronounced her name perfectly.

She waggled her fingers at him. "Hi," she managed to say. Why did the floor feel as if it were tilting? Did they have earthquakes in Cancún?

"This is Father Domenici." Antonio's lush, husky voice

held only a hint of foreign inflection. "He's offered to help us."

"Help us what?" she whispered.

"Get married, of course."

Melissa tried getting to her feet, fairly certain she wasn't going to make it. This had to be a joke, and her friends were probably behind it. The priest bore a suspicious resemblance to the older man who'd bussed their table when they'd arrived. The lengths those girls would go to!

Kath eased out of the way as Antonio held out his hand. "Father, this beautiful woman and I are going to be one tonight."

Joke or not, Melissa was aghast. She was also enchanted. Antonio helped her to her feet with a strong, reassuring grip. She wobbled only slightly as he presented her with a velvety red rose. He also had a delicate white lace veil for her head.

"For Melissa," he said, "the answer to a man's dreams."

Dream was right. The dulcet strains of a mariachi band filtered out from the restaurant, and Melissa could hear her friends buzzing in the background, but she had no idea what they were saying. Antonio's superior height forced her to tip her head back to see him, which made her dizzy—or was it the Mocambos?

This was her first opportunity for a good long look at him, and it *was*. Good, from his indecently sensual mouth to his dark, soulful eyes. The girls must have put him up to this. Otherwise, what could he want with her? Not that she was slim pickings, mind you. She had good teeth, shiny dark hair and long legs, which made her sound rather like a horse. She could still wear the same jeans she'd worn in high school. So what if she had to lie flat on her back and hold her breath to zip them up?

She doubted Antonio had ever had problems zipping up his pants. Or zipping them *down*. She smiled at the thought and glanced at him sideways. From what she could see, there wasn't an ounce of anything anywhere that wasn't absolutely necessary. His slacks fit as if they'd been tailored to his body. Narrow black satin bands ran the length of the outside seams, and the linen fabric caressed his thighs, straining ever so slightly when he moved. His snowy-white tuxedo shirt had a couple of buttons undone, which wasn't bad either, as long as you were partial to corded muscles and sun-bronzed skin.

Kath would have described him as yummy, and Melissa didn't doubt that any one of her friends would have leaped to switch places with her, in which case, the joke was on them. He'd chosen *her*. She didn't care to wonder why.

After a moment, Melissa realized that Antonio was leading her away from the table. Even more surprising, she was following, hand in hand. And she didn't seem to have any desire to stop him. Quite the opposite, it felt as if she could have gone anywhere with this man, done anything. How could that be?

She glanced back over her shoulder and smiled nervously at the girls.

"Where are you going?" Kath called.

"To the mission," Antonio replied.

"To the mission," Melissa echoed. "I lost the bet, remember."

"But you can't just marry him," Renee said. "You need a license and—"

"All I need is her." Antonio turned to face the three startled women and spoke in a voice of quiet resolve. "You begged every man in the restaurant to marry her and make a woman out of her," he said, "but that's not why I proposed. For some reason none of you can see it, but she *is* a woman—a beautiful, desirable woman who any red-blooded man would want—and I do."

You could hear the clunks all around the patio as jaws dropped.

Melissa was as bewildered as everyone else. Maybe this

wasn't a joke. She looked at her friends, and fought back a tiny bubble of hysteria. They didn't seem to know what to do, and she certainly didn't either. They had bet they could get a cute guy to marry her for just one night. Well, he was more than cute. And he seemed to want to marry her. Really want to, for some reason.

Now would be the time to ask some questions and find out what was going on, she told herself. Even if her girl-friends weren't involved, this had to be a practical joke of some kind. If she stopped for a moment, cleared her head, maybe this crazy rush of feeling would disappear, and she could get her bearings. Then again, maybe she didn't want the crazy rush of feeling to disappear. *She'd waited her whole life to feel like this.*

Suddenly she understood how a woman could let herself be swept away by an impulse that didn't make sense and might even seem reckless. This was what she wrote about in her articles, but never dreamed she would experience. It was just a fantasy, right? Sexy, dark-eyed strangers didn't really ask for your hand and say that they were going to be one with you that night. Not if you were Melissa Sanders, the magazine writer. She was a recluse, a spectator, not a participant. She lived vicariously through others, courtesy of her imagination.

But her imagination, wild as it was, could never do this justice. And that must be why she was following him out of the restaurant, hand in hand. That must be why she didn't want to stop, not even for a second. For the first time in her life, she was going to do what she and her girl-friends had always said they would do when they took their annual trip. She was going native.

MELISSA'S EYES blinked open. She vaguely remembered being woozy and needing to lie down for a second, but that was it. Had she passed out? Those Rum Mocambos tasted like fruit punch, but hit like a hammer.

Whatever had happened, she wasn't dreaming though it was still dark, outside beyond the curtains. She was lying on a bed with a man, curled up in his arms, and they were both fully clothed. That last part struck her as odd. How could they be fully clothed if—

She lifted her head from his shoulder. "Antonio?"

He was awake—awake and gazing at her as if that's what he'd been doing for hours. Melissa struggled to dredge up details. There'd been a wedding ceremony in a small Mexican mission with not one word of English in the vows, which had not concerned her at all at the time. Antonio had slipped a delicate gold-filigree ring on her finger, and afterward she'd signed something written in Spanish that might have been a marriage license.

Antonio had found a way to make everything seem wonderfully authentic, but of course, it couldn't have been. No priest would marry two total strangers who barely spoke the same language. Nor could Melissa be legally bound to a document if she didn't know what she was signing. The ceremony wasn't real, just a crazy romantic adventure, which had led to this, whatever *this* was.

"We're in bed," she pointed out. They seemed to be in a hotel room, and one that no ordinary waiter could afford. The wrought-iron posts of the king-size bed swirled up to meet a red satin canopy. She'd never seen anything as vibrant or beautiful. Crimson clouds floated above them and a silk leopard-print comforter cushioned them from beneath. Scented candles flickered from every surface, giving off luscious notes that reminded her of warm vanilla flan with a dash of cognac. There was even a golden cornucopia, spilling exotic fruit on the dresser top.

Did Latin lovers seduce their women with food?

"*Sí, cama,*" he said, patting the comforter. "That's Spanish for bed."

"Did we—I mean, of course we did—we're in a *cama*. But did we—"

"Consummate the union?"

He might have nodded. She wasn't sure. His dark, soulful eyes had a tidal pull that made her feel as if she were made of nothing but liquid.

"Be nice if I could remember," she said.

"How could you remember? You were asleep," he teased in his deep voice.

"We did it while I was asleep?"

He laughed. "You must have very good dreams."

"So nothing happened? You were just watching me dream?"

"Watching you dream in my arms."

Apparently there was a huge difference, by the tone of his voice. He was just too romantic to be believed. She might write about this sort of thing in real life, but she never had any illusions that it could happen to her. It still didn't seem real.

She plucked at her linen sundress. "Antonio, we're both fully clothed."

"That's because we didn't take our clothes off."

"But you married me." She pointed to the ring on her finger. "Why would you do that and then not have sex with me?"

His eyes darkened, if that was possible. "I married you for many reasons, one being to discover what makes your heart run wild. But I also married you to solve the eternal mystery of Melissa, and to prove your friends wrong. They may think they know who you are, but they don't."

"And you do?"

"No, but…" He tilted his head in thought. "How can I explain? Let's just say I saw the wishing well in your smile, and I want to find out how deep it goes." He traced her *un*smiling lips with one finger. "I want this to be a night that neither one of us will easily forget."

"A night? Just one night?"

"It all starts with just one night, Melissa."

She began to laugh. She didn't know what else to do. "Are you sure I actually woke up? That I'm not still dreaming?"

Pinch him, she thought. *If he yells, it's real.* But somehow she never got the chance. He took her hand as if she'd offered it to him on a platter. Was that how he would take the rest of her? As if she were something succulent that he wanted to sample and savor? That wouldn't be so bad. It wasn't like she'd ever been savored before.

"What makes Melissa's heart run wild?"

She tried not to react as he turned her hand over, exposing the inside of her wrist. She could see the delicate blue veins, the rapid pulse. She was watching her own heart flutter in crazy anticipation of what he might do.

He touched his lips to the tiny pulse and made it jump.

"Kissing wrists seems to work," she murmured, aware of the rasp in her voice.

Steady as she goes, Melissa. If you're going to write about this stuff, maybe you should give some of it a try. All the wicked things you've thrilled to in your mind. Bare lips on naked skin. A man's hands, hot and slow. That first forbidden cry of excitement.

"Want to bet it works with elbows, too?" he said with a slow smile.

She shook her head. "Not the same—" And quickly realized her mistake.

He trailed baby kisses up the inside of her arm. His breath was hot and moist—and his teeth deliciously sharp. When he got to the tingling flesh on the inside of her elbow, he helped himself. The nip sent a bolt of fire through her veins that made her dizzy and weak.

When she tumbled into his arms, he whispered, "Welcome home."

They rolled across the big bed, and Melissa's dress crept up to her panties. Antonio tried to preserve her modesty by pulling it down, but she barely noticed his efforts. They were flush up against each other, and her nerve endings had turned into friction sparks. The fire bolt zinged through her, its velocity thrilling. So this was what unbridled lust felt like. She hadn't realized it could come upon you that suddenly. Like a sneeze. You were fine one minute and reaching for a tissue the next.

Somebody should give her a box of tissues. She was on the verge of a fit. She wanted to kiss and bite. Be kissed and bitten.

"Why did you marry me?" he asked, watching her face.

Apparently he wanted to talk.

She swallowed a tiny sigh of frustration and shrugged. "Because I would very much like to get into as much trouble as possible."

"You married me to get into trouble?"

"Yes, definitely."

"What kind of trouble?"

"The kind where you do things you've only imagined doing."

His jet eyes sparkled with intrigue. "What's stopping you?"

"I've never been in trouble. I'm not sure I'd know how to get out."

"Let's get you *in* first."

He feathered the silky tops of her breasts with the backs of his fingers. His boldness left Melissa momentarily speechless, and the sensations left her shaking inside. He was playing in the neckline of her sundress. He hadn't even kissed her yet. They hadn't kissed and he was headed for first base!

The fire bolt flared in her belly. No part of her body was safe.

She watched with fascination the bronze hands that teased her blushing skin. Her nipples drew tight in anticipation of what he might do next. She made no effort to stop him, which only increased the tension. She'd always wondered what it would be like to let a man have his way with her, to be a wanton love toy, existing only for his pleasure, at least for a couple hours.

What an article this would make. *Let the man have his way, let him kiss and touch and play, and he'll be randy, night and day.*

It took too much energy to compose bad poetry, especially with the sensations spiraling through her. The fire bolt had split into ribbons of light, and she could barely concentrate on anything but their brightness.

Antonio seemed pretty intent, too. Apparently he enjoyed watching her breath catch in response to his touch. She trembled with delight as he bent to drop a kiss in the delicate cleft between her breasts. His mouth was warm and steamy, and she wondered if it could take her to the places where only her imagination had gone. She could still feel the way he'd caressed the back of her hand with his lips and his tongue. It had tickled so sweetly.

She made a purring sound as the lights ribboned through her again.

He met her gaze. "You remind me of a kitten," he said. "Big, innocent eyes, sharp little claws and very curious. What kind of trouble do you want to get into, kitten?"

She would rather have been a wild cat, but it was a start. "French-kissing, maybe?" She'd done it, of course, but a very long time ago, and she was anxious to get on with this makeup course in sexual fulfillment. Maybe she could write this off as research, and even if she couldn't, at least she wouldn't feel like a fraud anymore. She would finally have had some thrilling experiences of her own.

She decided to get more adventures. "Or fantasy role playing?"

"Rolling and playing?" He didn't seem to know what she was talking about.

"Maybe it would be easier if I showed you," she said. "Can I borrow one of these sheets?"

Together they worked the top sheet loose, a black silk beauty that would easily make a half dozen of the skimpy costume she had in mind.

"Don't go anywhere," she told him as she disappeared into the bathroom with the sheet. The marbled dressing room had a full-length mirror that Melissa couldn't avoid as she slipped out of her clothes. She wasn't totally uncomfortable with her rather average figure, but she didn't often look at herself naked. Her tummy could have used a few emergency crunches, and there would be no cheating with a push-up bra to enhance her B-cup breasts. Her butt wasn't bad, though, and her calves were nicely shaped, thanks to the yoga, no doubt.

Gaaaah. Was she really getting naked in the bathroom of a hotel suite with a man lying in wait on a jungle-print bed just outside the door? Did sexual fulfillment have to be this thrilling, *this* wild? She wanted the experience, but this was nuts. Blame it on the Mocambos. And she'd almost forgotten about that knock to her head under the table at the restaurant. Call her crazy, call her drunk, call this the school for sluts. *Or call it her chance to find out who she really was, as opposed to who she'd been pretending to be.*

She undressed down to her panties, knotted the ends of the sheet together over one shoulder like a black silk toga, and let the length of it trail after her like a train. She thought about leaving one breast wantonly exposed, but that kind of brazenness would have taken another thump to the head. She'd never behaved like this before and she wasn't going to hold back now, after almost thirty years of holding back. Moments later, she opened the bathroom door, raised her arms above her head and touched the frame on each side, as if she were lashed there by ropes.

Antonio had rolled to his side, facing her, and propped his chin with his fist. He could have been a *Playgirl* centerfold, except that he wasn't showing enough skin. He could have been one anyway.

He smiled inquisitively.

"Have mercy, Lord," she whispered. She almost giggled but swallowed the urge and continued. "Don't ravish me and fling me into the volcano."

Antonio cocked his head. "Excuse me?"

"I *said* don't ravish me and fling me into the volcano. You're the tribal king, and I'm the only maiden left in the village. You have to sacrifice me to appease the volcano gods."

He cocked an eyebrow. "Couldn't I just ravish you?"

"No! There has to be a blood sacrifice."

"Sounds a little harsh, don't you think?"

"No, actually, it's *wonderful,* see, because you can't do it. You can't fling me to my death, so you fling yourself instead. Oh my God," she whispered. "I love that. It's so noble. It's so you, Antonio."

He sat up and swung his bare feet off the bed. "I appreciate the vote of confidence, fair maiden, but I'm not *that* noble, and I have a much better idea. Let's keep it simple. Why don't we tease you until you beg me to ravish you?"

"What fantasy is that?"

He began unbuttoning his shirt. "It's the prim-and-proper-lady fantasy, where you pretend you're immune to my fondling and wicked suggestions, and I, being a gentleman pirate, do my best to prove that you're not."

"Not bad." Except that Melissa had a wicked idea of her own. She struck a wanton pose then blew him a kiss. Next, she gave her shoulders a little shake, startling herself with her own boldness. The move made her breasts bounce, and while she had his attention fixed on her décolletage, she reached under the sheet and gave her panties a tug.

Could she really do this?

His dark eyes lit with anticipation.

"Like what you see?" Encouraged by his interest, she

began to rotate her hips and draw the sheet up her leg, exposing a bit of creamy thigh.

Antonio watched her every move. "What's this fantasy called?"

"Shameless hussy."

"I like it."

His smoky voice could have set off a fire alarm. It brushed her senses with enough sparks to make her crazy with lust.

Antonio's shirt fell open as he rose from the bed, and the stark white material brought the tawny tones of his skin into sharp contrast. Unfair, she thought. His abs could have been classified as concealed weapons. They weren't just rippled. They were corrugated steel.

Show him what you've got, hussy. Level the playing field, so to speak.

Breathless, Melissa flashed more thigh and wriggled her hips, gyrating until the panties she'd tugged down were free of her hips. The silk material began to slide down her legs, and a thrill shot through her as it pooled around her ankles.

His gaze flared with passion. His beautiful mouth twitched.

With two strides, he closed the distance between them. Melissa's heart caught. She expected to be swept into his arms, kissed and plundered. Instead he smiled, watching her jump as he caressed her shoulder with his long fingers.

"You're toying with me," she murmured.

He gazed down at her, and she defied him with her eyes. If his soul was as black as his pupils, they were in terrible trouble, both of them.

"Like what you see?" she asked coyly. Two could play at that game.

"Oh, yeah."

"Then take it...if you can."

She tried to step out of the panties, but the touch of his

lips sent her swaying toward him. He locked his legs, bracing her, and reached up to place a hand over hers on the door frame. His other hand stole inside the sheet that protected her.

Melissa gasped. Not pretending anymore.

He growled softly as he found her naked skin.

The shameless hussy was shaking like a leaf. A moan welled in her throat. She kissed him back, and lights zoomed in her depths. Fountains splashed. This was better than her fantasies. A connection this thrilling couldn't be imagined. You had to feel it and let it feel you. You had to succumb.

Warm fingers found the small of her back, urging her closer. They crept down, those marauding fingers, getting more and more intimate with her defenseless derriere. But Melissa couldn't think about anything except the way he was laying sweet claim to her mouth.

His tongue swept her parted lips, and she moaned in appreciation, more eager than a shameless hussy should ever be to accommodate him. He drew back before she was anywhere near ready for the kiss to be over. She searched his eyes and saw the molten sparks of desire. *Good.* He was aroused, and that stoked her courage. Not breathing fire yet, but he would be.

She wanted this to happen. She needed it to. It would prove that she could push past her fears to her desires.

Back to the game. Now would begin the slow assault on his defenses, and she intended to be merciless. She would dangle the prize and then snatch it away. Give him sips but never let him drink his fill. This would be no easy conquest. He would have to take the prize from her…and make her glad that he did.

She willed the sheet to fall away and leave her totally naked. How lovely to brush her breasts and thighs against him, and watch the fireworks. She swallowed heavily, imagining the way he would kiss her and fondle her when she was nude in the doorway. Who would be at whose mercy then? she wondered.

"Has a woman ever driven you crazy with lust?" she asked.

"Never."

"Good." Her knee crept up the inside of his thigh. "Let me be the first."

She tried not to look surprised as she nestled his burgeoning erection. This night promised to fulfill her fantasies in many ways. In her book, she had once described the pleasures of a well-endowed man, but she'd never experienced them. Never experienced much of anything, really. Her pirate would have to be slow and patient with her, although she wasn't going to tell him that just yet. Let him strain at the leash a little more.

She pressed her lips together in a pouty smile and rubbed her leg against his shaft. It was hot enough to burn a hole in his pants. "Shameless enough for you?"

"I could devour you right here in the doorway."

Passion made his voice throaty and harsh. Melissa had to struggle to find hers. "Where would you like to start?"

"All of the really tasty places, like here—" Hot breath burned her ear as he whispered along her jaw to her mouth.

How could she hide her trembling breath from him? How could she hide anything? Her pulse was a mess, and if she'd been wearing panties, they would have been soaked by now.

"You can do better than that," she said. But she didn't sound terribly convincing, and he must have sensed weakness. He pressed his advantage, his fingers rimming the cleft of her buttocks and dipping between her legs to find the wetness there.

Pleasure zinged through her in a dizzying current.

"How's this?" His lips moved over hers, and the reverberations in his throat sounded like a sensual snarl. Long fingers pleasured her so sharply that her legs wanted to melt underneath her. Only she was trapped. The silk panties held her ankles, making it impossible to move without stumbling.

"Not bad," she got out.

But the whimper must have given her away.

In the space of the next several moments, she experienced one first after another, all of them at Antonio's sweetly plundering mouth and hands. He released her arms, and she waited for him to undo the sheet and let it fall from her body. Instead he knelt and raised it as slowly as a theater curtain, exposing her bare feet and unsteady ankles, the secrets of her calves and the pink baby skin behind her knees.

With a sound of satisfaction, he tucked the sheet behind her and secured it there.

His fingertips caressed the sensitive cords at the back of her ankles, purling upward to the bend of her knees. Melissa could feel her knees lock as he feathered the entire length of her shins. Heavenly. She didn't want him to stop, and yet it was maddening the way he drew out each touch to the breaking point.

Her thighs tightened almost painfully as he unveiled them. She wasn't sure she could handle much more, but he'd barely started. He opened the sheet to her waist and glanced up, as if preparing her for what came next. He pressed his lips to her mound and kissed her through the soft cap of curls. The sudden heat made her shiver with ecstasy. Her hands were still clutching the door frame, now the thing holding her up, or she would have buried them in his rich black hair. When had she lost control of this fantasy? She was supposed to be driving *him* mad with desire.

He cupped her buttocks, anchoring her as he brushed her still-hidden labia with his lips. His tongue stroked her secrets, searching for the nectar hidden in the rose. It swirled into crevices and flicked over nerve endings, nearly driving her over the edge. His warm breath dampened the dark curls, turning them into shiny ringlets. Or was it her own excitement making them so wet?

"Open your legs for me," he said.

She stepped out of the panties, anxious to give him access. She could have cried it was so delicious. But suddenly he rose—and left her aching for one more kiss.

"Not bad," she said faintly.

He laughed and picked her up in his arms, flinging away the dangling panties as if he never wanted to see them again. The sheet trailed behind them as he carried her to the bed. There wasn't time to protest as he laid her out, sheet and all, and took a moment to admire her that way. He dropped down to her feet and came up from there, spiriting the black silk away as he exposed her belly and breasts. He sprinkled kisses all the way up, lingering to let his tongue dip into her belly button and leisurely encircle her areolas. Velvet, that tongue.

He didn't stop until he had the sheet above her head, and she realized that her arms were entangled. Her breath snagged in her throat. He was going to leave her this way. "You're a devil," she cried softly.

She watched him rise from the bed to undo his belt and the clasp of his slacks. And he watched her watching. Talk about shameless. She couldn't believe the way he stripped down to the skin for her, clearly aware of her staring at him with wide, wondering eyes. He stepped out of his briefs, and she lost the breath she was holding. He was more than impressively built. He was intimidating. He moved toward her, but nothing bounced with his steps. His muscles were far too rigid for that. All of them.

"Think you're in enough trouble yet?" he asked her.

He ravished her senses slowly, arousing her until she could do nothing but whimper and plead with him to spare her. Even with the leisurely pace, she swiftly reached a point where one sensation burst like a star and melted into another, and soon it was all one glorious, mindless blur. Still, she was exquisitely conscious of the moment he mounted her, the moment he entered. The sudden pressure made her throw back her head in ecstasy. The aching sweetness brought tears to her eyes.

The experience of losing her virginity had been rushed, furtive and painful. This was as thrilling as her dreams. *More.* She begged him to pump faster and release her. But like a good pirate, he showed no mercy. He took his trembling prize all the way to the stars and back with slow and deliberate thoroughness—and made her desperately glad that he did.

Afterward, Melissa lay limp and breathing softly in his arms. But the vixen wasn't vanquished. She was only catching her breath. Some time later, as Antonio lay spent on the bed, she moved over him with the grace and cunning of a she-demon and aroused him to the same screaming pitch of desire that he had her.

Her sneak attack left *both* of them trembling, and when it was over, they slept for hours, but Melissa's body never truly quieted. It quivered in ecstasy the entire time she dozed, and at some point, deep in the night, he kissed the nape of her neck and whispered one last wedding vow, "I promise to keep you in trouble for as long as we both shall live."

MELISSA AWOKE with a soft gasp of surprise. She saw the man lying next to her in bed and realized she hadn't been dreaming. He was there. She'd married him. Or maybe she hadn't, but he *was* there. Dear God, what had she done? He could have been a serial killer, and she wouldn't have known. Everything was confused and fuzzy, but if she remembered correctly, she'd been more intimate with him than with any dream lover and she barely knew him. People sometimes poured out their hearts to total strangers. Was that what she'd done?

No, she hadn't poured out her heart. She'd poured out her most erotic fantasies.

How had this happened? Had she been drugged? Kidnapped? Sold into slave labor? Taken hostage and brainwashed?

Nothing so convenient as any of that, Melissa. Try consenting adult.

Careful not to wake him, she crept out of bed and looked around for her clothing. Panic rose inside her as she clutched a corner of the comforter to her naked body. Finally it came to her that she'd undressed in the bathroom. Maybe she *had* been dreaming. It was all so fuzzy in her mind.

No more Mocambos for her. Ever.

In the bathroom's full-length mirror, she checked herself for telltale marks. She did look slightly flushed and swollen in certain intimate places. Were those teeth bites on the inside of her thighs? She was lucky she hadn't pulled a muscle. All kinds of crazy questions buzzed through her head as she rushed to get into her clothing. Panic stirred again. All the more reason to leave before he woke up and confirmed her worst fears. If they'd really done the things she remembered, she didn't want to know.

She thought about leaving him a note, but there wasn't time. Something told her she had to get out of there before he woke and discovered her. Otherwise, she might not go. *Might not go?* What kind of crazy notion was that? He had incredible powers of persuasion, but she was sober now, with all her wits about her. Of course she was going. Just watch her go.

She straightened the straps of her dress and felt something snag on the linen. The ring. She'd almost left wearing the ring! A couple quick tugs on the band told her it wasn't going to come off easily. Desperate, she tried soaping her hand, but that didn't loosen it, either. She twisted and pulled, wincing in pain as the ring caught on her knuckle. Nothing short of metal shears was going to work, she realized in despair. She would have to find a way to return it to him later.

He was lying on his stomach as she came out of the bathroom. He'd thrown the pillow on the floor and twisted around so that the sheet just covered his sinfully sexy backside. She told herself not to look at anything, especially him, but a piece of paper on the bureau caught her eye. It was the marriage license. She picked it up on impulse and slipped it into her bag. The writer in her had taken over. Someday this would make a good story, if she ever had the courage to tell it.

She slipped out the door into the pink light of dawn, still unsure whether the odd warm glow that pervaded her body was really from sex or just from dreaming about it so vividly. By the time she got back to her hotel, she realized she'd left her shawl behind, the one she'd been searching for under the table when he'd arrived with the priest. Maybe she was destined to lose that shawl. Better than a few other things she could have lost. Like her mind. Or her heart. So much of what had happened confused and frightened her, but one thing she knew for sure. She wasn't going back for the shawl.

Chapter Two

What's sexier to a man? A hot imagination or a hot body? If you said imagination, you're right! And he's one lucky guy.

101 Ways To Make Your Man Beg

Kansas City
Two years later…

MELISSA SANDERS WAS in the stork position when her bedroom phone rang. She'd raised her left leg, bent it at the knee and grabbed hold of her foot, which sounded easy but wasn't. With her other arm she reached for the sky. he'd been working on the posture for six months, and this was the first time she'd managed to hold it without timbering like a felled tree. She was not the most co-ordinated of women, which was why she'd taken up yoga. Well, that and to help with her runaway imagination. She'd heard yoga centered the mind as well as the body.

Let the phone ring. This was a milestone. She wanted to hold the position for at least two—maybe even three—minutes. That was a mere fraction of the time that Tara, her yoga teacher, could hold it, but still impressive. Tara was a goddess.

"Melissa, you there? It's Jeanie from Searchlight Publishing, and I have to talk to you! Call me the second you get in. I have great news!"

Exhale slowly from the center of your being. Breath is the divine life force.

Melissa's life force hissed out of her like a punctured tire. She tried to abandon the position and felt a sudden, agonizing tightness in her lower back. She'd pulled something.

"I'm coming," she said, knowing Jeanie couldn't hear her. She worked the heel of her hand into the tenderness, wondering if she had any liniment in the medicine cabinet—and felt like thirty going on one hundred and five.

She hobbled to the night table next to her four-poster bed with the heirloom patchwork quilt her mother had given her. But all she got for her trouble was a dial tone. Jeanie was long gone. The woman did everything at warp speed, including talk, but then she probably had to. She worked for Melissa's publishing company, and she was in charge of the publicity campaign for *101 Ways To Make Your Man Beg,* Melissa's first book.

My first book. Melissa marveled, smiling through the pain. She was still a little bewildered by her good fortune. She'd been making her living for years writing freelance articles for women's magazines. The articles had gotten her noticed, and she'd been invited to submit a book proposal to Searchlight because of several pieces on imaginative sex she'd done for *Women Only* magazine. But she hadn't dreamed the publisher would actually want to buy it. That was a year ago, and just last week, *101 Ways* had been released.

Melissa punched in the number and got Jeanie on the first try.

"Are you sitting down, Melissa? Maybe you should," the publicist said.

Melissa groaned in anticipation. Sitting was going to hurt. Her back didn't seem to want to do anything *but* the stork position. She worked the area vigorously, with her fist.

"Okay, I'm on the bed. If I fall over, it'll be a soft landing. What is it?"

"Your first week's sales in the chain bookstores are phenomenal, and marketing wants to run with it. They're sending you on a two-week, ten-city media tour, and I'm coming with you. Isn't that the best?"

"Two weeks?"

"At least. We'll fly you into New York on Thursday, but here's the really exciting part. You're going to be on *Wake Up, America* Friday morning. Are you getting this?"

"*Thursday?* Two days from now?" Melissa had never been to New York, and she'd certainly never been on a media tour. Other than her yearly escapes with the girls, she didn't travel at all. Her writing assignments allowed her to work from home, and she did most of her research on the Internet. Besides, the trips she took inside her own mind were exotic enough.

"It's okay," Jeanie said. "I'll meet you at the airport and get you settled in your hotel, and I'll be there first thing Friday morning to pick you up for the show."

Melissa was too agitated to stay on the bed. A twinge made her groan as she rose.

"Melissa? Is there a problem?"

"I hurt myself, Jeanie. Where's your spleen anyway? Lower back near the kidneys? I think I may have bruised mine."

"Oh pooh, Melissa. You're always ailing with something. I think spleens are like appendixes, aren't they? Not really necessary? Besides, being hurt is out of the question. We've already booked you on almost every daytime show in existence. The airline is e-mailing you the tickets, so get yourself packed. It'll be fine."

"Jeanie, I really did hurt—"

But she was gone again, before Melissa could defend

herself. And it was probably true that she had a tendency to exaggerate medical symptoms. Her friends had stopped discussing their various conditions in front of her because she would invariably come down with them within days—TMJ, ADD, the heartbreak of psoriasis, which had turned out to be a couple of bug bites. Her damn imagination was always getting her into trouble. But it was also her bread and butter. She spent her time thinking up ways to make women's love lives more exciting. She, who'd had no sex in two years, and then it had been just a crazy fluke.

The phone rang again, and she jumped about a foot off the floor. *Ouch.* She really did need to get a grip. She'd be doing the tour in a back brace.

"Sorry," Jeanie said. "I forgot the most important part. Marketing wants you to bring Antonio with you."

"Antonio?"

"Your gorgeous husband, silly. The man you dedicated the book to."

Melissa sank down on the bed. This couldn't be happening. There *was* no husband, not the way Jeanie was thinking. Two years ago she'd married a man on a dare, and her one night with him had inspired the idea for the book. But it wasn't a real marriage, just a night of unbelievable passion. The man had driven her mad in the best possible way. He'd had her as naked as the day she was born and perspiring through every pore, and she hadn't even given a thought to catching a cold. There'd been moments when she couldn't remember her own name.

At any rate, she'd dedicated the book about revitalizing marital sex to her "husband" to give it credibility. Who would listen to a woman who'd never been married?

"Your readers will be crazy to meet him," Jeanie was saying. "Everyone at Searchlight is crazy to meet him. I mean, this is the guy who gives you orgasms by whispering in your ear, right? Wasn't that chapter eight—'How to Turn Him into the Lover of Your Dreams in One Night'?"

"Yes," said Melissa weakly. "Chapter eight."

Melissa forgot her bruised spleen. In the next thirty seconds, she debated every possible excuse she could think of. She was pregnant, she was dying, she was gay. She put her vivid imagination to the test, but nothing made sense. Nothing but the truth.

"Jeanie, don't hang up, okay? I need to tell you something."

"Oh my God, more marriage-bed secrets? You two will be a smash on the talk-show circuit."

Melissa wet her lips. "Jeanie, I've got something to tell you." She paused a moment, then biting the bullet, she blurted out, "There is no husband. Antonio does not exist."

Over the din of her pounding heart, Melissa heard a thud. Fortunately, it turned out to be Jeanie's phone, not Jeanie, herself.

"I'm okay," the publicist said, breathing hard. "I got up too fast. How can there be no Antonio? You dedicated the book to him! He lovingly waxes the hair from your inner thighs, Melissa! He nibbles on your elbows and removes your underwear with his teeth. I've been fantasizing about the man for a year, and now you're telling me he *doesn't exist?*"

"I can explain." And she tried. She told Jeanie everything. About the dare, about the one crazy night, about the most incredible sex of her life—well, almost everything—she did not mention that it was the only sex of her life worth mentioning.

"It wasn't a total fabrication," Melissa pointed out. "We did get married, sort of."

"You married him and never saw him again?"

Now Melissa heard repetitive thuds and imagined Jeanie pacing back and forth over her floor. Her poor publicist was clearly desperate to salvage the tour—and the book sales. Strong sellers weren't easy to come by, and it wasn't just Melissa's credibility on the line. It was Jeanie's, too, and the publishing company's. They had obviously never bothered to check on their author's credentials.

"Maybe we can still make this work," Jeanie said. "It was a bona fide union, right? Was there a marriage license?"

"Well, I signed something, a document in Spanish that looked sort of legal, but it was in Mexico. I'm not a citizen. It wouldn't be valid here, would it?" *Please say it wouldn't.*

"Do you still have it? And don't say 'sort of'!"

Melissa sighed. "Yes, somewhere."

"Fax it to me. Fax it to me *now,* along with all the information you have about the man—his full name, his nationality, the name of the restaurant where he worked, and when you last saw him. Send me everything."

"All right...but why?"

"Because I'm going to find your mystery husband, and I'm going to find him fast."

"Do you think that's a good idea?" She spoke to a buzzing dial tone. Jeanie was already hot on Antonio's trail, and there was probably nothing she could do about it.

Melissa fell on the bed, moaning at the twinge in her back. She tugged futilely at the delicate gold band that was still stuck on her finger after two years. She'd never been able to get it off, and she hadn't had the heart to have the band cut off. She'd explained it to her parents as a ring she'd had to buy because it got stuck on her finger, the wrong finger. They knew nothing about Antonio or the book she'd dedicated to him, and given that they lived a very isolated existence on their farm, with one television that hadn't worked in years, she didn't expect them to find out. On those infrequent occasions when she dated, she resorted to the "wrong finger" story, or wore a Band-Aid.

Maybe the ring had jinxed her. And what had she been thinking about anyway, pretending that she had a real husband? If Jeannie didn't find Antonio, her book was down the drain. The publisher might even sue her for misrepresentation. But if the publicist did find him, what was Melissa expected to do? Pretend she and Antonio were still married—and that they were the blissfully satisfied couple she'd written about, whose relationship was so hot they used their cell phones to leave each other erotic text messages?

She'd hoped writing the book would resolve her feelings about that night—kind of like exorcising demons—but it hadn't. She dreaded the possibility that Jeanie might find him. How crazy and complicated and *dangerous* would that be? Melissa had no idea how he felt about her after all this time. What if he was angry at her, or worse, delusional in some way? He could destroy her career with a word. It was a terrifying thought, but at the same time, she felt an undeniable fascination with the idea of seeing him again. How could she not? He was the catalyst for her wildest fantasies and a source of pleasure beyond description. His smoldering intensity was as sharply imprinted on her nervous system as it was vivid in her mind.

Antonio. Dear God.

Melissa sprang up and rushed out of the bedroom, heading down the hall to her office. She was supposed to be looking for a marriage license, but she had to find a copy of her own book first. What else had she written in that thing?

"I'LL BE FINE. I can do this," Melissa said. She sat next to Jeanie on the greenroom couch of *Wake Up, America,* patting the publicist's tightly clasped hands. "I really like the idea of picking couples from the audience and giving them the Naughty-Sex Quiz. That should be fun," she enthused, despite in truth feeling a bit leery about the idea.

"Are you ready for some tough questions?" Jeanie asked. "In the last segment, Bobbi will take questions from the audience, but even she doesn't know what they're going to be. The show's producers don't want to lose the element of surprise."

"I don't think I could be surprised," Melissa said dryly. "I've memorized the damn book."

"Where's your hubby, Ms. Sanders? How are you going to answer that one?"

"He's in London on business travel. I'm hoping he can join me soon." Melissa smiled and flashed the band on her finger at Jeanie. "See, I'm ready for anything. I'm even wearing a wedding ring."

"Hey, *good* thinking," Jeanie said. "That didn't occur to me."

Melissa felt an uneasy twinge as the gold ring glinted in the lights, but decided not to share its history with Jeanie. Maybe that's why it was still on her finger—to help her pull off this crazy tour.

"You thought of everything else," she told Jeanie. "It's going to be fine."

Of course, Melissa was certain she would be stricken with hysterical blindness during the broadcast and run screaming off the set. But other than that, it was a classic case of role reversal. Jeanie seemed more nervous than Melissa. There was more at stake than Melissa wanted to think about, so she was concentrating on being grateful that the booking hadn't been canceled. Antonio still hadn't been located, but the marketing department had made an executive decision to go ahead without him. *Wake Up, America* was too good a gig to pass up, and Melissa had finally convinced them she would be able make excuses for her missing husband.

Please, God, let him stay missing. It was much safer that way.

The greenroom door popped open, and the show's guest-wrangler—the harried young woman who'd been squiring them around all morning—beckoned for Melissa. "C'mon! You're up next!"

Melissa squeezed Jeanie's hand. "I can do this," she whispered. "I won't let you down."

Jeanie squeezed back, and some color returned to her ashen face. She began to straighten Melissa's clothing, dusting the shoulders of her navy pin-stripe pantsuit and straightening the starched collar of her man-tailored blouse. She even gave Melissa's shiny brunette pageboy a smoothing. It was probably a reflex action, but Melissa was encouraged that Jeanie was acting more like herself. Jeanie was about thirty-five and the perfect publicist, part brilliant sales strategist and part mother hen. There hadn't been much strategizing going on this morning, but at least she was starting to make familiar clucking noises.

The guest-wrangler grabbed Melissa's hand, dragged her out of Jeanie's clutches and quickly led her through the wings. Melissa heard a countdown, and then she was gently pushed onto a television set to tumultuous applause. The lights were surreal, like the spaceship landing in *Close Encounters,* but she could see a woman who looked like Bobbi Start rising from a couch and waving at her. She'd never seen the host through anything but her television screen. Now she looked as if she were a mile away.

Was that a symptom of hysterical blindness?

Melissa wouldn't have placed a bet on her chances of getting over there, but somehow she made the trip in seconds, and miraculously, there were no disasters. She didn't trip or fall. Her fly didn't unzip itself and her jacket didn't catch on anything and rip off her body like stunt clothing.

Did they have obedience schools for imaginations? She should have sent hers years ago. *Down, imagination, down.*

"Here's our sex expert!" Bobbi rushed over and hugged Melissa as she stepped up on the pedestal set. Bobbi's exuberance nearly knocked them both over, which the audience loved. They clapped and cheered, making Melissa feel as if she was in friendly company. She wasn't surprised the show was a hit. Bobbi projected that same sort of welcome to everyone. Tiny and boundlessly perky, the former Olympic gymnast was morning television's bright new face. She'd brought *Wake Up* to the number-two spot in the ratings, and the show was swiftly gaining on number one.

Who needs coffee, with Bobbi Start in the morning? That was the show's teaser.

"Melissa, Melissa, *Melissa*," Bobbi gushed as they sat down. "You naughty girl! This book of yours is quite an eye-opener. Or should I say mind-opener?"

Bobbi held up *101 Ways,* and Melissa blushed, mostly with pleasure. She'd been coached by Jeanie to think of herself as excited rather than nervous, which must mean she was *really* excited. Her insides were vibrating like one of those coin-operated motel beds.

"Please, yes, call it a mind-opener," Melissa said. "My goal with the book is to help women think out of the box, so to speak, when it comes to their love lives. I believe we should be as creative in our quest for sexual enjoyment as we are in our quest for bargains at the mall. Think how happy everyone would be—and how skinny. You know sex burns nearly seven hundred calories an hour. That's better than the treadmill."

Bobbi chortled. "But who could have sex for an hour?"

She doesn't know Antonio, Melissa thought.

One of the cameras had a blinking red light, which Melissa had been told meant it was on. She glanced at it and smiled, hoping to send Jeanie a signal. *See, I'm doing fine out here. Piece of cake.*

"Why don't we have some fun with the folks in our audience," Bobbi suggested. "Let's give a lucky couple the Naughty-Sex Quiz and see how they do. Do we have any volunteers?"

Hands shot up all over the studio, but one of the show's pages was already out in the audience with a couple who'd volunteered before the taping. The page introduced the couple as in their thirties, married ten years and stuck in the sexual doldrums.

Melissa scanned the crowd nervously. Okay, so she'd invented the quiz for her book, but it hadn't occurred to her that she'd be conducting man-on-the-street-type interviews. She greeted the couple with a smile, pretending it wasn't at all unusual to be casually probing into the intimate details of their lives.

"Do you indulge in sexual afterplay as well as sexual foreplay?" she asked them. "In other words, do you talk about your lovemaking afterward and tell each other what you liked?"

The man blushed, but the woman spoke right up. "What I'd like is to *have* sex," she said.

The audience tittered, and Melissa found herself grinning, too. "Not to worry," she said. "It sounds like a case of sexual batteries going dead. What you need is a jump start." She rubbed her hands as if warming them. "To get the current flowing again, try something I call erotic flashforwards. They're fun, highly stimulating, and they'll help you discover your own secret turn-ons."

"What are erotic flash-forwards?" Bobbi asked.

The husband seemed perplexed, too. "I flashed someone once," he said uncertainly. "There was a census taker at the door and it was hotter 'n hell that day, so I flapped my bathrobe to create a breeze—"

Bobbi jumped in again, apparently to save the audience's delicate sensibilities. "I'm guessing Melissa is talking about visualizing the kind of sex you'd like to have with your partner. Right, Melissa? Fantasizing?"

"Yes, exactly." She turned to the crowd. "And here's a homework assignment for *all* of you. Next time you're stuck in traffic or waiting in a line, use that time to daydream about what would thrill your soul if you were alone somewhere with your partner. It could be something you saw at the movies or read in a book, but don't limit it to the obvious. Sure, you could have your partner brush your hair, but maybe you'd rather have him warm your bottom with that hairbrush."

"Just when it was getting interesting!" Bobbi clucked with disappointment as the show's theme music began to play. "We have to take a short break, but stay tuned. Coming up next? How to make him sit up and *beg* for booty."

As soon as the cameras were off, the set buzzed with activity. A rather morose young man refreshed Melissa's water glass and Bobbi's iced tea. Flowers were fluffed and pillows plumped. A soundwoman checked the boom mikes, and a group of staffers huddled in discussions off to one side.

Melissa looked to Bobbi for approval and got a thumbs-up as the host leafed through her notes. "The next segment should be even better," she said. "I see we have some great surprises in store. These producers of mine are geniuses."

The guest-wrangler dashed out to powder Melissa's nose, so there was no chance to find out what Bobbi meant, but she wasn't too concerned. Things seemed to be going pretty well. Even the married couple had been cute without trying to be. When you talked about sex, you had a real advantage, she'd discovered. The subject was a minefield of double entendres. You couldn't go far without stepping on something. It was dangerous—and exciting.

"...three, two, one—"

Melissa barely got a sip of water before they were back on the air. Bobbi held up the book again, and one of the cameras zoomed in for a close-up. The cover appeared on the monitor, and the name Melissa Sanders appeared on the screen. It gave her quite a jolt. That was *her* book! There'd been a flurry of activity getting ready, and it hadn't dawned on her until now that she'd be seeing her own book on TV. It almost felt as if they were talking about someone else, and she was here by mistake.

"Let's talk about chapter five, Melissa. Some of these games sound like carnival rides—Joyride, Spin Cycle, Express Train to Blissville, Wing-Ding Swing and Sexual Paste. Oh, and how about this one—the Velvet Tongue. Care to tell us about any of those?" Bobbi said with a coy wink.

"Well, the Wing-Ding Swing involves having your partner push you in the swing, but not with his hands."

"My, my." Bobbi laughed. "Sounds like good coordination is required. How about Sexual Paste, hmm? You must tell us about that one."

Melissa laughed, too. "Sorry, you'll have to read the book. Sexual Paste is triple-X-rated and much too hot for daytime TV."

"Okay, but tell us this at least—which one of these games made your husband beg for more? Was it the Velvet Tongue, maybe?"

Melissa blushed. The interlude that had sparked the name Velvet Tongue was still achingly vivid in her mind, even after two years.

"Actually, Antonio inspired that game," she said softly, "but I'm not sure I should tell you how."

Bobbi rose, glancing toward the wings from which Melissa had emerged. "Well, then," she said in a tone lilting with intrigue, "maybe Antonio will tell us himself."

"What?" Melissa stared at Bobbi, who was now talking directly to the camera.

"Yes, folks, we have a surprise for Melissa. She doesn't know anything about this, but we've brought her husband over from London, where he was traveling on business. We thought everyone would want to meet the man who inspired the Velvet Tongue."

Bobbi flung out an arm. "Welcome, Antonio Bond!"

No ONE GASPED louder than Melissa as a tall, dark and exotically handsome man walked onto the set of the talk show. His glossy black hair was a little longer than current trends dictated, but he'd never seemed the type who cared about trends. It caressed the nape of his neck and fell onto his forehead, making him look ever so slightly disreputable, but in the sexiest possible way.

On the other hand, he could have been a spokesperson for the line of clothes he wore. The casually tailored slacks, black silk shirt and woven leather sandals gave him the look of a man who'd just flown in from the south of France. The shadowed jaw beautifully carved his angular face. This was not the waiter who'd dropped to his knees in front of her and proposed. And yet, it was. This was Antonio. He had that same intense, prepare-to-be-swept-off-your-feet quality.

He walked to Bobbi first and shook her hand, then turned to Melissa, who had not yet managed to stand up. His dark gaze locked in on her, glinting with dangerous lights. Apparently he was in no rush. The set's blinking red bulbs and ticking time clocks didn't seem to faze him as, with undisguised interest, he watched her efforts to rise.

With a tug of his hand, he pulled her to her feet and said for everyone to hear, "*Cara,* it feels like years since I've held you."

The audience sighed as he drew her into his arms. Melissa couldn't even breathe. Her pulse throbbed so hard it hurt, but this wasn't pleasure. She didn't know what it was. Fear, excitement, wild anticipation?

The audience couldn't hear what he whispered, and Melissa didn't catch all of it either, but it sounded like, "Don't expect to walk away from me again. Ever."

She glanced up at him, startled, but all she caught was his fleeting smile. Lord, he was impossibly gorgeous. Still. That mouth of his was every bit as smolderingly gorgeous as the night he'd laid a trail of fiery kisses all over her nude, trembling body. Why was this happening to her? On national television?

"It's just as beautiful as the night I put it on your finger," he said.

Melissa wasn't sure what he meant until he brought her fingers to his lips and kissed the woven gold band she wore. Her heart froze like a stone. It was the ring. She was jinxed, cursed. She would never escape him as long as that ring was on her finger. She could feel her imagination spinning away with her, and she made a desperate effort to stop it. Jinxes and curses were pure superstition. It was *him,* not the ring. *He* was her problem.

She needed some distance from him, but it felt as if she'd stepped onto a merry-go-round. If not for his arms around her, she would have tumbled off. The set swirled, and so did her thoughts. What had he actually said, and more to the point, what did he want from her? Maybe she was spinning out again, but could this be some kind of blackmail attempt? Was he after money? He'd never struck Melissa as that kind of man, but how well did she know his true character?

Jeanie should have thought of all this before she tracked him down.

Why didn't she tell me she'd found him?

Antonio sat down next to her, and never in her life had Melissa been forced to gather her wits so quickly. She knew Jeanie had been looking for him, but she hadn't been prepared for him to show up this way. In all honesty, she hadn't been prepared for him to show up at all. She hoped he'd been coached and knew what he was supposed to say and not say, but there'd been no sign of that so far.

She had no idea what to say either, especially to him. *Have mercy, Lord, don't ravish me and fling me into the volcano.* That should bring down the house.

"I can see this really is a surprise for Melissa," Bobbi

chirped. "Just look at her. She looks— Are you all right, Melissa?"

"I'm speechless," Melissa managed to say. "How did you find him?"

No, never mind! Don't answer that.

Bobbi was already addressing the audience. "Somehow, I have trouble imagining Antonio begging for anything, don't you?" she asked them. Heads nodded.

"Call me Tony, please," he said. He graced Bobbi with a fleeting smile, then shot a penetrating glance at Melissa. "I think my bride should answer that. Have you ever heard *me* beg, Melissa?"

Melissa tossed him a bawdy wink. "Well, of course." She turned back to Bobbi. "My whole book is based on personal experience." She was not going to let this man intimidate her on national television. He was supposed to be her well-satisfied husband, according to the book, and if he didn't know it, she would have to make that point somehow.

He leaned over and whispered in her ear, "Tell the truth, if you dare. And by the way, according to your book, I can arouse you to the point of orgasm this way. Is it working? Maybe you'd better let the audience think it is if you want to sell books."

Melissa whimpered, but not in ecstasy. Every single eye was glued on her. She considered doing her best imitation of Meg Ryan in *When Harry Met Sally,* but the humiliation factor was too great. She couldn't make those noises when she was having sex. Well, except with him, the rat, and she didn't intend to give him that satisfaction now. She was already having flashbacks of their wedding night. In Technicolor and Surround Sound.

She could hear the sensual growl in his throat when he'd stolen inside her toga with his hand and found her naked skin for the first time. She could smell the body heat rising off his skin, and feel the rush of her own blood as she realized how addictive his touch could be.

Somehow she had to hit Rewind and turn this video off!

Stalling for time, she reached for her cup of ice water. Her hand was shaking so hard, she could barely hold it steady, which gave her an idea. But could she do something that crazy? No, it was outrageous, much too risky.

Yes, she could do it. She had to. It was the only way to put him off balance and regain any kind of control.

She sucked in some air, flashed Antonio a nervous smile—and emptied the entire mug into his lap. It had to be freezing cold, but he didn't move a muscle that she could see. He just sat there, breathing through his nostrils, and did nothing while the audience gasped.

Bobbi sprang into action, looking for something to blot up the mess, and the guest-wrangler dashed over with a towel. She held it out to Tony, but Melissa grabbed it.

"It's okay!" She held up the towel, addressing Bobbi and the audience. "We're playing a game called Oops! You spill something on the gentleman's lap, and then you get to clean him up. It's very sexy. Right, Tony?"

Tony's glance had gone darker than a creature of the night's. Dracula didn't have eyes that black and endless. In an ominous voice, he said, "I don't know about Oops! but we have played a few games. The one I like best is the Runaway Bride and the Furious Groom—who takes his revenge when he catches up with her."

Melissa gulped audibly. She had little doubt that he was furious, and that she would pay for this in some unspeakable way. But that wasn't the only thing that concerned her at the moment. The audience had all been given free copies of *101 Ways*. She hoped no one would notice there was no such game in the book.

Chapter Three

Fighting is an underrated activity among lovers. It cleans the pipes and clears the air, and then there's make-up sex!

101 Ways To Make Your Man Beg

IT ALL BROKE LOOSE right after the show. Tony stood behind a screen, pulling on a dry pair of pants, which the guest-wrangler had found for him. On the other side of the screen, he could hear Melissa pacing, muttering about how she'd been betrayed and how Jeanie would hear about this. As far as Tony was concerned, Melissa had a few things to learn about betrayal, but that could wait until they were alone.

Alone. He could hardly wait.

The door opened and someone entered the greenroom. "Hey, terrific show!"

Tony recognized the voice as Jeanie's, the publicist from Searchlight. But Melissa didn't seem to share her enthusiasm for the show. She nearly squeaked with indignation.

"Why didn't you tell me about him?" she asked Jeanie.

Her anger gave Tony a small measure of satisfaction. If he had his way, she would squeak often and with feeling. And he *would* have his way.

"The producers wanted him to be a surprise," Jeanie said. "What could I do?"

Tony zipped up his pants. As he emerged from behind the screen, the two women were circling each other like combatants. He didn't realize they'd noticed him until Melissa stabbed a finger in his direction.

"A surprise?" she said. "He's not a surprise. He's a fatal mistake from my past. How could you spring something like this on me?"

Jeanie clasped her hands in an act of contrition. "I'm *sorry*. The show wouldn't take you without him, Melissa. They were going to cancel our booking. I found him at the last minute, and they made me promise not to tell you."

"And you agreed to that? Knowing my history with him, you still agreed?"

"I thought you'd want me to. It's for the book. Everything we're doing is for the good of the book, right?"

Tony wasn't exactly happy with either one of these women, but he was rooting for the one who hadn't just dumped ice water on him. The vestal virgin had changed, he acknowledged, watching her stamp her black spectator pumps. She'd gotten better at standing up for herself.

So much for trying to protect damsels being badgered by their girlfriends. At first his proposal two years ago had been nothing more than a gallant move to quiet her friends. But when he'd knelt down to ask for her hand and seen the look of utter disbelief in her eyes, he'd known he was going through with it. She didn't believe any man could want her.

And he couldn't believe that.

She was beautiful. Her translucent skin was tinged with the hot pink of blooming roses, her expression one of wonderment. When he'd run into her on the beach, she'd seemed as wistful as the Madonnas in the mission, but once they were alone in his room, she'd confounded him with the way she'd thrown caution to the winds. She'd sent his heart and various other parts of his body soaring, and he hadn't caught up with them since.

The guest-wrangler popped her head in the greenroom at that moment and made various hand signals that Jeanie seemed to understand.

"The limo's here," Jeanie said, beckoning to Melissa and Tony. "It will take us to the hotel, and we can talk this over there."

"What hotel?" Melissa asked.

"The hotel where you and Tony are staying."

"He and I are *not* staying at the same hotel."

Tony caught Melissa's glance, the one that said this was all his fault.

"It's just for appearances," Jeannie explained. "We need people to think you're married—and by the way, you are."

"Are what?"

"Married."

Melissa went as pale as death. "It's legal? Is that what you're saying?"

She tugged on the ring as if trying to pull it off, which Tony found highly ironic. The band had been in his family for years, and there was an interesting legend attached to it, if you believed in such things. He'd always wondered why she'd taken the ring with her. He could never really fathom that she'd stolen it, but now it was also hard to imagine that she'd kept the ring all this time.

Jeanie nodded with the authority of a magistrate. "Legal and binding. You signed your name to the marriage license."

Melissa gave out a little choking sound. "How is that possible? I thought it was all a joke, and the license was in Spanish. I didn't know what I was signing."

"No judge is going to buy that, Melissa. You stood with Tony before the priest, recited the vows and signed your name to the certificate. You knew it wasn't a funeral."

Tony had some sympathy for Melissa at that moment. News of her had certainly come as a shock to him, too.

He had obligations that didn't allow for treks to New York—binding obligations, both business and personal. He should have been furious at the news, but he hadn't been, not totally. Melissa had signed the form, but her last name was illegible. That apparently didn't make the union any less legal, but it was why he hadn't been able to trace her. She didn't know that, however, and he wasn't going to be the one to tell her. He was here because he had to be. Her publicist had made him a deal he couldn't refuse. But there was one other reason: He wanted to know how a woman could give herself to a man with such complete abandon and then walk away without a word.

"Melissa, are you all right?" Jeanie asked.

She held her chest and made little panting sounds. "I can't seem to breathe," she said. "There's something wrong."

Jeanie gave an exasperated shake of her head. Apparently she'd dealt with this before. "Melissa, you're fine. Now, let's get out of here. The limo's waiting for us."

Melissa's pants became gasps, and it sounded to Tony like the breathing problems he'd had as a child. Moving quickly, he came up behind her, clamped one hand over her mouth and held her nose with the other. His forearm pressed into the softness of her breast, and he could feel every crazy beat of her heart. He wasn't copping a feel, much as he might like to. He was trying to keep her from passing out, but apparently she didn't appreciate the good deed. Within seconds she'd broken out of his hold and was whirling on him.

"What do you think you're doing?"

"Just trying to help," he said. "It's an old remedy my mother used to use. You seem to be breathing better now."

Jeanie made a tiny gurgling noise that sounded like laughter, but Melissa didn't seem to be amused. She had her arms crossed over her breasts, and he knew exactly what that felt like. His skin still resonated with the steam heat of her flesh and the quick, hard beats of her heart. Two years ago she'd wanted his touch. She'd begged him for it, but he'd made her wait. He knew all about pleasure withheld. Its potential. Its power.

She'd been making him wait ever since.

"Let's go." He reached for her arm. "I'll help you."

She drew back, her eyes spitting fire. "I don't need help, thank you. Why don't you just throw me over your shoulder like a caveman and stomp off with me?" Obviously realizing what she'd said, she thrust out a hand. "Don't you dare!"

Tony's smile held little in the way of mirth. She had no idea how much he wanted to throw her over his shoulder and carry her off. His runaway bride had left him wondering what hit him. She'd given him a gift—one night of heaven—and then she'd snatched it away. He'd spent two years unable to get her out of his mind, two years obsessed with her wanton body and her heart-shaped face.

He and Melissa Sanders had some catching up to do. Call it unfinished business.

Her book was all about how to make men beg, but that wasn't how it was going to work. Someone might be begging, but it wouldn't be him. And he couldn't wait to be there when she found out.

THE BLACK LINCOLN sluiced its way through the rain-snarled streets of midday Manhattan, traversing the honking cabs, jaywalking pedestrians and death-defying bike messengers. It was exactly noon, and the storm clouds had picked the busiest hour of the day to burst. Runoff drains were overflowing and the block-long city buses drenched everything in their wake with their spray.

Spring had sprung a leak, and tempers were coming to a quick boil. Sirens wailed, and cabbies rolled down windows to shout curses in every language imaginable. But inside the limo the atmosphere was more restrained—

quiet and tense. No one said much of anything, except Jeanie, who was on the phone with booking agents, trying to juggle appointments.

Melissa was just grateful to have the show over and nothing else scheduled today. She had a book signing tomorrow morning and two interviews in the afternoon, back-to-back, and there would probably be more when Jeanie was done. But at least they had time to get this mess straightened out, the mess being Antonio—or rather, Tony—Bond.

Jeanie had done her best to put a good face on things. "The show was a huge success," she'd told them when they'd first got into the limo. "The audience was on the edge of their seats."

"At least their seats were dry," Tony had observed in a low, dangerous tone.

"Accidents happen," Melissa was quick to insist. "I had to make the best of it, didn't I?"

Fortunately, Jeannie had positioned herself in the middle of the squabbling couple. Otherwise, Melissa might have been singed by the look she got from Tony. It was as hot as the steam coming off the streets.

Now he was busy jotting notes on a legal pad, and Melissa was trying to peek over Jeanie's lap to see what he was up to. Naturally his handwriting was illegible. Someone else might have called it bold and dramatic, but Melissa wasn't feeling very charitable right now. It didn't surprise her, though, that he wrote boldly. He did lots of things that way.

"Excellent," Jeanie said to whomever was on the line. "You want Mel and Tony there two hours early for makeup and wardrobe? You got it. Thank you!"

She clicked off the phone, all smiles. "You guys are hot! Melissa, they've already shortened your name to Mel. Isn't that adorable? And apparently every booking agent in the country was watching *Wake Up*, because they're crazy for you two. I just firmed up four more shows, with six pending."

"Not so fast," Melissa said. "We have to talk about this."

"And we will talk." Jeanie dropped her cell phone in her huge Louis Vuitton backpack. "But first a word of warning, kids. I haven't had a reaction to an author appearance like this in years. Something is happening here that is bigger than all three of us, and if anybody in this limo is thinking about chickening out, let me just say this. *Don't.*"

"Thanks for taking the pressure off," Melissa mumbled.

Tony, however, seemed more than ready to negotiate. "I want game approval prior to the shows," he told Jeanie. "No more surprises like that Oops! game. Without that stipulation, I can't agree to the terms you've laid out."

"What terms?" Melissa asked Jeanie. "What agreement have you made with him? And why wasn't I told about any of this?"

"As I said in the greenroom, I wasn't free to tell you." Jeanie's tone was one of calm forbearance. *Hey, relax, everything's under control,* she seemed to be saying. "And as for Tony," she added, "we dragged him away from his very busy life. We had to find some way to compensate him."

Melissa peered at the two of them suspiciously. "And what way was that?"

Jeanie shrugged. "I can't really discuss the details of our arrangement with Tony, now, can I?"

Tony hadn't cracked a smile, but Melissa sensed that he wanted to. His expression, his whole demeanor, was a bit too innocent for her taste. He and Jeanie were in league in some way, and that struck her as just downright wicked. How could a publisher turn on their author like this? Of course, she was the one who'd started this whole thing by dedicating the book to him, but that didn't justify a conspiracy.

"Well, maybe I have some terms, too," Melissa said,

thinking fast to come up with a whopper of a list. "If we really are expected to stay in the same hotel room, then it has to be a suite. I want my own bedroom and bath. I'd also like a daily rundown of the schedule with background information on whom we'll be dealing with at each interview. Plus, Tony and I are obviously going to need some rehearsal time if we're to pull off this blissfully happy couple thing. And last, when all this is over, I want a divorce."

"No problem with any of that, including the divorce," Jeanie said amiably.

Melissa looked at her sharply. She hadn't expected it to be this easy. She'd thought someone would protest, possibly even Tony, but he seemed to be taking it all in stride, too. Maybe she should have added a little something like: *And meanwhile, there's to be absolutely no sex!* See if that got his attention.

"This is a two-week tour?" Tony asked, apparently confirming what he already knew.

Jeanie nodded. "However, Searchlight would like you both to be available for joint interviews for the next three months."

Melissa dropped back in the seat with a gasp.

Both Jeanie and Tony glanced over at her, and at least Jeanie had the decency to show some concern. "You don't have to live together," she told Melissa, "but you do have to be willing to make media appearances."

"How about two months?" Antonio suggested.

"One month," Melissa croaked when she found her voice.

"I'll leave it open for now," Jeanie said, "but whatever period we agree upon is final. If you want a quick and quiet annulment of the marriage after that, go ahead. I assume that's what you both want, isn't it? An annulment?"

"Of course," Melissa said, aware that Tony had echoed her. Apparently, with the right kind of connections, they could get an annulment even though the marriage had been consummated. She'd heard these things could be arranged with the consent of both parties.

Jeanie's relief was audible. "At least we agree about that. And by the way," she said, "I've been trying to recall if that Oops! game is in the book. If it isn't, we'll have to add it to the next edition."

The driver's voice came through the intercom as the limo pulled over. "Hotel Da Vinci."

Melissa was seated on the street side, and as she grabbed her bag and got ready to make a dash for it, the driver got out and came back for her with an umbrella. It was still pouring, and she would have to hurry if she wanted to save her brand-new suit and boots. Unfortunately, just as he opened the door, a cab roared by, and she was instantly drenched.

By the time Melissa got around the car and under the hotel's protective canopy, she was dripping like a drowned cat, and of course, there was Antonio, standing by the door, bone dry and looking impossibly dapper. Some people had all the damn luck.

"Things have a way of balancing out, don't they?" he said as she shook off the water and walked over to him.

"Beast," she whispered. "I am not having sex with you, so don't even think about that."

He gave her a puzzled look. "I haven't thought about it in two years. Why should I start now?"

"Yeah, like I believe that. You've been thinking about it every damn day, just as I have."

"Really?" The smile that had been lying in wait suddenly appeared.

Melissa's heart quickened. She clearly had his attention now. He was eyeing her as if she were a cream puff on a dessert tray.

"Every damn day?" he said. "I can't wait to hear about it."

A HOT, STEAMING BATH with essential oil of jasmine and mounds of lovely bubbles. That was the way to beat stress. Melissa's sense of well-being seeped back into her by degrees as she soaked in the deep well of the claw-footed tub, behind locked bathroom doors. She'd found a basket of bath accessories in the hotel suite's sumptuous marble bathroom, and she'd immediately chosen that room and the adjoining bedroom for herself. When she was done with her bath, she was going to have a glass of white wine from the ice bucket on the coffee table. When they'd entered the suite, the wine and a tray of appetizers had been waiting for her and Tony, compliments of Searchlight.

Jeanie was the one who'd chickened out. Once she'd arranged for the suite, she'd left them at the elevator, suggesting that they needed some time alone to talk. In theory, yes. But, in reality, Melissa wasn't ready to talk to the man she'd exposed so much of herself to. It was a dare, a crazy dream of a night, and she'd had too much to drink. Maybe it had seemed like a chance to experience all her fantasies with no one the wiser, but that was supposed to be the beginning and the end of it. She'd never imagined he would show up in the flesh, and she would have to deal with him, not to mention everything she'd done with him.

Well, that wasn't exactly true. She'd imagined it all right. She'd even thought about waking up one morning to find him standing in the doorway of her bedroom, one arm braced above his head, watching her with the deliberate calm of a wolf on the hunt.

Think you're in enough trouble yet?

Melissa let out a soft moan of despair. She closed her eyes to the disturbing image, but she couldn't shut him out of her senses. He'd kept his promise. She was in plenty of trouble now. But was she going to pay the rest of her life for one reckless night of pleasure? While she was writing the book, she'd tried to tell herself that it had been about research. But that was ridiculous—an excuse, not a reason. She'd wanted to be with him. Wanted it with every cell of her being. But that still didn't explain why she'd done it. Why with him and no one else? Why that night? And why had she gone so far? Abandoned didn't begin to describe her behavior.

Something about him had allowed her to take the risk of claiming what she wanted, and that's what alarmed her now. She'd walked through the doorway of her own volition, but it felt as if someone else had opened the door, as if *he'd* opened it.

How could she be sure he wouldn't do it again?

Suddenly everything was spinning. She was back on the merry-go-round, her heart racing, her thoughts awhirl. The force of it should have made her dizzy. She *was* dizzy, but there was something strangely exhilarating about it, too. She felt alive, empowered.

She didn't want him to open that door again...did she?

No! No, of course not. And even if she did, there was too much at stake.

Melissa sank lower in the tub, trying to relax and recapture the serenity. Remembering had brought back all the confusing feelings, and she needed to let them dissipate. But the steaming bath had done everything it could. In fact, it might be making things worse. She needed a glass of wine and a good night's sleep. If only she could talk to Kath. She and her friend had always confided in each other, and men were Kath's area of expertise. But the suite seemed eerily quiet, and hotel walls were notoriously thin. She didn't want to chance being overheard.

She left the tub, having already decided the phone call would have to wait for a better time. Tonight it would be the wine and the good night's sleep.

Moments later, still damp and jasmine-scented, she slipped into a fluffy terry robe, tied it around her and let herself out of the locked bathroom. She was almost surprised to discover that there was no one waiting outside the door, poised to ambush her. She was being silly. He'd probably put that night behind him, too. But then why was he here? She didn't know why he'd bother, unless money or some kind of revenge was involved. He couldn't make much on a waiter's salary—unless he wasn't a waiter anymore. There was a lot she didn't know about Tony Bond. But did she want to know?

The wine seemed like a better and better idea.

She slipped into the main room of the suite and found it glimmering with afternoon sunlight. The focal point was a sunken living room with a drop-out window seat that seemed to rest on top of the city. Melissa's gaze was drawn to the man standing in front of the panoramic view, looking out at Central Park. He'd already opened the wine, poured himself a glass and put the bottle back in the bucket. He'd obviously decided to get comfortable, too.

He was wearing a T-shirt and jeans that rode the crest of his hips. Maybe it was his stance, but she didn't remember him being quite so tall and imposing. The room had a Kentia palm that had to be close to six feet, but he had it beat. Of course, she'd been horizontal most of the time she was with him.

She brushed the distracting thought aside and concentrated on him, her mortal foe. Either he was one of the fortunate few who had natural tone, or he'd spent time in a gym. Waiters did some heavy lifting, but not enough to create those biceps. His muscled arms were golden in the light, and even his bare feet had taken on a bronze cast against the plush white carpet.

Bare feet. Plush pile. Was there something incredibly sexy about that? Or was she still suffering from post-traumatic stress disorder where he was concerned?

He had his back to her, but the picture that zinged into her mind was quite different. She saw him turning and walking toward her, a man crossing the room to join a woman lying on a bed. A naked man, muscled and golden from head to toe. Aroused like a stallion from head to toe. Even his nostrils were flared.

Melissa's thoughts came screeching to a halt. She couldn't go there. Could not. She shouldn't even be in the living room with him. It wasn't safe. The flashbacks flew like bullets when he was around. Maybe she could pour herself some wine and disappear. If she was quiet he would never notice.

"You're sneaking off again?"

Melissa froze. That was his voice, but she wasn't sure how he'd caught her until she saw her own reflection in the mirrored windows. He'd known she was in the room from her first tiptoe.

"Sneaking off?" she said.

He turned around, framed by the sunlight. His gaze was unflinching. "You know what I mean."

Of course she did, but— "I didn't sneak off. I just left."

"Without a note? Without a word?"

She hesitated in an effort to steady her voice. "I should have left a note. I meant to, but I was embarrassed, and I thought you might be, too. I wanted to spare both of us that awkwardness."

Did he believe her? She hoped so because she had just realized it was true. She had been trying to spare them. "I wasn't sure you were any more ready to face me than I was to face you." It didn't explain why she'd left, but it did explain how.

He gazed at her, perplexed. "Not ready to face you because I'd made love to you?"

"Well, it was a little more than the missionary position."

She shuddered, hoping to dodge the bullets of memory and knowing she wasn't fast enough. Had he forgotten how he'd laid her out on the leopard-print spread with her hands entangled in the sheet above her head? He didn't remember how helpless she'd been, and how she'd nearly cried because his touch was so sweet, so wicked, so right, so wrong...*so everything?*

"We let our imaginations run," he said. "We didn't throw up barriers. Maybe that was a little adventurous for a woman like you, a little dangerous."

"A *little* dangerous?"

"Melissa, I got down on one knee and proposed to you. That was dangerous."

She glanced up at him, startled and flushed. "That was a gesture. You were just being kind."

"I don't marry all the women I feel kindly toward. In fact, I haven't married any of them but you."

"Why did you marry me?" She met his gaze and saw her reflection swirling behind him, as if the room had moved. Uncanny, but that happened all the time with him. The whole world felt as if it were moving, like the horses on a carousel, galloping around the cornice at the center. Somehow, he made her feel as if he was the only stable element on the plane where they existed, wherever that plane might be. He was the cornice. Everything else fell away.

She glanced at the gold band on her finger and wondered if wearing it had anything to do with the effect he had on her. Wishful thinking, that. If the ring was responsible, then all she had to do was get it off, and she was free. It couldn't be that simple, could it?

"I'm not sure," he said in measured tones. "Why did you leave?"

She had a plane ticket? He hadn't asked her to stay? She didn't think the marriage was real? He was such an accomplished lover she thought he might be a gigolo? She was scared to death?

"It all happened so fast." She took a sip of the wine, more to see if her hands were shaking than for any other reason. "It was chivalry, right? You were trying to rescue me."

He frowned at her. "Is that wrong?"

"Probably not wrong, but hardly the basis for a lasting marriage."

"I've heard worse reasons."

What did that mean? Melissa didn't understand him. He didn't operate according to any rational rules. Her gut was telling her that he was some kind of Don Quixote, rescuing the needy. He had a savior complex, and she had made the mistake of needing to be saved that night, at least from her girlfriends.

"Why are you here?" she asked him.

He walked toward her, the sunlight at his back, masking his expression. "Maybe I'm curious. Would that be reason enough for you? I saw a woman on the beach, and I thought I knew who she was. No one else had a clue, but I had several—and a strong desire to solve the mystery."

Melissa tried to speak, but her voice had lost its strength again. Amazing how he could do that to her. Amazing how he could make the earth move. But she had to make it stop moving. She had to, or someone was going to fall off the edge. And she knew it would be her.

She cleared her throat. "How could you possibly know who I was?"

"The better question is how could I not know? It was right there, crying out for recognition. I'm surprised everyone didn't see it."

"What was crying out? You just said I was a mystery."

"Maybe I said too much."

"You're not going to answer my question?" That brought a flash of anger. "If this is some kind of game, I don't want to play."

"I saw needs, your needs. I saw a hunger in you for more, but something was holding you back. That was the mystery. I didn't understand why you didn't go after what you wanted, claim it."

"I did go after it," she insisted. "I'm the expert on that,

if you'll remember. I've written an entire book about women going after what they want."

He smiled. "You did, and you didn't, which is all part of the puzzle."

"So that's what turns you on, a good mystery?"

"No, it's the hungers of the human spirit that turn me on. It's unrequited love and lost dreams. But mostly, it's women who are terrified of being needy."

Melissa gaped at him. So this *was* about her being needy. That's how he'd seen her, as desperate for his attention? In need of sexual healing, maybe? She turned away from him, wondering if she should be as deeply offended as she felt. In fact, she *had* been needy and desperate that night. But she could have lived her whole life without having him know it.

Her hands were shaking, and she kept thinking she should set her wineglass down. Instead, she took a good long drink.

"I'd really like to put that night behind us, if we could."

"Why? It happened."

The wine ripped at her throat. "Just because something happened is no reason to drag it out and analyze it to death. Sometimes it's just as good a reason not to. I'm going to bed."

She didn't bother to look back as she walked out of the room, still clutching her glass. She was more than likely wrong about him anyway. Unrequited love? Needy women? Don Quixote was beginning to bear a passing resemblance to Don Juan, and that wouldn't have surprised her, either. Nobody got that good in bed without some experience.

Personally she liked a guy who tilted at windmills.

But the real question was why she cared which one he was.

Chapter Four

Retire your vibrator, girls. His tongue is trainable!
101 Ways To Make Your Man Beg

SHE WAS ENCHANTING. Marching out of the room with her dark hair pinned up and bouncing on her head. Her slender body drowning in the white robe. Trailing a mist of jasmine. Haughty. Hot. And everything the word implied.

She had enchanted him. Tonight. Two years ago.

Maybe it was those Bambi eyes. When she'd turned them on him in the restaurant, he would have fought mythical dragons to save her from harm. But tonight those big brown eyes had suddenly looked wounded and accusatory, and he had no idea what he'd done to hurt her. Or that he *could* hurt her.

Tony glanced down at the swirling wine, lifted the glass and took a swallow. Now, *there* was a twisted yet strangely exhilarating thought. He had the power to hurt her. Would he want to hurt her? She had hurt him and, human nature being what it was, he wouldn't mind a little payback. But this was more than that. If he was right, she had just inadvertently revealed a vulnerability—and that's what had him intrigued. Maybe she still had some feelings for him. The way she'd disappeared that day two years ago had made him question whether she'd ever had any.

A platter of appetizers—everything from pâté and oysters to Norwegian smoked salmon stuffed with cream cheese and chives—waited on the wet bar. He was duly impressed, even for a man who knew his way around a restaurant kitchen. He helped himself to some salmon, savoring the pungent flavors and tender texture—and fleetingly thought about ordering up some dinner. Melissa's publisher had flown him in late last night, and he'd been up early this morning for the talk-show taping. There hadn't been time to think about food, and he should have been hungry, but he wasn't.

He poured himself more wine, although chardonnay wasn't a real favorite. Most Americans had yet to discover the pleasures of a really fine rosé. In Europe some prized it more than red or white, but here it was largely thought of as unsophisticated. Just one of the many things about this country that mystified him, that and one particular woman.

The slant of the sun's rays through the living-room windows said it must be around seven. Sundown. Too early to retire to the bedroom with her book, but that was exactly the plan. Jeanie had given him a copy with instructions to get it read and quickly, but he'd only had time to skim the chapters. It amused him that Melissa had made him sound like a porn star. The woman had quite an imagination. Their night together had been erotic, to say the least, but she'd given him credit for things he'd never heard of. He was going to have to do his homework to find out exactly what the Velvet Tongue was, although he could imagine.

Maybe he should go directly to the author.

He'd become fairly familiar with her tongue that night, as she had with his. And he could still remember exactly how she tasted—delicate and sweet, yet as deeply intoxicating as the finest French rosé. He could have drunk her all night long. She had made his head swim and his muscles go mindlessly hard. What more pleasure could a man want than that? Vital signs on full alert. Vital juices flooding his loins.

That's probably why he wasn't hungry tonight. His blood was rushing elsewhere. And why he couldn't sustain a thought that wasn't about her.

He set down the wine. He didn't need anything else blunting his instincts. She was doing a fine job. Two years and she was still in his blood? That was too long for any man to be preoccupied. Okay, obsessed.

He walked to the bedroom at the opposite end of the suite from hers and thought about the distance between them. Not just the span of a hotel room. They were from different worlds although he'd done enough traveling to feel comfortable in most situations. He wasn't just the backwater waiter that she might think. And more important, his life had changed in the past two years. He had moved on, and obviously so had she. He knew what the crystal ball had in store for him, and it didn't include a runaway wife who wrote about sex games but was afraid to play them.

Accomplish what you came to do and go, he told himself. *Make it a clean break and go back to your life. Your real life.*

But there was just one thing stopping him. One question he had to ask.

One question that only she could answer.

A LONG EVENING stretched ahead of Melissa. That should have been a relaxing thought, but she dreaded the unscheduled time. With her imagination, who wouldn't? It wasn't even 7:00 p.m., which gave her the entire night to think about how many different ways things could go wrong, and they all started with Antonio. If he was after revenge and trying to ruin her career by exposing her as a fraud, he might well bring down Jeanie and Searchlight as well. He could also be a double-dealing blackmailer, intending to strip her of every penny she made. Or he could decide to take up where they left off—and strip her of other things, like her clothes. Forget about her virtue. That was long gone.

Of course, there was always the possibility that he might be here simply to get the marriage annulled so he could move on with his life. She had a news reporter's tendency to gloss over mundane realities in favor of catastrophic possibilities. But regardless of his motives, one thing was clear. She was going to be forced to submit to all the possible risks and indignities of Antonio Bond, because without him the book could bomb.

She'd been lying on the bed leafing through magazines, and she grabbed one to fan herself. Either the room was stuffy or she was coming down with a fever. With any luck it was some virulent new strain of flu, and they would have to cancel the tour. Of course, fevers also signaled dread diseases like meningitis and malaria. She hadn't been bitten by any mosquitoes lately, so it was probably meningitis.

An inflammation of the lining of the brain. Oh, joy.

She whisked her cell phone off the night table to check her voice mail. That should distract her. If any of her friends had caught the show, she expected some startled messages. Kath and the girls knew about the book tour, but nothing about Antonio, the well-kept secret.

The first message was from Kath, followed by one from the whole gang, who were at a restaurant where the four of them met for dinner whenever they could. Listening to her friends' excitement worked like a tonic, and Melissa found herself laughing with them. Kath did the talking, but the other two could be heard cheering her on, and occasionally stealing the phone to make some cheeky comment.

"Melissa, you bad girl, you vixen, you *slut!*" Kath said. "You didn't tell us your 'husband' was going to show up.

You didn't even tell us you *had* a husband. Isn't that the waiter from Mexico? Did you actually marry him for real, or is this just a great publicity stunt?"

Both, Melissa thought. Apparently, fate reveled in mixing the bad with the good, just to keep things interesting.

"Melissa, it's Renee. Congratulations on the book *and* the man. An*tonnnnio*. Just saying his name makes me lubricate. I can imagine what shape you must be in. And speaking of that, I spilled some water in my date's lap last night. He loved it!"

Melissa rolled her eyes. Crazy women.

Pat Stafford added her two cents'. "So, are you two on your second honeymoon? I hope it's every bit as wicked as the first. You *have* to call and tell us everything!"

Melissa had never gone into detail with her friends about the night with Antonio, not even Kath. She'd been too thrown by the whole experience. It had taken her months to come to terms with what she'd done, but eventually, just so the girls would stop bugging her, she'd begun referring to it as the night of her life. That had started them guessing, and some of those guesses had inspired ideas for her book. But in reality the girls never got close to guessing at the sheer wild heat of that night, which was saying something.

No wonder I'm nervous, Melissa thought, clicking off her messages. Her friends knew very little about the dark side of Melissa Sanders. Only a near stranger knew how truly slutty she could be.

She called Kath back, knowing this was her friend's investment-club night, and left her a message that Antonio was a surprise arranged by her publisher—more of a shock, actually—but everything was fine. She couldn't say much more than that. There was no explaining this mess in a voice mail, and she really didn't want to encourage any more group messages. Besides, there were those thin walls to think about.

She couldn't call her parents, either. They also knew nothing about Antonio. She'd intentionally left them with the impression that her book was a self-help tome about the perils of dating. That had seemed a safe enough story. Their farm was light-years from the nearest bookstore, and they didn't have a TV that worked.

Melissa fell back against the pillows. The bedroom had French doors that opened onto the balcony, which really wasn't a balcony at all. The heavy wrought-iron railings allowed just enough space to open the doors and step out. But the bedroom *was* stuffy, and she didn't want to go in search of a thermostat and run the risk of encountering him again. Better to let some fresh air in, no matter how noisy it was out there.

She rose from the bed and opened the doors to the din of traffic. It was well after rush hour, but the taxis were still honking and squealing their tires, jockeying for position. Fifteen floors up, she tilted over the railing to look down and had a horrifying vision of a woman leaping to her death and the morning papers announcing that it was the newly infamous author of a kinky sex manual trying to escape her whispering husband.

Overcome by dizziness, she stepped back from the balcony. A breeze washed over her, warm and steamy from the rain, but nothing could have cleared her buzzing head. Her composure had evaporated. She turned back to the room, wondering what in the world she could do to distract herself. She had a book signing in the morning and radio interviews in the afternoon. She'd already laid out what she was going to wear and come up with some cute phrases to inscribe in the books.

She really ought to try her hand at conspiracy thrillers instead of self-help books. That might be a way to put her antsy imagination to practical use.

The chilly sound of her own laughter made her shiver. She had on nothing but her silk nightgown, and her bare arms were clammy with goose bumps. Her skin prickled and stung, making her wonder if she really had come down with something. Was that a rash on her hands? Wasn't that one of the symptoms of Lyme disease? She pictured Tony calling 911 and riding with her in an ambulance to the emergency room. Searchlight would send flowers, of course.

Time for a physical, she thought, heading for the bathroom.

The rash didn't show up well in the soft lights of the bathroom. In fact, she couldn't see it at all, which was a relief. That didn't mean she wasn't sick, though. The green coating on her tongue was very suspect, although it might have been from the green-apple candy she'd been nursing earlier, but she didn't think so. Her eyes looked a little yellowish, too, as she pulled down the lower lids. Yellow eyes meant hepatitis, didn't it?

Her pulse was too fast and her skin damp. This wasn't good.

She grabbed a cloth and soaked it in cold water to mop her forehead, but when she looked up, she thought she saw another reflection in the mirror. It didn't go away, even when she blinked. Now she was seeing double? What was that a symptom of? No, wait, it looked like a man's reflection. Someone had come up behind her!

She screamed, twisting the rug beneath her as she turned. Her feet flew out from under her, and she tumbled into his arms.

"Tony," she gasped. "What are you doing here?"

He scooped her into an embrace, cradling her with the tenderness that a wide receiver would a football. "I thought I heard you screaming," he said.

"I'm screaming because you're in my bathroom."

She was too off balance to push him away, but she wanted to. He helped her get to her feet, and she hurried to extricate herself. Her nightgown was all over the place—everywhere except where it should be. Nearly exposed breasts blushed at him, one nipple peaking from behind a silk strap.

"I'm fine," she said, pressing her hands to his chest for leverage. That might have worked, but she made the mistake of glancing up at him as she stepped back. It was as far as either one of them got. Their gazes caught and drew them back together like rebounding springs.

All the crazy energy of that electric moment surrounded them like an aura and held them exactly where they were. She didn't want to push him away anymore. She didn't even try to save herself as he cupped her face and whispered something low and sexy in a language she didn't understand. It sounded like French. How many languages did this man speak?

There was a section on kissing in her book, but it didn't begin to do this justice. His lips touched down tentatively, brushing sparks across the surface of hers. He made a noise that sounded like relief, and she yearned to hear it again. He didn't actually lift her off the floor. It just felt that way. His hand stroked her face, urging her to give him more. His mouth coaxed and beguiled, seducing her to open up and surrender everything he wanted. Everything she had. And suddenly it was everything she wanted, too.

"You taste like apples," he whispered, "and I'm hungry."

I am, too. Her throat tightened and ached with longing. She wasn't even sure she'd heard him right, but the feelings suffused her. They reminded her of her one and only night with him, and suddenly she couldn't imagine why she'd felt compelled to run away. His mouth was perfection. How could anything ever surpass this need to be lost in drowning passion?

She was just about to wrap her arms around his neck when he broke the kiss and released her. She panted for breath. "Why did you do that?"

"Kiss you," he asked, "or stop kissing you?"

"The first thing." She wasn't sure herself.

When he finally spoke, his voice was almost as breathless as hers. "There were times when I thought I'd dreamed that night. I had to know."

She could see by his expression that he was serious. His dark eyes shimmered with intensity. He'd come in here and kissed her because he thought it might have been a dream. That was exactly how she felt. How she'd always felt. But they couldn't both have dreamed what happened. It *had* happened and she'd been staggered by the passion that had ignited between two virtual strangers. It could have burned her to ashes. And even though she'd run away, being with him had forced her to question nearly everything about herself and her life.

After days and weeks of wondering if she might hear something from him, or even—romantic fool that she was—if he might come in search of her, she'd finally decided it had been spontaneous combustion, like what could happen to leaves piled up too long. She'd gone too long without sex and, in the heat of the moment, she'd burst into flames. The insight had helped her set her fantasies aside, but the experience had stayed with her, nonetheless. It had motivated her to write an entire book, and perhaps she owed him something for that.

"Listen, I'm sorry," he said.

"No, it's all right." She drew a breath and cast her eyes down. "The truth is, I need to tell you something. There wouldn't be a book if I hadn't met you. It feels a little awkward saying that, considering the way things began, and the way they ended, but it's true, and—Tony?"

She'd felt him step away, but it startled her when she looked up and saw him disappearing through the door. She had the feeling he hadn't heard anything she'd said, but she didn't have the strength to stop him and start again.

Let it go, Melissa. You tried. Center yourself and give it a couple of good breaths. A yoga position was out of the question, but she did manage some slow deep breaths, which calmed her a bit. Even if she'd been able to kid him about this having anything to do with the book, she couldn't kid herself. One kiss, and they'd been very close to another meltdown—or at least she had. That kind of erotic chaos wasn't going to work for this book tour, no matter how sexy her book was. There was too much at stake, not the least of which was her famously shaky grip on reality.

She drew a nightgown strap off her shoulder and peered at her reflection, turning in front of the mirror to check her back. She didn't find any visible marks, although it seemed as if there should have been some after something so shattering. She really did have to get things under control—herself at the very least. Under the circumstances, she couldn't trust Jeanie to help. She and her publicist seemed to be at cross-purposes lately, which meant she, Melissa, would have to do it herself.

Rules of engagement. That's what she needed. Ironclad rules so that no one was in any way confused about acceptable tour conduct. And she knew exactly what the first rule would be: No kissing except in public places!

TONY HAD THE SHOWER going full bore before he had his clothes off. Conveniently, he wasn't wearing much. He pulled the T-shirt over his head and shucked his jeans, practically in one motion, leaving everything in a pile on the floor of the bathroom. He was already barefoot.

The shower stall was a work of art, its floor-to-ceiling glass textured like ocean waves, with a heavy door held by two gleaming brass hinges. It appeared to be free-floating, swinging shut behind him with soundless force. The steaming hot spray needled him in three different places along the length of his body—his shoulders, his lower back and his bum.

He imagined the showerhead was meant to massage

aching muscles, but all he needed right now was water, and the more the better. Showers had been known to save his sanity. They cleared his head when life crashed through the center divider of the road and sideswiped him. In this case, he may have been the one who'd gone through the divider, but he had definitely been sideswiped. And by a kiss.

The trembling leaf was still a temptress in disguise.

She was fireworks on a summer night. She had the power to hold the eye and the mind. Worse, she didn't seem all that aware of her allure. Of course, he hadn't heard her scream just now. What a lame excuse to go to her room. But he had to know, and she'd given him her answer without saying a word.

She was not a figment of his imagination and neither was their sexual chemistry. That night two years ago had affected him more than he wanted to admit. It had etched itself into his soul, and it was all real. So, where did he go from here?

He ducked his head under the spray, soaked his hair and shook off the excess water. There was a nook in the marble wall with several choices of shampoo. He took the only one that sounded vaguely masculine—Autumn Orchard—and worked it into billowing suds. By the time he was ready to rinse, he had begun to get his thinking back in line.

He wasn't here to win her back. He wasn't even here to pick up where they'd left off, although, God, he'd like to. All of his dark urges aside, he'd put Melissa and their marriage behind him and get on with his plans for the future. He had responsibilities to uphold and promises to keep that went beyond business obligations. They were personal and private. Jeanie Trent, the publicist, had promised a quick and quiet annulment if he went along with the happy-husband charade, and he'd agreed to it. They'd also mutually agreed to keep his real reasons a secret, even from Melissa. Why? Because Jeanie was afraid that Melissa might have backed out if she knew the truth.

For everyone's sake he needed to keep it a game, never let it get real. He had to pretend to be the passionate, sexually satisfied husband—and do it well enough to convince a national-TV audience. But it could never be anything but a charade, even temporarily. That's why he was in the shower. And why he might never get out of the shower again.

He turned in the spray, facing the vertical line of showerheads. One of the jets pummeled his shoulders, another his abs, and the third, his pelvis. As he looked down, he was reminded of a well-known Bible story, only in this case, it was an erection parting the seas. The lowest jet ricocheted off his hardened shaft like a wave crashing against the rocks. That was the impact she had on him.

Maybe if he turned the tap to cold?

Better yet, he would wash up, get the hell out of this steam bath, get some clothes on and find a way to occupy himself. Of course, what he should be doing was reading her book and preparing himself for their upcoming performances. But somehow he didn't think that was going to help his current condition.

He grabbed a container of liquid soap, also Autumn Orchard, squirted some of it on his chest and began to scrub. Foam rose from his amber skin and filled the stall with the scent of ripening apples. His hormone-weakened mind conjured up images of a man and woman romping in an orchard, hiding behind the fruit-laden trees, and falling onto the grass into each other's arms to make love. Particularly riveting was the skirt she wore and the way he slid it up her thighs to reveal a dark delta of succulent, apple-scented curls.

Eyes closed, Tony soaped himself with determination. The feel of his heaving pecs made him move down to his abdomen, but the tight muscles there offered little comfort as he massaged them. When his hands came into contact with his own engorged organ, it was like megavolts of electricity rocketing through him.

This was hell, and he had two more intensive weeks of it. After that the torture would become intermittent, but he would still have his thoughts to contend with. Of course, there was an easy way out. He could give himself some quick relief. He'd done it before, but he wasn't going to take that route tonight. He'd pleasured himself while fantasizing about Melissa Sanders for the last time. Better to endure and keep his edge than bow to the secret pleasures of a woman he couldn't have.

It had rocked him to see that wedding band on her finger. She was clearly driven to succeed, but he hadn't expected her to take it that far. Jeanie had told him Melissa wanted the money to pay back her parents and make their lives easier. Apparently they were Midwestern farmers who'd sacrificed to send her to college and give her the opportunities they'd never had. He had a feeling her ambitions might not be as selfless as all that, but even if her hard-luck story was true, he still had a score to settle.

She'd married him, bedded him, and vanished without a word. He'd woken the next morning and gone into a full-blown panic, searching for her. When he hadn't found her, he'd called the hotel where she'd been staying. They had given him the news that his new bride had checked out and flown home.

That night he'd sat out the night in his darkened living room, deadened to everything but the heavy thud in his chest. If it was naive to feel betrayed over what was essentially a one-night stand, then call him naive. He'd lived with those feelings until very recently, and he wasn't going back there now. And bringing himself to orgasm with her sweet face in his mind would be another betrayal.

When he stepped out of the shower, he grabbed a terry bath sheet and began vigorously toweling himself. His blood had cooled by the time he was done. Good, he thought. Of course, he knew the heat would return, and he'd have to fight his response to Melissa again. He wasn't *that* naive, but he'd won the battle for now. And meanwhile, he would enjoy flushing out the real Melissa Sanders. Trembling leaf? Or shameless hussy in disguise? It was his sworn mission to find out.

Chapter Five

One of my personal favorites is the Happy Gardener
game. What could be more fun than having your
flowers fertilized and your bush trimmed!
101 Ways To Make Your Man Beg

IF YOU HAD A NIGHTMARE twice, did that make it recur-
ring? Once, when she was a child, Melissa had dreamed
of being lost in a never-ending cornfield. The field seemed
to circumnavigate the earth it was so big and so dark. She
was eight years old, small for her age, and the rustling
cornstalks looked as tall as trees. Her mother called from
somewhere in the distance, but her voice grew fainter.
Melissa was going the wrong way, but no matter which
way she turned, her mother's voice receded until it faded
to nothing.

Now she was dreaming again, lost again in a forestlike
maze that could have been cornstalks, and someone was
calling her name.

"Melissa!"

She stirred. That didn't sound like her mother.

"Melissa, wake up!"

It felt as if something was shaking, as if everything was
shaking. Now she was dreaming about earthquakes. She
opened her eyes, and through a haze of sleep, she saw her

publicist. Jeanie was at the foot of the bed, gripping the bedpost like a furniture mover.

"What are you doing?" Melissa asked.

"Trying to wake you up!" Jeanie gave the post another sharp tug. "Let's go, let's go! I have a car waiting out front, and you're going to be late for the book signing."

Moments later, maybe seconds, Melissa was in the bathroom, washing her face and wishing she hadn't taken that over-the-counter sleeping pill. She did look rested, though. In fact, she looked positively healthy. There was a glow to her skin she hadn't noticed before and didn't know how to explain. It couldn't have had anything to do with *him*, of course. You didn't glow over a man when the attraction was purely physical. And it was. Even he would have agreed to that. Lust could keep you up all night with overstimulated nerves. It could drive you to sleeping pills. But it couldn't make you glow.

And then there was that incredibly overdramatic thing he'd said about having to know if it was a dream. He had come up behind her in the bathroom, caught her off guard and blown her mind—again. He was good at that. For a moment he'd had her thinking they might have shared something deep and moving, that he'd been touched the way she had. But how much wishful thinking was that? It certainly wasn't reality. There wasn't any reality where they were concerned, and she had to remember that. He was so damn persuasive, so damn Latin…if he was Latin.

With men like Tony, it was the grand gesture. They were the knights in shining armor, appearing at the last minute to save the day. In her case it had been night, but she'd definitely needed saving. He'd probably pitied her, and she couldn't tolerate that. She was no one's fixer-upper, thank you.

She peered into the mirror as she patted her face dry and checked the whites of her eyes. They were clear, too. She would have to make a note of the sleeping-pill brand. They were great.

Teeth next. She loaded her toothbrush with whitening paste. A total makeover would have been her first choice, but there hadn't been time. She was doing the best she could with what she had. Jeanie had just gone to round up Tony, which gave Melissa a chance to think about the book signing as she began to work on brightening her smile.

She'd been asked to do a short lecture first. They would probably want Tony to sit right next to her at the signing, looking like a stud in perpetual heat. Apparently the two of them were supposed to strike sparks off each other every time they spoke or touched. That shouldn't be too tough. They were combustible in each other's company. A touch from Tony came with sound effects. She could hear the hiss of a match being struck, and then *whoooosh*. Fire.

No, no. No touching. There was not going to be *any* touching. With him, touching was a gateway to other things.

Melissa was just about to rinse, when she heard a cry of alarm that sounded like Jeanie.

"Melissa! Come here!"

That *was* Jeanie. Melissa dashed out of the room, the toothbrush still in her mouth and foamy bubbles coating her lips. She found Jeanie in the living-room area, turning in a circle, her hand on her forehead.

"What's wrong?" Melissa asked.

"What's wrong? We're going to be late for the signing, and one of my authors is missing. It's every publicist's nightmare."

Melissa blotted her face with the sleeve of her bathrobe. It was gross, but not as bad as foaming at the mouth. "Are you talking about Tony? He's not an author. *I* wrote the book."

"The point is, Melissa, he's *missing*. He's not in his room. He's not anywhere in the suite."

Melissa's hopes soared. "Missing? Are you sure? Jeanie, that's fabulous!"

Jeanie's glare threatened bodily harm.

"Of course he's not missing," Melissa rushed to assure her. "He probably went down to get a cup of coffee. He'll be back in a jiff."

Then again, he might be on a plane to London or somewhere even farther away. He could have been kidnapped or comatose in some emergency room, mowed down by the same bus driver who'd splashed her. Fantasies were better when there was a little poetic justice involved.

Jeanie went to search the hotel while Melissa finished getting ready. Twenty minutes later, she was dressed in the powder-pink linen skirt and twinset she'd put out, but Tony still had not appeared. Jeanie had been down to the lobby. She'd checked the hotel's restaurants and its lounge, gift shops and health spa, but he was nowhere to be found.

"Okay, we go without him," Jeanie said. "You'll have to make some excuse."

"Like maybe he got exhausted from all the begging?" Melissa grinned and Jeanie gave her another warning look.

"Do you want to sell this book or not? And what's with that outfit? This is not afternoon tea, girl!"

Melissa checked herself out. "What do you want, a femme fatale? This outfit is lightweight, it's within my budget *and* my comfort zone."

Jeanie's sniff was audible. "I'll settle for a woman who looks like she could have written a book about hot sex."

"Excuse me? Have you heard of Dr. Ruth? I'd like to say that I more than hold my own on that playing field, thank you."

Jeanie directed Melissa to the door. "Let's make a deal," she said as they left the suite and walked toward the bank of elevators. "You expand your comfort zone, and Searchlight will expand your clothing budget."

Melissa brightened. "Deal."

On the ride down, she fussed with her outfit, wondering if a shorter skirt might do the trick. What wasn't within her comfort zone was Tony's disappearance, now that she'd had time to think about it. The focus would be totally on her now, but maybe that wasn't an altogether good thing. The book might suffer for it. Still, it was a trade-off. Her life would be infinitely less complicated without him around. How could that not be good?

"STOP!" Melissa shouted. The town car lurched to a halt, sending both Melissa and Jeanie into a forward slide.

Jeanie clutched the hand grip, juggling an enormous disposable cup of coffee. "What is it? We're late!"

Melissa pointed out the car window. "I think I see him! Look over there at the entrance to the park." As they were pulling away, she'd noticed a man across the street in Central Park. He had Tony's height and dark hair, and he was huddled with a slender young woman and two uniformed officers. He seemed to be arguing with the policemen.

"That's him, isn't it?" Melissa tapped the windowpane. "I'm sure that's Tony. I'm going over."

"No, Melissa! You'll get killed."

"I'll be right back." Melissa let herself out of the car, dodging cabs as she made her way across the street. She could hear Jeanie shouting at her, but she didn't stop. She had to know if it was Tony with the police, and what had happened. Some crazy reasons ran through her mind, including the possibility that they were trying to arrest him. With mixed feelings, she realized she might be about to discover the truth about what kind of person Tony Bond really was.

As Melissa approached, she heard the woman speaking in a language she didn't recognize. It sounded a little like Spanish.

"*Por favore, ajude-me encontrar minha crianca!*" the

woman cried, clutching a shawl around her shoulders as if she was freezing.

Both the officers shook their heads. "No comprendez," one of them said.

But Tony did seem to understand. He spoke to the woman in her language, and Melissa realized he was trying to interpret for her and convey her concerns to the police.

"She's asking you to help her find her child." Tony spoke to the larger of the officers, a burly redhead with a round, ruddy face. "She says her little girl is lost."

"Did she see anyone approach the child?" the officer asked

Tony asked the woman that question, and she shook her head. "*Ajude-me encontrar minha crianca!*"

She'd begun to sob, which made understanding her even harder.

Melissa hesitated a few feet away, not wanting to interfere, and yet wishing she could help ease the mother's anguish. She could only imagine the horror of losing a child. The woman attempted to explain what had happened in badly broken English, and Tony continued to interpret.

"She says they were down by the lake," he told the officers. "She was sitting on a blanket, reading, while her daughter fed the ducks. But she dozed off—only for a minute, she says. When she opened her eyes, the child was gone."

"*Per favore!*" the woman keened.

The ruddy-faced officer shook his head as he spoke to Tony. "Sorry, but we're not down here on lost-kid detail. We're after a robbery suspect. You need to find one of the park cops."

Tony's voice was hard-edged. "Sorry, but I found *you*, and as I understand your job, it's to protect the vulnerable. What's more vulnerable than a lost child, especially in a park like this?"

Jeanie dashed up at that moment. "Tony, Melissa, we have to go. We're late for the signing."

Melissa grabbed Jeanie and hushed her. By now the terrified mother was in tears and begging anyone who would listen to help her. An elderly couple had stopped and overheard some of the conversation, and the older woman exhorted the police to find the child, shaking her cane at them. A few other passersby stopped, too, apparently out of curiosity. Melissa wanted to speak out, too, but she sensed that this wasn't the time.

Tony was involved in a stare-down with the two men. "I'm asking you to find the little girl," he repeated.

The redheaded officer took a look around, seeming to realize for the first time that they'd attracted some attention. The young mother wailed out her grief.

"All right," he conceded. "We'll start a search, and when the park detail gets here, we'll turn it over to them."

"I'm coming with you," Tony told him. "You'll need me to interpret."

"Tony, you are not!" Jeanie stepped into the fray.

One of the passersby spoke up. "I'm an interpreter with the U.N., the woman is speaking Portuguese and I speak it also. Can I help?"

Jeanie didn't give anyone time to respond. She turned to the redheaded officer. "Now, can we go? These are my authors and they're late for a book signing over on Madison."

"We'll handle it," he told her. Turning to Tony, he said, "We'll find the little girl, and everything will be fine."

Tony reluctantly agreed. He explained to the grateful mother that the two policemen would help her find her little girl, and he would check back to see that they did. Meanwhile, he pulled out a card, jotted down the name of the bookstore where the signing was to be held and gave it to the officers, asking them to keep in touch.

"Good work," Jeanie said. She hooked Tony by the arm, and at the same time, gripped Melissa's hand. The message was clear. They either went willingly or they would be dragged back through the traffic.

Once they were safely in the car again, Jeanie gave Tony a verbal pat on the back. "What you did was wonderful," she said. "Don't you think so, Melissa?"

"Wonderful, yes." Melissa couldn't disagree. He was always doing wonderful things. More proof of a complex, as far as she was concerned, that Don Quixote thing.

She leaned around Jeanie. "I didn't know you spoke Portuguese, Tony."

"I speak several languages," was all he said. "It comes in handy."

She could imagine. Multilingual. Why did that word sound so naughty? Or was that just the way her mind worked these days. When you wrote sex manuals, everything began to take on lurid connotations.

"English will be fine for the book signing." Jeanie was already pushing buttons on her cell phone. "I'm calling to tell them we're on the way. Melissa, do me a favor and burn that twinset when you get back to the hotel. And Tony, the dark shirt and slacks might be a little dramatic. You two are supposed to be sexual dynamos, not Donnie and Marie."

Apparently someone came on the line, because Jeanie began explaining and making apologies. Melissa glanced over to see Tony checking out her twinset. He mouthed the words, "I like it."

Melissa blushed foolishly and looked away. She'd never had a chance to sit down and talk to him about her rules of engagement. There certainly wasn't time now. She should be rehearsing what she was going to say at the signing, but as it turned out, Jeanie wasn't done with them. As soon as she clicked off the phone, she began lecturing them on their relationship.

"The public is expecting a man and woman who can't keep their hands off each other," she told them. "Most of them can't remember what that's like, if they ever knew. They're counting on you to remind them—and may I be candid?—you're reminding me of a couple of cyborgs. Please, please, *please*, crank up the heat. Hold hands, cop a feel, steal a kiss."

She swiveled back and forth between Melissa and Tony, giving them instructions like a referee in the ring. "Melissa, when you and Tony are sitting next to each other, I want your hand on his thigh at all times, and don't let those fingers lie idle. Stroke him!

"Tony, if even half of what she's written about you in the book is true, you know what to do.

"Melissa, unlash that corset and give up the goods, girl. This is your man, your stud muffin, your tiger lover. I want to see some squirming. I want you and Tony to give this crowd the impression that you can hardly wait to get back to the limo and have sex, okay?"

She continued her swiveling until one of them spoke. And it wasn't Melissa, whose lips twitched nervously when she tried to smile. Tony managed a husky "Sure."

"Good," Jeanie said. "We're going to wow this crowd, and do you know why? Because tomorrow morning, you two are booked on *Nice Girls Do*. Yes, I can see that you're dumbstruck, but I'm serious. It's only the biggest morning show in the country right now. Their ratings are unbelievable, their demographics perfect. The audience is made up of married women, ranging from their twenties to their fifties, and they're going to make everyone connected with this book filthy rich!"

Melissa was dumbstruck all right. Her publicist had no idea what she was asking of them. Fortunately, Melissa had picked up on the word *rich*, and it had reached out and grabbed her like a lifeline. Rich was good. Rich could make all the difference, and she needed the money for so many reasons. Of course, she wanted financial independence and security. She also wanted the chance to make something of herself after laboring in obscurity for so long. But her first obligation had always been to pay her parents back.

She'd been diagnosed with rheumatic fever in grade school and suffered a damaged heart valve. The valve had been surgically repaired, but her parents had no health insurance, and the cost had been staggering. Melissa had lost a year of her life, and her parents had lost their financial security. They'd been struggling ever since, but it hadn't stopped them from mortgaging their home so that she could go to a good college.

Melissa owed them everything, including her life. There wasn't anything she wouldn't do to ease their financial worries—and this was her chance.

She'd also written the book to empower women and to make them understand how vital and potent and in control they were when it came to their relationships with men. In many ways, it had been a defensive maneuver because she'd never felt more out of control than with Tony Bond. She'd left their hotel room shaken, confused and running for her life. Thrilled to her core, yes, but running from the bewildering feelings like a madwoman. She didn't want other women to have to run. She wanted them to accept their feelings, celebrate them.

She crossed her fingers, and glanced over at Tony, who surprised her by giving her a wink that actually made her smile.

"Prepare to be wowed," she murmured, hoping she could do it.

"Ms. SANDERS, have you and your husband always had a good sex life?"

Melissa tilted an eyebrow, trying to look coy and provocative. Not for the benefit of the woman who'd just asked the question. Melissa wanted the audience to think that she was choosing from such an array of answers, she couldn't make up her mind which delicious tidbit to share. But, in fact, she was scrambling to come up with anything that wasn't an outright lie.

"Good doesn't begin to cover it," Melissa said. "Crazy, wild, impulsive, erotic, romantic, even dangerous. And that was just the first night."

The woman blinked, possibly in surprise, and sat down. Other hands flew up.

This was only going to get worse, Melissa realized. Given what she'd written, these people felt as if they could ask her anything. The turnout was amazing by book-signing standards, according to Jeanie, and there were several reporters in the crowd, including one from *The New York Times*.

The store's events director had arranged twenty rows of chairs in a large semicircle with a podium at the front, where Melissa stood. Tony sat at a table next to the podium, where stacks of Melissa's book waited to be signed. She'd spoken briefly about *101 Ways* and read an excerpt, and just now she'd opened up the floor to questions. The crowd had filled every seat and spilled over to the back of the room, where people stood three deep, her publicist among them.

Melissa watched Jeanie make a log-rolling gesture with her fingers, as if to say, "More, more! Spill every juicy detail, even if you have to make it up as you go."

Hands flew up. Lots of hands. Too many for Melissa to ignore.

She nodded at a woman in a straw hat with a big flower on it, mostly because the woman looked safe.

"Are you and your husband as kinky as the book makes you sound?" she asked, peering out from under the flower. "Did you really do that thing with the pearl necklace, and does Antonio do gardening work like it says in the book?"

So much for safe.

"Gardening work?"

"Trim your bush?" the woman asked innocently. "Isn't that what it says?"

Antonio made a choking sound, which Melissa ignored. Some of the audience members gasped, some howled. Melissa forced herself to laugh along with them. However, she wanted to tell the questioner that she'd just ruined it for women wearing straw hats. Melissa wouldn't be calling on another one soon.

She held up her hands to restore order. "Just some fun suggestions," she explained. "They're in the chapter on 'Things Your Mother Didn't Want You to Know!'"

A young Generation Xer jumped up next, giggling. "Do you have Antonio's name tattooed somewhere?"

Jeanie waved frantically, trying to get Melissa's attention. She cupped her hands and mouthed the word *yes*.

"No," Melissa said firmly. She waited for the next question, but the crowd clearly expected her to continue. Finally, she relented with a sigh. "That doesn't mean I don't have a spot reserved—but don't ask me to show you where it is."

Jeanie grinned and gave her a thumbs-up.

A man at the back who'd been scribbling on a spiral pad raised his hand. "Your book tells women to watch their men undress," he said. "It also tells them to switch underwear with their mates because of the sensory turn-on."

"That's true," she said. "It has to do with the softness next to your skin, the scents of perfume or musk."

"Are you wearing Antonio's shorts today?"

Melissa's smile was swift. "I'm delighted to know that you read the book."

"Was that a no?" the man asked.

"We have matching thongs. Does that make it a yes?"

Antonio glanced up at her, and Melissa blushed. Okay, so that was a fib. Occasionally you had to stoop to conquer. After all, newspaper space was worth something, wasn't it?

"Could we see them?" the man asked.

"I don't think we want to get arrested." Antonio spoke up before Melissa had a chance to respond, and his quelling look seemed to back the guy off.

A tabloid reporter, obviously. More hands waved, but Melissa had answered all the personal questions she was going to. "Enough about Antonio and me," she said. "We're here to talk about your men, ladies. You must have some questions."

The woman in the straw hat raised her hand again. "Should a woman ever say no to a man?"

"Of course. Regularly. Make him wait for it. Make yourself wait. The anticipation that builds will have you hot as a firecracker when you do say yes."

"Do you have an example?"

Melissa had a beaut. Unfortunately, she couldn't share it. Antonio had been a master at making her wait on their wedding night. She didn't even want to think about how he'd had her body thrumming with anticipation. Certain parts had been screaming, but he hadn't given in to her demands. He'd lightened the kisses to nothing and slowed the touches until she was writhing. He'd actually told her to hold back her climax as he whispered every wicked thing he was going to do to her. But she couldn't, and his dark smile had told her that was exactly what he'd intended.

She glanced over at him and saw a shadow of that smile now. He was reading her mind. *He knew.* Melissa's breath turned to fire in her throat, and she actually thought she felt a strange sound rising up. Thank God, Jeanie chose that moment to speak up.

"How about some questions for the man who inspired the book?" she said.

Melissa didn't have a chance to agree before a sexy brunette popped out of her seat and smiled enticingly at Tony. "Would you come whisper in my ear?"

Everybody laughed at that one, except Melissa.

"Sorry," Tony said. "My mouth is already spoken for—and so is Melissa's ear."

Melissa wasn't sure she liked that answer, either, but her stomach certainly did. It was a butterfly farm.

A woman with a notebook and a very brisk voice spoke up. "What kind of work do you do, Mr. Bond?"

"I hang around the kitchen a bit."

"Really?" She cracked a grin. "You could hang around my kitchen anytime. Where's your favorite place to have sex?"

He laughed. "The kitchen, of course."

"How convenient," the woman quipped. "Do you also cook?"

"Cooking is foreplay," he said. "The sensual turn-ons are incomparable—the velvet of a sauce with real cream, the tart juices running from a bitten peach, the sizzle of prime meat on the grill. It's all very sensual."

"Mr. Bond, what nationality are you?"

She hadn't noticed who'd asked the question, but apparently Melissa wasn't the only curious soul.

"A bit of a mutt, I'm afraid," Tony said. "My mother was Hispanic, my father European." He tapped his chest. "There are too many nations in here to count."

Melissa glanced at her watch, hoping it was time for the questions to end and the signing to begin. But apparently the brunette hadn't given up. She jumped back into it with a question for Tony, uttered in a voice so breathy and laden with sexual possibilities that it could have steamed stamps off envelopes.

Melissa felt as if her blood pressure had just hit the high-normal range. At least.

"What makes a man like you so incredibly sexy?" the brunette asked.

Tony didn't seem to have a ready answer. In fact, he went so quiet that Melissa looked over at him, only to find that he was looking at her, too. The expression on his face made her breath stop. She didn't just feel it catch. This wasn't one of those situations where air was quivering in your throat, waiting to be expelled. She actually stopped breathing.

She wasn't at all sure she was going to like this.

What in the world was he going to say?

Chapter Six

Nurture your inner vixen. Embrace her! She's been suppressed, repressed, oppressed and rejected. By you! It's her turn!

101 Ways To Make Your Man Beg

MELISSA TORE HER GAZE from Tony's and turned to the hushed crowd. The gallery of expectant faces left her searching for something fitting to say. Anything, for that matter. Jeanie made a throat-cutting gesture, which Melissa took as a signal to end the question period. Unfortunately, the clever sign-off she'd planned had vanished—along with the glass of ice water she could have sworn was sitting on the podium.

Hallucinations? That could be heatstroke, malnutrition, brain damage, and take your pick of mental problems.

She cleared her throat and thanked them all for coming. "If you'd like a personally autographed copy of *101 Ways,* I'll be happy to sign one for you, and even if you don't, come on up and say hi, please."

A crisis averted. Except that it wasn't.

Tony rose from his seat before anyone else could. "This lady asked me a question," he said, addressing the brunette, who beamed. "She wanted to know how a guy like me got to be—I think the word she used was *sexy.*"

Melissa stared at Tony, helpless. Now every eye was riveted on him.

"The answer is simple," he said. "If I'm sexy, she's the reason why."

"Who, the hot brunette?" a male called out.

Scattered laughter broke out in the audience. Melissa felt a burning pain just above her breastbone. She actually felt as if she'd been stabbed. Why was he doing this?

"Yes, the hot brunette." He turned to Melissa. "My wife."

He said it with enough edge to make Melissa narrow her gaze and peer at him. His dark eyes sparked with secrets, and her heart tilted. What was he doing now? She thought she saw his jaw muscle tighten, as if he'd quelled some errant emotion. But she couldn't be sure, and the next thing she knew, he was taking her hand.

He brought her fingers to his lips, and she could hear sighs coming from the audience. She understood the women's reaction. He could be romantic beyond belief. He turned her hand over, smoothed it flat and pressed his lips to the tender middle of her palm. Warm breath eddied and caressed her skin. Melissa almost sighed herself.

She could barely feel his mouth on her flesh, and yet it was a delicious sensation that brought back all the other delicious sensations his mouth could elicit.

When he turned back to the audience, he spoke to the brunette again, who wasn't looking quite so confident of her powers of seduction. Melissa didn't allow herself to feel smug, but, okay, it was a *nice* moment, and this man had provided her with more than a few of those.

"It has very little to do with me," he told the brunette. "What man is sexy without a woman to inspire those feelings in him? It's all about her, that special woman, the one whose smile can set fire to a man's heart."

The brunette shrugged, apparently conceding the battle, but not the war. "Okay, so what's your secret?" she asked Melissa.

Tony picked up one of Melissa's books. "All her secrets are in here."

Melissa laughed along with everyone else, but she wasn't quite sure how she felt about what Tony had just done. His grand gesture probably had every woman in the audience yearning for a man like him, one who would choose his woman over a femme fatale, and even put the seductress in her well-deserved place. Who wouldn't yearn for a man like that, if it was how he really felt? Melissa would have given anything to be so adored. But then, somehow he'd brought it all back to her book, and that had given her pause. It was a brilliant pitch—and probably nothing more.

Melissa's imagination churned, never a good thing in a situation like this. Tiny doubts exploded into big ones, and within seconds she had very nearly convinced herself that his vow was just another grand gesture. It wasn't all about her. It might have little or nothing to do with her. If anything, it was probably all about the book, which meant it was all about money. What had Jeanie said? That everyone involved with the book was going to get filthy rich?

With chilly politeness, Melissa removed her hand from Tony's and excused herself to go sign books. The ring he'd given her glinted in the bright lights like golden lace. Melissa resisted the urge to tug at it. She'd never been able to get the wedding band off before. Why should that change now? And it might look a little odd giving him back his ring at a book signing. Besides, she couldn't completely discount the possibility that she was overreacting. She'd been known to do that.

Jeanie pulled out two chairs at the signing table and motioned for Melissa to sit down. Unfortunately, the publicist wanted Tony to inscribe the books as well.

"You know, as a husband-and-wife team?" Jeanie said.

She flashed a smile that was probably meant to disorient Melissa with its brightness.

Melissa stepped around the table and reminded Jeanie under her breath that *101 Ways* was a hefty manuscript— one hundred and fifty thousand words—and Tony hadn't written so much as one comma.

"But he did provide the motivation, did he not?" Jeanie whispered back. In a louder voice, she added, "And I'll bet the ladies lining up for autographs might enjoy having Antonio's signature."

"Yes!" rose in a chorus from the waiting women.

"Of course," Melissa agreed with a tight smile. There were too many people around to say what she really thought—that Jeanie and Tony should go into the publicity business together. That they could have planned this entire campaign—and maybe they had.

The signing table had two chairs, and Jeanie came around to stand behind Melissa and Tony, apparently to help them get settled. "You do want to sell books, don't you?" she whispered as she poured Melissa a glass of water and began opening copies of *101 Ways* for her to sign.

Melissa had a ready answer, but she held her fire. The truth was, she did want to sell books. She had very good reasons for wanting to sell books, and it wasn't entirely clear to her why she wasn't thrilled that so many people were lining up to buy hers. Nearly everybody in the audience seemed to be there—and Antonio was undoubtedly a big part of the reason.

Okay, she thought as she signed the first copy and chatted with a bubbly young mother of three, who said she couldn't wait to read the chapter about all the things she wasn't supposed to do. Okay, this was why she, Melissa Sanders, was here. She was an author with a first book that she believed had something to say to women. What did she care why *he* was here? She hadn't seen the man in two years. What could it possibly matter what he did or why he did it? As long as he helped sell books, that was enough.

Right? *Right.*

"Embrace your inner vixen," she said as she signed the words in the woman's book. She passed the book to Tony, who wrote, "Happy gardening!" The young mother seemed to love it.

Melissa vowed to remember her priorities. She threw her energies into the signing, laughing and joking with the crowd and reminding herself what a miracle it was that they'd actually given up precious hours of their lives to listen to her speak and to purchase a book she'd written. She even joked with Tony and the women who attempted to flirt with him, which was most of them. See, she was a mature adult. If she had any hang-ups where he was concerned, they were now insignificant to the point of being inconsequential. It had been one night of her life. One night. Two years ago. How much could that have meant to either one of them?

Things picked up from that point on. She and Tony signed steadily, and they'd gone through two stacks of books, when Melissa heard a commotion and looked up. A small crowd had gathered at the entrance of the store. As she craned to see around the line of customers, a police officer appeared.

Melissa gave Tony's foot a kick under the table.

"It's the officer from the park," she told him, pointing out the tall redheaded man who was headed their way. A woman trailed behind him, tears streaming down her cheeks. She looked like the mother who'd lost her child.

Melissa had a bad feeling. The officer had a look of grim determination on his face, but when he reached them, he presented the woman to Tony with a good-natured grin. The woman had a little girl in tow behind her, hanging on to her skirts.

"She insisted on coming here to thank you," the officer said.

Tony immediately got up and went to the woman. He hugged her gently, letting her cry to her heart's content and thank him for helping to save her daughter. The room seemed to have been hit by a tidal wave of emotion, and even Melissa felt a tug on her heart. When the mother was more composed, Tony released her and knelt to talk to the child, whose big dark eyes lit up with surprise. He was speaking her language?

A shy smile slowly replaced the child's pensive expression, and by the time Tony had finished brushing her curls from her face and telling her how beautiful she was, the little girl was beaming and telling him the story of her great adventure. The mother smiled through her tears, and even the policeman looked misty.

Tony interpreted the little girl's chatter. "She says her balloon got away from her, and it could run faster than she could."

Who *was* this man? Don Quixote? Don Juan? Or some sort of gold digger? He couldn't just be after money, could he?

The whole room was smitten with him, Melissa realized. She took a visual poll of the women waiting in line. If she read their expressions correctly, they didn't have any question about who he was: a white knight in a world very low on courage and chivalry. Several of them gazed at him with wistful eyes, as if they'd love to take him home to meet the parents, or in some cases, the children.

Melissa felt a little twinge in the area of her rib cage and acknowledged that it could be the irrational jealousy that was no longer bothering her. Then again, she might be coming down with something, in which case, the diagnosis was pretty much a no-brainer. What she needed was an Antonio vaccination. On the other hand, if she'd already been bitten, shouldn't she be immune?

INCREDIBLE AROMAS brought Melissa out of her bedroom to sniff the air. That afternoon's radio interviews had been long, and Jeanie had suggested dinner afterward, but Melissa could think of nothing but the hotel suite and its beautiful bathtub. Tony had come back with her, and he'd suggested room service, but Melissa had pleaded exhaustion, and they'd gone to their separate rooms.

Now, bathed and ready for bed, Melissa was rethinking room service. But then the savory scent of onions and mushrooms, sizzling in hot butter, had seeped under the double doors and filled her bedroom, so she'd decided to follow her nose and investigate. The tantalizing smells had to be coming from the suite's kitchen.

Her silk gown and kimono rustled against her legs as she walked, and her bare soles were chilly against the marble tiles. She should have put on some clothes, but those smells were irresistible, and she was hungry. Her empty stomach would not be denied.

The suite had a full kitchen in its media room, with a built-in barbecue and spit for grilling, brushed-chrome appliances, copper accents and gleaming granite countertops. Subtle recessed lighting softened the modern, dramatic design. The room was worthy of a magazine spread, but the first thing Melissa noticed as she entered the room was the tiered plate of appetizers and the generous glass of red wine that had been set out.

She spotted Tony behind the counter, working at a chopping block. The wine was probably for him, although he seemed completely engrossed in what he was doing.

Another woman might assume that she was expected, even that this production was for her benefit. But not Melissa. She never assumed anything of the kind when it came to men. And besides, he had said he liked to cook. Maybe this was how he entertained himself.

"What smells so good?" she asked.

He turned immediately, surprising her. Maybe she was

expected. His eyes seemed to light with pleasure at the sight of her, and that alone could make a girl's footsteps falter. But this girl was driven by hunger, a physical imperative. It encouraged her to cross the large room and sit down at the counter, despite that the man on the other side was achingly handsome in nothing more than casual slacks and an open dress shirt. He had a white ribbed T-shirt on underneath, snug enough to reveal the muscle definition in his abs, although she didn't know why she was looking. She wasn't *that* hungry.

"Have some wine," he said, abandoning his chopping block to join her. He brought a half-filled glass and came around the counter.

"It's a very nice cabernet." He held up his own wine. "Medium-bodied, smooth and a bit fruity."

She picked up her glass, and they touched rims with a musical clink.

"But also saucy and impertinent," he added as she took a sip, "like the woman who's about to drink it."

It was all Melissa could do to hold in the wine. Her snick of laugher had a gurgling sound, and she waved a finger at him when she finally managed to swallow the cabernet. "That's not fair. You're not supposed to make someone laugh when they're taking a drink."

"Bad timing," he admitted, sliding the appetizers toward her. "Please, help yourself to some chow. I promise not to crack any jokes."

Greedily, Melissa surveyed a tantalizing array of Spanish tapas. There were empanadas, roasted poblano chiles that Tony explained were stuffed with three kinds of cheese, and some other scrumptious-looking tidbits that she couldn't immediately identify.

"Thanks," she said, helping herself to a bulging, golden-brown empanada. "You just whipped these up, right?"

She was kidding, of course, but he wasn't.

"They're still warm from the oven," he explained. "I

called the concierge this morning and told her what ingredients I needed. They were in the fridge when we got back tonight."

"Wow," Melissa said, honestly impressed as she bit into the oozing meat pie. She'd had empanadas before, but these were spectacular. They were stuffed with finely ground pork, onions, green peppers and raisins, and lightly seasoned with cumin.

"Delicious," she said. "And so is the wine."

They clinked glasses again, and this time he made a toast. "To getting to know each other," he said, "two years later."

"And you thought we'd start tonight?"

"If you're willing."

She looked up and purposefully met his gaze. Maybe it was time to stop the avoidance behavior. After all, he couldn't hypnotize her with a look...although with very little effort, he did seem able to create that sensation in her stomach like a cork bobbing on the ocean.

She drank deeply, uncomfortably aware of his lips against the edge of his wineglass. Such a mouth he had. Beautiful. It should be against the law, that mouth.

He'd thought of everything. She hadn't even noticed the appetizer plates, forks and napkins on the counter. He took a plate, speared himself a chile and cut a large wedge out of it with a fork. She continued to eat her empanada with her fingers. It was too late for manners.

She nearly finished her wine and was pleasantly relaxed by the time he refilled her glass. Amazing how a little alcohol expanded her comfort zone with this man. He was on the bar stool next to her now, but it seemed to her that they were really very far apart, although their knees did bump occasionally.

"I have a crucial question," he said.

She glanced at the ring, anticipating him. "If I could get it off, I would give it back to you."

"What?"

"The ring, of course."

He frowned. "The ring is yours. I gave it to you."

"But it looks valuable, like an heirloom." She fingered the gold latticework. "You must be curious why I'm wearing it."

"I *know* why you're wearing it. What has me curious is why a woman would want to wear a man's underwear."

She gave him a look. "That's the crucial question?"

"Humor me, I'm going somewhere with this."

"Okay...but can't you imagine why she would?"

The tines of his fork tapped against the plate. "Well, normally I would say because it allows her to be intimate without even touching. She can feel the fabric against her skin and that tells her how it must feel against his. She can't *not* think about him while she's wearing his briefs."

"Even his T-shirt," she said, trying not to glance too obviously at the one he wore under his shirt. "A woman can tell by the scent whether or not a T-shirt was worn by her mate. Her senses can identify him, even when she can't. They've done scientific studies. Intimacy changes our brains. It makes us bond."

"Hey, I believe you," he said. "I do."

With that he got up from the counter and went to the dining-room table where a small gift bag overflowed with sparkly strips of tissue paper. Melissa had completely missed seeing it when she came in the room.

"This is for you," he said.

Surprised, she took the bag and thanked him. She felt around inside and pulled out a glossy red cylinder imprinted with the brand name Brief Encounters. Two slinky black thongs were inside the package of men's underwear.

He leaned over and whispered, "Now you don't have to lie about the matching thongs."

"I'll wear yours if you wear mine." Her voice sparkled with challenge.

He took one of the thongs from the package and

stretched it this way and that. "Couldn't we just use them as slingshots?"

"Chicken," she murmured.

His eyebrow tilted with interest, and suddenly the skimpiness of her kimono seemed to hold some appeal. "So...she really is a shameless hussy?"

Melissa gave him some chin. "Did you ever doubt it?"

"Several times, like when you wouldn't come out from under the covers, and when you fainted."

"I didn't *faint*. I swooned a little. All good hussies know how to swoon."

"Now you're going to tell me it was all an act?"

She snapped the thong he held, and smiled. "I guess you'll never know, will you? And speaking of chicken, how's dinner coming?"

"Let's check it out." He rolled off the stool, and she followed him into the kitchen, aware that the wine had gone straight to her head. Her cheeks felt warm and her tongue fuzzy. Not much chance she'd pulled off the hussy imitation, though. He was no dummy—and she was no hussy, except in her dreams.

"We're taking a detour to northern Italy for the entrée," he told her. "It's a pasta dish made with raviolis stuffed with chicken, porcini mushrooms and pears in a white sauce. I use sauterne wine for the sauce and the finishing touch is pear nectar."

"Pears?" she said. "In ravioli?"

"You're going to love it, trust me."

Trust him. Just the thought gave her shivers. But they were rather nice shivers, she realized, surprised at the awareness. She was enjoying being this close to him without feeling the need to have her guard up. If the situation had been different, and they hadn't had so much crazy history between them, they might have been friends.

As well as lovers. No matter what the circumstances,

they would have been lovers. Melissa couldn't imagine it not being sexual with him.

"Now I have a question for you," she said. It occurred to her that she might already have her answer as she watched him palm each one of the pears, apparently trying to decide which one was ripe enough. "What's so sexy about cooking?"

"What's not sexy? Have you ever peeled and sectioned a peach? Felt that juice running through your fingers?"

He looked up at her. "A wok makes some of the most sensual noises I've ever heard. The oil crackles and hisses as it hits the pan. Those are like the sounds of a female in heat."

"A female animal?"

"A female anything. When you're hot, you're hot. How about the spitting fire of a grill as it seals the flavors into an aged cut of meat? Or the delicate work of filleting and boning the tender flesh of freshly caught fish?"

She didn't dare speak. Her voice wouldn't have sounded in any way natural. The way his hands caressed those pears was positively obscene.

"There are tactile sensations, too," he said. "The springy feel of al dente pasta. And smells, like the simmering richness and mystery of a good soup stock."

They should be discussing business, Melissa realized. How to handle the tour, the interviews and the media. Her rules of engagement. Those things had all seemed so crucially important to her this morning. Now they barely seemed to matter. What mattered was knowing more about him, anything she could find out, and this might be her only opportunity. Was she crazy? Was it the wine? Or was this more of the spontaneous combustion that had set her life afire two years ago?

Lord, how her heart raced. Despite what he'd said today, it wasn't she who inspired him to be sexy. It was the other way around. His mind was as sensual and ripe and succulent as the pears he was sectioning. And his body was as hard and steely as the knife blade. In a terrifying moment of awareness she realized that they were going to make love again. Possibly even tonight, although he didn't know that. He wasn't intentionally trying to seduce her. He was merely cooking.

He wasn't planning it. She was.

Chapter Seven

Seduction is a lost art, and a man should be seduced with every wicked wile in a woman's arsenal.
101 Ways To Make Your Man Beg

EMBRACE YOUR INNER VIXEN. Melissa was dangerously close to taking her own advice. She urged her readers to use their God-given sensuality, but she'd only done so once in her life—and even though the experience had been wildly sexy, it hadn't been wildly successful, or she wouldn't have fled the scene like a criminal. Maybe that's why she was thinking about trying it again, if that's what she was thinking about.

It could be the booze talking. Spirits and Antonio Bond seemed to be a lethal combination for her. But what a way to go.

Oh, shit, it *was* the booze talking. She wasn't this gutsy, and she never said shit.

He had his back to her now. He did little more than rinse various pieces of fruit in the stainless-steel sink, but she could see all kinds of intriguing movement beneath his shirt. The muscles fanning across his shoulders were the most noticeable—and the most sensual by far. They rippled like running water, leaving an indelible impression of the natural power in this man's body.

Melissa wasn't sure she'd ever seen a man as comfortable in the kitchen. He moved around as if he owned the place. His confidence could have been intimidating, but other qualities became apparent as she watched him. Patience, for one.

He didn't rush at anything, even removing the annoying sticky label from the apple. He peeled the paper slowly, coaxing it with his thumb and forefinger until it lifted like a leaf in a breeze. Afterward, he took his time rinsing the fruit, and seemed to enjoy the feel of it in his hands. Water sluiced through his fingers and pooled in his palms until it overflowed. The man seemed to have a powerful thing for apples.

That was how he moved in bed, too, she remembered. Confident, knowing, and yet always patient, always lingering long enough for her to respond, as if he had absolutely nothing else to do in this world other than make her shudder with pleasure.

"I've been meaning to ask you something." She toyed with a napkin corner.

"What's that?" He didn't bother to turn around, which was fine with her. She'd just as soon he didn't notice that she'd turned the napkin into origami. He might think her nervous.

"I was just wondering why you used that word today at the bookstore. Remember, when you called me your wife?"

"You *are* my wife." He glanced over his shoulder at her, a possessive edge to his voice. "Besides, it felt right at the time."

"Right in what way?"

She saw his shoulders rise, as if he'd taken a breath. "It made me feel close to you, I suppose." He went quiet. "If that makes you uncomfortable, I won't use the word again."

Melissa smiled. Those were some pretty good reasons. "I don't mind."

"I've been meaning to ask you something as well." His voice rose above the splash of the water.

She stopped torturing the napkin. "What's that?"

"Why did you write the book?"

Melissa shrugged. She'd been asked this question many times. "I wanted to empower women to explore their own sexual needs. Believe it or not, many women still need permission to feel pleasure, and I want them to be able to give it to themselves. Permission, not pleasure, although there's no reason they shouldn't do both."

He turned off the water and dried his hands on a fluffy towel. A stainless-steel colander filled with fruit sat in the sink. He picked it up and brought it back to the counter. "Is that what you did the night we were together, give yourself permission?"

"In a way, yes, I suppose I did."

"All by yourself? Is that the idea? Or does the man have something to do with it?"

Melissa had to grin. Men and their egos. "Of course you had something to do with it." She wasn't sure it could have happened with any other man, but that much of a boost he didn't need.

Her book was actually lying open on the counter. "You were reading *101 Ways?*"

"It covers a lot of ground." He pulled a cutting board from beneath the counter and then selected a sectioning knife from the butcher block nearest him. "Especially to have been inspired by just one night."

She was beginning to see where this was going. "It's true we had only one night together. And granted, what we did was—hmm, what's the word?"

"Extraordinary? Radiant? An out-of-body experience?"

A smile quirked. "Yes, all of that. But it was still just one night. We did a lot, but not enough to fill a whole book."

Tony set the freshly washed fruit on the counter and began lining up the peaches, pears, apples and plums, as if they were beauty contestants. "So where did the rest of it come from?"

She'd been watching his hands. Now she looked at his face. He stared down at the fruit as if he'd just seen a spoiled spot, his forehead tightly knit. She was right about where this was going. The ever-confident man in the kitchen—and the bedroom—was feeling a little insecure, perhaps?

"Why do you ask?"

Tony shrugged as if it was no big deal. "A woman as beautiful as you, she must have many lovers, of course."

It was the first time she'd heard his perfect English slip—and for some reason, she laughed out loud. He raised an eyebrow.

"It's nothing," she said, shaking her head. "I watch too much television. I just had a flashback of Ricky telling Lucy she had some 'splaining to do."

He didn't seem to know what she was talking about. Maybe they didn't have Lucy where he lived. Where *did* he live?

"There haven't been any other lovers." She wasn't counting the one disastrous experience before him, even though, technically, it did count. "I haven't been with anyone since you."

His countenance softened a bit.

"My readers would probably be terribly disappointed if they found out that I'm not the wild woman that they— and apparently, you—think I am."

"And all those games and techniques in the book?" he asked. "There are one hundred and one of them, according to the title."

"I made most of them up." She wasn't about to tell him that he had been at the center of her lurid imagination the entire time she'd written the book. There was no good reason for him to know that each kiss, nibble, tickle and touch described in her book had been performed by him in the deep recesses of her mind.

"I am a little curious about some of those games." He retrieved an enormous orange from a bowl nearby and rolled it under his palm, releasing some of the citrus essence. At the same time, he tipped his head toward the far end of the counter, apparently indicating the book.

Melissa picked it up and read the chapter heading. "Ah, yes," she said, "'Nooks and Crannies.' Now, *that* I didn't make up. Well, not exactly, anyway. I may have embellished a tad."

"The book needs a glossary." He pretended to be perplexed. "I know what nooks are, but I'm not sure about crannies."

Something emboldened Melissa, perhaps the subtle invitation in his voice. Whatever the reason, she slid off the stool and took the book with her as she walked around to the opposite side of the counter, where he was working.

"Maybe I should teach you a lesson or two." Her smile carried a flirtatious invitation of its own. "Think of it as a rehearsal," she said. "You'll need to know these things when we're making public appearances."

Tony regarded her with obvious interest. "Is that right?" His voice deepened to something very close to a sensual growl. "Be my guest."

Melissa set the book down and picked up a paring knife. With one easy stroke, she cut the orange he had been rolling in half. Its fresh, pungent aroma wafted between them as she settled one of the halves in her hand.

"'Nooks and Crannies' is about learning the most intimate details of your lover's body," she explained, using her best talk-show voice. "It's about exploring those sensual places we usually ignore."

"That sounds deliciously...dirty," he said.

She took his hand and held it, palm up. "It can be," she replied softly as she squeezed some orange juice into his cupped palm. "Now, watch and learn. You'll be tested on this later."

Tony's grin was slow in coming, but lovely and sensual. The heat of his hand set loose a flurry of erotic shivers that headed straight for her depths.

She lifted his hand to her lips. "This is about fingertips and tongues," she said, her voice dropping to a whisper. Feeling like a kitten at its saucer, she slowly licked the juice from his palm, using only the tip of her tongue. There was no liquor involved, but there could have been, given the sharp head rush she experienced. The sensation of her soft tongue against his textured flesh, combined with the tangy flavor of orange, was intoxicating.

What was she doing? What *was* she doing?

Her heart quickened, but she got no answer to her question—and probably wouldn't have listened anyway. Apparently she wanted to do this more than she wanted to stop, no matter how risky—and despite knowing what had happened before. That might be why she had to do it, because she *had* messed things up so badly before.

As with so many of the fantasies in her book, Tony had been the genesis for this one as well. Somewhere in the darkest hours of that one night together, she had drizzled papaya juice on his naked, reclined body and licked up every last drop. Even where it trailed into his belly button and then lower still.

The memory of how she had pleasured him with her tongue and lips was excruciatingly sensual. Melissa closed her eyes and took his fingers, one by one, into her mouth. She sealed her lips greedily around each as she slid it in and out, her tongue flicking teasingly. From above, she heard Tony's breath as it snagged in his throat. She was no mind reader, but she had a pretty good idea what he must be thinking, imagining. And it wasn't his finger she was laving.

He touched her jaw, urging her head back up. "My turn," he said. His gaze burned her tender skin.

Melissa wet her lips, his taste still on them, as Tony chose a ripened plum from the cutting board. He slit it in half and gently squeezed it, bringing a flood of juice to the surface. "Tilt your head back," he said, cradling her neck as he held the dripping fruit to her mouth. Without saying a word, he ran the fleshy part of plum along her lips, painting them with sweet red juice.

When her lips were covered, he leaned forward and whispered, "This doesn't mean anything, you understand?"

"Of course not. We're just rehearsing." Had her voice been any softer it couldn't have been heard at all.

The tip of his tongue was feathery light as he brushed it along the fullness of her lips. She could feel a sound forming in her throat, and keeping it there was one of the hardest things she'd ever had to do. He wasn't actually kissing her. It was more like tasting, she told herself. But it was enough to make her shudder in the sweetest places, shudder like wheat fields in the wind—and to remember in detail all the unspeakably sexy things they'd done.

She wanted him to pull her close and kiss her as succulently as he had in their honeymoon suite. How wonderful to be pressed to the hardness of his body and enveloped in his strong arms. Couldn't he feel the desire burning through her? She must be hot to the touch. But if he'd picked up on her vibes, he was doing a remarkable job of restraining himself.

He stopped tasting her, and Melissa sighed. She wanted more of that, more of anything even close to that, but apparently he had other plans. He eased her hair away from her ear, and she felt coolness brush her skin as he again painted her flesh with the juice. This time it was her earlobe and the curve of her neck. The sensation was maddening and thrilling at once, followed by a more deeply erotic pull as his warm breath tickled the sensitive flesh along her lobe.

His lips moved along the delicate curves, suckling. "This must be a cranny," he murmured.

Melissa was too breathless to protest. To her it was definitely a nook, but as long as he kept doing what he was doing, he could call it whatever he wanted. Her breasts ached to be touched. They were hot and swollen against the rustling silk of her kimono. She closed her eyes and imagined the robe was his thumb pads caressing her nipples, teasing them, occasionally pinching them. He had done all that to her, and not just in the book.

With exquisitely slow strokes, Tony began lapping the juice from her neck. The plummy fragrance was rich in her nostrils, and Melissa had begun to identify with the pulpy fruit in more ways than one. It felt as though she could dissolve into juice herself.

She didn't want him to know how crazy she was to be with him, not unless he was crazy to be with her, too. These things had to be equal, or it could be too embarrassing to live. Asking him was out of the question, and she couldn't see him with his head nuzzled in the hollow of her throat. But her arm hung between them.

She moved slightly. Her hand brushed his thigh and came into contact with all the evidence she needed. He was plenty crazy. If he got any crazier, the zipper of his pants would be an endangered species.

Tony groaned when her hand "accidentally" grazed his shaft.

She could feel his fingers curling into a fist, capturing her hair, and suddenly everything was real and immediate. He drew her head back, exposing the full length of her neck. When Melissa opened her eyes, she saw the desire burning in his. There was no mistaking what he intended to do.

She reached for him, already lost in the power of his kiss. She could feel it all through her, sizzling on her lips and radiating in the echo chamber of her senses. When his mouth closed on hers, she would fall into him, giving in to all the strange and wonderful hungers she felt. In the swirl of her thoughts, she also understood that she wouldn't stop him if he swept her up, spread her out on the counter like a sumptuous gourmet meal and ate her alive.

But his mouth didn't close on hers, and eventually Melissa realized that he was looking at her in a different way. Passion shimmered in his eyes like night fires, but there was a different quality to it. He was in control again.

"We are just practicing, right?" he said.

His question had officially put an end to their rehearsal, and they both knew it. "Yes, of course," she said, smiling too brightly. "I think Jeanie's going to be proud of us, don't you? Maybe we could put in a request for fresh fruit at our next talk show."

She hoped her voice was steadier than it sounded. She could barely talk. She was shaking all over.

Very quickly they were back to code again, side by side. The fruit was on the cutting board, and Tony had picked up the towel. While he went to the sink to wash his hands, Melissa tried desperately to collect herself. Despite her intentions, it had turned into one of those embarrassing moments, and she didn't know when or why.

Was he as affected by this as she was? He seemed to be doing almost as good a job of avoiding her as she was him. But even though she'd just been rudely rejected, it felt as if something else was going on here. That in itself was progress. She had spent most of her life imagining men rejecting her because she wasn't attractive enough or wasn't something enough, but Tony had never acted as if he didn't find her attractive. Quite the opposite, to her continual surprise.

Maybe he was being noble, taking it upon himself to prevent a repeat performance of what had gotten them into this mess in the first place. She liked that a little better than the idea of rejection, but not much. She didn't have the answer, but a couple of things seemed reasonably certain as she headed back to the other side of the counter, where it was safe. One—she wasn't nearly as devastated by his withdrawal as she would have expected. And two— if she couldn't make her own man beg for sex, what right did she have to tell others how to do it?

TONY STOOD in his darkened room, gazing down at the city. Under the streetlights, a row of horse-drawn carriages stood, waiting for customers. Not much business tonight, except for the occasional tourists. Manhattan's well-heeled natives either cabbed it or walked to their glamorous destinations.

A walk to the State of Maine wouldn't have cooled him down, unfortunately. Payback wasn't everything it was cracked up to be. Just his luck that he had a hard-on that wouldn't go away. And he wasn't much closer to accomplishing his sworn mission than the day he'd sworn it. She might be a born trembling leaf—and he suspected she was—but she could do a damn convincing hussy when she put her mind to it.

Still, it wasn't a fair fight. He had a big advantage.

Jeanie had convinced him the tour would be a disaster if Melissa knew the truth about his situation, and he'd accepted the publicist's assessment. She'd told him Melissa had a chance at some sorely deserved success—and he didn't want to be the one to ruin that for her. He had some skin in the game, too, but it was different for him. He knew what was going on. He knew why he'd had to put the brakes on their relationship, and she had no idea. He probably shouldn't have let it go as far as he did tonight, but the woman was delectable, sweeter than any plum juice. Those wild little noises she made in her throat had *him* wild.

Still, he shouldn't have. When he'd come back to his room from their book signing, he'd discovered a dozen messages on his cell phone, some of them tagged as urgent. People were counting on him, waiting for him. He couldn't let them down. And yet, he'd had no desire to answer any of the calls, only a nagging sense of obligation.

That should have told him something—and it did. He had a problem. Still. After Melissa had disappeared from Cancún, he'd spent considerable time trying to convince himself that she'd run off because she was a flight risk— a love-'em-and-leave-'em kind of woman. The type who had no interest in attachments or commitments. That was the easiest way to explain why she'd left so suddenly and mysteriously—and it had allowed him to blame it on her.

But a part of him had known all along it wasn't the truth. She was frightened. She'd never done anything like that before, except maybe in her head. She had unlocked a part of herself that longed for expression that night. That was the only way to explain her unbelievably erotic behavior—and she probably felt ashamed afterward, maybe even dirty. What a tragedy.

Tony had treasured every sigh she'd surrendered to him, every rule she'd broken and vulnerability she'd exposed.

He'd wanted her back for years. Maybe he still did.

And now, with his lips afire from their broken kiss, he was coming to grips with another truth. Melissa Sanders wasn't just trying to empower other women to accept their sexuality. She was still trying to empower herself. She had something to prove, and that alone meant he had better avoid her like Samson should have avoided Delilah. The stronger she got, the weaker his willpower became—and neither of them needed the chaos that could cause.

"IS THAT what you're wearing?" Jeanie tilted her head as she entered the greenroom and got a look at Melissa's outfit.

"What's wrong with it?" Melissa had spent hours this morning trying on one outfit after another, hoping to find something sexy, but not too sexy. It was no piece of cake trying to look like a hooker and Betty Crocker at the same time. She'd finally chosen the silk jersey wraparound, which, granted, would have been sexier if it had fit. It was a smidge too big, and she'd attempted to fix that by sewing in some extra snaps at the bust and skirt opening.

"Pardon the expression," Jeanie said, "but you look frumpy. What's with all these snaps? You look like you climbed inside a burlap bag and tied the top shut. Show a little skin, hon."

Jeanie undid two of the snaps at the bust and two at the skirt opening. She stepped back and nodded. "That will have to do, I suppose. Make sure you cross your legs and dangle your high heels from your toes. Tony likes that."

"How do you know?"

"Well, duh. All you have to do is watch him. You dangle and zoom, he's there, all eyes. I think our boy has a foot fetish."

Melissa laughed. "You think so, huh?" Interesting that Jeanie was giving her advice on how to attract Tony. If she'd known they were licking fruit juice off each other last night, she might not be so concerned.

"Dangle anyway. Speaking of Tony, where is he?" Jeanie asked. "We're up next."

Melissa checked her watch. "He said something about having to make a call. That was nearly ten minutes ago. He should be back anytime."

They hadn't come in with Jeanie this morning. The publicist had an early appointment, so she'd taken a taxi. Melissa and Tony had been driven to the studio in a town car provided by the publisher. She'd felt too embarrassed to be chatty, and Tony had offered little more than a good-morning. He'd concentrated on his morning cup of Star-bucks coffee, seeming moody and distracted. She had a feeling he might not have slept well. Or maybe it was the phone call he'd made this morning. At any rate, it was a long, quiet ride.

"I hope he's not late," Jeanie said. "We don't want to have to raise another search party." She plucked at Melissa's dress again, undoing another snap on the skirt.

"Did you kids go through the book last night?" she asked. "Did you practice fielding questions? Do you think you're ready? This has to sizzle, you know."

"We practiced," Melissa assured her. "It sizzled."

The guest-wrangler stuck her head in. "It's time. Ready?"

Melissa headed for the door, followed by Jeanie. As they entered the wide hallway that led to the set for the *Nice Girls Do* morning show, Tony joined them. He was dressed in a light, single-breasted linen suit that looked as if it could have had a designer label in the collar. His shoes looked expensive, too. How did he afford such pricey clothing on a waiter's salary? Of course, it was none of her business. He might very well have gone into hock to get some decent clothes for the tour—and for that, she should be grateful. Or he might have blackmailed Jeanie out of a few bucks.

As she passed a full-length mirror at the very end of the hall, she stole a look at herself. She *did* look frumpy.

Nice Girls Do was in the middle of a commercial break, and Dr. Darlene Love, a sex therapist and the show's host, hurried over to welcome them. She was well into her sixties, but with the kind of bubbling energy that made Melissa want to ask her what vitamins she took.

"Melissa and Tony? *Sooooo* nice to meet you two," Dr. Love said, giving both their hands a shake at once. "Listen, just relax and have fun, kids, the more fun the better. I'll be announcing you as soon as we're back on air."

With that she hurried back to the set, completely ignoring an adoring gaggle of audience members who vied for her attention. And they called her Dr. Love?

A voice-over announcer could be heard, and the host's round beaming face flashed on the studio monitor. She was holding up Melissa's book to a chorus of applause.

As they walked onto the set, Tony said under his breath, "No tricks today."

He could have saved his voice. Tricks were the last thing on her mind, right after sex, which didn't bode very well for this show, which was supposed to sizzle. Somehow they had to make America believe they were the world's horniest couple, an honor they'd just been given in the promo for the show, when they didn't even want to be in the same room. Tony was acting as if she had a contagious disease. Maybe she did. Her breath was a little short.

They took their seats on a crushed-velvet sofa the color of the plum juice that had been all over Melissa's face last night. Not a reminder she needed, thanks. Apparently Tony did think she was contagious. He sat at the opposite end of the couch, the big dope. What was wrong with him? Maybe she'd just go plunk herself in his lap and tickle him.

"Well, let's get right to it." Dr. Love graced them with a slightly loopy smile. "What do we women have to do to get our men to beg for sex?"

"Bite them," Melissa said, remembering the host's remark about fun. "A little nip on the neck or the earlobe is a sure sign that a woman's in the mood, right, Tony?"

"Teeth marks all over me," he said, deadpan.

"Oh, my," Dr. Love murmured. "Could we see them?"

Tony didn't answer, and the doctor's smile faded. "Do you two always sit so far apart?" she asked. "Is that in the book?"

With a glance at Tony's dark countenance, Melissa hastened to explain. "See, this is a little game we play. He gets grumpy, and I coax him out of his mood, no matter what it takes. There's nothing a man loves more than a persistent woman. Right, Tony Baby? Hmm, Tiger Lover?"

"Bite me," Tony said in a low voice.

"See—he loves it. They all do."

"Really?" The doctor sounded unconvinced. "That's the secret to your white-hot relationship? Grumpiness? Biting?"

The audience tittered.

"Just kidding, of course. Communication is the key." All too true, but not nearly exciting enough for the *Nice Girls Do* show. She searched her brain for some way to spice things up, and finally tossed it to Tony. "Wouldn't you agree?"

Say something provocative, Tony, please. Tell me I'm crazy. Naked vacuuming is the key.

"Communication," he echoed with all the enthusiasm of a performing parrot. "It's *all* about communication."

The smile on Dr. Love's face drooped noticeably, and Melissa knew they were doomed. This wasn't going badly. It was the turnpike at rush hour. It wasn't going at all.

Dr. Love stole a glance at her blue note card. "Oh, it's time for the call-in segment! Goody, right after this break, we'll take some exciting questions from our viewers." Her tone said please, God.

As the show went off the air, Darlene Love's smile turned into bared teeth. "What's going on?" she asked Melissa and Tony. "Is this some crazy publicity stunt? How do you two manage to have sex at all? You barely look at each other."

Poor Jeanie was jumping up and down in the wings, trying to get their attention, and Melissa knew she had to do something.

"My fault. It's the game." Melissa sprang from the couch and plunked herself in Tony's lap, much to his moody surprise. "He just needs some coaxing."

Under her breath, she warned him, "If you let me down now, I'll push you over the hotel balcony when we get back."

"I'm taking you with me," he said.

Steam hissed through Melissa's nostrils. He really was impossible. If only she had another glass of ice water. Anything would be better than sitting on his lap, goo-gooing and playing kissy-face. But when the stage manager began the countdown to airtime, Melissa did exactly that.

"Isn't that sweet?" Dr. Love cooed. "Our guests are demonstrating techniques for make-up sex. Let's hope they can break away from each other long enough to talk to our first callers—a Mr. and Mrs. Earnest Sanders. Have I got that right? Melissa, I think you may know these lovely folks from the State of Kansas."

Melissa had been blowing little puffs of air in Tony's face. One of them got stuck in her throat. Caught like a fish bone. This couldn't be.

"Mr. and Mrs. Sanders, is there anything you'd like to say to your naughty daughter and son-in-law?"

"Melissa, is that really you? Your father and I heard about your book at church last Sunday. The minister held it up and told the whole congregation what a great help a book like yours could be to married folk. We went out and bought it, and I must say—"

"Mom?" Melissa would have recognized her mother's prim-and-proper voice anywhere. But she didn't know what to do. Her brain had frozen solid, so her body decided for her. Melissa's respiratory system reacted to crises like a blow-dryer did to overheating. It shut down the plant. She stopped breathing altogether. No air, either way. She couldn't inhale or exhale.

She clutched her throat and waved her hand, trying to get someone's attention. But no one seemed to understand that she was in danger of suffocating. She could die right there onstage. And finally, Dr. Love let forth with a peal of laughter.

"Would you look at that!" she said. "Our outspoken author is speechless. Isn't that cute?"

Chapter Eight

As aphrodisiacs go, the mind is the most potent, but never underestimate a great tush on a guy.
101 Ways To Make Your Man Beg

MELISSA FIGURED she must be several shades of blue by now. She could hear her mother's voice droning in her head, which meant she wasn't dead yet, but she still couldn't make herself breathe. It felt as if her lungs were caught in a vise.

"Melissa, your dad and I tried that crazy game in chapter five. What was it called, Ern? Ride the Wild Pony? He had to see the doctor for his sacroiliac, but we're very proud of you, dear. When do we get to meet your handsome Tony?"

Dr. Love's eyebrows shot up. "Your parents haven't met your husband?"

Melissa let out a strangled gasp, and finally people began to realize that she was in trouble. Tony scooped her up in his arms and put her on her feet.

Dr. Love jumped up, too. "What should we do?"

"Give me some room," Tony said, waving the host away. "We've been through this before. It's her breathing."

Melissa fell against Tony as he clamped a hand over her

mouth and pinched her nose shut. Not this again! She struggled, but couldn't break his hold. God, he was strong. She was smothering, and he was going to finish her off! Was that his plan?

Let go of me. Let go already! She couldn't scream at him, except mentally.

She tried to step on his toe and missed. Desperate, she kicked back with her high heel, meaning to hit his shin. She hadn't intended to hurt him, but she aimed too high.

"Oof!" Tony released her, doubling over in pain, and Melissa stumbled forward, sucking air into her lungs.

"These kids play rough," Dr. Love said. "Time for a break, folks. When we come back, we'll bring out our next guests—and hear this! It's the entire cast of *Girls Behaving Badly.*"

FORTUNATELY, Melissa's breathing made a rapid recovery. She was fine by the time she and Tony got backstage. And he was only limping slightly, but his mood didn't seem to have improved at all.

"It was an accident," she said, hazarding a glance at him. "I swear it was."

"One more accident like that, and I'll never have children."

"I'm *sorry.* Is there anything I can do?"

"Please, no! I can still walk."

Melissa decided she was only making it worse and went quiet, but by the time they reached the hallway to the exit, Tony seemed to have rallied. She checked with him again. "I'll live," he said, shrugging it off. "How about you? How's the breathing?"

"Oh, I'm fine." On second thought, she added, "I really would appreciate it if you'd stop trying to smother me."

"Deal, if you'll quit going for my crotch."

They both managed wan smiles, which quickly faded when they got a look at their devoted publicist. Jeanie stood stock-still in the middle of the hallway they'd just entered. Her mouth hung open like a sprung garage door. Her eyes seemed distant and remote. Melissa wondered if she was in shock.

The guest-wrangler flew by them as if they were invisible. On her way to pick up the badly behaving girls, no doubt.

"Jeanie, it wasn't that bad," Melissa said, speaking low so as not to jar her.

Jeanie blinked. She looked at them as if she'd been in a hypnotic trance and someone had snapped their fingers. "Not that bad?" she said. "Not that bad? It was a *disaster*." She focused on Melissa. "You didn't tell your parents you were married? You didn't even tell them you'd written a book? How did you expect to get away with that?"

"The same way you expected to get away with passing me off as her husband?" Tony ventured.

Jeanie glared at both of them. "I think you need another publicist."

"Jeanie, no! My parents will be fine." Melissa couldn't swear that was true, but Jeanie obviously needed humoring. Melissa was just grateful her parents weren't too upset. She hadn't expected them to become a part of her fan base, but it shouldn't have surprised her. They'd always supported her in everything she'd done.

"They would never do anything to hurt me," she assured Jeanie. "They just didn't know. I'll speak to them. I'll ask them not to call any more shows."

"They probably sold more books than we did," Tony offered. "That Wild Pony business will make a great story."

Jeanie huffed. "Damn right they sold more books than you two bozos did. You acted like you couldn't bear the sight of each other. And by the way, I didn't buy that make-up-sex game for one minute. I'm sure no one else did, either. You two have to get some chemistry going. You're duds in the fireworks department!"

Jeanie had her purse open, already searching through it for something, most likely her cell phone, which meant she was probably out of danger, as far as shock went.

"Go back to the hotel and wait for me," she told them, an ominous edge to her voice. "This calls for drastic action, and I have some thinking to do."

With that she turned on her heel and marched for the exit, leaving Melissa and Tony to stare after her with some trepidation.

LATER THAT EVENING, Tony answered a brisk knock at the suite's door. He knew before opening it that Jeanie would be on the other side. She knocked the way she walked and talked—with speed and determination.

"Where's the other lovebird?" she asked as she brushed past him.

Tony closed the door and followed her into the living room. "She's on the phone with her parents, assuring them that I saved her life on the show today. Nice folks. She put me on the line, and we all had a good chat. They've agreed not to call the police."

"You must have made quite an impression," Jeanie said, setting a loaded shopping bag on the living-room coffee table. "Did they really like the book?"

"They've already started an online fan club." He grinned, indicating the bag she'd brought. "What do you have there?"

"Salvation...I hope." She marched to Melissa's door and called, "Come out of there, Ms. Sexpot. We have work to do."

"And just what are you trying to save?" Tony sank to the sofa and folded his arms. It was beginning to look like a very long evening.

"Our collective asses, if you must know. We have to turn you two into red-hot lovers." Jeanie rapped on Melissa's door. "Chop-chop. I'm serious."

Tony heard some kind of female grumbling and supposed Melissa was no more excited than he was about this apparent crusade of Jeanie's. A moment later Melissa appeared, casting a suspicious gaze upon the scene in the living room.

Slitty eyes flattered her, Tony realized. He had to be going nuts. Slitty eyes didn't flatter anyone but Clint Eastwood.

Melissa dropped into an overstuffed chair by the window.

"And I'm so happy to see you, too," Jeanie said with an overly bright smile. "Now, down to business. Tomorrow the two of you will be demonstrating some of Melissa's techniques, in person, on live television."

"Oh no, we're not," Tony and Melissa said in near unison.

"Oh yes, you are," Jeanie chirped. Tony wasn't sure but he thought he recognized a woman on the verge of hysteria. Her cutting sarcasm and sharp-edged smiles were her only defense.

"I've already taken care of everything," she said. "The venues have been notified as to what they'll need, and I have a list of what you'll be doing tomorrow."

She handed each of them a sheet of neatly typed paper, along with a copy of Melissa's book. "Go to the chapters I've marked and study them as if you were cramming for finals. I've highlighted each of your copies, so really I've done all the work for you. All you need to do is learn, memorize and practice. Practice, practice, practice. The entire key to this is practice. You need to look relaxed and natural as you're demonstrating. If you don't, I swear I *will* kill you both."

She flashed them another blinding smile and began rifling around in her bag of tricks. "There now, that wasn't so awful, was it? What have I done with the Ginseng Revitalizing Tonic in a Capsule?"

She produced a huge bottle of pills and plunked it down

on the coffee table. "Two of these, three times a day, on an empty stomach. I can personally vouch for their effectiveness. They'll lift your spirits, sedate your nerves and focus your mind. These babies can take the edge off a razor and give you a lovely little buzz to boot. Go at it, kids, with my blessings."

With that, she pivoted like a drum major and headed for the door.

"You know, they have decaf," Tony said.

Jeanie spun around, that god-awful smile still plastered on her mouth. She waggled her index finger toward the book in his lap. "Practice, mister, and take your pills. Melissa, tomorrow, I will dress you myself. Good night, dearies."

After she left the suite, Tony considered locking the door. "She seems a little tense, you think?" he asked.

Melissa was looking over her sheet of paper. She appeared very pale now, as if she'd been bitten by a vampire and left to die. "I have a feeling we'll be joining her soon."

"Why?" Tony didn't wait for an answer. He skimmed his own sheet of instructions, and felt the blood draining from his face as well.

"We can't do this on television," Melissa said under her breath. "They'll arrest us!"

"SEXUAL PASTE? She wants us to pretend we're stuck together? *There?*"

Melissa was afraid to look up from her instruction sheet. She and Tony were on the sofa, surrounded by the contents of Jeanie's care package and, just like a man, Tony had already begun flipping through his copy of *101 Ways,* looking for the first warm-up exercise on Jeanie's list.

"This is like being joined at the...uh, hip," he said, looking over at her.

"Actually, it's worse—or better, depending on how you look at it."

Melissa had spent so many hours on her book she knew its contents inside out, an advantage Tony didn't have at this point. She also knew what to expect from the games and exercises on Jeanie's cheat sheet. There was no way to demonstrate them without some very suggestive touching and physical contact. It would be great for the talk-show circuit, but deadly for those nights alone in the hotel suite together.

Melissa was still a little shaken from the *Nice Girls Do* appearance, and her parents' call wasn't the only reason, although it had certainly cooled her jets. She'd also realized after last night that seduction was a tricky business, with ramifications beyond the bedroom. Playing games with a man you were legitimately married to was one thing. An unknown quantity like Tony, quite another.

"Maybe we should take our herbal supplements?" Melissa picked up the bottle Jeanie left. A pill that could energize, calm and tranquilize all at the same time sounded damn good to her, but her only interest at the moment was tranquillity.

"Maybe later," Tony said, eyeing the pills. "Are they safe?"

"Jeanie takes them and she hasn't keeled over yet." Melissa opened the lid and spilled out two of the capsules. "I'm starting now, *before* I require hospitalization. Come on, be brave."

But Tony declined when she offered him the bottle. With a sigh she put it back on the table. Jeanie wanted them to take the herbs, and she hoped Tony wouldn't be difficult. Men did tend to be difficult about taking pills. Maybe it was a macho thing. Then again, maybe he had the good sense not to trust what lurked inside the pungent-smelling brownish capsules.

"Tony, there's no way we're getting out of this," she said, telling him what he already knew. "I hate to admit it, but Jeanie's right. Today was a fiasco, and not just because of my parents. If we blow it again tomorrow, I'm afraid it'll be all over."

He laid his book and paper on the massive coffee table. "You don't think we came off as the world's horniest couple?"

She had to laugh at that. "Maybe the world's most hostile. But I suppose after last night, we were just trying to protect ourselves."

Tony rose and slipped his hands into his pockets. He'd taken off his suit jacket earlier and loosened his silk tie at the knot. Even in relaxed mode, he looked good. Hot, in fact. Too hot for her poor overworked circuits.

"Speaking of last night," he said. "That retreat on my part wasn't about you. I need you to know that."

"What was it then?"

He affected a shrug. "Maybe I don't want the kind of collision we had before. One car wreck in a lifetime is enough."

"That's how you think of it, as a car wreck?"

"It did some damage," he said.

His somber expression made her think it was a lot more damage than he was willing to say. She wasn't the one who'd been left, but it had never occurred to her that he would want her to stay. And when it appeared that he'd made no attempt to find her, she'd assumed the worst.

Melissa eyed the pills again, wondering when they would kick in, if ever. Everything was moving too fast, especially her thoughts. But as she stared at the bottle, an idea came to her that made her think the pills might be working.

"Do you think if we practice enough we might desensitize ourselves to the point that the games wouldn't get to us? You know, like when someone says a bad word so often it loses its shock value."

"I don't think it's quite the same thing," he said.

She blew out a long breath and rose from the chair. "In that case, I think we need to agree in advance of any practicing we might do that there won't be any sex. In fact, let's not even think about sex. Let's just suck it up and do what we have to, you know, like performers and prostitutes and politicians."

"No thoughts of sex? I can't guarantee that."

"Okay, we can think about it, but we *can't* do it."

"Agreed. However—" His gaze traveled down the length of her body, lingering on the openings of the wrap dress she hadn't yet changed out of. "If we're going to try the Sexual Paste game, you might want to put some pants on."

The rules of engagement at long last. Ten minutes later they were back in the living room. Tony had changed from suit and tie into jeans and a blue cotton T-shirt. Melissa wore a pair of workout shorts and a racer-back sports bra. Like two dancers about to rehearse their routine for the first time, they met in the center of the room.

"I'm all yours," Tony said. He placed his hands on his hips, one of his many mundane gestures Melissa found downright erotic.

"The Sexual Paste game is actually very easy." She forced herself to sound detached and professional. "It's supposed to be played in the shower, but we'll have to pretend that part. But do keep in mind that this would normally be done in the nude."

Tony's eyes glinted with interest. "I can do that."

She chose to ignore that. "Here's how this works. If we were really in the shower, the first thing we would do is lather each other with soap. Tonight, we'll have to fake it. You do yourself and I'll do myself."

The glint became a frown. "That's no fun."

Melissa shot him a warning look. "Hey, this can be sexy. It's the anticipation phase, like foreplay."

"If you insist."

And Melissa did. Insist. "Now, after we're both wet and slippery, we take turns touching each other, but we're not allowed to touch, you know, the goods. You can touch fronts and behinds, but no primary sexual zones."

"Which are?"

"Well, technically, nipples, labia and vagina on a woman. I'm not allowed to touch your—" She had it in mind to be subtle, but her gaze dropped like a rock to his crotch. "Manhood."

"I don't think I like this game." Tony pretended to grumble.

"You will, trust me. It requires some patience, but you're good at that. This is about getting to know your lover's body in a slow, tactile way."

"So I'm going to put my hands on you?"

"Yes, but it's more than that." Melissa sighed. "It might be better if I just showed you. Whatever part of my body I place against yours has to stay where it is until the game is finished. That's where the paste part comes in. Like this."

She stepped close to him, close enough to catch the light woodsy scent of his cologne, and gave him the once-over. She took her time looking him up and down, demonstrating correct procedure. He was a sexy guy. She was a sexy chick, getting an eyeful, and so on and so on. No big deal. They could do this.

Actually, Melissa knew he expected her to place one of her hands on him, but she decided to try something else. Instead, she pressed the inside of her right calf against the outside of his left calf.

"See? Now I'm stuck to you."

Tony gazed down at their conjoined legs. "This could get very interesting," he said. "So I don't actually have to use my hands yet? I can use any part of my body I want?"

Melissa nodded, her heart already pounding. It was now her turn to be shamelessly surveyed from head to toe, and Tony took his own sweet time with it, too.

"Maybe I'll do this." He pressed his right thigh to her left thigh. They both had to spread their legs a bit to keep their balance, but they remained joined through the process.

"What about the soap part?" Tony asked. "Why are we all slippery if we can't rub each other?"

"In a sec." Her voice was beginning to fade on her. There didn't seem to be enough air when she got this close to him. Melissa's next move was a rather bold one. Maybe those pills really had started to work. She reached around and placed her hand on his right butt cheek. It was a hard, rounded muscle, and she could feel it flexing under her touch. Unfortunately, her brain wanted her to see the action, too, and she had a rather intense flashback of another time she'd curved her hand to his beautiful bronze behind—and watched muscles rippling wildly from the effort to gain control.

The things she'd done to this man. The things he'd done to her!

She had to give him some credit, though. Until now she had only seen flashes of the deeply sensual nature that she knew was hidden in his gaze. That seemed to be changing. His chest rose and fell more slowly than it had just seconds ago. And his eyes had narrowed and focused as if he, too, was imagining the forbidden.

"I can touch you anywhere?" he asked. The thickness in his voice betrayed him.

"Anywhere except those primary sexual zones I mentioned." If she didn't find her breath soon she'd be reduced to sign language.

Apparently Tony decided one bold move deserved another. He moved his hand upward and cupped the fullness of her left breast. He lifted it gently and squeezed its softness. Her sports top was a bra in itself, and only the thin cotton material separated his flesh from hers. Melissa nearly whimpered under his touch, but the resistance her mind threw up was futile. There were too many sensory reminders! There'd actually been a time that night in Cancún when all he'd had to do was brush his tongue over her nipple, and she'd come close to peaking. That was how wildly responsive she'd become as the hours wore on, and their honeymoon suite became a fantasy realm. She wondered what would happen now if he were to brush his fingers over her tender nipples.

It didn't take long before they were as intricately pressed together as they were going to get. All that remained was their lips. "It's your turn," Melissa said. "You should probably kiss me now."

"Where?"

"Wherever you can reach."

She knew his options were limited. He had access to her forehead, cheeks and lips. Maybe her neck, too. She hoped he stayed away from her neck. His kisses there made her insane.

Tony had made his decision. He pressed his lips to hers and began nibbling, teasing her. She wasn't sure if that was fair or not. It seemed he was breaking the rules, but she wasn't able to correct him. Her own mouth had decided to play along.

She broke the kiss enough to speak, which was probably against the rules, too. She couldn't quite seem to remember what the rules were. "This is where the soap comes in," she said, her lips murmuring against his. "We're supposed to slide ever so gently against each other. Only a fraction of an inch, no more than that. Okay?"

Every nerve ending in her body lit up as Tony began to move. His palm rolled her breast with light pressure, and she moved against him, creating a riot of pleasure. Such wild sensations. Holding the position made her thighs tremble. He teased her budded nipples with the pad of his thumb. Slow and deliberate. Back and forth, making her nerve endings sing. Lord, so sweet. *So intense.*

They had to be breaking some rules, right?

His hipbone nudged hers, causing her legs to sway. He turned in to her and caught her back against his chest, re-establishing his hold. His body made contact with hers in several startling places. His groin nestled her derriere, the hardness between his legs was unmistakable. She didn't need to see it to know it was there. She could feel it sliding toward the crack of her other cheek. Now, *that* would be breaking a rule!

"You're not moving," Tony whispered.

She rolled her breast against the heat of his hand, and a sharp thrill rewarded her. Tony groaned into her mouth as she toyed with his knotted glute. Even their calves created friction sparks. Whether by accident or design, his hands curled tighter, forcing her closer. One wrong move, and they would be on the floor.

It didn't help that Melissa felt tipsy. She tingled every-where. Her face was flushed, her head muzzy and light. Was it the herbs or him?

"Don't forget to breathe," he said.

"Breathe? What's that?" She broke away from him with a soft gasp. She could only take so much of this, and Tony seemed to have the same problem. They both backed off a good foot. Melissa avoided looking at him as she tried to catch her breath.

"There's a problem," he said.

"Only one?"

"Well, one big one."

Melissa glanced up and right back down as she saw what he meant. The protrusion in his jeans pressed firmly against his fly. It was a good size, big enough to hang a hat on, as she'd once quipped in an article called "Ten Signals He's Interested."

A sound squeaked out of her. Laughter? Where had that come from?

"Well, if that happens," she said, "at least Jeanie won't be able to say we're not turning up the heat. In fact, I think you should do everything you can to have an erection on the air just to keep the woman quiet. Think of the reaction."

"You mean *after* they take me to jail? Or before?"

More squeaky laughter. She sounded like a bicycle with bad breaks. Still, this was fun. She couldn't remember the last time she'd enjoyed anything as much, not since the tour started, for sure. And if Jeanie's pills had anything to do with it, she might decide to take them on a regular basis.

"Want to try another game?" she asked him.

"And risk a blowout? I think my erection and I are heading for the showers, thanks just the same."

"Chicken!" she called after him as he adjusted his jeans and made his exit. At least she had a front-row seat to catch a view of his retreating derriere.

THE LUMINOUS DIAL of Tony's watch told him he wasn't going to get any sleep that night anyway. Still fully dressed, he let himself out of the bedroom and walked the entire length of the living room, coming to a stop at her bedroom door. Was she wandering around in the dark, too? He hoped so. Insomnia should be mutual.

For several seconds, he stood there, breathing, feeling what she'd done to his body and his mind. Breasts weren't supposed to burn a man's hand with their softness. The pressure of her rounded bottom against his manhood wasn't supposed to leave him engorged. Not all night. Hard. Ready. Aching to be inside her. Aching for some relief from this madness. Even his thighs burned from the tension.

What the hell was he going to do about Melissa Sanders Bond? His wife. The woman who couldn't get her wedding ring off or catch her breath half the time. He'd had no doubt about his intentions when he'd gotten here— and they hadn't included a 24/7 erection. Or standing in front of her door obsessed with the thought of spreading her legs and tasting the apple sweetness of her sex.

This was ridiculous. Pathetic.

He took a step back, turned…and stopped. A flash of light had caught his eye. Moonlight streamed through the windows, bouncing off the gigantic bottle of pills. Jeanie's pills, the ones that could take the edge off a razor.

He rubbed the roughness of his unshaven jaw as he debated.

They couldn't hurt him. They were herbs.

And his edges were sharp enough to cut paper, for Christ's sake.

A moment later, he had the bottle in his hand. He poured out a handful, stared at the pile of brown capsules for all of sixty seconds—and downed them like candy. There, that was done. One of the more sensible decisions in his relationship with her. They tasted like shit, so they had to be good for him, right? At least maybe he'd sleep.

"NOW THERE'S A SEXY OUTFIT," Jeanie said as she stepped back to appraise Melissa's ensemble. They were alone in a large, sumptuous dressing room, and, true to her word, Jeanie had picked out Melissa's clothes for the late-night talk show that would start taping in less than twenty minutes. Melissa stepped carefully—and rather awkwardly— to a ceiling-to-floor mirror to survey the damage. The heels of her sexy black stilettos felt six inches high.

Lord, her reflection would have made an underwear model blush. Jeanie had insisted that she shimmy into a clingy black skirt that wasn't quite a mini, but short enough. What put it in the sexpot category was the center seam. An alarmingly deep slit pointed north, taking your glance—and your imagination—along with it.

Melissa took a test step and noticed how provocatively the slit opened up. Her top was a cropped jacket with some detail stitching on the hem and sleeves. Under the jacket was a low-cut black camisole.

"I can't wear this out there," she said, her voice a low moan.

"Yes, you can, and yes, you will," Jeanie said. "You look great. If this doesn't get Tony's attention, nothing will."

"It isn't Tony's attention I'm worried about. Look at this slit, Jeanie! One wrong move, and I'll be facing obscenity charges."

"You have panty hose on. What are you worried about?"

"Indecent exposure, maybe?"

"Here, take a pill," Jeanie said, searching through her tote. She produced a smaller bottle than the one she'd left at the suite, but the capsules were the same. "Take two."

Melissa took two and popped a third for good measure. She'd been taking them regularly, and they left her pleasantly relaxed yet energized. At times, her blood rushed and she felt a little giddy. But it was a lovely sensation, actually. She didn't mind it at all. Maybe another one? Four? Mmm, no. She was mellow enough.

Eighteen minutes later, she and Tony were sitting side by side on a leather sofa stationed next to the talk-show host's desk. A former stand-up comic, Larry Gunderson had a rather breathtaking overbite and slightly crossed eyes with pupils that roamed freely, even when he looked straight at you. Melissa was reminded of Groucho Marx from old clips she'd seen on the Comedy Channel.

Larry had asked all the usual questions, and either Tony or Melissa had answered with more than enough sexual innuendo to elicit giggles and gasps from the audience. Everyone seemed pleased, even Jeanie, who for the first five minutes of their interview had stood in the wings, wringing her hands. Now she was smiling, laughing along.

Larry leaned toward the two of them as if he was about to whisper something. "I've been told," he intoned, "that you've agreed to demonstrate one of your games." He gave the audience a wry glance. "Waddaya think, folks? Want to see a man beg for sex on national television?"

Hoots and howls brought Larry out of his chair. He waved extravagantly toward a curtain that opened to reveal the frame of a shower stall in the middle of a bathroom set.

"My stage is your loo," he told Melissa and Tony. Turning to the cameras, he said, "We do things right here on the *Larry Gunderson Show*. We even have flesh-colored bodysuits for our sex experts to wear. Can't wait to see that, folks? Stick with us. We'll be back right after this commercial break."

The bodysuits came as a surprise to Melissa, and naturally there was only one screen for her and Tony to change behind. Why would a married couple need separate screens? Melissa's resembled a two-piece tankini, and behind the screen she turned away from Tony, planning to put on as much of it as she could before taking off her clothing. She managed the bottoms easily, but as she began to work on the top, she felt some air on her backside, and a sharp sensation.

"Hey!" She shot Tony a look over her shoulder. He'd snapped her spandex tankini bottoms, and she couldn't retaliate. Her arms were tangled in the camisole she was trying to take off inside her jacket. But she didn't miss the dark and dangerous sparkle in his eyes. This was nothing like the *Nice Girls Do* show. He looked ready for anything. His rakish smile made her knees weak, and she needed her wits about her to get the tankini top on. Thank God, the suit fit. Someone must have given the producers their sizes. Jeanie, the woman who would barter her soul to sell a book? Who else.

Tony already had his Speedo-style suit on, and he seemed more than interested in Melissa's predicament. As she shed her jacket and camisole, he nuzzled her neck, his warm breath caressing her ear. "Need some help?"

"I'm fine."

"Yes, you are," he whispered.

"Tony, what are you doing?"

"I'm whispering in your ear—and making plans to molest you."

"On national television?"

"Anywhere, Melissa, anywhere. I'd like to drag you into the nearest closet, lock the door and never let you out."

Melissa didn't know what to make of him. Either he'd lost his mind or something wicked had taken possession of Tony Bond's soul. She wondered if it had anything to do with Jeanie's pills. They'd certainly worked their magic on Melissa. Her heart raced pleasantly and she blushed for no good reason. All day she'd been smiling over nothing, and she wasn't the slightest bit worried about exotic illnesses.

But Tony wasn't taking the pills. It couldn't be that.

When the curtain came open moments later, Melissa was all set to explain the game to the audience. Her tankini strap had been carefully miked. She only needed to speak clearly. But try making sense while a man was looking at you as if he wanted to devour you, starting with your trembling lips.

"Everyplace we touch, we stick," she managed to get out.

Tony pasted the outside of his calf to the outside of hers, and when she cupped his behind, the audience roared with approval. The two of them had agreed to go with most of the routine they rehearsed last night, except for his hand on her breast. No doubt the crowd would have loved it, but Melissa didn't think it was appropriate, even for late night.

She was also trying to avoid any possibility of another

meltdown in front of God and everyone, although she wasn't certain God watched Larry Gunderson. She hoped not. Whimpering in front of the late-night audience would be embarrassing enough—and she didn't trust herself not to whimper if Tony touched her that intimately. He had a way of making her feel as if no one else existed, and that could only get them into trouble tonight.

"Your turn," she told him.

He leaned close. "I can't wait to get my hands on you," he said under his breath.

A gasp resounded as the mike picked up Tony's sexy warning and broadcast it to the room. Melissa barely heard the clamor. She was too startled at what he actually did with his hand. Her breast was supposed to have been off limits, but he touched it anyway, cupping her tenderly enough to elicit the whimper she feared. Her legs nearly gave way when she registered the searing heat of his skin. She was terribly weak. Was it because she hadn't expected this? Or because that's what he did best, make her terribly weak?

He was dangerous, out of control. *What had come over him?*

Somehow she swallowed back the sound in her throat. She even steadied her legs, but as his fingers closed over her flesh, she lost touch with everything else for a second. She knew this was wrong, against the rules, an infringement, but she couldn't seem to hold that thought. Or any thought. Every nerve ending was in shock, quivering. And she was engulfed with the sweetest kind of need. *How did he do that to her?*

She had no idea what came next. Anything? Oh, yes, the kiss. Was she supposed to say something, do something, or just be kissed to the brink of oblivion by this sexy, reckless man?

"Tony, don't kill me." She tilted her face up to him, and their mouths touched. Tony's soft moan resounded like thunder, but Melissa could only hear it in her mind. Nothing else existed but him. He lifted her off her feet and enfolded her in his arms, pasting their bodies together from lips to toes. They'd broken the rules, but Melissa couldn't remember what game they were playing anyway, so it didn't matter.

He was still whispering in her ear, vowing that he was going to have his way with her the minute they got back to the suite. Maybe in the limo.

"Have your way with me," she said. "Yes, *do*."

The curtain came down on their sizzling kiss, and Larry Gunderson could be heard saying, "I think that's all we need to know, folks. Show's over. Let's go buy the book."

"HOTSY-TOTSY! You two are barbecue starters."

Jeanie's excitement filled the town car. The show had been taped live, so it was late in the evening when the three of them returned to the hotel. Jeanie talked nonstop during the drive back, congratulating them on their astonishing performance. Melissa didn't say a word. She couldn't get past the noise of her soaring heart. Tony was quiet, too, but she could feel the tension pouring off him.

Jeanie wanted to celebrate. She offered to buy them a nightcap in the hotel's lobby bar, but Melissa begged off. Too tired, she said. Tony used the same excuse.

Their next ride was even more silent, just the two of them in an elevator all the way up to their suite. Silent. Tense. Vibrant. The air seemed to shimmer before Melissa's eyes, the way heat shimmers on a summer day.

Tony used his key to open the door, and Melissa stepped into the darkened room. She didn't bother to turn on the lights as Tony snapped the door shut. She dropped her bag to the floor and turned to face him. His embrace was quick and tight, his kiss immediate and desperate. And hot. Steaming hot.

Melissa kicked off her dreaded heels and pressed herself to him as intimately as she had on the talk show. No, that wasn't intimate. This was. She didn't even try to pretend that his touch didn't burn her flesh. Just being near him dragged her into a deep pool of desire.

Their hands created a frantic flurry as they began undressing each other. There wasn't time to speak. Words would only get in the way. They both seemed to understand that this was inevitable, preordained after their one night together two years earlier.

A sense of joy flooded Melissa. This time they would make love. He wouldn't change his mind. She couldn't bear that. How many times had she fantasized about the way he would find her again, sweep her into his arms and make love to her with wild abandon? She'd imagined it just like this, him taking her wherever they happened to be, without a word. He wouldn't change his mind. Not this time.

Chapter Nine

Don't think of it as rejection. Think of it as an invitation, a challenge, or better yet, a dare.
101 Ways To Make Your Man Beg

TONY WAS A MAN BESET by demons. Melissa's naked skin brought a thrill of pleasure as drugging as the most potent opiate. And just as illegal. He couldn't do this. Some part of his mind had been telling him to stop all night, but it didn't have a chance against the fires roaring in his blood. He was drunk, high, over the moon. Maybe he'd taken too many of those damn pills, he thought but at this same time knew it wasn't about pills. She was the drug.

Her nails ripped him sweetly. She kissed him like a kitten, with hungry, feeding bites of his lips. She sucked on his tongue. He shuddered and kissed her back. Brutally. A moan caught in his throat. This wasn't a conscious choice anymore. Maybe it never had been.

They dropped to the floor and sprawled in the deep nap of the carpet. Their heat-slicked bodies entwined like rope. Knotted like rope. God, it was beautiful. He wanted this heaven to last forever, just the naked wonder of her body sliding against his. But not as much as he wanted to feel her tighten with pleasure.

That was his drug of choice. His pleasure. Hers.

They rolled, and her cool hair brushed over him like a breeze. She was on top of him and below him, rolling and touching, on top and below. Moonlight poured silver all over her liquid curves. She threw back her head, and he ran kisses down the ice-white slope of her neck. Her breasts were small, luminous moons. Her swollen pink nipples begged to be kissed.

He captured a rosy nub in his mouth and rolled his tongue around it. She bit back a cry of surprise. He drew on her gently to let her know how that felt, but it was the hard pull that she liked. She arched up, as if surrendering herself to the carnal delight. To the heat of the fires. To him.

Tony, don't kill me.

Those were her words. Could she actually die from this? He could. He could die.

They fell to their sides, and he searched her face, wondering how she made him feel powerful and vulnerable at the same time. A God and a beggar. He wanted his power back, all of it. But he wanted her, too, and for some reason, he couldn't get near her without experiencing every damn emotion known to humankind. Why was that?

Melissa sensed the change in him. She moved over him and braved the fire that lit his eyes. An emotion flared within him that she'd never seen before, and for a second, it frightened her. Passion or anger? She never got her answer. A more urgent concern took hold as she straddled him. The width of his hips forced her to open her legs wide, sending dark thrills spiraling through her.

All she could think about was this wild beauty she felt when she was with him, if beauty could be felt. She gloried in being on top, on all fours, and letting her breasts swell like ripening fruit. Not since their last time together had her body been this sensitive and needy. His erection brushed against her inner thigh, unleashing the years of frustrated longing.

She was instantly wet. He was hard enough to break.

The ache to be joined with him was enough to make her cry.

"Take me," she whispered.

A roll of her hips, a rock of his and he was deep inside, exactly where she needed him to be. He let out a moan, the sound muffled by the nipple he was suckling. Melissa felt it vibrate through her breasts like a low-voltage current. Nerve endings tingled that she didn't know existed.

He lifted her with his arms, laid her out on her back and sheathed himself all over again in her writhing body. Melissa cried out in surprise and delight. She reached out blindly, found his rocking hips and dug her fingers into the firm flesh. She pressed him into her, greedy, unable to get enough, until suddenly, it was enough. *It was too much.* Too sweet and sharp. Too wild. Her climax was unexpected and urgent. Pleasure broke like a cloudburst. For minutes she ceased breathing and existed on nothing but bliss. And then all at once she was gasping.

Don't forget to breathe.

Tony reared back, and a growl of sweet anguish ripped through him. He was magnificent above her, his body rippling with the deep feelings of completion. His jaw spasmed, and the constriction in his throat sounded like a cry. As he collapsed, he pulled her into his arms and held her as if she were his only source of sustenance.

They rolled again, this time landing on their sides, still joined and throbbing with feeling. Melissa clutched him with every muscle in her body. She never wanted him to withdraw, but her legs ached from the strain of squeezing him.

"My God," Tony breathed, "what just happened?"

"I don't know." She couldn't have explained it either, but she understood his astonishment. Their coupling had the force of a breathtaking accident. One moment they'd been separated by mute tension, and the next they were tearing at each other's clothing. Now they were naked on the floor and stunned from the collision. Still vibrating. Still rolling end over end.

She closed her eyes and had a silent conversation with her roaring heart, but nothing would quiet it. He pulled out, and then gathered her close again. She could hear the roar of his heart, too. It was oddly reassuring. She rested her face in the cradle of his shoulder, and his heart pulsed against her cheek. But as the mad rush of his blood gradually transformed into the long, steady rhythms of sleep, she was lulled into the depths with him.

Sometime later, she felt herself being lifted and carried to the bedroom. It was still dark, and she had no idea how late it was. Groggy, she clung to him as he settled her on the bed and drew the comforter over her. He stepped back as if he wasn't going to join her, and Melissa protested. How could they not spend the night together after they'd become a part of each other? They'd been as close as a man and woman could be.

"We'll talk in the morning," he said.

Even in her sleepy state, she picked up the finality in his tone. "What's wrong?" she asked.

"It can wait until tomorrow. Go back to sleep."

"No!" She couldn't see his expression in the dark. "Are you sorry we made love?"

"I'm not sorry about anything. But I'm not sure what the hell happened, and I feel responsible. Sex should be a mutual decision, not a random impulse."

"I thought it was a lovely impulse." She reached for him, but he wasn't there. "Tony, come back. You're not responsible for anything. I'm a consenting adult."

"Get some sleep."

His voice had gentled, but the click of the bedroom door told her that she was alone. She sank back on the pillow, overcome by a sense of despair. As an only child to older parents, she'd always felt alone in some ways, but never more so than at this moment. She could no longer question that Tony was attracted to her. He wanted her. He just didn't want to want her.

TONY STRETCHED OUT on the bed naked. He'd thought about putting on some pajama bottoms in case someone walked in, namely Melissa. But the room was dark, and he needed to cool down and think. He didn't like anything about the clumsy way he'd had to put her off, but there hadn't been much choice. What else could he have said under the circumstances? He still didn't know what the hell had happened tonight. It wasn't the first time he'd given in to a forbidden impulse, but this was different. He'd made a pact with himself not to take it that far— and he never broke vows. At least never before.

When had he lost control? It hadn't felt gradual, more like falling off a cliff into a pit of oblivion. Erotic oblivion. He'd been fine one minute—or reasonably so—and sinking with concrete tied to his ankles the next. He still didn't understand how she did it—and it had to be her. He wasn't like this with other women. He'd always had the control he needed when he needed it, even in his twenties. He made the moves, set the pace. But with her, he did insane things.

Like ask her to marry him.

Like break vows.

What was her secret? Why was she his Delilah?

He knew what had done him in this time. Crazy as it seemed, watching her struggle with the bodysuit had been the tipping point. He'd seen her naked from just about every possible angle, but her determination to sneak the spandex suit on under her clothing had confounded and enchanted him. Who did that?

He smiled. Couldn't help himself. All that tugging and wriggling? Much sexier than if she'd just stripped. Odd how that one incident had started a blaze that had whipped itself into a firestorm. Odder still how hot he still was now.

Could this really be a chronic case of sexual heat? He held the back of his hand to his forehead, wondering if he was coming down with something. Chills? Fever? Maybe a weakened condition could explain his lapse. Not to take anything away from Melissa. The woman was lethal. Few men would have put her in the category of femme fatale, but they would have been wrong. Mata Hari had nothing on her. Being around Melissa was like getting ambushed with one of those illegal date-rape drugs.

A sigh escaped him. This was bad. Now he was imagining illnesses, disasters and sabotage. He was turning into her!

He reached over to switch on the bedside light and knocked something to the floor. As he snapped the light on, he saw the bottle of pills Jeanie had insisted he and Melissa take. He'd downed a handful last night, and taken more during the day. He picked up the bottle and scrutinized the label. Ginseng, of course, but the rest of the ingredients were even more exotic. There was also red Korean ginseng, wild green oats, yohimbe, damiana, ylang-ylang, *Jasminum grandiflorum*, ginkgo biloba and zinc gluconate, to name just a few.

The list was long and every one of the ingredients sounded like an aphrodisiac to him. He knew yohimbe increased blood flow to the penis, which was the last thing he needed. Several European drug companies were competing to market the herb. What the hell had Jeanie been feeding him? It was a wonder he wasn't out accosting women on the street.

BY MORNING Melissa had decided that Tony was either a professional gigolo with a wealthy woman in every port or a secret agent for the publishing police, out to catch her and Jeanie in an act of consumer fraud. The latter made more sense. Gigolos didn't marry starving writers, which he'd done with great enthusiasm two years ago. Of course, maybe he'd spotted her creative potential and predicted their one night would inspire a bestseller. That would mean he was clairvoyant. Or a talent agent.

He'd told her they would talk today, and she already knew what he planned to tell her, unless she beat him to it, which she intended to do. Antonio Bond had rejected her for the last time.

She threw back the comforter and went straight to the bathroom, where she looked herself over in the mirror while she checked her pulse. Naturally, it was racing. Unfortunately, she wasn't ill. She looked in the pink of health, a woman in full bloom. No one would believe she was dying of some mysterious illness, for which the one symptom seemed to be horniness.

Dropsy. By the time she'd picked up her toothpaste tube for the third time, she'd diagnosed herself with the nervous disorder. Not dramatic enough, though. Or fatal, either. Horniness, now *there* was a fatal illness.

She wove her hair into a single fat braid, determined not to look in any way fetching. A little mascara, a little peony-pink lipstick. This was not the woman who just last night had fondled a gigolo's butt and offered him her breasts. Absolutely not.

The bedroom closet was the next step in the desensualization of Melissa. What to wear for a confrontation with the man with whom you'd had red-hot and very wet sex on the floor? Something that shrieked I'm not interested. A nun's robes? A burka?

She laid out several things and finally decided on a black linen sundress that was relatively prim and proper, if you didn't count the fact that it showed some cleavage and some leg. Once she had it on, and a matching pair of sandals, she checked herself out in the mirror. Actually, just the right amount of cleavage, she decided. Why not taunt the boy a little with what he would never have again? Not as long as he lived.

She took a turn in the dress, smoothing the fabric and adjusting zippers and bra straps, until finally she was satisfied. You would have thought she was getting ready for her first prom. That alone indicated the severity of her hang-up with him. She'd just spent forty-five minutes trying not to look sexy, yet make him drool with desire.

She bent a little to test the cleavage. Perfect. *Melissa, you look good enough to be the man's breakfast melons.* She was ready to go, but something held her back. Possibly the fear that she might be mistaken for a fruit cup and lustily consumed. Or slowly savored?

She looked longingly at the phone on the nightstand. Maybe she should call Kath to discuss this. No, she knew what her friend would say. *Have sex with him, Melissa! As often as you can. The rest of us would kill to be where you are—in a suite with* Antonnnnio. *His whispery voice gives me the shivers. Does it really make you orgasmic?*

At that point, Melissa would have hung up the phone. Interesting that the so-called sex expert had nothing but sex maniacs for friends.

She mentally squared her shoulders and left the bedroom. As she walked into the living room, she felt the warmth of the morning sun beaming through the floor-to-ceiling windows. Just beyond the open French doors, she saw Tony out on the balcony. He sat at the table in his robe, reading the paper and absently caressing the coffee-cup handle. The view was spectacular. Not him, of course, Central Park. Nothing Melissa loved more than a panorama of leafy-green trees and sunny blue skies. The impossibly handsome gigolo added zero to the scenery as far as she was concerned.

The aroma of freshly brewed coffee drifted from the kitchen, but she decided against it. Her nerves were alert enough. Since the French doors were already open, she made shuffling noises to alert Tony that he had company.

He didn't look up as she walked out onto the spacious deck. She waited a moment, taking in the veranda's bright contrasts. Bright red poppies and lush white orchids abounded in glossy black pots. The teak patio furniture had blue-and-white-striped cushions and a fringed umbrella that looked like an enormous sun hat. On the table, a large silver tray overflowed with goodies. Apparently he'd ordered up a continental breakfast. There was a thermal urn of coffee, pitchers of juice, a basketful of crusty rolls and pastries, and tiny crocks of honeys and jams.

She shuffled again, waited some more. Still he didn't look up.

Well, isn't this a cozy setting? she thought. The man at breakfast, reading his paper and drinking his coffee. The little woman waiting to be acknowledged.

Finally he peered at her over the sports section of *The New York Times,* and she forgot she was annoyed. Just for an instant she marveled that his eyes could be so dark on a sunny day. It would be possible to lose your way in the black of his pupils…and she had.

"Last night," she informed him. "That can't happen again."

He went back to the paper, muttering, "You're darn right it can't. You can't be trusted."

"Excuse me?" She stared in shock at the newsprint that hid him. When he didn't respond, she walked over and pushed the paper down. She was already shaking her head. "*I* can't be trusted?"

"That's what I said."

"I wasn't rolling around on the floor all by myself, Mr. Tiger Lover. *We* can't be trusted."

The paper hit the deck. He held up the bottle of herbal supplements that Jeanie had given them. "You think these sex pills might have had anything to do with it? They're loaded with ginseng and Chinese aphrodisiacs."

"Sex pills?"

"As in aphrodisiac."

She folded her arms. "What are you saying? That we were drugged?"

"We've been guzzling sex pills. You can draw your own conclusions."

Melissa picked up the nearly empty bottle and skimmed the list of ingredients. "They're herbal supplements, just like Jeanie said, and if anyone's been guzzling them, it's you. I never took more than the prescribed dosage." She studied him through narrowed eyes. "You have been acting oddly. How many of them did you take? Maybe we should go to an emergency room and have you detoxed."

"No emergency rooms. I was trying to make a point about the pills and what we did last night."

Ah, yes, last night. She set the bottle down in front of him. "Nice try, but I don't think it had anything to do with a few pills. I think it's us, you and me. We're like a lit match and a gasoline leak."

"With a wild green oats chaser." He rose and pulled out a chair for her to sit down. It was all very gentlemanly, but she liked being taller than he was. He offered coffee and rolls, but she couldn't be bought off with bribes, either. He helped himself to a warm French roll from the basket, broke off a crusty chunk and buttered it generously. Polite to a fault, she waited until he'd refilled his cup and was settled again before she continued.

"Just for the sake of argument," she said, "let's say the pills are having an effect. We can stop taking them. That's easy. How do we stop our—"

"Ourselves?"

"Our glands. This attraction we have is a physical thing, like a drippy faucet. Once the water's turned off, the leak is gone."

As she talked, Melissa watched the butter melt into the steaming roll and run over the side. Equally fascinating was the way several drops clung to one of his fingers, and he caught them with his tongue. His lids drooped for a second, as if he was savoring the sensuality as much as the flavor.

A breeze fluttered the flowers, and Melissa's stomach felt as flimsy as the poppy petals. She knew the sandy softness of his tongue.

"You think our attraction's just physical?" He took a bite of the roll, revealing a flash of white teeth as he began to chew. His jaw muscles made slow, beautiful work of the crunchy roll. It was like watching a dance.

"I do," she said. "Absolutely."

His tongue darted in search of buttery crumbs. "And how do you propose we turn off the water?"

God, he was sexy. Those eyes. That mouth and velvet tongue. Maybe she could just wade in the water for a while. Dip in a toe?

"I don't know," she said. "That's why I'm here, watching you lick butter off your lips. Maybe for starters, you could stop doing that? You could also stop doing that thing with the handle of your coffee cup?"

That produced a frown. "I can't eat or drink?"

"It's not the eating or drinking. It's the sexy stuff you do with your lips and hands. A grown man is not supposed to put his fingers in his mouth, okay? And you don't hold things, you caress them. I'm not saying you do it on purpose, or that you know I'm watching, although sometimes I wonder…like when you adjust yourself."

He held her gaze, daring her to look as he reached down at that very moment and rearranged things. Naturally her mind conjured up lewd images of what was happening beneath his robe. Those tan fingers moving dark and dangerous parts. He'd probably planned it that way. Maybe it was all a carefully constructed plot to drench her brain in hormones and impair her thinking. Maybe he wasn't Tony at all. Maybe he was an impostor, a saboteur sent from a rival publisher to drive her mad with wanting and ruin the entire tour.

Honking drifted up from the street below. The breezes lifted, the flowers fluttered, and Melissa's stomach joined the dance.

"Well, now I don't have to wonder," she said. "You are doing it on purpose."

"Like you're playing with your bra strap on purpose? I'm not the only one who adjusts things. You're always fiddling and fussing."

Damn, she was worrying her bra strap again. She didn't know whether to stop—or defy him and boldly continue. "It's a nervous habit. Not sexy at all."

"It's the sexiest thing I've ever seen. I'm insanely jealous of your bra right now."

She stopped. He didn't. He gave her low-cut sundress a lingering inspection with what could only have been called a smoldering gaze. Her face flushed. Her nipples burned.

"Listen here," she reminded him, "I don't whisper erotic things in your ear. Do you remember what you said to me last night? It was indecent, and that was on the *Larry Gunderson Show.*"

"But I wasn't the one wearing a skirt up to my ying yang, now, was I?"

"I didn't know you had a ying yang. Darn, I could have put that in the book."

He lifted the coffee urn. "Are you going to sit down and have some breakfast?"

"No, but if I did, I wouldn't play with my coffee cup."

A dark eyebrow arched. "And I don't play with my pearls or dangle my high heels from the tip of my toes."

"You wear pearls and high heels, too? This may be all the information I need to plug the leak."

His voice faked a husky tone. "I can plug any leak you've got, baby."

"See, that's what I mean. You shouldn't say things like that. You shouldn't even think things like that. You have to stop nibbling on my ear and touching me—especially those barely there touches, they're the worst—" She shivered as she experienced a flashback of those touches. "And this is big," she told him. "You have to stop looking at me like you want to drag me into the nearest closet and lock the door."

"Then maybe you should stop licking fruit juice off my palm."

"I was demonstrating something! And as far as my clothing goes, Jeanie ordered me to tart it up."

"So you haven't been flirting with me?"

Flirting? He thought that was flirting? She'd been flat out trying to seduce him. Her skirt swished as she walked past him to the wrought-iron railing and looked down on the city. When she turned back, his gaze was locked on her like radar.

"Okay, here's the bottom line," she said. "I'm setting some boundaries, and if either of us crosses them, there will be terrible consequences."

"Like what?"

"I don't know, but they will be terrible. I'll start, but feel free to jump in."

"Shoot."

She made a face. "Don't say 'shoot,' okay? That's a dirty word when it comes out of your mouth."

"That's one of your boundaries?"

"No, it's a polite request. I may have several more of them over the next few days. Meanwhile, boundary number one— No more smoldering, peel-me-like-a grape looks from those bedroom eyes of yours."

"Agreed. No more high heel dangling from those slutty toes of yours."

"No more whispering smut in my ear, thank you!"

"Fine, but you're not allowed to call me Tony Baby or Tiger Lover—and no more checking out my equipment."

"That was two, and I have never checked out your equipment."

She crossed her arms, and he rose from the chair, mirroring her. She squared her shoulders. He did, too. It was a standoff, but she had the last bullet.

"No more touching, kissing or sex, except in public. Do you agree?"

Melissa barely got it out before Jeanie breezed onto the patio, all decked out in a bright metallic pantsuit.

She gave them both a quizzical look. "What's going on out here? Why didn't anyone answer the door? I've been knocking and knocking."

Melissa turned away, arms still crossed. She didn't want Jeanie to see how upset she was.

Tony tried to ply the publicist with coffee and rolls, but Jeanie wasn't to be diverted. Melissa could hear it in her voice.

"What's going on with you two?"

"Nothing," Tony insisted.

Melissa turned at the same time, aware that her face must be flushed. She certainly felt hot and bothered. "Everything's fine, Jeanie."

Jeanie's eyes narrowed with suspicion as she looked from one to the other. "Okay then, you'll be excited about my good news. Your autographing's been canceled, so you have a free morning."

"That's the good news?" Tony asked.

"No, no, I have a much bigger surprise. We're going to crack Nielsen ratings records with this one." She stopped short, looking them both over. "Okay, what is going on with you two? Something's different. Have you been fighting?"

Melissa started to protest, but Jeanie was already shaking her head. She looked from one to the other, taking in their rigid posture, their folded arms and red faces. But it was probably the deep denial and profound guilt that gave them away. Body language was hard to hide, and Jeanie was a human lie detector.

"Oh my God," she whispered. "You two had sex! You did, didn't you? You had *sex*."

Chapter Ten

If you're smitten, kitten, let him hear you purr.
101 Ways To Make Your Man Beg

"HOW DO YOU KNOW we had sex?" Tony asked Jeanie. "Do we glow?"

Melissa gave him a warning look. "Stop talking like that or Jeanie will think she's right about us having sex."

Jeanie's *tsk* dismissed any hope of plausible deniability. "Oh, of course I'm right," she said. "Anyone would see it. Just look at the two of you. You're giving off enough heat to melt the polar caps. Global warming is *all* your fault."

"It was an accident," Melissa said. "It wasn't supposed to happen, and it never will again."

"Global warming?"

"No, the sex!"

Jeanie winked, and Melissa knew enough to throw in the towel. No sense prolonging the agony. Jeanie would have figured it out anyway—and not given up until she had a confession. Still, Melissa couldn't believe they were as bad as Jeanie claimed. She made them sound about as subtle as two wildebeests in heat.

Jeanie helped herself to a croissant and began to pick at it, popping feathery bits into her mouth. She'd dressed for spring in a striped slacks outfit that made her look like a pink-and-gold rainbow. Bright and pretty, but a little out of character for Jeanie, who usually wore black. Melissa had noticed something subtly different about her lately, but couldn't put her finger on what it might be. Was Jeanie glowing, too?

"You don't have to justify anything to me," Jeanie said. "You're adults and can do as you please in private. And it might not be the worst thing that could have happened, considering my news."

"Oh, God, the surprise," Tony said with a groan. Melissa groaned. Everyone groaned but Jeanie.

"Now, don't get negative," she warned. "I can honestly say that I've never come across a hotter promotional opportunity than this one, and it wasn't even my idea."

She peeled off another strip of croissant and nibbled it, making them wait.

"Well?" Melissa helped herself to a hard roll from the basket on the table and began to pick at it out of nervousness. The crumbs dropped to the balcony floor. In the blue skies above, a small flock of birds began to circle.

Jeanie finally relented. "Okay, you've both heard of reality TV, right?"

Melissa had. "That's where people get paid to be under surveillance around the clock. Cameras watch you floss your teeth and drool on your pillow while you sleep. They have no shame. They'll even record the gross stuff guys do, like scratching their privates and breaking wind."

"Sounds like fun."

Tony's comment elicited sharp looks from both women. He bowed out with a shrug and returned to his chair. Wise man, Melissa thought.

Jeanie addressed herself to Melissa. "You've been watching the wrong shows. The reality television I'm talking about is where *the* top-rated network chooses an absolutely fascinating couple and documents their absolutely fascinating relationship for a short period of time."

"How short?" A small mountain of crumbs had accumulated at Melissa's feet, and several eager birds were perched on the patio umbrella.

"Twenty-four hours."

"Hours? Did you say *hours*?"

"That's a nanosecond in the great scheme of things," Jeanie argued. "You wouldn't trade twenty-four hours for a lifetime of fame and fortune, would you?"

"Twenty-four hours of humiliation can feel like a lifetime."

"Oh, pooh." Jeanie dismissed her with a head shake and went to work on Tony. "Care to guess who the chosen couple is?"

"Are you looking at them?"

"That I am." She beamed, apparently charmed by his sense of humor. "You guys were so incredible on Larry Gunderson's show that the network is in a dither. They want you for your own reality show."

"Our schedule is booked solid," Melissa said.

"I've cleared the way," Jeanie assured her.

"How? When's this supposed to happen? Is there time to rehearse? We'll never be ready." Melissa threw out everything she could think of, but Jeanie was unflappable.

"The producers want to start this afternoon—and what's to rehearse? Their goal is to capture your relationship."

"We don't have a relationship!" Now Melissa was worried. "We're faking it, or did you forget?"

"Who was faking last night?" Jeanie asked in a superior tone.

Melissa threw up her hands, accidentally lobbing what was left of her roll over the balcony ledge. The birds dive-bombed in formation, and some poor passerby on the street below whooped in surprise.

"Tony, speak to her," Melissa pleaded. "Tell her we can't do this. Tell her why."

Tony tilted back in his chair and rubbed his unshaven jaw with one hand. "Sure, as soon as I find out what it is we can't do. Jeanie, what's the deal? What kind of show is this?"

"There won't be a camera focused on the throne, if that's what you're thinking, but there will be cameras in every room of the suite, including parts of the bathroom. For example, there'll be one trained on the shower stall, so you should let it steam up before you go inside."

She pressed on, clearly excited. "The network is betting millions of viewers will tune in to watch American's hottest couple behind closed doors. Viewers want to know how you keep it passionate, and secretly they're hoping they can do the same.

"Tony, tell her no. Tell her *why*."

Melissa wasn't giving up, and neither were the birds. Some of them had already returned and were eyeing Jeanie's croissant. She popped the last of it in her mouth and washed it down with a glass of orange juice. Melissa could have sworn the birds looked crestfallen. She knew how they felt.

"What's with you two?" Jeanie said. "It's not like you'll have to fake anything. You're human torches. Just be yourselves, and the rug will catch fire. Fight if you have to. The American public will love it when you make up."

How did she know about the rug? Was the suite bugged? Melissa struggled to quell her paranoia. Jeanie obviously didn't get it. They didn't want to be human torches, or at least Tony didn't.

"Maybe this isn't such a good idea," Tony said.

See. She was right. He didn't.

"It's a fabulous idea," Jeanie insisted. "The producers plan to organize the footage into episodes and air them on consecutive nights. They're predicting a forty share for the first show. That's twenty million people. If they pull even half that, we would reach more people with this gig than the rest of the tour put together."

The numbers gave Melissa a twinge. She'd written the book to break out of the negative spiral she was in. She barely made the rent with her magazine articles. This one show could turn the tide. It could be her ticket out.

"Did you hear me, Melissa? Did you hear those numbers?"

Tony tried again. "Jeanie, Melissa and I have been working out some ground rules for our *relationship*, and they don't include setting rugs on fire."

Jeanie picked up another roll and began to pace, apparently unaware of how much danger she was in. "All right, how about this?" she said. "You do this show, and your obligation to the tour is over. I'll cancel the rest of the schedule."

Tony looked intrigued.

He glanced over at Melissa, and her stomach dipped. She felt as if she'd been sitting in a rocking rowboat too long. He wanted to do it. He wanted to be free of his obligation—and of her. She'd been leaning toward doing the show, too, but Jeanie's deal meant everything would be over in twenty-four hours.

"We'd both be free to go our own way?" Melissa asked in a faint voice. "Will Searchlight let you do that?"

"They may not like it, but what can they do? I've already made a verbal offer to both of you. Will you do it?"

Jeanie waited, oblivious to the birds circling her head. Melissa stayed silent and so did Tony. Apparently no one was going to crack first.

"I guess we need some time to talk it over?" Jeanie bestowed a motherly smile upon them. "That's fine. I have plenty of things to do. I'll call you in fifteen minutes for your decision. Deal?"

"Deal," Tony said, coming out of his chair. "I'll show you to the door."

"Not necessary." Jeanie was already on her way back inside. "You talk her into it, Tiger Lover. I'm counting on you."

The front door slammed, and the two accidental lovers were alone again.

Melissa closed her eyes and wished the rowboat would stop rocking and the birds would stop circling. Maybe she was ill. Or pregnant. Could you get morning sickness after being pregnant one night?

"Want some coffee now?"

Tony's voice coaxed her. Melissa shook her head and wished she hadn't. "The cameras are going to be on us every second," she said with an ominous tone worthy of the late Vincent Price. "They'll expect us to touch, kiss, dangle high heels and fondle pearls. Everything we said we wouldn't do."

"Melissa? Why are your eyes closed?"

"I can't deal with this."

"Open your eyes. It's all right, baby. It's going to be fine."

His velvety tones made her heart pound. They reminded her of that moment in Cancún when he'd dropped to one knee and proposed. He hadn't wanted to be free then. He'd wanted to be tied to her, a knot that could never be undone.

What a foolish girl she was, thinking these things.

She opened her eyes and looked into his accusingly. "You promised you wouldn't look at me like you wanted to drag me into a closet, remember?"

"Right, I did—and I won't. It'll be hard because I want to drag you into every closet I see, but I won't."

Yeah, sure. "We agreed not to touch or kiss, either."

"That's true, *except* in public." He smiled at his own brilliance. "And what could be more public than television?"

"Or more fantastically awkward. Think about it,

Tony." He really did want to do this, in front of God and everyone. She didn't understand that at all—unless it *was* about wrapping things up and going on his way. Well, let him, dammit. She was fine before he got here, and she would be fine again. She hadn't even wanted him here. Her life had been rolling along quite nicely. Like a parade.

Suddenly she was more angry than hurt. That made it easier.

"If you feel that strongly," he said. By his look he'd picked up the edge in her voice.

She felt like tearing up more bread, but the growing flock of birds could have been auditioning for a Hitchcock movie. "No, I'll do it," she snapped. "Let's just get it over with— and while we're at it, let's get this whole tour over with."

"Are you sure?"

"Yes." Twenty-four hours, and she'd be done with it. She would take the money and run. He would get his annulment. Jeanie would probably get her own publishing company, and everyone would be happy.

He was still studying her as if he didn't know whether or not to believe her. "How about this?" he suggested. "No cameras in the bathrooms or bedrooms. I'll make that a condition of our being on the show. Would that make you feel better?"

Not really, but she couldn't admit it. And he wouldn't get it anyway. He really had no idea what was bothering her. "I doubt if they'll go for that. These shows have cameras everywhere. They don't want to miss a thing."

"Fine, then we won't do the damn show. Sound like a deal?"

A phone rang, and Tony fished his cell out of his bathrobe pocket. It hadn't been fifteen minutes, but Melissa could tell it was Jeanie from the conversation. Tony told her they'd come to a tentative decision and glanced over at Melissa for confirmation. She bit her lip and nodded. She was still biting her lip when he hung up the phone.

"Jeanie's going back to the network brass with our conditions. If they can come to an agreement, the camera crew will be here at one," he said. "That gives us better than three hours. Jeanie suggested we come up with a game plan. She likes the idea of several different scenes, blocked out like a stage play."

"What happened to 'just be yourself'?" Melissa sniffed.

"It'll be all right," he said. "I know you're nervous, but we can do this. Only a flaming exhibitionist could get sexy under twenty-four-hour surveillance."

"But we won't *be* under surveillance in the bedroom."

That gave him pause. "Maybe we shouldn't have insisted on those conditions."

"Maybe we shouldn't have agreed under *any* conditions," she muttered.

He scooped up the herbal supplements and shook the bottle. "If we do the show, these are history. No more drugs or alcohol in our systems, making us do crazy, impulsive things. We'll be sober as judges."

Melissa sank down in the chair next to him. It was true that all of their "accidents" had happened when they'd been under the influence. She'd been tipsy on Rum Mocambos in Cancún, and she'd been drinking wine that night in the kitchen when she'd had the bright idea of seducing him. And then, of course, there was last night on those ginseng things. She was still reverberating from that.

With a flick of Tony's wrist, the herbal supplements went the way of Melissa's roll—over the side of the balcony. Just as quickly the circling birds were gone. They'd formed another military formation, but no shouts came up from the street this time. Instead, someone yelled, "Hey, thanks, I could use a lift!"

Melissa wondered if anyone would catch her if she dived over the railing.

"What's the verdict?" Tony asked. "I'll back whatever you want to do."

Whatever I want, Tony? Really? Let's forget the reality show and bring some reality to this relationship. How about admitting that it was about us last night and not about some silly herbs? Or that you're still wildly attracted to me and not here for some other sinister reason? How about that, my pretend husband? Let's stop pretending.

A tiny fire burned bright within Melissa. Her desire to know the truth was almost as strong as her desire to protect her heart. And for a second, she thought she might actually say everything she was thinking. Let him answer those charges. Let him speak up in his own defense. But of course she didn't do it. She'd already put her hand out there and had it slapped too many times. She'd learned her lesson. Much smarter to laugh it off. Make some clever comment and be done with it. This was all for the good of the book, right? The network, the Neilsens and everyone else concerned? It was what she'd always wanted, right?

The now-familiar pep talk ran through her head: *You may never get another shot like this, Melissa. It's your once-in-a-lifetime. You wanted to break out, and this is your chance. Besides, it isn't just about you. Imagine how many people you'll be letting down if you don't follow through.*

She glanced over at Tony, managing a grin. "Think you could arrange for Jeanie to take a fall from this balcony? One of those freak accidents that will have New York talking for years to come? We could say we left her out here with the birds, but only for a moment."

"*Melissa.*"

"Okay, okay. I said I'd do it, and I will." She sat up in her chair and figuratively dusted herself off, waiting for him to join her. They had some serious negotiating to do.

"Okay," she said, all business. "How are we going to play this, hot or cold? The audience is going to be expecting hot. Everyone's going to be expecting hot, for that matter. But I'm thinking we could fudge. Maybe we could get by with lots of sexy talk."

Tony nixed her idea immediately. "They'll want action, and if they don't get it, they may just keep shooting until they do. You said you wanted to get this over with, so let's give them what they want."

"Flip a coin," Melissa suggested. "Heads, we give them hot talk and lots of it. We scorch their earlobes with our double entendres. Tails, we give them—" She saw where that one was going and stopped.

"Tail?" Tony grinned, fished a quarter out of his pocket and tossed it high in the air.

Melissa watched the coin twist and turn and glint in the sunlight. She said a little prayer.

"BABY, oh, baby, you taste like every kind of delicious…"
"You like that, do you?"
"Mmm, I need more honey."
"Where would you like it this time, Pooh Bear?"
"Right here in my mouth."
"My, my, look at those big sharp teeth."

Melissa scooped up some crème brûlée on her finger and got most of it into Tony's open mouth. The rest she smooshed on his lower lip and promptly nibbled off with lusty smacking and slurping noises. She also put a dollop of crème on the end of his nose and licked it up with her tongue. The buttery-rich taste made her purr with pleasure.

Tony added to the noisiness with a satisfied growl or two. A very happy bear, that one. And a hungry one, too. He popped her finger in his mouth, as if it were a lollipop, and drank up every last drop of crème brûlée. Melissa's stomach floated like the weightless cork it was. This adventure in food had been his idea, and quite an adventure it turned out to be. He'd whipped up the crème brûlée and a chocolate mousse, and they'd ordered up pies, puddings and a jar of peanut butter from room service.

Where would the mousse taste best? She hadn't tried that yet. His eyelashes? Earlobes. Maybe his toes! She still hadn't finished the lemon meringue pie on his chin, and he'd left some butterscotch pudding on her elbow. Thank goodness she'd worn a washable teddy. His cotton briefs were headed for the hamper, too.

"Cut!"

The bellowing voice startled Melissa, and she sat up straight. She'd almost forgotten the camera crew was there. Maybe it was the frosting that had practically glued her lashes together. She would have to shower for hours to get the gunk off.

"We're taking a break," the show's young male director announced to his crew. Tall and lanky in designer-label jeans, he turned in a circle, addressing everyone. "Go get some fresh air, people. I need a word with our *stars*."

Melissa and Tony exchanged a look. The only star on the set was their director. Jeanie had introduced him as *the* Bat Bohanan and raved about his background directing music videos. Right now Bat didn't look happy, but Melissa had no idea why. Surely he wouldn't accuse them of holding back. They'd done everything but throw food at each other. What did he want? *Animal House?*

Melissa had lost the coin toss. It was probably a loaded quarter, but she was a woman of her word. Tony wanted action, and action he would get. He might even wish he hadn't been so lucky. Talk about pretending. If this had been an Olympic event, she could have taken the gold.

Bat sauntered over to them, his hands on his hips.

"Is there a problem?" Melissa asked, blotting meringue from Tony's chin.

"I thought cuts weren't allowed," Tony chimed in. "Isn't this reality TV?"

"That *is* the idea." Bat anchored his sunglasses in his

dark blond hair, apparently to better scrutinize his stars. "Which is why I'm going to have to ask you two to stop hamming it up. Just relax, okay. Turn down the volume. This show is about who you are in your real life."

"Hamming it up?" Melissa batted her sticky eyelashes, pretending innocence. He probably wasn't going to buy this act, either. "But this *is* how we are in real life. We're all over each other all the time. Really."

One of Bat's eyebrows nearly went vertical. "You sit on each other's laps and smear food on each other?" He glanced at Tony for confirmation.

"Absolutely," Tony said. "She eats chunky peanut butter off my thighs. For breakfast," he added.

Melissa didn't dare smile. Both Bat's eyebrows were involved now.

"You don't think that might be laying it on a little thick?" he said. "And I don't mean the peanut butter."

Melissa concentrated on pulling a strip of drying crème brûlée from her cheek. Tony dipped up some of the chocolate mousse on his finger and ate it. Bat cleared his throat. Loudly.

"Okay, Tony was kidding about the thighs," Melissa admitted. "I am a peanut butter fanatic, though. I even put it on broccoli."

"That's sick," Tony murmured. "You're not getting near my thighs again."

"Are you sure you guys are married?" Bat squatted down, peering at the two of them like a high-school counselor with troubled students. "Wouldn't most husbands know their wife's weird little food quirks? I'm divorced, but my ex was a sushi nut, and nothing I could say would convince the woman that God put seaweed in the ocean for the fish. The point is, I *knew* her quirks. I could probably have finished her sentences if she'd stopped talking long enough. We had our own shorthand language, inside jokes, special looks."

Hard to argue with that, Melissa conceded. If Jeanie had been here, she would have had some clever answer up her sleeve, but Bat wouldn't let Jeanie on the set. He'd warned her several times to stop coaching his stars, but she hadn't listened. Of course, Jeanie wouldn't. And of course, she'd refused to leave the set. Bat had been surprisingly masterful, cupping her elbow and hustling her out the door. Melissa suspected this was the first time anybody had manhandled Jeanie and lived to talk about it.

Bat frowned at them. "To be perfectly honest, you two act like you're on a blind date."

"So would you if your eyes were glued shut with frosting."

Melissa chuckled merrily at Tony's quip. "Isn't he adorable?" She smiled in the face of Bat's skepticism and gave it her best shot. "Actually, Tony and I have worked very hard to reestablish the crazy unpredictability of courtship. You know, when it's all brand-new, and you're a little off balance. That newness keeps things very…"

"Tense," Tony offered.

"And that's good?" Bat said.

"Oh, very good." Melissa and Tony spoke in unison.

Bat nodded, but he didn't look convinced. "So what's the story?" he said. "How did you guys meet?"

"It's a great story," Melissa assured him. "But could we take a shower first? If all this food dries, you'll have to put us through a car wash to get us clean."

"You guys want to take a shower?" Bat popped up and yanked his cell phone off his belt. "Hold on long enough for me to get the crew back here."

"No, I didn't mean that you should be involved," Melissa said. "Give us some time to get cleaned up, and we'll start all over again, the real deal this time. Tony and Melissa exposed, okay?"

But Bat was already on the phone, ordering his crew back. "No cameras in the bathroom," he told his assistant director, "but we can get a shot of them walking into the spa with their towels on. Once they're inside, they can toss the towels out. You won't see anything, but you'll get the idea. If any bits and pieces show, we can always blur them."

Naked in a tiny shower stall with Tony? Blurry bits and pieces?

Not what Melissa had in mind.

Tony had the decency to look uneasy, too. But nothing could be done to deter Bat, and he hadn't breached their agreement in any way. The director couldn't have known that he was testing this crazy married couple to their limits, possibly even breaking their will to resist. He probably thought he was giving them a chance to calm down and cool off. *Naked in a tiny shower stall with Tony?* Melissa could almost hear her resolve snapping like a twig.

Within moments the camera crew had descended on the suite like a swarm of locusts. Melissa and Tony were being ushered into her bedroom, told to undress behind a screen—another screen!—and given towels that looked as if they would barely cover the essentials.

MELISSA STILL HAD her towel wrapped tightly around her as she entered the shower stall. Tony had already tossed his, and she tried not to look at any of his bits and pieces, but she had a challenge on her hands. He took up more than his half of the stall and he stood boldly facing her. She could tell him to turn around, but then she'd be dealing with the rear view. A quarterback's shoulders and rock-hard glutes.

"Come on in," he said in his velvety rogue's voice.

"I am in," she said in her witchiest voice.

Melissa dealt with stimulating mental imagery for a living, and even though she had limited personal experience, she knew what she liked. Those ads of naked men with water streaming all over their bodies were like an electrical current to her nervous system. Here she was *in* the shower with one of them. A girl could get electrocuted.

"Melissa! Throw that towel out here."

Bat had opened the bathroom door and shouted at her. Melissa ignored him, gripping the soggy material tighter. The terry cloth grew heavier and heavier as the spray soaked her down.

"Turn around," she told Tony, mouthing the words and making circling gestures with her hand.

"I don't want to," he mouthed back.

Obviously he wasn't going to show her the same courtesy she had him. Staring hard into his eyes, she whipped off the towel and snapped it over the stall. Naked. Both of them. Naked and glistening like starlight. The water pricked her bare skin like needles and aroused her nipples to rosy peaks. She didn't have to see it happening, she could feel it. He could, too. His eyes on her were as physical as his hands would have been. He might as well have been molesting her...and she loved the very thought.

Despite everything, she did.

There it was, the shameful truth. She *was* a hussy, but only for him. She hadn't been pretending at all. Not ever. She was in heat for this man. Out-of-her-mind-in-heat. She would do anything, cry like a baby, purr like a kitten. No self-control at all. She was a lost cause, and for some reason that thrilled her. Now she just had to be sure he didn't know it. How about that for a mission impossible?

Tony took in her taut, dripping curves with a rueful smile. He seemed to understand that this was going to be a painful lesson in restraint. She glanced at herself and saw what he saw—a silvery gown flowing over pink and white flesh. She did love water on a naked body.

"You look beautiful," he said, not bothering to disguise the words.

Melissa put her finger to her lips, signaling Tony to keep his voice down. No microphones were allowed, either, but

Melissa wasn't taking any chances on being overheard in any way, even by the naked ear.

He coaxed her closer with a crooked finger. He wanted to whisper in her ear, but she knew where that would take them. She edged closer, trying not to come into contact with his male protrusions.

"Bat is going to want us to talk about how we met," he said, half whispering, half mouthing the words. "Are you up for that?"

She nodded, absently aware of wonderful smells. Honeysuckle and clover. Had to be the soap. "Might as well tell them what happened. It's the truth."

"Except the part about you running out on me?"

"What?" She pretended not to hear him, and the crooked finger invited her closer.

Bat could just be heard muttering about uncooperative artists as he shut the bathroom door. Melissa breathed a little easier. She had been terribly nervous about being naked with Tony in the cold light of day—and sober at that. But maybe this wasn't so bad.

As fragrant steam rose around them, Tony pulled her into the circle of his arms and whispered in her ear, "We have to do this more often."

Their knees bumped and other parts touched. His arm brushed her breast, and she could feel him twitch and harden. Somewhere inside her a coiled spring of desire tightened.

"What?" she whispered back. "Play dodge the erection?"

He laughed. "No, meet in the shower. This is the only place they can't see or hear us."

He spoke the truth, and Melissa couldn't blame the whole situation on Jeanie. This was too diabolically inspired, even for her. The same fickle gods who'd put her and Tony together in the first place must be conspiring against her. Did they want her to make love with him again? Was it written in the Book of Life in the chapter on Melissa and Tony? They'd probably sent the birds, too.

Tony reached around her for something, and his erection teased her thigh. She had visions of stroking him, but knew that would invite disaster. The unintentional contact was bad enough. One deliberate touch, and Bat would be hearing some noises he wasn't supposed to hear.

Tony stretched even farther, and she locked her arms around him for balance. "What are you doing?"

"Getting this." He showed her the bottle of shampoo he'd taken from a nook in the shower wall. "There's whipped cream in your hair and I'm in a perfect position to get it out. Close your eyes."

She didn't even argue. She just gave herself over, knowing that having his hands in her hair might well send her to places she wouldn't be able to get back from. He squeezed a dollop of shampoo into his palm and drenched the stall with the sweetness of honeysuckle. Melissa felt as dizzy as a kid playing Spin the Bottle for the first time. She didn't want to slip on the shower tiles, so her only choice was to stay close to him and let him steady her against his body as he turned her around. He began to massage her scalp, working the rich shampoo into clouds of foam.

"You'll need to bend over to rinse," he whispered.

Melissa shuddered at the erotic image that flashed before her eyes. There was only one way to bend over in this stall, and that *would* be inviting disaster. Glorious, mindless disaster. If ever there'd been a moment when she had to stop herself with this man, it was now. This moment. *Stop.*

Chapter Eleven

Don't believe the popular wisdom. Men love intimacy rituals. Want his undivided attention? Let him shave your legs, his way.

101 Ways To Make Your Man Beg

TONY FELT MELISSA SHIVER under his hands, and his body zinged like a lightning rod. He grimaced at the pressure of overengorged veins and tightly cinched skin. If the lightning rod got any bigger there wouldn't be room in the shower for both of them, unless—

No, no, no, don't go there, Bond. That's begging for trouble. Kinky sex is the path to chaos and ruin.

So, of course, he didn't want to walk the path, he wanted to run.

Oh, the joys of sex from behind. Just the thought put him in a state of pulsing carnal bliss. And it was all for a good cause. Perfect way to save space. They would no longer have an awkward encumbrance between them. She was probably tired of bumping her butt against it anyway. And he was damn tired of being a human battering ram.

"Bend over?" she said. "I'm not sure that's a good idea."

"No, not a *good* idea." His voice was tellingly husky. "It's an excellent one."

She craned around to look at him, her eyes wide and

questioning. A glob of shampoo melted onto her forehead and headed straight for that blinking gaze. Another slid to the bridge of her nose.

She winced and scrubbed at the suds. "Ouch, that stings!"

"See what I mean? Rinsing is a must."

"Okay, but I can do it." She waved him away, but there was nowhere for him to go unless they changed positions entirely. Which might be an interesting dance.

She nearly banged her head against the wall when she tried to tilt forward. The second try, her feet went skating on tiles slippery with shampoo. Fortunately, it was a tiny rink. The third was her last solo effort. Teamwork had its advantages, lucky for him.

"Hey," she called back to him, "hold on to me so I don't fall."

"No problem. I've got you." He slipped an arm around her waist and watched her bend like a ballerina. Her beautiful bottom tilted up at him invitingly, and the sheer sensuality of it made his jaws ache. He sucked in a breath, but it didn't help. Heat rocketed toward his already steaming groin. With one well-placed thrust, he would drive it home. A groan caught hard in his throat as the idea resonated in his mind. God, how many problems he could solve with just one hot, aching thrust. The way she was wriggling, he wasn't certain she didn't have the same thought.

"Are you doing anything back there?" she asked. "I don't feel you doing anything."

"Would you *like* me to do something back here?"

The beating water had already washed most of the suds from her hair, and he hadn't touched her yet. Not the way he wanted to.

"Am I too far away?" Her behind swayed, pressing toward him. "Can you reach me now? Is that the problem?"

God, woman, don't press your luck. I'm about to

launch the shuttle here. With all her wiggling and squirming, she'd nudged his penis up and back until it was pointed toward the ceiling. Soon it would be burning a hole in his belly. Men had died this way, as he recalled. The cause of death was blood loss, all of it from the brain.

He bent over her to rinse her hair, and the pressure wedged him gently in the slippery cleft of her cheeks. She let out a moan that sent pleasure knifing through him. Did she want him to take the path of chaos and disaster? Beautiful chaos. Sweet ruin. His mind was as tightly focused as his shaft, and he could think of no greater satisfaction than to be encased in her while they were both encased in this steaming waterfall.

Not going to happen, Bond. You made a vow. To yourself.

He wound her drenched hair into a long knot and drew her head back, letting the spray catch the last of the soapy residue on her forehead. Her sigh turned into a smile as she reached back to touch his clenched arm. She couldn't quite make contact, but it was a privilege watching her try. From his vantage point, he could see her breasts shiver as she moved. Was there any sexier position to a man than having a naked woman bent forward in front of him?

God, he was ready, so ready he ached. But the physical pain reminded him he was being tested, and he intended to pass this time.

"Do it," she whispered. "I want you to."

Had he heard her right? No, he must have been hallucinating. But just in case, he asked, "Do what?"

"You know *what*."

"Do something else to your hair?"

"Tony, put it in, for heaven's sake. Do it!"

"What are you talking about? Sex?"

The frantic tension in her voice made him suspicious. Desperation was written into everything she said and did. She was throwing in the towel, giving up the battle with her good intentions. He'd lost that battle last night, and entered a world of pleasure and pain, heaven and hell.

Desire flashed like a match in the dark as he thought about making love to her again. Even his butt muscles clenched.

"Please," she said. "Let's just get it over with. You know we're going to do it anyway. We'll never last twenty-four hours. You're harder than the showerhead, and look at me! Naked and upside down in this tiny stall. Just do it, okay? Take me, dammit. I want you to."

Lord, was he being tested. "We can't—"

"Why not?" The pitch of her voice veered even higher, bordering on a cry of frustration. "Tony, why can't we? It's not like we're ever going to do it again. This will be our last time. The show wraps tomorrow afternoon, and we'll go our separate ways. Do you really want to be as hard as a plumbing fixture all night long?"

"It'll be all right. We can hold each other."

"Oh, don't be ridiculous. Do me and do me now!"

Okay, now he *was* hallucinating. Every drop of blood had evacuated his brain. "We agreed not to. We have ground rules."

Ground rules. How lame was that?

She gave him a sexy little bump with her butt, possibly unintentional. But at the same time, he heard a strange sound in the bathroom. It sounded like the click of the bathroom door. Bat and the crew must have heard her yelling, even over the noise of the shower. He hoped they didn't pick up what she'd said.

"Well?" she pressed. "Are you going to do it before or after I drown?"

"Shhhhhhhh." He placed his hand over her mouth and brought her back to a standing position. Half turning with her in his arms, he gestured toward the shower-stall door, letting her know that something was amiss.

"I forgot all about the crew," she whispered.

"That's what they're hoping you'll do."

She bowed her head, shaking it, as if in despair.

"Hey, it's all right," he said.

"No, it's not."

She could have been crying as she turned and gazed up at him through the spray. She looked embarrassed—inconsolable—and he felt as if his heart were going to twist out of his chest. He understood her frustration. He felt it, but as sympathetic as he was, he couldn't give in to it.

God, she *was* crying. Tears filled her eyes, and she tried not to let him see. She turned away, and he tugged her back, gathering her into his arms. She resisted him at first, but finally she rested her forehead in the curve of his shoulder and sighed.

The sound nearly broke him. It cut into him as nothing else could.

A moment later they were clinging to each other in the heart of the waterfall. He locked his arms around her, aware of the deep satisfaction it gave him to comfort her. But as the water crashed around them, and his head cleared, he asked himself the question that had rocked him last night. What the hell had happened? They were like two stars on a collision course. It was cosmic, and fatal. She was a total enigma to him, a mystery without a solution. Why had fate dropped her into his lap two years ago? And why again now? Apparently the first time had been impossible for her. This time was impossible for him.

But he wasn't going to think about that right now. He'd waited too long for this, for her.

"LOVE AT FIRST SIGHT. Do you believe in it?"

Bat directed his question to both Melissa and Tony. He'd been quizzing them with personal questions for the last fifteen minutes—with the cameras rolling. Most reality shows shot for extended periods and edited huge volumes of material into weekly episodes. This one was more like a newsmagazine with a looming air date and a tight production schedule. Interviews with Tony and Melissa would connect the candid segments.

"Well, not in the sense of Cupid shooting arrows." Melissa started to elaborate, but Tony spoke over her.

"We'd better believe in it," he said, "because that's how it happened, for me at least."

"Tell me more." Bat jumped in, forgetting for a moment to be cool.

Melissa was more than a little curious, too. She reached around the back of her neck, where perspiration slicked her fingertips. The air-conditioning ran at full blast but couldn't compete with the heat of the lights the crew had set up in the living room. The extraordinarily humid weather outside didn't help, either.

"Melissa doesn't know this," Tony said, "but I saw her first."

He rested his hand on her bare knee with a familiarity that startled her. Bat had wanted them to be interviewed on the living-room couch in the robes they'd put on after their infamous shower. Melissa wasn't certain how much of the shower activity the mikes had picked up, but she would have been uncomfortable anyway. She'd exposed far too much of herself, and not just physically.

"She was on vacation in Cancún with some girlfriends," he said, "but she used to take a walk every morning, alone, and she went past my restaurant."

"Your restaurant?" Bat motioned for one of the cameras to move in.

"The cantina where I worked," Tony said. "I started going in early because I didn't want to miss her. She looked so unhappy."

Melissa stared at the hand on her knee. "I looked unhappy?"

"You guys have never talked about this?" Bat hooked his sunglasses on the crew neck of his T-shirt.

"I didn't want to scare her off," Tony said, seeming caught up in the memory. "It felt as if I'd been given an opportunity, but I only had one shot. If I missed, she'd be gone, like a deer in the woods."

"And you were the hunter," Bat said.

"Corny, I guess, but true."

"I looked unhappy?" Melissa's heart had taken on a strange, erratic pattern. He'd been watching her for days before the morning they'd met?

Tony transferred his gaze to her, and she was struck by the length of his lashes, the depth of his expression. You could almost believe he meant what he was saying.

"I couldn't figure out how to approach you," he said. "I'm glad I did, though, because the night you showed up in my restaurant, I knew I was right."

"Right about what? My being unhappy?"

"About having fallen in love with you at first sight."

Melissa couldn't think what to say. She just stared at him, wide-eyed and stricken. Why was he doing this? He shouldn't make light about such things. No one should. You could get hurt joking about this stuff.

After what seemed like an eternity, Bat made a throat-cutting gesture, signaling a break.

"Okay," he said once the crew had shut everything down, "it's late, and the guys need a break. So do I, for that matter, but you two won't be alone. The cameras never sleep around here. How about some pillow talk right here on the couch? Tony and Melissa, why don't you keep your robes on—that way it'll look like you sleep nude—and continue this conversation."

"It's clothing that stimulates the imagination, not nudity."

Melissa's statement made every man in the room look at her as if she was certifiably crazy. She didn't have the energy to defend her statement. She didn't have the energy for anything at the moment, and especially not pillow talk with tripods and wall-mounted cameras directed at them.

"I have to go to the bathroom," she said. Bat and his crew were still watching her as if she might be a danger to society. With a measure of satisfaction, Melissa realized she'd picked the only room in the suite besides the bedroom where they couldn't follow her. Bat had tried to talk her into a wall-mounted camera in the bathroom, directed at her vanity so they could capture her cosmetics rituals, but she'd said no. She must have known she would need a refuge from all of them.

"IT'S ABOUT TIME you answered your phone! I've been leaving you messages for days. So? Are you having fun yet, just the two of you?"

The cheery question made Melissa wish she *hadn't* answered. Still, how could she not have? She was in the bathroom, taking off her makeup, and her cell phone had started playing the theme from *Last of the Mohicans*. Hard to ignore.

"Kath, I'm sorry. I haven't had a moment."

Melissa had no way of letting her friend know that she and Tony were on a TV show, or that this conversation might be caught by the ultrasensitive sound system. The producers had expressly forbidden them from telling anyone about the show, even friends and relatives. If the conversation was caught on tape, Kath would be told afterward—and given a chance to have the footage involving her omitted if she didn't want to participate. Melissa just hoped Kathy wouldn't ask any awkward questions that would require Melissa to say more than she wanted the mikes to pick up.

"Melissa, you there?"

"Kath, I'd love to talk to you, but it's pretty late here."

"Oh, right, there's that time-zone thing! Sorry, am I interrupting anything?"

"No, it's not that."

"Melissa," Kath blurted, "I met a guy, and I used one of your role-playing exercises on him."

"Really? Which one?"

"Shameless Hussy."

"Oh, my goodness, Kath, what happened?"

"I created a stalker. The man won't leave me alone. He sends me flowers. He writes me love letters. He begs to give me pedicures!"

Melissa smiled. Shameless Hussy was inspired by her night with Antonio, and apparently it was a foolproof way to get yourself into trouble. She should have started the chapter with a disclaimer.

A knock on the bathroom door preceded Tony's husky voice. "Are you decent? I hope not." He waited a moment, then opened the door and looked in, just the way a curious husband would. He certainly had the role down.

"Can a guy get a little bathroom time?" he asked.

"Sure, I'm done here." Melissa began clearing the counter of her makeup remover, cleansing pads and alpha hydroxy moisturizer. "I can finish my phone call in the bedroom."

Tony loomed in the doorway, blocking it as she approached. "Where are you going?" he said. "We love to be in the bathroom together, remember? It's one of our intimacy rituals. Chapter eighteen, I think."

He raised an eyebrow, indicating the bathroom door, which probably meant the camera crew hadn't left yet.

"Oh, right, our intimacy rituals. How silly of me."

"Might as well hang around and finish your conversation," he said. "This won't take me long."

"*What* won't take you long?"

"What I'm about to do."

Apparently he wanted it to be a surprise. She watched him study his reflection in the mirror. He ran a hand over the stubble on his face as if he was going to shave. What a perfect idea that was. "Let me get your shaving balm," she said.

"I have it right here." He crouched to search the cabinet under the sink.

"Intimacy rituals?" Kath was saying, obviously having overheard. "Isn't that sweet? Is he going to whiz? And by the way, what category does he fall into? Power tools or lethal weapons?"

In her book, Melissa had created a section about pet names for the male organ, and encouraged her female readers to use them, swearing that men loved to have their penises given macho names. Power tools and lethal weapons were two of the name categories.

"Kath, I really should go."

"Probably lethal weapons. He looks like he'd have a pistol to me."

Melissa lowered her voice. "Tony can be found in your grocery store's produce section."

Kath gave out a little squeal. "He's a cucumber?"

"A plantain."

"Isn't that a great big ol' banana?"

"A great big ol' banana from south of the border."

"Oh my God, Melissa, I'm so jealous."

"As well you should be. G'night, Kath."

Tony gave Melissa an inquisitive look as she clicked off the phone. She smiled brightly, the picture of innocence. He had his secrets. She had hers. She was starting to wonder if he'd really just come in here to shave.

Intrigued, she watched him unzip his leather travel case and paw through it, looking for something. A brisk citrus essence teased her senses as he pulled out a dark green bottle of cologne, some nail clippers and a cuticle brush. A wicked-looking straight razor appeared next, and his smile told her that he had finally found what he wanted. Must be a Latin thing, she thought.

"There is no smoother shave," he said, catching her eye in the mirror.

Melissa couldn't help but notice his heavy five o'clock shadow—or think about what the texture of his skin would be like when he was done. Cool satin. But when men shaved before bed, it was usually in preparation for one thing. Sex.

"You're going to use that on your face?" she asked.

"No, I thought…your legs. Have you ever had the experience?"

Her stomach dipped wildly. "Tony, I don't think so. I'm still trying to recover from having my hair washed."

He nodded and began to lather his jaw with a creamy white meringue that looked good enough to eat. "Let me know if you change your mind."

Melissa drew her lower lip between her teeth and bit down, trying to contain her excitement. She already had.

"SOFT ENOUGH?"

"Like a baby's bottom," Melissa said, smoothing her hand over the satiny skin of her calf. She sat on the vanity seat, and Tony was cross-legged on the floor, cradling her foot in his lap as he put the finishing touches on her ankle. Apparently, some very delicate maneuvering was necessary down there to negotiate the anklebone and the various other subtle curves.

Melissa sat very still, enjoying the new feelings. His fingers were warm and firm, and the straight edge tickled rather than scraped, as she'd imagined it might.

The "experience" of having her legs shaved hadn't been bad at all once she'd gotten used to the idea. Tony had wielded the wicked-looking razor with great care and finesse. Most of the time she'd felt as if there were boa feathers gliding over her skin. She'd actually found it relaxing, an unusual feeling in her relationship with Tony.

He finished up with the razor, rinsed it in the sink and

wiped the remaining cream from her skin with a steamy towel. She could almost feel her pores opening and sighing with happiness.

"Now what?" she asked.

"Whatever you'd like. Some lotion, maybe?"

Her ridiculously eager smile must have given her away. He snagged a porcelain bottle from the countertop behind him, poured some lotion in his palms to warm it, and began to massage her calves.

Melissa's eyelids fluttered. Now, that was nice. She could have slithered right off the vanity seat it was so nice. By the time he'd worked his way down to her toes, she was so relaxed, she was having trouble sitting up. This man's hands outperformed even Jeanie's pills. Even her mind was floating like a cork.

"How's that feel?" he asked.

"Mmm," was all she managed.

He rose from the floor and helped her to her feet, catching her as she swayed.

"What's next?" she asked, still floating. Such a lovely thing, floating.

"I think it's bedtime for baby."

MELISSA SNUGGLED deeper under the crimson silk sheet that she and Tony had pulled up over their heads. There were no cameras around, and the crew was gone, but they were both a little paranoid by now. And, anyway, having their own little tent created a feeling of safety and privacy they hadn't had since the show started.

Tony had propped a fist against his jaw, his head and drawn-up knee serving as tent poles. His dark features were bathed in rosy light, but his expression was one of confusion and tenderness. He seemed on the verge of asking Melissa a question, but she had to ask one first.

"You didn't mean any of that, right?" she said. "About love at first sight?"

"A big ol' banana?"

Apparently love would have to wait until they'd discussed produce. She'd lost the battle against nudity, so she was careful not to look anywhere but his eyes as she spoke. "Would you rather I'd said a string bean," she asked. "Could we talk about love now?"

"Sure, right after we finish talking about sex. Just for the record, string beans are a really unfortunate choice of side dish. They look bad, taste bad and sound bad. And while we're on the subject of sex, what did you mean by every damn day?"

"Every damn day?"

"That's what you said at the Plaza when the driver let us out—that you thought about our wedding night every damn day."

"I said *you* thought about it every damn day."

"And I quote—'You've been thinking about it every damn day, just as I have.'" He lifted his head, fixing her with his sexy expression that said I'm gonna love you within an inch of your life. "You included yourself, and you were furious at me."

"Well, that's nothing new. I've been furious with you for two years."

"Yeah? Well, it's mutual."

Somehow that encouraged her. Must be a sign of her desperation. "But you didn't mean that love-at-first-sight stuff, right? You just said that for the cameras."

"Actually, I did."

She punched her pillow, flopped her head down and sighed. "That's what I thought."

"I meant it, Melissa. I fell in love with you that first morning."

She stayed flat on the pillow. "You never told me."

"I would have if you'd stayed."

She shushed him without even thinking. It was habit by now. "I couldn't stay," she told him, mouthing the words.

"I'm not a fixer-upper, and you're not Don Quixote, even if you think you are."

He lowered his voice, too. "Am I supposed to know what that means?"

"You said I looked unhappy. That's a weird thing to be attracted to. Are you sure it was love and not pity?"

"Melissa, are you angry at me for falling in love with you?"

"I just don't understand why."

"Who knows why people fall in love? It's chemistry. You were the most irresistible unhappy woman I've ever seen."

"Um, sure," she said, wishing she could believe him. Obviously her self-esteem wasn't up to the challenge. But then why would it be, with him wanting her, rejecting her, wanting her again? If he had been so madly in love with her back then, why couldn't he make up his mind now? Of course, he might be protecting himself the way she was. Or protecting something or someone else. Whatever it was, she just knew he wasn't telling her everything.

She really didn't know which way to go with this. He was saying things she wanted to hear, and even that frightened her—that she *wanted* to hear them. Talk about thin ice. She could hear it splintering.

"Okay," she said at last, "let's say I buy this love-at-first-sight business. That was two years ago. How do you feel now?"

Of course, he didn't answer that question. And of course, the way he lifted his head and fixed her with his darkening gaze made her stomach float away—like a balloon on a string this time.

Chapter Twelve

There's a reason they call it making love. Put your heart as well as your body into it, and the sex will soar.
101 Ways To Make Your Man Beg

IT WASN'T Melissa's question that left Tony momentarily speechless. It was the answer that had almost spilled out of his mouth. He couldn't believe the thoughts that were rolling through his head. They were crazy, *impossible*. He felt his chest squeeze tight as he tried to talk, and maybe it was just as well. He wouldn't have made any sense anyway.

Melissa looked ready to pop, too. If her eyes got any bigger, they would tip her over. God, she was lovely. Clothes on, clothes off, she was irresistible in a way that had nothing to do with her looks. All that trembling expectation that the next ship on the horizon would be hers, all that sweet despair when it wasn't.

"Love you?" He cleared his throat of its huskiness. "I'm out of my mind, Melissa. I'm not safe on the streets I love you so much. They should put crazies like me in straitjackets."

Suddenly her brown eyes crinkled, taking on an expression of suffering. "You really shouldn't make light of things like that," she said.

He jabbed a finger at the silk ceiling above their heads and mouthed the words, "The walls are paper, and the cameras are likely still running." She was born for reality TV. They loved it when people made fools of themselves for the entertainment of millions.

"I'm not making light," he said, enunciating in case she'd been overheard. "I've never been more serious, Melissa, I promise you. I adore you, I do."

She looked more stricken with every word, and worse, she seemed to be sinking into the mattress. Maybe he should have stayed with the speechlessness. What had he done now?

"This is all a joke to you, isn't it?" She turned away from him and curled up, apparently so that he couldn't see her beautiful naked ball of a body. "You're not in love with me and probably never were," she went on in muted tones. "It must be the money. That's why you're here. It's the only thing that makes sense."

"What? What are you talking about?"

"Shhhhhh! The walls are thin."

"I don't care about the walls, Melissa. To hell with the walls."

He gave her shoulder a gentle tug, hoping that she would roll over and open her arms to him. He could almost imagine her coming into his embrace and letting him make it all right. Now, *there* was a *serious* thought.

But it wasn't to be. She stubbornly kept her back to him.

"I don't give a damn about the money," he said, lowering his voice. "If you believe anything I say, believe that."

"Then why are you here?"

He couldn't tell her, and that angered him. He should never have made the promise to Jeanie, but it had made sense at the time. The payback he'd had in mind for Melissa was strictly personal. He'd never intended to harm her career. He knew how committed she was to doing something with her life—and to paying back her parents as well. He admired that.

A silence fell around them, broken only by the catch in her breathing.

He contemplated her hunched shoulders and made a decision.

"You," he said. "That's why I came back. All I thought about was you...every damn day."

"You don't mean that," she mumbled into her shoulder.

"If there's a Bible anywhere in this suite, I'll swear on it."

Her breath seemed to whistle in her throat. For a second nothing moved other than the blink of her eyelashes. He gave her another gentle tug, and this time she did turn, rolling toward him with grace and urgency. The anguish in her expression was the sweetest thing he'd ever seen. One bright tear slid down her cheek.

"Get over here," he said, collecting her like a bundle of perishables.

She held back at the last minute, her hand on his biceps. "You came back just for me? You don't have some kind of deal with Jeanie?"

"It's not the kind of deal you're thinking of. I'm here because I want to be." He stumbled over the words because they weren't what he wanted to say. He didn't know what he wanted to say, but right now she felt like the only thing in his life that mattered. He couldn't grasp all the ramifications of that for his future, but he knew it was huge. It would change everything.

His throat felt as if it were paved with sand. "There's no reason in the world that I want to be here right now, except you, Melissa. You're my reason. Just you."

She fell into his arms, a heap of sighs and gooseflesh. "I think I'm falling in love with you," she said, struggling to control her voice. "Even if you don't love me, I think I am."

Her confession cut straight through him. He closed his eyes and worked on breathing normally. Only one of them should be losing control under these circumstances, and she was clearly already over the edge. He needed to be strong, but this was crazy. His temples throbbed, and his throat was on fire. The sensations made him profoundly uncomfortable, but if he stopped to figure out why, he might lose this feeling, this feeling that his heart was about to burst. And he hadn't felt this way in years, not since the morning he first saw her.

He brought up her chin and looked into her eyes.

Tenderness and lust consumed him in equal measure.

"This *isn't* for the cameras," he told her. "I love you, Melissa. I don't need to think about that. I know."

She made the strangest gurgling noise he'd ever heard. He had a hunch she was trying to say something but couldn't. He knew what that felt like, but never got the chance to tell her. Her fingers slid over his mouth, touching him in ways that made her needs known. The delicate pressure brought every one of his nerve endings alive. Her warm breath riffled his hair, but it was the dreamy softness of her breasts that ripped a sigh out of him.

He kissed her lightly and all hell broke loose. Desire sizzled between them. Tony's jaw clenched with how sweet it was. Heat jetted through his nostrils. She arched her back, and he pulled her under him, capturing her with the weight of his leg. She couldn't move, nor did she seem to want to.

Another sexy sound purred in her throat as she touched him intimately. Her fingers trailed softly along the inside of his thigh until she reached his sac. She cupped his testicles, lifting their weight in her palm, and blood flowed like a river into his already hard shaft. That was all the encouragement Tony needed.

He reached down to gauge her readiness and found her warm and wet. Her petals quivered under his touch.

"Tell me what you want," he said. "A velvet tongue, a wild pony, a very happy gardener? Your wish is my command."

"No games," she whispered. "All I want is you, and I can't wait another moment."

The thought of stopping may have entered his brain for a nanosecond. But he couldn't stop. He had a million reasons—imperative reasons—and none of them mattered. Only one imperative existed in Tony Bond's mind—making love with her. Now, in this suite, under these sheets, and stone cold sober.

"We can't make any noise," she whispered as he moved between her legs.

"The hell we can't. I'll get up and disable every damn camera."

"No!" She clutched at him. "Don't go anywhere."

A sharp sensation made him realize that she'd sunk her nails into his flanks. Every muscle fiber knotted in wild anticipation. She pulled him into her, and they both groaned with the savage joy of it. One thrust of his hips, and he was engulfed in the tight, slick heat of her. This was right. This was what they were made for.

He sank his fingers into her hips and locked the two of them in sensual combat. Heaven couldn't be better than this. Nothing could. He was sheathed in her luscious flesh and the desire to go slowly was the only thought that existed, the only reason he existed. She curled her legs around him, urging him into the rhythm of deep, mindless thrusting, and he surrendered with a hungry shudder. Pleasure moaned through him.

"Tony, it's love," she murmured. "Not liquor or aphrodisiacs. It's love that makes us so crazy."

Something wrenched deep inside him. She'd written a book full of erotic tips to make men beg, but there was no way to capture this in a book, this wildness she called love. You had to feel it. If he was begging for anything, it was to take her back into his life, into his heart.

He could feel her cresting. Her entire body tightened, especially the muscles that caressed his shaft, and she didn't intend to let go of him. A powerful urgency built inside him. He slowed his thrusting to delay his release, and she cried out, cursing him softly. She twisted frantically, urging him to pump, to bring her to completion.

"I feel it coming," she whispered. "Deeper, faster."

"I will do neither," he said, kissing her passionately. He kept his thrusting slow as she screamed into his mouth and came apart in his arms. Somehow, he held out against the terrible pressure building inside him, but when she raked his back with her nails, he lost the fight for control. Their bodies bucked and pounded, his climbing toward a release that felt as if it could rip him apart when it came.

She sobbed his name and a sensation more intense than pleasure flooded him. Something hot and wet stung his eyes. Tears? No, impossible.

When their breathing had quieted, he pulled her close. Almost immediately, she dozed off with her head in the crook of his shoulder and her leg draped over him. He listened to her rhythmic breathing deep into the night, never closing his eyes. He was glad that she trusted him enough to sleep easily. Knowing she felt safe gave him the sense that he might have done something worthwhile, despite this crazy mess of a book tour. But she didn't know what was coming, and he couldn't tell her. He could only pray that everything went well.

The crew would probably be back by the time they woke up, but Tony had a news flash for Bat Bohanan, and he didn't care whether the director liked it or not. In fact, Tony had a news flash for several people, and he sincerely doubted whether any of them would like it, starting with Jeanie.

The sense of relief he felt had been a long time coming. He took a deep breath and let it go. He could hardly wait to put his plan into motion.

MELISSA AWOKE to a sunlit chamber. Surrounded by a rich golden haze, she wondered for a moment where she was.

Gradually, she realized two things. She was no longer hiding under a canopy of silk sheets, and she wasn't in Kansas anymore. She'd also misplaced a bed partner. Or should she say husband?

"Tony?" She rolled over and checked out the bedroom, but didn't see him anywhere. She had no idea who might be around, so she didn't want to yell, and she didn't want to jump out of bed, either. Not nude anyway. Odd that the suite was so quiet. She couldn't hear the crew at work, and the bedside clock said 9:00 a.m. They should have been here long ago.

Another feeling crept into her awareness, but this one she couldn't put into words. Just a tingle of dread beneath her breastbone.

She shivered and sat up, covering herself with the sheet. Even the spring sun couldn't warm her up, but she wasn't going to let a fleeting mood bring her down. Last night had been wonderful. Shockingly wonderful. She was in love. Correction, *they* were in love. Who would have guessed? Apparently it had surprised him, too.

She smiled, remembering the look on his face when he'd admitted his feelings. Confession looked good on him. The only time he'd been even more uneasy was when she'd blurted out her feelings.

Time to find him and shock him again.

Inspired, she slipped on her robe and made a dash for the bathroom. She took a quick shower, toweled off and hurried to get dressed behind the screen. Having no idea what was on the shooting schedule for that day, she chose a khaki skirt and a red sleeveless turtleneck top in a lightweight cotton knit. For underwear, she slipped on one of the matching thongs Tony had bought for them. And nothing else. Breezy, to say the least.

Her butt did not fall into the category of thong-worthy, and she had no intention of a permanent switch from her one hundred percent cotton bikinis, but it would be fun

to see Tony's reaction when she revealed her fashion secret. She would show him at some appropriate time—or
better yet, inappropriate. She loved surprising him. That
could have been why she was born.

The suite appeared deserted as Melissa walked through
it. For a second, dread skittered back, tapping her with
cold fingers, and then she saw Tony out on the patio. His
white Polo shirt gleamed in the sunlight, and a pair of
khaki shorts showed off his long bronzed legs as he sat at
the table. Bent over a legal-size tablet, he seemed completely absorbed in whatever he was writing, but he closed
the notebook when she called his name.

"I missed you," she said, her voice breathy as she
joined him.

He was already on his feet, and she marveled at how fit
and robust he looked this morning. His black hair was as
rich and lustrous as onyx. His dark eyes were dangerously
bright, and his mouth was curved in a sensual smile. Love
must agree with him. As for her, love did crazy things to
her heart.

He opened his arms, and she wrapped herself around
him like a ribbon on a birthday gift. "Last night was wonderful," she said. "Did you miss me this morning?"

"Fiercely, but I didn't want to wake you."

"What are you writing?" She gazed up at him. "The se-
quel to my book, maybe? *101 More Ways* or *How To
Make Your Woman Beg*?"

"Neither, but that last one's a good idea." He laughed
and released her. Too quickly, in her opinion.

"Here, sit down," he said, pulling out a chair for her.
"I'll get you some coffee. We need to talk."

He poured her amaretto-scented coffee and set about
slicing her some coffee cake laced with cinnamon and
walnuts. Melissa sipped the coffee, but she was too nervous to eat anything, no matter how delicious the cake
smelled. She assumed their talk would have something

to do with the lovemaking—or maybe the missing camera crew.

Despite her nerves, her stomach rumbled at the sight of food, and she tried to remember how long it had been since she'd eaten. "Where's Bat this morning?"

Tony poured himself a cup of coffee and sat next to her. "When I got up, there was a voice mail from him saying he'd reviewed last night's tape, and they have everything they need for now."

"They have everything they need?" Melissa mouthed the words. "What does that mean?"

"You don't need to whisper anymore," Tony pointed out. "There's no one here but us."

"Were we noisy, do you think?"

"Even if we were, no one's going to know. I'm going to have a look at the footage and veto anything that's embarrassing. They had plenty of material without including last night."

"Do you think they'll agree with that?"

"They will if they don't want a hot-blooded Latin on their hands, threatening to block the show's release. I suspect I could find some publicity-hungry lawyer to take our case, and that's not the kind of buzz they're looking for."

He sounded serious, and Melissa didn't imagine Bat would want the show held up. She relaxed a little and broke off a bit of her cake, then looked up at the sky to see if the birds were back. No sign of them. A good omen, she hoped.

"You said you wanted to talk. Was it about the meeting with Bat?"

"Actually, no. I have a meeting set up with Jeanie this morning. In fact, I need to get going. With the traffic, it will probably take twenty minutes to get to the Searchlight offices."

"You need to talk to Jeanie? Why can't you talk to her here?"

Tony leaned over and took her hand, cradling it in both of his. He kissed her fingertips. "It has to do with my agreement with Jeanie and Searchlight. There may be forms involved, but it won't take long, I promise."

"What's going on, Tony? You're not going to tell me?"

"I'll tell you everything. In fact, I'll tell you my life story, right *after* I've talked with Jeanie."

He rose from the table and Melissa got up with him to walk him to the door. It didn't seem that she had any choice. "Am I going to get any clues?" she asked. "How about a game of Twenty Questions? Does this have anything to do with that secret you've been keeping?"

He angled her a quizzical look that told her she'd hit a nerve. But the man could cover well. His enigmatic smile gave nothing away.

"Aha," she said. "*Aha.*"

"Everything to do with it," he admitted.

"Aha!"

He laughed and pulled her into his arms for a goodbye kiss. "It will be all right, I promise."

His lips brushed hers fleetingly, but his main interest seemed to be in finding her left hand. Melissa presented it to him, and he fingered the ring she wore.

"Here's a secret," he said. "This band won't come off because it's not supposed to. It means our love was never meant to end."

Melissa gazed at the ring's woven braids of gold. "Did you just make that up to make me feel better?"

"No, I didn't make it up. The ring has been in my family for years. My mother gave it to me before she died, and she told me what her mother told her—that the ring means unending love. Of course, I didn't believe it at the time."

"Of course not."

"But then you couldn't get it off your finger, and I began to wonder."

She resisted the impulse to laugh. Maybe it was nerves.

"This is silly, but I actually wondered if the ring brought us back together."

"I did, too," he admitted, kissing her again. "Now go have your breakfast and relax. Our obligations to Jeanie and the tour are over. You have nothing to do today but wait for me to come back and explain everything."

"I'd rather you made love to me."

"I'll do that, too."

Giddiness brought a lilt to her voice. "I think you talked me into it."

"WELCOME TO MY humble abode." Jeanie called to Tony from her desk, beckoning him into her small office. "I'm just finishing up here."

A phone pressed to her ear, she waved him to an over-stuffed chocolate-brown and white couch. Tony remained standing, and she nodded at him, smiling brightly. Perfectly okay with her, she seemed to be saying.

He'd called at the last minute and she'd had to squeeze him in between her other commitments, so he hadn't expected her to be waiting for him. He hadn't expected her to be so cheerful, either.

Her office intrigued him. The small rectangular space had been made larger by the artful use of mirrors and false windows depicting the city skyline. A vividly blue aquarium set into the wall was, in fact, a screen saver for some kind of flat-screen monitor. *Nothing is what it seems,* Tony thought. Life was a series of charades, and his life might be the greatest charade of all. Maybe it was fitting that he end all that right here.

"That was one of the reality show producers," Jeanie said as she hung up the phone. "He's excited about the footage, says it's going to be a ratings blockbuster."

"Is that right, a blockbuster?" Tony made no attempt to disguise his irony. "Will we get our own talk show?"

Jeanie shrugged. "Stranger things have happened. And

by the way, I told him you'd asked to see a rough cut of the show before it airs. He said it could be arranged."

"Fast work, I appreciate it." He'd only asked her that morning when he'd set up the appointment with her.

"We aim to please. What else can I help you with?"

Jeanie wasn't one to equivocate, and Tony decided to come straight to the point. "I want out of our agreement," he said. "Melissa has a right to know what's going on, and I want to tell her. The tour's over, so it shouldn't have any effect on the promotion of the book."

Jeanie settled back in her chair, appearing to reflect. Finally, she said, "You're in love with her, aren't you?"

He didn't confirm or deny it, but Jeanie had obviously made up her mind.

"Melissa knows virtually nothing about you, Tony. Are you going to tell her that you aren't a waiter? That you own restaurants around the world and—"

"And maintain quality control by anonymously waiting on tables? Of course, I'm going to tell her that. I'm going to tell her everything."

She arched an eyebrow. "Everything? She won't react well."

"I have to take that chance."

"I can see that, but I don't want her hurt, Tony. This has nothing to do with the book or with Searchlight. I like Melissa. I care about her welfare."

"For God's sake, Jeanie, so do I."

"Then wouldn't it be easier if you just left, went back to your life and let her go back to hers. Do you really want to entangle her in your affairs?"

"I want her with me, and whatever that takes, I'll do it." He had conviction enough for ten men, but Jeanie had made a good point. His situation was messy, and Melissa could be hurt no matter how hard he tried to shield her.

"I know what you're thinking, Jeanie," he said, "and I won't let that happen. I'll do anything to protect her."

"I hope so." She scrutinized him like the mother of a budding teenage girl. At last she rose to shake his hand. "You take good care of her, hear? Any complaints and you'll have me to deal with."

Jeanie obviously had more to say, but their handshake got interrupted by a rap on her office door. Tony turned around to see Bat Bohanan himself loitering in the hallway. He had on his usual jeans and cotton Polo shirt, sunglasses hanging in the open neck.

"Bat, what a surprise," Jeanie said, blushing hotly.

The director jammed his hands into the pockets of his jeans. "I was in the area," he explained.

The awkward silence told Tony that he was the one interrupting. "Me, too," he said. "Just leaving."

He slapped Bat on the arm, and they briefly gripped hands. Tony glanced back at Jeanie to say goodbye, and noticed the red mark on her neck. Maybe it was her flushed skin, but the mark looked suspiciously like a love bite.

On his way out the door, Tony shot the director a grin. Now he knew why they called him Bat. He also knew why Jeanie was so cheerful.

A CLOCK CHIMED throughout the suite, and Melissa looked up from the suitcases lying open on the bed. She'd been trying to decide whether or not to pack while she waited for Tony to return. She had no idea where she would go once she did pack, but she needed something to do that would make her less anxious about his news. He'd said he loved her and everything would be all right, but she couldn't seem to make herself believe that.

If one was packed, one could always go. It was a rule of life.

More chimes. They rang and rang. Maybe that wasn't a clock.

The doorbell! She headed for the living room on a run. Tony must have lost his key card.

Puffing from exertion, she flung open the door. "That was quick," she said. "Oh, sorry, I thought you were—"

It was a woman at the door, not Tony. Melissa didn't know what to say for a moment, especially since this particular woman looked as if she was about to cry. She'd folded her arms, tilted her chin high, and her lush dark lashes blinked furiously.

Beautiful, exotic, defiant, hurt. All those thoughts flashed through Melissa's mind as she realized she hadn't said anything. "Can I help you?"

"Please, may I speak to Antonio?"

"Do you mean Tony? He's out. Is there anything I can do?"

The woman's almond-shaped eyes flashed angrily. "I think you have done quite enough. I want to talk to Antonio, please."

Odd that she called him Antonio. Melissa had begun to wonder if she was dealing with an overzealous fan. That happened when people became public personas, and Tony had proven to be extremely popular with the ladies on the tour. On the other hand, the woman had a Latin accent, and maybe this was all a mistake. She wanted some other Antonio.

"Are you sure you have the right room?" Melissa asked. "It's a big hotel. Could I call the desk for you and check?"

"Are you Melissa Sanders and did you write a book called *How To Make Your Man Beg*?"

"Yes, I did, but I still don't know what you're talking about."

"I'm talking about your husband." Her chin trembled violently, and she seemed on the brink of tears again. "He h-happens to be my fiancé."

"Your fiancé?" Melissa's first impulse was to shake her head. She'd never heard anything so ridiculous. Either the woman was out of touch with reality, or this was some kind of joke. On the other hand, maybe she *was* an obsessed fan. She was highly agitated and making wild claims. Both were red flags from what Melissa knew.

Stay calm, Melissa told herself. *If you're calm, she will be. If you don't panic, she won't.* She nodded at the woman reassuringly, trying to assess how dangerous the situation might be. At the moment, she appeared more hurt than angry. Now all Melissa had to do was get to the phone and call security without alerting her that anything was wrong. That shouldn't have felt so overwhelming, but she could hardly hear herself think. The sense of dread had returned, and it wasn't quiet anymore. It was screaming in her ears that something was terribly wrong here.

Chapter Thirteen

A sensual massage, role playing, sex toys…all of these are secondary. If you want to reach the heights of ecstasy, your heart is all that really matters. It gives meaning to all the rest.

101 Ways To Make Your Man Beg

MELISSA CONSIDERED her options. She could slam the door and lock it, but if the woman tried to block her, Melissa would have a fight on her hands. Right now she looked too distraught to put up much of a struggle, but anything could trigger her, and delusional fans could be violent. Melissa decided to try something she hoped was less risky.

"If you'll wait here a minute," she told the woman, "I'll try and reach Tony by phone. Who shall I say dropped by?"

"Tell him it's Natalie de la Cruz, his *fiancée*. Ask him what I'm supposed to do about the wedding? *Our* wedding. We were to be married next month."

Her batting eyelashes couldn't stop the tears that welled and spilled over. She fished a delicate lace hankie from what looked like a Gucci bag and tried to stem the flow, but failed miserably. Her lovely face was awash. Even her shoulders shook as she battled with her emotions.

Melissa shouldn't have been sympathetic, but suffering in any form was difficult for her to witness. As a child on the farm, she would mourn for weeks when one of the animals had to be butchered. She never got used to it, and finally her worried parents stopped altogether and bought what little meat they could afford at the market.

"Miss de la Cruz," she said, "would you like to come in and sit down while I call him? Perhaps that would be easier for you."

The woman peeked over the lace of her handkerchief, studying Melissa as if uncertain she could be trusted. Finally, she nodded, but her expression changed when Melissa touched her elbow to guide her inside.

"Where did you get that ring?"

Melissa glanced at the wedding band. Her visitor's horrified gaze was fixed on the delicate gold lace, and Melissa's first impulse was to say it was a friendship ring or something left to her by a relative, anything but the truth. Instead she remained silent.

Tear-stained and defiant, Natalie de la Cruz presented her hand in the way of engaged women everywhere. A huge emerald-cut diamond sparkled on her ring finger, left hand.

"Tony asked me to marry him on Valentine's Day," she said. "The ceremony will be at Tattershall Castle in Lincolnshire."

"How nice for you." Melissa wished she'd slammed the door.

Natalie sniffled and brushed right past her, her high-heel sandals echoing on the marble tiles of the foyer. Her ebony tresses fluttered with the breeze she created, and she didn't bother hiding that she was casing the place, apparently intent on finding someone lurking behind a doorway.

Melissa followed her into the room. "There's no one here but me."

"Are you going to call Antonio?" Natalie's elegant white silk pantsuit rustled as she turned to Melissa.

Noisy creature. "Yes, of course. I'll do that now." Melissa had never intended to call Tony. Her original plan had been to call hotel security and have them deal with Miss de la Cruz. Now that seemed like a very good idea.

Melissa casually walked to the wet bar and lifted the wall phone receiver. "Why don't you have a seat there by the window and make yourself comfortable. It'll just take me a minute."

Natalie hovered, watching as Melissa's finger dropped to the red button on the panel.

"What are you doing?" She rushed over, sandals tapping, hair fluttering. "If you're calling security, go right ahead. They'll come and escort me out, but you won't be rid of me, Ms. Sanders, because I'm telling you the truth."

Okay, Plan B. Melissa hung up the phone without dialing. "Miss de la Cruz, would you like some tea? If you'd just sit down somewhere, anywhere you'd like, I'll go fix some."

"Nothing, thank you."

"Are you sure? Biscuits? Tea and some lovely English biscuits? No?" *Plan C.* Melissa could feel the strain in her smile. "Let's try this. Since I don't know when Tony's coming back, why don't I have him call you? You could write him a note and leave your number."

Melissa indicated the hotel stationery near the phone. She was inviting Miss de la Cruz to sit and compose—the note, as well as herself.

"I'm not writing any notes, and I'm not leaving."

Now the woman's behavior was simply rude. Melissa couldn't help but wonder if someone had put her up to this. A practical joke? More reality TV? Whatever was going on, Melissa had run out of plans. "I wish I could help you, but—"

"Help me?" Natalie de la Cruz's dark eyes sparkled with anger. She clenched her tiny fists. "This is how you help? By trying to steal my fiancé? I saw the two of you on CNN in London. My whole family saw it. Now everyone's consoling me to my face and making jokes behind my back. I'm a laughingstock!"

Out of patience, Melissa marched straight to the door. "I'm going to have to ask you to leave," she said. "If you don't, I *will* call hotel security."

Melissa braced herself for an explosion. But Natalie began to cry again. This time she sank to the sofa and broke down in convulsive sobs. The lace hankie couldn't begin to contain her anguish. When she tried to speak, her voice wobbled and cracked.

"I'm not going until I—I see him," she said. "He hasn't called or written in days. I won't be treated like this."

Melissa had thought the woman was faking, but no one except a consummate actress could have faked this display of emotion. Her pain was palpable. That didn't mean she wasn't delusional, however.

"Please do sit down," Melissa said, "and I'll make us some tea. I don't know when Tony's going to be back, but if it's that important, you can stay. I'm sure he'll clear this up."

Natalie seated herself on the large sectional sofa, still blotting her tears. If she was a kook, she was a wealthy one. Her pantsuit was almost certainly an Armani creation, and she carried herself like a woman accustomed to the finer things. Her legs were crossed at the ankle, her posture impeccable.

Melissa left to get the tea. It only took her a few minutes to put together a tray, but that was more than enough time for unwanted doubts to creep in. She didn't want to think about whether or not her visitor was telling the truth, but the nagging concerns wouldn't go away. Tony had been harboring some kind of secret since he arrived.

They'd even talked about it, and he'd promised that everything would be explained when he got back from his meeting with Jeanie.

Melissa returned to the living room with the tray of tea and various goodies that she knew wouldn't be eaten. Sometimes just the presence of comfort food was enough.

She poured a cup and offered it to Natalie. "How did you and Tony meet?"

Natalie balanced the saucer on her knees and took a sip of her tea. She let out a quick sigh of appreciation. "It wasn't nearly as interesting as his whirlwind encounter with you." Bitterness tinged her voice. "But I did meet him at a restaurant, just as you did."

Melissa nearly dropped the bone-china cup she was holding. "How did you know we met at a restaurant?"

"Tony told me, of course."

Melissa just managed to get the china safely to the table. Natalie could only have known about that through Tony. Melissa had never revealed publicly how she and Tony had met until yesterday on the reality TV show, which hadn't aired yet.

Could she be telling the truth?

The door lock clicked before Melissa could ask the question. Both women looked up as Tony entered, a smile wreathing his handsome face. His gaze was locked on Melissa as he came through the foyer and entered the living room. He didn't seem to see Natalie at all.

"Tony?"

He stopped, confused. He glanced from Melissa to the woman who'd spoken.

"Natalie," he said. Disbelief swept over his face, and his entire countenance changed. The room seemed to go dark, as if the sunshine had been snuffed out by clouds.

Melissa thought she was going to be ill. He knew this woman.

Natalie's cup and saucer clattered to the table. She rose, wobbling on her heels. "I'm sorry, Tony, but I had to come. Are you angry with me?"

His face clearly asked, *What the hell are you doing here?* Instead, in a calm voice, he said, "I started a letter to you this morning."

Natalie gestured toward Melissa. "She doesn't seem to know anything about me, Tony. Why didn't you tell her?"

"I had good reasons, Natalie. The same reasons that you and I agreed not to tell anyone why I had to come here. We did agree, Natalie."

Her cheeks turned an angry red. "I didn't tell anyone. You did. You showed up on CNN with that woman, playing some game called Sexual Paste."

Tony registered surprise. "CNN in London? Since when do they air American talk shows?"

"Apparently marriages around the world are in need of some hot sex. See what a wonderful public service you provided? You and *her.*" She jabbed a finger toward Melissa.

"You knew I would be posing as Melissa's husband. I explained the situation before I left."

Posing? Melissa felt as if he'd slapped her.

Natalie's reaction seemed almost as strong as Melissa's. She glowered at Tony as if she wanted to slap him. "Tell her how much I mean to you, Tony."

"Natalie, why are you here? Why are you doing this?"

"Tell her how you proposed to me." She thrust out her hand. "How you bought me this ring."

Tony's jaw flexed. "The ring is a family heirloom, Natalie. *Your* family. I didn't buy it."

"But we're engaged to be married! Tell her that, dammit!"

"Tony?" Melissa could hardly get his name out.

The edges of Tony's mouth had turned white. Finally, he spoke to Melissa. "It's true," he said. "Natalie and I are engaged, but this is not how I wanted you to find out.

I just spoke with Jeanie, and I was coming back to tell you everything."

Natalie wasted no time vindicating herself. "You see. It's all true, everything I said. His marriage to you may be a fake, but his engagement to me is real."

Melissa couldn't make herself believe it, even now. "Is this for real, Tony? There aren't any cameras running, recording this?"

He heaved a sigh. "I almost wish there was."

"You're going to marry her? That's why you wanted the annulment?"

"Give me an opportunity and I'll explain how all this happened, Melissa. But not this way. Let me take Natalie back to wherever she's staying first—"

Natalie swooped like one of the birds on the patio and linked her arm in his. "Come on, darling, let's go. There's a car waiting for us." Her fingers curled around his wrist.

Tony pried her hand free and turned to Melissa. His voice grated like car wheels on gravel. "Will you hear me out, please, before you decide that I've been intentionally deceiving you? There's so much you don't know."

Melissa couldn't even nod. "Does she know about us?"

"She knows about our past…but not about our future. I'm going to need some time with her. Is that all right? It's only fair that she understands what's happened."

"Of course," Melissa said. "But there's no need to take her anywhere. I'll leave. I'll go right now."

She started for the door with no thought except to get out of the suite. Why hadn't she packed those suitcases?

Tony caught her arm and drew her back. "Where are you going?"

"Why didn't you tell me?" she asked him, her throat burning with pain.

"That was Jeanie's condition. It was the only way she would agree to a quick annulment of the marriage once the tour was over. She said you wouldn't go through with the tour if you knew I was engaged."

Laughing wasn't possible. Otherwise, Melissa would have been hysterical.

"I'm sorry it happened this way," he said, "but I'm not sorry it happened. I wanted to tell you. I wanted you to know everything."

She nodded, although in truth she couldn't hear anything but street traffic and screaming birds. Had someone left the balcony door open? The next thing she knew she was in Tony's arms, and he was talking to her, only to her.

"It will be all right," he whispered. "Melissa, I promise it will."

She wasn't able to cling to him the way she wanted to. Her arms wouldn't work. Nothing would work. "Tony, I'm afraid."

He held her against his chest, cradling her head with his hand. Natalie's toe-tapping could be heard, her impatient mutterings.

"I have to tell her about us," he said. "And I have to do that now. I should never have let it go this long."

"Go," she said. "Talk to Natalie. I'm all right."

"Stay here while I'm gone. Do you hear me, Melissa? *Don't go anywhere.*"

He released her, and she sank into the chair behind her. Her legs wouldn't hold her. Tony hesitated, but she waved him away.

"Please, just go," she said. "I'll be all right."

Reluctantly, he took Natalie by the elbow. Melissa couldn't watch them leave. She was heartsick. Quite a secret he had. His fiancée was one of the most beautiful women she'd ever seen, and she obviously loved him madly. Why would a man ever want anyone but her?

She had just begun to berate herself for being a gullible idiot, when the door to the suite banged open and Tony strode back in.

"What is it?" she asked him.

"I love you," he said, hesitating halfway across the room from her. "No matter what happens, don't ever doubt that. I *love* you."

Melissa was instantly terrified. "What's wrong?"

"Nothing, I just couldn't leave that way, without telling you."

She rose from the chaise. "Tony, what is it? Please, tell me. Oh, God—"

He stepped back, and she realized he wasn't going to tell her. Something had made him come back inside, and either he couldn't or wouldn't explain it. Reflexively, she began to pry the wedding ring from her finger. If she could get it off maybe the pain would stop ripping at her heart. Her knuckle burned as she forced the band over it. Blinded by a grief she barely understood, she held the ring out to him.

His face drained of blood. His cheeks sucked in with a ragged breath.

"Keep it," he said. "This is as close to begging as I will ever come, Melissa. Please, I want you to keep it."

She didn't have the energy to argue. The room seemed to spin, and she closed her eyes. Only for a second, but she thought she felt his lips on her forehead and his voice whispering that he would be back. The only thing that registered in her mind was the resounding click of the door as he left.

The ring fell through her fingers to the floor. It was an accident. One moment it lay cradled in her palm, a symbol of something precious and permanent, and the next, it was swallowed up in a white sea of carpeting. Lost.

She dropped to her knees, searching for it in the rug, fiber by fiber. *It was an accident. She hadn't meant to drop it.*

"ANTONIO, before you say anything, let me speak. There's something I need to tell you, and it can't wait."

Tony didn't like the sound of Natalie's pronouncement, but he felt an obligation to let her have her say. He was about to do something he would have given anything to avoid. It would change the course of both their lives, and he already knew the pain that could cause. Natalie deserved his undivided attention now, as well as his understanding.

"Glenlivet on the rocks?" She walked over to him with the drink she'd prepared, an ice-filled highball glass brimming with his favorite scotch. She'd even turned on the soft jazz he loved. Her hotel room was actually a spacious suite with expensive furnishings and a beautiful view of the city. The French antiques and fresh-cut flowers were all very much Natalie's thing.

"Thanks." Tony sampled the amber liquor, wondering why he couldn't taste it—and why he had never been able to feel what he should have for this woman. Her beauty defied description. Men turned in their tracks when she walked by. Traffic came to a halt. All the usual clichés. But none of that had ever moved him. Natalie had been a friend since their childhood days in Cancún. They'd grown up together, and their families had been pushing them at each other since they were teenagers. Tony had resisted until his mother's death last year made him realize it was time to stop drifting and make a decision about the direction of his life. He'd needed to let go of the past.

But he'd made the wrong decision, and for the wrong reasons.

Natalie held up her glass and clinked it against his. "To us," she said.

The back of his neck tightened. Was she saying goodbye or toasting to their future? He couldn't tell by the odd edge in her voice. Her smile seemed distorted, too.

"Natalie, there isn't an us," he said softly.

"What do you mean?"

"That's what I came here to tell you. Things have changed. Everything's changed."

"What the hell do you mean?"

"There isn't going to be a wedding."

She stepped back, her dark eyes lighting with a mix of shock and outrage. Her face reddened until it looked as if her skin were on fire.

Watching her reaction, Tony got the first glimpse of what he was actually dealing with. She wasn't just hurt, she was furious. Hell hath no fury...

The words that came out of her mouth were low and tremulous. "I won't let you go, Antonio."

MELISSA WAITED out on the balcony with the birds. She sat at the table, under the umbrella, absently aware of the sun beating down on her exposed knee. She was going to have quite a sunburn. With great effort she shifted her chair around and moved her entire body into the shade. Lord, it was hot. She ought to get up and make herself some iced tea. Her throat felt dry enough to crack.

The poor birds were as listless as she was, perched on the balcony railing, facing the patio door. Tony had an entire welcoming party waiting for him. The doorbell had rung not long after he'd left, and Melissa had nearly died of heart failure, but it was only the workmen coming to dismantle the wall-mounted cameras. That's when she'd come out to the balcony. She hadn't even noticed when they'd left.

She glanced at her watch, wondering what could be taking so long. Nearly two hours had ticked by. She could easily imagine Natalie becoming hysterical, and Tony, being Don Quixote, feeling compelled to stay with her until she was calm. Considering what he'd gone there to tell her, that could take a good long time. Natalie had not seemed very stable, and Tony really was too heroic for his own good. But his poor welcoming party would die of heat-stroke if he didn't hurry.

She shivered reflexively. Thank God for the heat. It seemed to insulate her. It kept her from moving, from thinking. All you could do was sit and wait in weather like this, like a sunstruck bird perched on a railing. Not even the notion that a dreaded disease was the cause of her shivering had entered her mind, which was a shame, really. Nothing could keep you occupied like a good hysterical illness. The only thing that hurt at the moment was her knuckle, where the skin was raw and fiery.

"MELISSA, it's Jeanie. Tony just called me from Kennedy."

The phone receiver nearly slipped from Melissa's hand. It was wet with perspiration. "Kennedy? What's he doing there?"

"He's going back to London."

"He's leaving?" Melissa whispered. "With Natalie?"

Jeanie cleared her throat. "Yes, sweetie, I'm afraid so."

A crushing weight pressed on Melissa's body. For a moment she couldn't think or breathe or do anything. The weight felt heavy enough to snuff the very life out of her, but then it was gone, and she began to shake.

"Of course, he's gone," she said, fighting to get the words out. "What man wouldn't go anywhere with that exotic creature."

"Melissa, *you're* the exotic creature. And he didn't go with her because she's beautiful."

"Why, then?"

"I wish I knew. He doesn't love her, I'm certain of that. He was at the airport, and either she was right there with him, or he couldn't hear me well. He thanked me for trying to help, but he didn't answer any of my questions."

"What questions?"

"Like what the hell he was doing? Like had he lost his mind?"

No such luck, Melissa thought. "Tony knows what he's doing. He knows." She swallowed over a raw, aching lump. "Why didn't he call *me?*"

"I don't know, but he asked me to tell you how deeply he regretted not being able to come back. He said he'd kept his promise, and one day you would understand. He also said that he'd kept his promise to me, although I don't know what he meant."

"What was his promise to you?"

"That he would protect you and not let you be hurt."

Laughter stabbed at Melissa's throat like a thousand sharp stickpins. "He promised *me* that everything would be all right. I'd say he fouled out on both of those, wouldn't you?"

"This has to be devastating for you. I'm sorry, baby."

"So am I, Jeanie." It was all Melissa could manage. Her eyelids burned, but she couldn't let herself cry. That would be admitting how bad this was, that it *was* devastating. It wasn't pride stopping her, it was pain. How would she ever deal with that much heartbreak? It would snuff the life out of her.

"Can I ask what you're going to do now?"

She unwound her legs and sat forward on the living-room couch where she'd been curled up since she'd come indoors. Her whole body ached. This may have been the first time she'd moved in several hours. "Go back to Kansas, what else?"

"Why don't you stay in New York a while longer? I haven't canceled all the appearances yet, and it would be easy to book more. At least you'd be busy and not sitting in your apartment brooding. You could even stay in the suite, if you wanted."

"I can't stay in this suite, Jeanie."

"Does that mean you'll stay in New York? I'll make arrangements to get you moved immediately. Another hotel, maybe the Peninsula. It's lovely there."

Jeanie was gone before Melissa could protest. How many times had that happened? Melissa sat there, shaking her head, dazed. She couldn't decide whether to call Jeanie back or go and pack her bags. She chose the latter. It seemed certain she was going somewhere, and that was all she cared about right now.

The last rays of sun slanted through the living room as she rose from the couch and stretched the stiffness from her body. A rich amber glow lit the room, magnified by windows that stretched from floor to ceiling. It was an effect worthy of a cathedral. Melissa should have been savoring it, but another flash of light had caught her eye.

She let out a little gasp of relief. Or was it dread?

Something gold glinted in the white carpet.

"WELL, it's all over now. You're free to go back to Kansas, Dorothy." Jeanie reached over to pat Melissa's hand. "If you want to, that is."

A brave smile seemed to be in order, but Melissa wasn't feeling particularly brave. She stared out the window of the limo, wishing Jeanie hadn't just reminded her that they would soon be back at the Peninsula Hotel, and some decisions were in order. She'd just completed her last day of book signings and the tour was officially over.

"Click my heels, and I'm home?" she said. "Maybe that's exactly what I should do."

"You're sure that's what you want to do? Go back to Kansas?"

Melissa shrugged. "What else is there?"

Jeanie peered at her with concern. "In case you haven't noticed, you have a hot book that's only going to get hotter after they air your reality TV show. The world is your oyster, Melissa. Be a celebrity, get a place here in the city and go to A-list parties. You can stay with me until you get settled. I have plenty of room."

"And the fact that my 'husband' walked out on me? That he's having our marriage annulled so he can marry someone else? What's going to happen to the book when that gets out?"

Melissa had received the latest missive from Tony's attorney that morning. He seemed determined to kill her, little by little, just the way he'd seduced her. Or had she seduced him? She didn't remember anymore. All she knew was the growing bitterness she felt toward someone she had once loved dearly.

In the two and a half weeks since he'd left, Melissa had kept the emotional demons at bay—barely—by working from dawn to dusk. Sleepless nights had been spent jotting notes for a new book idea that had nothing to do with sex, men or marriage. She'd titled it *The Joy of Celibacy,* but her heart wasn't in it. What joy?

When the attorney letters had started coming, complete with legal forms for her to fill out and sign, she'd wondered why they didn't just clamp her to a revolving board and start throwing knives.

"Okay, the annulment could be scandal fodder," Jeanie admitted. "At some point the media's going to find out, and we have to prepare ourselves for that. But it's not necessarily a bad thing. The fact that your husband deceived you takes nothing away from the book."

Melissa could hardly believe what she was hearing. How could it not affect the book? "To be honest," she snapped, "I don't give a damn about the book anymore, but that's *all* you seem to care about. And Tony didn't deceive me. You did."

Melissa's outburst surprised both of them. She'd been too stunned by Tony's abrupt departure to deal with it until now. She hadn't even realized how angry she was at Jeanie.

"I apologized for that," Jeanie said, quick to defend herself. "In fact, several times."

"I know you did. I just wish you'd told me about Tony's engagement. None of this had to happen, Jeanie. I wouldn't have let myself get involved with him—and I wouldn't be feeling like roadkill on the highway." Grief washed over Melissa, and her chin began to tremble. "Oh God. Just forget it. Let's change the subject, okay? Could we talk about something else, please?"

Jeanie brought her fingers to her mouth with a look of absolute horror. "I didn't realize, Melissa. Really, I didn't. I could see that he was falling for you, but I didn't know you were in this deeply. You seemed to be doing fine."

Pain thickened Melissa's voice and made it throaty. "Of course I'm doing fine." Of course she wasn't doing fine, but Melissa had to say it. Jeanie finally understood what she'd done, but it really wasn't her fault that Melissa had fallen in love.

"What can I do?" Jeanie asked. "How can I help? Please, tell me."

Melissa shook her head. What could anyone do? "I don't want to live in New York, that's for sure. I want to be as far away from the city and its memories as I can get, even if it means falling off the edge of the earth."

Melissa pulled at the ring on her finger, and then saw what she'd done. It wasn't there. Phantom-ring syndrome. People who lost a limb felt it for years afterward, sometimes their whole life. In her case, the sensation of wearing the tight band had burned itself into her nervous system. Was she doomed for the rest of her life to feel a ring that wasn't there?

"What are you doing?" Jeanie asked when Melissa bent to reach into her purse.

"Looking for something." Melissa's purse was on the floor by her feet. She kept valuables in a hidden zipper compartment, and it only took her a moment to find the delicately scrolled band.

"Here. Send this back to him." She put the ring in Jeanie's hand. "You must know where he is."

"Melissa, I can't. Ask me to do anything else."

"But you're the one who created the terms of the agreement—book tour, quick annulment, remember? You should send it back."

"He didn't give it to me."

Melissa was doomed. The ring seemed to symbolize her greatest downfalls and mistakes in life, and apparently it would always haunt her. She returned the band to her purse and then made another painful request of Jeanie.

"Tell me what he said before he left."

"Are you sure you want to hear it again?"

Melissa nodded. "Tell me. I'm still trying to make sense of it."

Jeanie went through the brief conversation again, and by the time she was done, Melissa was staring out the window once more, her vision blurred by tears. "I just don't understand. If you'd heard the things he said to me, Jeanie, his passionate declarations of love, his promises."

"Melissa, don't go there. You'll only make yourself miserable."

"Like I'm not miserable already?"

Jeanie sighed. "Maybe it was some kind of honor thing. He made vows, had obligations over in Europe, and he believed he had to keep them. He's staying true to who he is, his culture, and what he promised to do."

"He promised to be with me. He said he was going to make it right for us."

"Maybe he couldn't."

"Then he should have told me himself."

"Maybe he couldn't do that, either."

Melissa brushed away the tears and turned to Jeanie. "Do you know something? Are you holding back again?"

"I wish I did, sweetie. I'd tell you in a minute. I promise I would. I'm guessing just like you are."

Melissa's conflict about Tony and the ring was so great she felt as if she had to do something to resolve it. He'd told her the ring wasn't supposed to come off. It meant their love was unending. But the ring had come off, and their love had ended. He was marrying someone else, and she couldn't hang on to a wedding band from a sham ceremony anymore. Even if she didn't realize it, she'd probably been trying to keep hope alive when the situation was hopeless. She was afraid to end it and face the pain. But she hadn't been protecting herself from the pain, not really. She'd been prolonging it.

By the time they'd reached the hotel she'd made a decision. "I don't want to guess anymore, Jeanie. I want to get on with my life. Give me Tony's address, and I'll send back the ring."

Chapter Fourteen

Don't stare too long out to sea. What you're looking
for may be right behind you.
                  101 Ways To Make Your Man Beg

"TO MELISSA, whose dirty mind has vastly improved my
love life!" Kath Crawford raised her Lemon Drop mar-
tini high and saluted Melissa, who sat across the table.

Renee Tyler chimed in. "Guess who's retired her vibrator, thanks to chapter thirteen."

Pat Stafford followed suit, and the toasts got more
risqué.

Melissa smiled as her faithful friends lifted their glasses
and drank. The four of them were at Maggiano's in Kansas City, an Italian restaurant where they'd met to celebrate Melissa's return home. She'd actually been back
over three weeks, but with four busy women, it had been
difficult coordinating schedules.

It had been nearly double that time since she'd seen
Tony or heard from him. Six weeks today. The time she'd
spent with him felt like a fever dream now, something
dredged out of her unconscious by extreme circumstances.
The first time had felt that way, too. Maybe such intensity
was never meant to be permanent, rings and legends
notwithstanding.

"My pleasure," Melissa said, bowing her head. "Literally."

Kath grabbed her menu. "Which pasta is it that looks like a big long tube?" she asked. "Cannelloni? I'm craving it."

Pat snorted. "We'd better warn the waiters to wear codpieces."

"Their loss," Kath rejoined. "I have that Velvet Tongue thing down."

Melissa winced. "Do you think we might order dinner, *ladies?*"

Everyone deliberated over their menus, and Melissa finally decided on eggplant parmigiana, mostly because it bore absolutely no resemblance to the male organ. It turned out to be a good choice, but she had little appetite. Fortunately the dinner chatter was brisk and funny. Prior to the get-together, Melissa had caught up with each one of the girls individually on the phone—and made one request for tonight. No talk of Tony. She desperately needed to be distracted, she told them. She'd received the final annulment papers yesterday. She didn't tell them it had knocked the breath out of her. They were friends. They knew.

"Excuse us, but aren't you the nice lady who wrote this book?"

Melissa looked up to see a beaming older couple, hovering near the table. The white-haired woman was holding Melissa's book and a ballpoint pen. "Sorry to interrupt your dinner," she said, "but would it be possible to have your autograph?"

"Of course." Flattered, Melissa took the book and the pen. As she inscribed the title page, the woman chattered nervously about her husband, an elderly, stooped gentleman, who was leaning heavily on his three-pronged cane.

"Howard here doesn't have a flat tire anymore since we tried that Over the Moon game," she said. "He really liked that one. His shoulder's out, though. Could be dislocated."

It took Melissa a moment to figure out what a flat tire was. "I'm so sorry about your shoulder," she told Howard, genuinely concerned as she returned the book. Perhaps she would have to write one for seniors. "Maybe the Sexual Scrabble game would work better for you?"

"No worries," Howard croaked. "The doc's going to put me in a sling. We can hardly wait to see how that works, right, babe?"

His wife blushed. "Right, Howie."

Melissa's friends had gone quiet, but she could feel their eyes burning into her.

As the happy couple left, Renee stifled a giggle. "Your book should come with a disclaimer, Sanders. 'Don't try this at home!'"

It got a laugh, but Melissa wondered if Renee was right. Had the whole world gone sex crazy? And was her book responsible?

By the time dessert was served, the discussion had moved to the next getaway.

"How about Alaska this year?" Pat suggested. "Anchorage has a very favorable ratio of men to women."

"Men," Melissa grumbled. "Haven't you girls got anything else on your mind but penis-shaped pasta and men?"

"You may have had something to do with that," Kath reminded her.

There was little Melissa could say, especially with all of them looking at her again. Apparently she'd improved everyone's love life but her own. Certainly her parents had never seemed happier. After they'd heard at church about their daughter's bestseller they'd immediately gotten satellite TV in order to catch her appearances.

"You know we've read *101 Ways* from cover to cover," her mother had said proudly. She and Melissa's father had showed Melissa their dog-eared copy the day they welcomed her home. She already knew about her dad's sacroiliac from the *Nice Girls Do* show. Thank God they hadn't given her any more specifics.

They'd also been supportive when she'd explained about Tony. Her mother had hugged her hard and said something about time being the healer. Her gentle father had talked about finding his gun—and Melissa had loved him for it.

The Maggiano party didn't break up until midnight, and Melissa got teary as she said good-night to her friends. She drove back to her apartment feeling less alone than she had in some time. She had loving parents and supportive friends. She'd written a book that was changing people's lives, hopefully for the better. Surely her father's back and Howie's shoulder were exceptions in her readers' experiences.

She had much to be grateful for, much to look forward to—and in time she might even believe that. Right now the irony of her situation was almost too much to bear. Everyone in her life was blissfully happy, and as much as she wanted to be able to share in their happiness, it made her feel all the more lonely and bereft. Nor did it help that they were happy because of her. What kind of cosmic twister was that? Right now all she wanted to do was go home and sleep, and maybe not wake up until the clouds cleared and the sun came out again, however long that took.

But as she pulled up to her apartment house and parked at the curb, she noticed a limo taking up the space of several cars. It was parked a couple cars in front of her, and just inside the glass doors of the building, waiting in the small lobby, was someone Melissa knew.

Melissa's heart broke into a run that winded her before she was even out of the car. *What was Natalie de la Cruz doing in Kansas?*

"MS. SANDERS," Natalie said as Melissa entered the lobby. "Thank God, you're here. Can I talk with you? I know it's late, but this is important."

"Of course." Melissa hesitated, wondering if it was

safe to invite her up to the apartment. The beautiful Natalie de la Cruz looked drawn and disheveled. Her delicate features were pinched, her jet hair tousled. Red flags had gone up the moment Melissa had seen her anxious expression. Still, she was Melissa's only link to Tony, and what if something had happened to him?

Not five minutes later, Natalie was seated on Melissa's living-room couch, fidgeting with the gathers of her plunging peasant blouse, while Melissa fixed them both a drink. Natalie had asked for cognac, and it just happened that Melissa had been given a bottle for Christmas some years ago. She'd never tried the stuff before, but this might be a good time to start.

Melissa handed Natalie a snifter with two fingers of cognac and sat down next to her. "Are you all right?"

Natalie took a slug of the brandy, rocking the snifter in both hands. Or was *she* rocking? Her nerves were contagious, and Melissa could have used a slug herself, but she could barely get the snifter to her mouth. The fumes were so strong they made her want to sneeze.

"I've made a terrible mistake," Natalie said. "And I've left Tony." She'd begun to shake. Even another healthy drink of the cognac didn't help.

"Leaving him was your mistake?" Melissa asked a bit confused.

"No, I had to leave, or he would have."

Now *Melissa's* hands were unsteady. She gave the cognac another try and failed again. The fumes burned her eyes. "I don't understand."

Natalie looked up from the swirling liquor. "The day I came to your hotel suite I did something terrible. Tony called it emotional blackmail, and maybe it was. I threatened him with the one thing I thought might get to him...and I was right."

She stared at Melissa so intensely that Melissa finally said, "Me?"

"Yes, you. I told him I'd ruin you unless he came back to London with me that very day. I threatened to call a press conference and tell the world that your marriage was a fake, that you'd married Tony on a dare and hadn't seen him in years."

She slugged down some cognac, her mouth twisting bitterly. "That was all it took. He agreed to go with me and to say nothing to you about his reasons. I insisted on that, too, because I wanted to hurt you as much I wanted him back. But, of course, the instant he agreed, all was lost. His willingness should have told me how much he loved you—and that he would do anything to protect you—but I was too angry to see it then." Natalie presented her hand defiantly. "See, no ring. It's official. Tony and I are done."

"I—I'm sorry." This time Melissa got the snifter to her mouth and took a deep drink. The fumes didn't faze her. She probably wasn't breathing.

"Don't be. It would have happened whether you came into his life or not."

Natalie rose and walked away, her back to Melissa. She stopped by the bookshelf on the far wall and began to leaf through the collection of magazines that had published Melissa's articles.

"Tony and I grew up together," she explained. "Our fathers were business partners, and it was always assumed the two of us would marry. I was several years younger, quite naive and completely enthralled with the idea. I think Tony went along with it because it was expected of him. But when our parents pushed him, he stood up to them."

"Why? He thought you were too young?"

"I wish it had been that. He said I was like a sister to him, and he refused to marry me. His father kicked him out, and none of us saw him again until his mother died last year. He arrived just before she passed, and she begged him to marry and carry on the family name. It was her last wish."

"And he proposed to you?"

She released a sigh. "He did, and of course, I said yes. I was still naive. I believed the arrangement would work, but you can't force someone to love you. Tony agreed to go through with the marriage, even after what I threatened to do to you, but it would never have worked. He became remote and distant. He even opted out of a business deal with my father that would have made him a fortune." She hesitated, her posture rigid. "One day I woke up and realized that he would never love me the way I needed to be loved—the way he loved you."

Something brought her around to face Melissa, maybe just the relief of getting the story all out. "It would have been a marriage of convenience at best. At worse, he might have ended up hating me. I didn't want that."

Melissa wished she had something more than sympathy to offer. Natalie had done more damage than she would ever know, but she'd been deeply hurt, too, and it couldn't have been easy for her to come all the way to Kansas to admit these things.

Melissa tried to thank her, but Natalie waved her off. "I had to," she said. "I couldn't have lived with myself otherwise."

"What will you do now?" Melissa asked.

"Who knows? One day there will be someone else. But perhaps I'll read your book first."

"*101 Ways?*" Melissa feared for the men in Natalie's future. The drink had warmed her up considerably. She flirted with the idea of another slug, but wasn't sure she'd be able to get up from the sofa. Pretty good stuff, that cognac.

"Do you have a place to stay?" she asked Natalie. "There's only one bedroom here, but the couch is comfortable."

Natalie glanced at her watch, a heavy stainless-steel piece with an incongruous diamond-encrusted face. "Thanks," she said, "but the limo waiting outside is mine. I'm catching a red-eye back to New York, and I'm late."

As Melissa rose to walk her to the door, Natalie thought of something else. She spun around, her dark eyes glinting with purpose.

"I almost forgot to give you this," she said, fishing in her jacket pocket. "It came in the mail after Tony had already moved out. He doesn't know you sent it back."

Melissa recognized the ring box immediately. Her throat burned with resignation as she opened it. The lacy gold ring glowed, picking up every light in the room. She would never escape this ring. Even if Natalie hadn't returned it, somehow it would have followed her the rest of her days.

"Here, take this, too," Natalie said. "It's a letter Tony started to me when he realized he'd fallen in love with you. It will mean more to you than it ever could to me." She drew a crumpled piece of paper out of her pocket, and Melissa recognized it as stationery from the Hotel Da Vinci.

Melissa took the letter, wondering if she would ever be able to bring herself to read it. She began to smooth the paper's edges.

"You'll find Tony at a lovely old restaurant in Brussels," Natalie said. "If you still love him, you'll know what to do."

"What? I should go there?"

"Of course you should! He's pining for you, Melissa. But he'll never make the first move. He believes he's ruined your life, and you're better off without him."

With that, Natalie dashed out, leaving Melissa to stare at the door and wonder what she should do. Had Tony ruined her life? It was true that he'd disappeared with barely a word, but she'd done the same thing to him. Maybe there was some kind of balance in that? It was all so confusing.

She went to the couch and sat down, cradling the ring box in her lap while she opened the letter.

Natalie, by the time you read this, I will be on my way back to London to meet with you and try to explain what's happened in my life. I know you haven't heard from me recently, and I apologize for that. I've had some realizations that we need to talk about. How do I explain my heart to you? How do I tell you all that has happened to me since I've been gone? Please let me try. And if you can, read this letter with an open mind. First, know that I have always cared deeply about you. I wish I could love you the way you deserve to be loved. But those feelings aren't there. I would have given you my heart gladly, except that I didn't have it to give. I lost it two years ago...

That was as far as he got with the letter, but Melissa didn't have to read another word.

BRAMBLE ROSES lay like a coverlet across the cottage's thatched roof. Spilling over the eves in lacy bowers, fat pink blossoms created an awning for the row of shuttered windows below. A tourist on the cobbled lane would never have taken the quaint old structure for an exclusive restaurant. It looked as if it had sprung life-size from the pages of a Grimm's fairy tale.

Fourteen Rue des Fleurs. Street of flowers? Even the address was quaint.

Melissa might have missed the restaurant if not for the sign painter working out front. He'd just finished painting the establishment's name on the Dutch door's glass upper panel, and now he was hard at work on something below it. Melissa couldn't read what it said, but she thought it might be the proprietor's name.

A hand-written card filled one windowpane, pronouncing the restaurant open for business. People milled around inside, but Melissa couldn't tell if they were waiters or customers. Was Tony one of them? Her heart seemed to float at the possibility. What would she do when she saw him? Probably expire. All the blood in her body would rush to her toes, and she would go into cardiac arrest and have to be taken to the hospital, where they would hook her up to life support. Doctors would huddle over her, fighting to save her life, and Tony would pace the halls, cursing, begging, tears in his eyes.

That's how she would make her husband beg.

Chill, woman! She gave her imagination a mental thwack, silencing it.

The sign painter gallantly opened the door for her as she approached.

"*Merci,*" she said as she slipped inside. It was two in the afternoon, and a number of diners still lingered over lunch and glasses of wine. Delicious smells of sizzling butter and garlic emanated from the kitchen, making Melissa's stomach rumble. She'd flown all night, and she'd slept and eaten very little. It had been a whirlwind decision and a whirlwind trip. But now that she was here she had no idea what she was going to do.

The restaurant was as charming inside as out, with long white linen tablecloths and fresh-cut roses everywhere you looked. Lining the walls were intricately carved wooden booths with curtains for privacy. Everything down to the china appeared to be handcrafted. But no sign of Tony. She hoped he still worked here. He seemed to have an almost nomadic existence—Cancún, London, now Brussels.

She spotted a table near a large potted plant that looked as if it might give her some cover. A place to observe without being observed. Head ducked, she walked over and sat down. The menus were parchment sheets, hand-written in a beautiful script that resembled calligraphy. Fortunately, they were plenty large enough to shield her face.

She could read very little of the totally French menu, but
pretended to study it anyway. Within moments, she heard
someone coming her way.

"*Que voudriez-vous?*" her waiter asked in a deep, sensual voice.

"I don't speak French."

"What would you like, *mademoiselle?*"

A glance beneath the bottom edge of the menu revealed
the man's shoes. They were woven leather sandals. Although she couldn't see his feet well enough to recognize
them, she did recognize the voice. If he'd whispered at that
moment she would probably have had an orgasm.

"What's your special?" she asked.

"Special, *mademoiselle?*"

"Yes, don't you have a luncheon special?"

"Ah, the seafood stew with mussels. Would you like
that then?"

She continued to speak into the menu. "No, thank you.
I'm not fond of mussels. *Unless they're attached to a certain man. Those I rather like.*

"Do you see something you are fond of?"

"Yes, I do."

"What would you like, *mademoiselle?*"

In a very soft, very deliberate voice she said, "Actually,
I'd like you on a skewer for leaving me the way you did.
If I can't have that, perhaps you'd like to propose. Again."

The menu dropped and so did Antonio's jaw. Melissa
dangled her high heel from her toe and casually played
with the pearls at her neck.

"How many times does a man have to marry you?"
He laughed out loud. "How many times, my lost-and-
found wife?"

He pulled off his apron, tossed it aside and tugged her
to her feet. "Smile for me," he said, holding her at arm's
length so he could look at her. "Smile and set fire to my
heart."

Melissa smiled through tears of joy. She burned with happiness and another emotion that might have surprised him—pride. He would never know what courage it had taken for her to make the trip, not having any idea what to expect or whether he would even want to see her. Two years ago, she had run from him as fast as she could, but today she was facing her fears. Today she'd run to him. In the past few weeks, with everything they'd been through and all the risks they'd taken, she'd grown enough to open herself to love.

He brushed a tear from her cheek, and his own eyes got misty.

"I want this relationship," she whispered. "I want you. I'm not afraid of my feelings anymore."

"I'm scared to death of mine." He shook his head, laughing. "Isn't that great?"

"It's perfect."

The rays that crept through the windows filled the room with gold, and reminded Melissa of something. "Look." She held up her hand to show him the ring that sparkled almost as brightly as she did. "It does seem to bring us back together."

"Never take it off. I want it to keep us together this time."

She nodded. "Let's don't mess with the legend."

Tony seemed to realize that they were attracting attention. He led her over to a quiet corner where Melissa gave his face a tender touch and draped her arms around his neck. She couldn't resist the impulse. She didn't want to jeopardize his job with a public display of affection, but she had to be close to him. She ached to be close.

Desire growled in his throat as he kissed her, a fiery little touch of his lips that left her yearning for more. Just as she was going to whisper something desperately erotic in his ear, he eased them apart, holding her at arm's length.

"Are you hungry?" he asked. "Would you like something after your long trip?"

"Hungry for you," she whispered. All she really wanted was him and one of the bottomless feather beds the country was noted for, but he obviously wanted to feed her—and cooking really was the sexiest form of foreplay when he did it.

"Yes, I'm starving—and this place is beautiful," she assured him.

"You like it?" He swung around, throwing his arm out, as if to introduce her with pride to his place of employment.

Melissa looked around her, taking it all in again. The lowering sun filled the room with a rich pink haze. Bramble roses curtained the windows, and outside at the door, the sign painter put the finishing touches on the last of his handiwork. He'd just finished painting the proprietor's name on the glass panel.

DNOB OINOTNA?

Melissa had never been able to read backward, but she glanced at Antonio and noticed his secret smile. What was that all about? she wondered. Next he would be telling her that he wasn't really a waiter.

Epilogue

One year later...

"TONY! What have you done to me?"

Melissa awoke to an alarming discovery. She couldn't move her arms. They were above her head and held fast by what felt like silk tethers. Her legs weren't going anywhere, either. Her ankles had been hitched to the bedpost with what appeared to be black silk scarves. When she raised her head and looked around, she could clearly see the predicament she was in. What she couldn't see was Tony.

"Tony? Where *are* you?"

He didn't answer, and her mind began to spin, whipping up its favorite dish. Panic. Maybe he didn't leave by choice. They were in a foreign country. What if he'd been kidnapped? It could have been revolutionary forces, if there was any such thing in Cancún. Whoever took him intended to hold him for ransom, and they'd left her bound to keep her from calling the police. But they wouldn't have used silk scarves, would they? And they probably wouldn't tie her to the bedposts, either, in her satin teddy.

No, this was the work of a cunning criminal, the same safecracker who'd stolen her heart.

She tugged at the ties and felt them tighten. Slipknots! She really *couldn't* move. Screaming probably wouldn't do any good. Tony had taken the hotel's honeymoon suite for old time's sake, and it was in a wing by itself. This was the room where they'd spent their wedding night, the room she'd fled.

So where had he gone? And what was she supposed to do in the meantime? Admire the red satin canopy above the bed? Count the folds in the ruched silk? Fat chance with her bent for paranoia. She'd already thought of several natural disasters that could happen while one was tied to a bed, helpless.

Screaming didn't seem like such a bad idea as the moments wore on. She took a couple of preparatory breaths, readying herself to shout, "Fire!" when the door to the room swung open. Tony walked in with a tray of breakfast rolls, coffee, juice and the morning paper.

"I see you're awake," he said as amiably as if he always brought breakfast to bound, half-naked women.

"You see that, do you? Do you also see that I'm tied up?"

He set the tray on the chest at the foot of the bed and barely gave her a glance as he poured coffee and slathered crusty Italian rolls with butter and jam. Finally, a cup of coffee in hand, he took the time to check out the situation, *her* being the situation. He actually folded his arms like an artisan inspecting his handiwork, and she detected more than a hint of self-satisfaction in his expression as he perused her spread-eagle legs. She must have kicked off the sheets sometime during the night.

He probably felt pretty good about himself that he'd managed to lash her to the mast without even waking her up. The pirate.

"You should wear black silk more often," he said. "It's good with your coloring."

"You mean my bright red face?" It would have given her great satisfaction to stick her tongue out at him, but that could have been mistaken for an invitation. The very coolness of his manner told her that he was in a dangerous mood. Her husband didn't ignore her unless he wanted her attention.

Okay. Two could play this game. She could be cool.

"May I ask why you did this?" she said. "And may I assume that you weren't going for a Scout badge?"

"It's this room," he admitted, looking around. "The last time we were here together, you disappeared on me. I wasn't taking any chances."

Melissa caught his fleeting smile and realized that he wasn't kidding, not entirely. It would kill him to lose her again, and this was his way of telling her. Her throat tightened so swiftly that she couldn't clear away its huskiness.

"The last time we were here, I was young and foolish," she said.

"And now?"

"Now I'm young and hungry." She strained against the ties, forgetting they were slipknots. "Get me out of here, m'lord, *please.*"

"Not so fast, vixen." He brought a bowl of fruit from the tray and sat down next to her on the bed. "Maybe I should feed you?" He plucked two grapes and popped one in his mouth. The other he kissed and offered to her.

Melissa allowed him to caress her lips with the grape, but she refrained from opening her mouth. Make him wait for it. What chapter was that anyway?

"Apparently she's not that hungry?" he said. "Then perhaps she'll appreciate my other surprise more—and reward her captor with a kiss."

"Your *other* surprise?"

Melissa didn't bother to hide her nervousness as she watched him take a newspaper from the tray. What was he going to do? Swat her like a naughty house pet? Now, *that* had possibilities.

He sorted through the sections until he found the one

he wanted, and then he thumbed through several pages and snapped open the paper. "Here we are."

The page he showed her was in the arts section. And right before Melissa's eyes was an ad for her latest book, *Begging Is Half the Fun!* It took up the entire page, and Melissa was totally dazzled by it. There were quotes from reviews she hadn't seen yet. Good quotes. A couple of raves even.

She tore her gaze from the ad and looked up at him, thrilling to his proud smile. "Untie me and we'll celebrate," she said.

A wicked gleam lit his eyes. "Let's celebrate and then I'll untie you."

Her face really must be bright red by now, heated by what his idea of celebrating might be. "How would we do that, m'lord?"

"Here's a thought." He bent closer. "Maybe we should make a baby so you can write a self-help book for parents."

That *was* a thought. She had a better one. "Maybe we should make a baby because it'll have your beautiful dark eyes."

"And your luscious lips."

He leaned over and kissed her, and Melissa no longer cared that her hands were tied. In fact, she rather liked it. That was the beauty of being a writer. *Research.*

THE SWEETEST TABOO
Alison Kent

To Muna Shehadi Sill and Jolie Kramer—
over 200,000 words written
and men remain a mystery!
Ain't it grand!

This one is for the man to whom I said, "I do."
I love you, Walt.

Chapter One

HE WAS PLAYING THE blues again.

The melancholy and menacing low-down sounds wound their way through her bedroom's open window, conjuring wild and reckless images in her wandering mind. Feet tucked beneath her in the bedroom's overstuffed reading chair, Erin Thatcher placed the open copy of Anaïs Nin's *Little Birds* facedown on the quilted throw covering her lap.

With her hands resting on the chair's padded arms, her head sinking into the cushioned back, she closed her eyes and listened. The rhythm worked the magic she'd come to expect from the sultry sounds, arousing the parts of her body the erotica had wickedly stirred to life.

She wanted to indulge in the sensations, to let the music take her places she hadn't visited in far too long, to offer her experiences rich with the sensual encounters and adventures her reading of late reminded her she was missing.

The guitar strings stroked velvet fingers the length of her neck, caressing her skin from her chin to the hollow of her throat. The singer's voice filled her ears with dirty words and sweet nothings, whispered suggestions of bodies belonging together and loving long into the night. Hearing so much in the music said a lot about the silence in her life.

Oh, the crowd at Paddington's On Main was noisy enough, but the downtown Houston, Texas, wine and tobacco bar was her career. A career she loved. A career she'd been destined for since first visiting the U.K. with her parents, standing but knee-high to her Granddad Rory behind the counter in his quayside pub deep in Devon's lush countryside.

But it was not a career that met her personal needs and desires. Neither her regular customers nor her co-workers—no matter how much she enjoyed the interaction with both—touched that part of her soul that knew there was more to life than the endless hours she devoted to work.

Hours she knew Rory would never have wanted her to spend, but how could she do any less? Paddington's was her legacy from the granddad she'd already lost. And she would do everything in her power to keep the bar afloat.

After all the years he'd devoted to her upbringing, the sacrifices he'd made on her behalf, the remorse of letting him down would be too much to bear. She couldn't chance losing his dream, not when she wasn't certain she'd ever recover from losing him.

Right now, however, at this moment, the one thing of which she was selfishly feeling the loss, the one thing her life was missing above all else, was intimacy of the most basic sort. One man and one woman. Simple and to the point.

She had friends galore, both here in town and in cyberspace. It was, in fact, the literary erotica her online reading group had chosen to read this month that had her so restless, furthering her discontent with this one part of her life—the only part of her life—in which she felt lacking.

And now he was playing the blues again.

She wanted to know who *he* was.

He'd lived in the loft above hers since, several months before, she'd moved into the newly converted, one-hundred-year-old hotel on the edge of Houston's theater district.

They crossed paths in the mail room, the tomblike space too small for the two of them and the mutual attraction which hovered like a heavy cloud of bone-soaking rain.

They ran into one another in the garage. His classic black GTO lurked at the end of the row where she parked her Toyota Camry, a darkly menacing presence lying in wait.

They passed each other coming in and out of the elevator on the ground floor. Neither gave the other wide berth. Instead, each seemed to have the need to test unspoken limits, to brush clothing, to breathe the same air, to measure the fit of bodies...

Enough already!

Pushing her way up out of the chair and dragging the quilt behind her, Erin padded across the hardwood floor of her bedroom, her socks slip-sliding on the smoothly grained surface. She pulled back the simple muslin panel along the antique brass rod and climbed into the window seat, tugging her sleep shirt over her updrawn knees and cocooning herself in the warm cotton knit and the quilt.

It was dark here, away from the single lamp she'd left on for reading. Here in the very corner of her room, far from the hallway door and the rest of the pitch-black loft, six stories above the ground. It was dark and it was cold and the clock was ticking its way toward 3:00 a.m.

But from here she could hear the muted noises of the traffic below, watch the brake lights and blinkers of the cars leaving the city's nightlife behind. And she could smell the smoke curling from the end of the cigar he inevitably smoked while the blues made love to the night.

She could so easily picture him, leaning on the window ledge, elbows bracing his weight, hand holding the dangling cigar, thumb flicking ashes from the end. He always wore dark colors—navy, burgundy, black and pine. Tonight, unseasonably cool for early October, her imagination dressed him in a crew-neck cashmere sweater.

He'd wear it loose, rather than tucking it into his jeans. The hem would bunch loosely around his hips, inviting her hands to explore the tempting skin beneath. He'd have on expensive black leather boots and his hair, cut short only on the sides and the back, left overly, rebelliously long on top, would fall over his forehead, to his darkly slashed brows and starburst lashes, skimming eyes an incongruously light shade of green.

Why she was playing fantasy dress-up, she had no idea. Except, perhaps, for the possibility that she'd never been easily intimidated. And that single personality quirk inspired her to figure out why the idea of actually sharing the building's tiny, slow-moving elevator with the man set her temperature on the same upward climb.

Or why she checked his parking space each time she pulled into hers, the skin on the back of her neck prickling hot at the thought of being caught alone with him in the ominously gloomy garage. Or why the click of his key in his mailbox, echoing in the small basement, resounded through her body like a shot to the heart.

Okay. Now she was exaggerating. He had to have at least one or two redeeming qualities or he'd wouldn't be living where he lived. She knew exactly the type of invasive background checks mortgage companies and tenant associations put a body through...unless that body had paid cash, another possibility that had occurred to her as the man hadn't kept any sort of regular hours since she'd known him.

Except she didn't know him. And so she shouldn't be noticing his comings and goings.

She was noticing both and far more. Things that a sane and practical woman would have the sense to ignore. Or at least to pass off as surface attraction. Shoulders accentuated beneath dark fabric. Legs confident in their long, rangy stride. Hands large enough and strong enough to palm a basketball. Or a woman's throat.

Erin shuddered. She had to be at least six degrees of sick to find his formidable aura intriguing. Her sex drive might be steering her thought processes but she'd be damned before her brain forgot how to apply the brakes. Brooding good looks did not serious boink material make.

For all she knew, he could be a thug of the highest order. The possibility of bodies beneath the floorboards wasn't much of a concern considering he lived on the seventh floor and she lived underneath on the sixth. Trafficking in narcotics or currency or plutonium, however, wasn't so easily ruled out.

Okay. Now she was borrowing libelous trouble. But wasn't trouble par for the Erin Thatcher course. If math and memory served her correctly, curiosity had already snatched away at least four of her nine lives.

Those were relationships, Erin. That's not what we're talking about here.

What was she talking about? Sex with an improper stranger? Ha! If *that* wouldn't make a perfect *Cosmo* headline, she didn't know what would. *Wait a minute.* A flash of memory flickered over her head and ruined the moody ambience. Throwing off the quilt, the music and her imagination, she jumped to her feet, sock-shushing her way back across the room. Hadn't she just seen another article...

She flopped belly first onto her bed, flipping through

the pages of the magazine she'd picked up earlier today. The magazine with the article that had caught her eye. The article about finding a Man To Do before saying, "I do!" Not that she planned to say any such thing any time soon.

But she did like the "go for it" sentiment behind the article. How cool it would be to ignore practicalities. To make entertaining conquests. To collect raunchy stories to share with her girlfriends. Not to mention having a hell of a lot of healthy naked fun.

And, thinking further, she knew two other single and sexually frustrated females who could benefit from a little living it up with a scandalously inappropriate man. Tess and Samantha both deserved to take a tumble with their own highly desirable Mr. Wrong.

Along with Erin, both women belonged to Eve's Apple, an online reading group devoted to literary temptation, from sensory enticement to intellectual appeal to the most basic and provocative exploration of adventurous sex.

Sex that not a one of the three of them were having.

Erin reached across to her bedside table where she'd left her laptop last night after spending too many hours in her office working on the budget for Paddington's upcoming anniversary celebration.

Settling back into the pillows propped against her headboard, she began composing an e-mail that she knew would raise at least one eyebrow in both Chicago and New York City.

From: Erin Thatcher
Sent: Wednesday
To: Samantha Tyler; Tess Norton
Subject: Magazine Article on Doing Men
Considering the reading group's recent fixation with liter-

ary erotica, I decided a themed and attention-grabbing subject line appropriate. ::snort::

Speaking of the group (and don't get me wrong—I adore the diversity of the Eve's Apple membership), whose idea was it anyway to spend an entire month reading Anaïs Nin? Did we need another reminder of the sad state of our sex lives? I can't believe I've let myself become so consumed with work, especially when Rory taught me better. And now with this do-or-die anniversary celebration for Paddington's...

Figures, doesn't it? The one time I could use a man to help me shag off a bit of this frustration I don't have one. Which brings me back to my subject line.

Here, girls, we have a veritable smorgasbord of unsuitable men. ("Rascals, rakes and rapscallions!") The type of man no girl in her right mind would settle down with but, hey, we're talking about a fling. At least I'm talking about a fling.

The article's title says it all: Men To Do Before Saying, "I do!" We know we'll eventually do the right thing with the right guy, but wouldn't it be great to do it all wrong first? With no guilt and no worries?

What do you think? Samantha? With all you're going through? Couldn't you use an uncomplicated sex fest? And, Tess. One of the men mentioned is The Playboy. How conveniently perfect, don't you think? <wink>

Why let men corner the market on fun when we girls have the same urges and needs? We can't possibly get into any trouble if we do this with our eyes wide open, right? Me, I'm taking The Scary Guy. Yes. The one I told you about. The one living upstairs.

I know, I know. You're both wondering if I've lost my mind. But you know I've never been one to jump out of my skin and these days its happening round the clock. Even now. I have goose bumps like you can't imagine. My bedroom window's open and I can hear his music and I can smell his cigar and I want to feel his hands.

I'm not sure how to pull this off since every time I see the man I forget how to put two words together. How do you tell a guy you don't even know that he's just won the bloomin' sex lottery? Love you both!

Erin scanned the e-mail for typos then hit Send before changing her mind. She shut down the system and returned her laptop to the bedside table, switching off the lamp and snuggling into down feathers and plush Egyptian cotton. She was ridiculously hedonistic when it came to the haven of her bed. And a haven was exactly what it was.

This one room was her personal sanctuary. She refused to bring business through the doorway, keeping Paddington's and all it entailed to her home office or the larger office she kept at the bar. This room was for dreaming, for reading, for letting her imagination run wild and indulging when she had a partner with whom to share her fantasies.

She'd meant what she'd said in her e-mail to Samantha and Tess. A relationship would come in good time for all of them. But this wasn't Erin's time. She had no ticking biological clock, no urge to hyphenate her last name, no desire to redecorate the red and gold harem of her bathroom with his and hers monogrammed towels.

Right now her focus had to be on Paddington's end-of-month anniversary celebration.

The bar had belonged to the grandfather who'd taken her in at the age of eleven, after a trip to the Serengeti had taken her parents and left her in Rory Thatcher's capable hands. He'd gone so far as to move from England to the U.S., wanting her to be comfortable growing up in the country she called home.

Rory had taught her not to pour all her energy into work but to save the best of everything she had for living. For the past year, she hadn't lived much at all. She'd worked her fanny off seeing to his dream of keeping Paddington's alive in the States after giving up the English pub that had been his life long before Erin had been born.

When he'd left this world three years ago, he'd only been fifty-seven, too bloody young to die. He'd lived a full and blessed life, right up to that very last minute. And Erin wanted to live the same. To grab the brass ring. To go for the gusto. To do all the things advertising guaranteed would make life the best it could be.

She smiled softly to herself as she began to drift off to sleep. She'd left her window open. Though the breeze was a little bit chilly, Erin remained warm, burrowed down in her bed and wrapped up in her imagination. The heat of the music blew warm liquid notes over her skin. The heated aroma of the richly smooth cigar teased her nostrils.

But it was the heat of The Scary Guy's hands as she imagined them roaming beneath her bedcovers and over her body, his fingertips tap-dancing the length of her breastbone, his widespread palm cupping the curve of her waist, his thumb tugging at the elastic edge of her string bikinis, that set her on fire.

Her hands became his hands, her fingers his fingers, the pleasure she found enhanced by sharing his taste in music and the imagined smoke of his fine cigar. Sensation became unbearable. Her skin burned and sizzled and sparked. Dampness grew, seeping and spreading from her sex to her thighs.

And her touch, his touch, swept upward to the source, stroking along either side of the tight knot of nerves where sensation centered, slipping through the slickness he drew from her body, fingering the soft pillow of her inner core where the pleasure of waiting bordered on pain.

When she finally came, she reached for the edge with abandon, crying out her release with a breathless catch, a sob of exquisite satisfaction that wanted to know his name. Replete, exhausted and tingling still, she turned to her side and curled her body around the lingering high.

It was only then, when the night closed around her and the silence set in, that she realized the music had stopped. Erin held her breath and, swore above the beat of her heart, she heard the beat of his.

Chapter 2

He watched her from the shadows fringing his world. Shadows that protected him from prying minds, prying eyes. Her mind, her eyes, her certainty that she held his salvation in the palm of her hand.

She was innocence embodied. Chaste and uncorrupt. And he was going to take her down, drag her to the gutter, show her the reality of the life he called hell.

She thought she knew him. He'd seen the brash confidence in her eyes. And he'd seen more. Flickers of quick-witted fear. A switchblade-sharp awareness. Vigilance. Watchfulness. She knew the truth. That once he got his hands on her she wouldn't want him to let her go.

He was certain that was the reason she hovered on the edge of his existence. He wondered how long caution would keep her curiosity bound. If her strength of character could withstand the destruction of her faith in mankind. In him. In herself.

Raleigh Slater choked back the crazed laughter eating at his throat. She wasn't the first. There had been others. Women who'd driven to the brink of his twilight, headlights cutting through the fog that concealed his dead end. He wasn't giving this one time to shift into reverse. Not until he'd fed her a taste of what she'd driven this far to find.

She'd never even know. She'd swear she'd been dreaming. That what she'd felt moving over her body while she slept had been nothing but the workings of her mind. Only Raleigh would know the reality of his possession. That what she'd thought she'd imagined, in truth, she had lived.

Sebastian Gallo saved the document and shut down his notebook computer. He'd had enough. Deadline or no deadline, he'd had enough. He needed a beer. He needed several. But he'd waited too long to go out.

The bars were closed for the night and now he'd have to put off until tomorrow what he needed to do today—to find a dark corner at Paddington's On Main and watch Erin Thatcher pretend he didn't make her sweat.

He needed to feel that edge, that cutting, biting awareness that he'd learned back when he was living on the streets and honed during his years in lockup. It was what kept him alive and kept him going. Fueled his high-performance artistry. Jump-started the creative bitch of a muse currently giving him hell.

A hell separate from her usual attempts at rewriting every word he wrote. No, this hell was harsh and demanding, a foot-stomping insistence that he set aside what she considered an unhealthy concentration on the macabre to write the book aching to break free from his heart. That's when he had to remind her that he didn't have a heart—the very reason he and Raleigh Slater got along so well.

Yep, he and Raleigh had more than a thing or two in common, but it was this latest obsession with a mysterious woman that was going to cause the both of them more than a man's fair share of trouble. Raleigh's problem was easily taken care of. Backspace. Delete. And his fictional world was set dead to rights.

The disruption to Sebastian's well-ordered life required more than fancy finger work. He needed sleep but was afraid his mental gears were wound too tightly to shut down. The cigar hadn't helped.

And the music, the blues, usually soothing in a twisted sort of way, had done nothing but speed up the beat of his heart, pumping blood into parts of his body that remained on edge no matter the intensity of his physical workouts. Or the long hot showers that followed.

He swore he'd heard her voice. After the music had stopped and before he'd put out the cigar and moved away from the window to reread the pages he'd written. The sound had crashed around him like lightning. White-hot electric jolts had nearly taken him out of his skin.

Now, minutes later, he wasn't sure if what he'd heard had been all in his head, a sound from the city street below, or the cry of a woman in the throes of pure bliss.

Sebastian laughed under his breath, muttering a curse that had nothing to do with the woman living below him and everything to do with his obsession instead. He shucked off his sweater, scratched the ball of black wool over his chest before tossing it to the floor at the foot of his bed where it skidded up against the clothes he'd worn yesterday and the day before. One of these days he'd have to find time for laundry. And, he cringed, for the dishes in the kitchen sink.

His boots came next, the metal buckles hitting the hardwood floor with a sharp clatter. He released the button fly of his jeans and headed for the shower, stopping only to scratch Redrum behind the ears. The black cat lay curled in a ball of sleep and fur on top of the room's highboy dresser.

At Sebastian's touch, she stretched, yawned and returned to ignoring him which she did so well. He chuckled before leaning down and, in a voice husky and rough from rarely speaking to anyone other than his agent or the cat, purred into her ear.

"Yes, cat. You do your job well." A job that entailed nothing more than reminding him of his invisibility, the condition once a hardship but now a valued commodity.

Redrum's cold shoulder was easy to laugh off without causing Sebastian any grief. Or distracting his creative muse as Erin Thatcher had managed to do. It was all Sebastian's fault that she affected him any way at all. His obsession had actually taken him to the mailroom where he'd discovered her name. She had no idea she'd picked up a stalker, though he, at least, did his stalking in his mind.

Raleigh Slater stalked women between the pages of the New York Times bestselling horror novels Sebastian wrote under the Ryder Falco pseudonym. But in Sebastian's world, a solitary existence of his own making, an isolation nothing like the years he'd spent forcibly confined by the courts in juvenile hall, the only real stalking was done by Redrum.

The black cat did her damndest to sneak up on the pigeons that fluttered on and off the loft's windowsill. Rats with wings, to Redrum's way of seeing things. To Sebastian's, too.

Reaching the bathroom enclosure—the dressing area and separate custom-designed shower space nearly half the size of his bedroom—he shucked off his jeans and boxer briefs, scratching all the body parts needing scratching before stepping beneath the blistering spray that rained down from three separate shower heads on three separate walls.

For the past sixteen years, since his release at age eighteen from the lockup where he'd spent his formative years, Sebastian had considered his showers as much about relaxation and clearing his mind as about cleaning his body. When he'd finally convinced himself he could deal with permanence, he'd made sure to allow the money and the room for the bathroom he needed to accomplish those goals.

For too many years he'd been allowed but a fifteen-minute shower four times a week, a shower shared with other boys considered a threat to society or to self. At least one out of each week's four soap-and-self-defense sessions resulted in a fight, a near riot...or worse. Sebastian had managed to escape unscathed and undetected.

Because the day he'd been taken from the street where he'd lived alone since the scrappy age of eleven, he'd made a promise to himself, a promise that he would never look to another human being for security or sustenance or support.

He chuckled to himself, wondering if he'd really been eleven at the time he'd been picked up by social services. Or if he'd been closer to twelve. He'd changed his age with the changes to his body, finally deciding on sixteen when his voice dropped and his balls dropped and the hair on his face began to grow as thick as that in his crotch.

He hadn't given a damn what age the courts declared him. He'd made up his own mind—relying on remembered images of candles and crushed cupcakes and little toy trucks—and counted forward.

Even now he had no idea how old he really was. All

those ages and dates were as much a part of his imagination as Raleigh Slater.

Or as much as the fictional fantasies he wove of Erin Thatcher.

Sebastian reached for the bar of soap and ran it over his chest and armpits, working up a lather before stepping back beneath the spray to rinse. He kept his eyes closed, the hazy fog so thick he couldn't see much of anything. He could barely even breathe. His skin burned from the stinging heat of the water. And from the mental picture of Erin. A picture of her sharing the heat and the steam. A steam that intensified as blood pulsed through his veins.

He stepped out from under the shower, moved to the back of the spacious enclosure and reached again for the soap. Suds slid down his slick skin, through the hair growing low on his abdomen into the thatch cushioning his sex. His hand was warm and soapy when he took his dick in his hand. He leaned his forehead on the forearm he'd braced on the wall and spread his legs.

Water pummeled his back and his buttocks as he began to stroke away the tension he'd had building for days. Eyes screwed up tight, he imagined Erin on her knees, her short sleek auburn hair slicked back, her big silver-bright eyes looking up into his, her mouth forming the perfect O, her lips plump and pink and wrapped around him.

He wanted to get her on her knees. He wanted to see the cherry-ripe tips of her breasts pucker and pout. He wanted to know how much of her body she shaved and how her baby-bare skin would taste when he sucked her into his mouth.

Sebastian threw back his head and silently roared, straining beneath the release that grabbed hard between his legs and jerked his lower body forward. He thrust

hard, thrust repeatedly, spilling himself into the soap-
scented steam when he wanted more than anything to spill
himself into the welcome warmth of Erin Thatcher's body.

Chapter Two

"I'M GOING TO HAVE TO clone myself or forget ever getting the rest of this party planned."

Erin shoved empty mugs and pitchers into a tub beneath Paddington's bar, a full circle in the center of the high-ceilinged room with interior walls of exposed red brick. Booths ran along both the left and the right, and clusters of tables sat scattered across a high-gloss concrete floor that reflected track lighting from overhead beams.

Frustrated, she shoved the heavy glassware a little too hard and ended up splashing beer the length of one pant leg. "Great. Just great." *Count to ten, Erin. Count to ten.* "And, of course, I didn't get to pick up my dry cleaning and don't have a change of clothes in the office."

Cali Tippen, the wine and tobacco bar's number one waitress and Erin's number one friend, dumped her empties into the trash and spun her serving tray onto the bar before offering Erin a commiserating pat on the back along with a clean rag. "Eau de Budweiser, huh? I doubt anyone will notice it over the Parfum Merlot or the smoky essence of *Le Cigare Cubain*."

"Tell me about it. The smoke in this place? Even with the phenomenal exhaust system I installed during the remodeling, I go home reeking." Erin grimaced. "And I'm still looking for a daily shampoo I can use daily."

She sighed. She pouted. Neither did her any more good than did the shampoos. She was never going to get over missing Rory. His matter-of-factness. His ribald humor. His huge meaty hands that crushed despair and meted out comfort with the same soothing touch.

A touch Erin longed to feel again. Especially on eat-a-worm days like today when every time she turned around she expected to see him looking over her shoulder, reassuring her that he was happy with the way she was running his place.

His place. Not hers.

She shook off a rush of melancholy. Chin-length strands of hair brushed the skin beneath her ear, a scratchy irritating tickle that renewed her aggravation. "All those specialty hair products and I have nothing to show for the expense but burnt straw."

Cali reached out and tugged on one of Erin's auburn locks. "Your hair is as soft and gorgeous as always. And if you need a change of clothes, I have an extra pair of work pants hanging in the car."

Erin took the rag Cali still held and did what she could to mop up the mess that had soaked into her pant leg from ankle to knee. "I'd take you up on the offer, except for one obvious problem."

Cali paused, frowned, glanced from her ankles to Erin's, from Erin's waist back to her own. "Hmm. Why do I always forget about your long legs?"

"Yes. Erin Thatcher. Redheaded stick figure. I know. I know," Erin groused, tossing the useless rag in the bin when what she really wanted to do was pull out her dry hair by the roots.

Except then she'd be forced to buy a wig and she

couldn't afford to buy herself a beer. Not with this party looming and getting more complicated and expensive every time she turned around.

Enough already!

Her bitchy mood was getting on her own nerves; she couldn't imagine why on earth Cali was still hanging around. Except that best friends did that sort of thing for one another. And right now Erin couldn't have imagined having a better best friend. Or needing one more.

Looking Erin up and down, Cali grinned. "The red hair and the legs, I'll give you. But stick figure? Not a chance. You've got two serious bumps going on upstairs."

Erin smiled and returned the wave of a regular customer, an upscale professional type who'd settled onto one of the bar's swivel-back stools. She moved to draw a draft beer. "I look like one of those long green bugs with bulging headlight eyeballs. At least you have proportions."

"Right? Take two parts short legs, one part J-Lo butt, throw in a couple of perky Britney Spears knockers and there ya have it." Cali handed Erin another frosted mug for one of the Rat Pack wannabes needing a refill. "Oh, did I forget to mention the extra fifteen pounds that this recipe *so* does not call for?"

"Puh-lease. You are a walking, talking recipe for s-s-s-sex," Erin teasingly whispered into Cali's ear before delivering the mug to the customer who'd joined his buddies for their daily, post-workday bull session and even now sat cutting the head of a cigar.

Impatiently twirling her tray around on the bar, Cali waited for Erin to get back before growling out a frustrated response. "Being a sex recipe isn't doing me a bit of good seeing as I don't have anyone to cook with."

Her back to the far side of the bar, Erin turned her attention to the girlfriend who'd been her number one rock the past three years and now appeared to need a bit of shoring up herself.

With a surreptitious tilt of her head, she drew Cali's attention to the man behind her sitting alone at the bar. "I'm not sure that sexy blond number back there wouldn't jump at the chance to stir you up."

Blue eyes as bright as the frustrated heart she wore on her sleeve, Cali peered furtively, hopefully beyond Erin's shoulder and sighed. "He is dishy, isn't he?"

And he was.

But Will Cooper was also the study partner Cali had been assigned at the beginning of the fall semester's screenwriting class. That meant an automatic conflict of scholastics and pleasure. As obvious as was Cali's interest in Will, she clearly had reservations about pursuing him outside the boundaries of brainstorming and critique.

Erin looked back at Will—who sat poring over a sheaf of handwritten notes, his head bent, gold oval-framed glasses perched on the end of his nose, the hand holding his yellow number two pencil rubbing back and forth over his spiky, sun-bleached hair—then she turned her consideration to Cali.

"What exactly *is* going on between you and Will? Tell me again why you can't have your yummy man cake and eat him, too?"

Cali rolled her eyes, then gave a little shrug, a little sigh, a little bit of a pout. "Oh, Erin. I like him so much. We have a total blast working together in class. And playing together after class. I don't want to mess that up. Will is a really good friend and good friends don't grow on trees."

"Good friends can make for good lovers, you know." Erin grimaced at the hollow-sounding words. Rather than offering the empathy intended, the sentiment came across as a weak effort at placating her friend's misgivings.

Thank goodness Cali was sharp enough, not to mention knew Erin well enough, to get it anyway. "Well, duh. I wouldn't want a lover that wasn't a friend. But I wouldn't want to lose Will as a friend because we didn't work out together in bed."

Friends and lovers.

Funny, but Erin hadn't even thought about sharing anything but the joy of sex with her Man To Do. She hadn't thought about introductions and small talk and changing her sheets. She definitely hadn't thought about mornings-after, or face-to-face encounters with the man she wanted only for his body and what he made her body feel.

And that was fine. Absolutely fine. Nothing wrong with a completely physical, emotionally-free affair. She sure didn't have the time or the energy for anything more.

Nose scrunched in thought, she shook her head. "I don't know, Cali. I can't see you and Will having a bit of trouble working things out in bed."

Cali glanced toward the front door as one of the couples who regularly frequented Paddington's walked through and slipped into their usual booth in the room's darkest corner. She pulled two wineglasses from the rack overhead and picked out a perfect Pinot Noir before sending Erin a pointed glance. "If you're seeing me and Will in bed working at anything then you're nothing but a voyeuristic pervert."

Erin chuckled. "The very least of the kinky urges I'm fighting today."

"And what's that supposed to mean?" Cali asked, focused on arranging the objects on her serving tray.

Lips pressed together, Erin frowned. It was best friend confession time. As much as she relied on Tess and Samantha for cyber support, a real life girlfriend had the advantage of being able to reach out and smack Erin back to straight thinking.

She took a deep breath and blurted out, "I'm planning to seduce a man."

Unfazed, Cali patted her apron pocket and came up with the corkscrew she needed. "Well, all I have to say is that it's about damn time."

Leave it to Cali not to mince words, especially when it came to Erin's dating drought of late. Of late? Who was she kidding? More like her dating drought of the last three years. One relationship disaster after another. Men resenting the time she put into Paddington's. Or finding her unapologetically outspoken nature a turnoff.

Which was why her Man To Do fling was not going to be a relationship. It was simply going to be fun. "True, though this time I'm planning to seduce a man I don't even know."

"So, you'll find him, you'll get to know him and... bang." Cali lifted a brow, lowered her voice. "So to speak."

"Well..." This was where it got more complicated. "I've decided to skip the get to know him part."

Cali hoisted the tray onto the flat of one palm and, glaring at Erin, grumbled under her breath. "Your sense of timing never ceases to amaze me. You always drop your best bombs when my hands are full."

"I'll fill you in when you get back." Grinning, Erin tilted her head toward the dark corner where the couple who'd come in minutes before already sat intimately embraced. "The Daring Duo is waiting."

"Well, they'd better keep waiting until I get there." Cali gave an exaggerated shudder. "I *so* do not like walking up on their funny business."

Erin had a feeling Granddad Rory would've shared

Cali's sentiment to the point of giving the couple his famous heave-ho. Then again, if Rory'd still been the one running Houston's Paddington's On Main, the bar would have attracted an entirely different clientele.

Times like this Erin couldn't help but wonder what Rory would think of what she'd done with his dream. Or what he'd think of her. She smacked Cali on her backside, sending her on her way. "It's not funny business. It's the business of romance."

Cali skittered two feet away and out of Erin's range. "Maybe so, but we're in the business of wine and cigars, a little Sade and Dido and even a little U2. Not the business of groping beneath the table."

Erin delivered a pointed glance in Cali's direction. "Be thankful Mr. Daring hasn't taken to groping her above the table. And that Ms. Daring hasn't taken to doing a lap dance for him."

"Trust me." Cali shuddered. "I'll be the first to scream should I walk up on that scenario."

With Cali gone about her business, Erin glanced the length of the bar. All the customers were set with drinks and in deep enjoyment of rich smoke and good conversation. She glanced out across the dimly lit room, wiping down the bar as she did, and taking pleasure in the richly burnished booth toppers and the lush color scheme of indigo and bloodred wine.

Tonight's crowd was small but the hour was still early. The after-work rush began around six, reaching its peak close to nine. Between nine and eleven, neither Erin nor the servers found but the rare moment to take more than a quick bathroom break. The way she figured, the longer she held it, the more money the cash register was socking away.

Having revamped Rory's beer hall into an upscale establishment better suited to Main Street's revitalized urban scene, she'd done well her first year of operation, not quite turning what could be called a profit, investing what she did make back into the venture, definitely breaking even. Her five-year projection was finally taking on the guise of reality, looking more like an actual business plan every day when she worked on the books.

But if the end-of-month anniversary celebration bombed after her huge financial outlay, she was going to be up a certain creek lacking even the semblance of a paddle to save her sorry hide, not to mention drowning with all those wasted years of Rory's work swirling down the drain behind her.

But she couldn't think about that now. The thinking she did now had to be positive and productive or the resulting stress would put her into a too early grave. The Halloween anniversary party was going to be the talk of the town.

And it damn well better be after all the hair-tearing it had taken to come up with the battle-of-good-and-evil, black-and-white theme. She'd already planned her own mistress of ceremonies costume and only hoped she had the chutzpah to pull it off with half the necessary aplomb.

With Cali making her way back to the bar, Erin sent a quick glance around to find the other servers efficiently covering the tables, affording her a few minutes to slip into the office and drag Cali with her. Taking hold of Cali's hand, Erin didn't give her girlfriend the chance to say no, or what the hell, or anything else.

Once the door shut behind her, Cali pushed a hand back through her short mop of blond Meg Ryan curls and stared at Erin like she'd just taken a leave from her senses as well as from the bar. "You'd better make this fast. I'm afraid to leave The Daring Duo without a chaperone for more than five minutes."

"Here. *This* is what I wanted to show you." Erin picked up the magazine she'd brought with her to work. She flipped to the page she'd dog-eared and handed Cali the article to read.

"Men To Do Before Saying, 'I Do!'" Cali glanced up from the page of five men standing in a line-up, a height chart on the wall behind their heads. They were all over six feet tall. And built. And gorgeous in a male modelicious unreality as opposed to the very real, real-man appeal of Erin's fantasy. "You're kidding me, right?"

"Not at all." Erin's sigh was heavier than she'd intended, especially after swearing off her earlier bad mood. "I'm tired, Cali. Tired of double standards that let men get away with casual flings while focusing on their careers. Tired of working and never having any fun. And, quite frankly, I'm tired of going to bed alone."

Scanning the article, Cali lifted both brows, whether in judgment or in consideration it was hard to tell. "Okay. I can understand where you're coming from. Having a Man To Do does sound tempting." She caught the corner of her lower lip between her teeth and chewed, then flipped to the second page. "It's just the idea of going for it that would freeze me up. I am too much of a wuss."

"A wuss? You? When did that happen and where was I that I missed it?" Cali's attraction for Will was obviously giving her more trouble than she'd admitted to Erin. And, yeah. Erin could see how it would be tough, deciding whether to answer the call of body or brain.

She gave her best friend an encouraging smile. "You have more guts than anyone I know. That's why I let you hang out with me. I need the moral support and the example. Plus, you make me look really good."

"Does that mean I need to go after Will to show you

how it's done?" Cali giggled, her laughter holding a twinge of desperate hysteria to go with her way too-wide eyes.

Aiming to jolt Cali's self-esteem, Erin socked the other woman's shoulder. "It hasn't been that long, moron. I still know the basic tab A into slot B, how-to-ride-a-bicycle mechanics. It's just…"

Cali picked up Erin's trailing sentence. "It's just what?"

Sighing, Erin leaned back against her desk, a hand on either side of her hips. "It's just that damn female inclination to involve emotions. And I don't want to get emotional about this. I don't want to get distracted and obsess over what to wear and whether or not I need to shave and if he's going to call."

Cali simply shrugged. "So, *you* call. And wear what *you* want to wear. And go prickly if you don't feel like shaving. If this is going to be a purely sexual liaison, then don't wig out playing mental games with yourself."

Erin nodded. Her girlfriend was right. Uncertainty had no place in her personality. Or her plans. Setting her sights on a Man To Do was the perfect example of a positive step toward solving a particular problem. It was not an issue requiring an undue measure of emotional angst.

In fact, it didn't require anything but the involvement of her very ready and needy body. She could do this. She would do this, she thought, and stomped her foot for emphasis. "You're right. I'm not going to wig out. In fact, this is going to be nothing but fun and games."

"Good girl." With a sigh of finality as she glanced at the article and a shrug as she closed the pages, Cali handed the magazine back to Erin. "If it goes well for you, who knows? Maybe I'll give it a go."

"With Will, right?" Erin so wanted to see the couple together but it was her turn to worry about Cali wigging out over a friend and relationship she couldn't afford to lose.

"We'll see." Cali headed for the door, stopping with her hand on the doorknob. "I think I'll put my study skills to use and observe you from afar, take notes, analyze, form hypotheses and all that."

Erin teasingly frowned. "What? You save the close-up examination for The Daring Duo?"

"Ugh." Cali screwed up her nose and grimaced. "Thanks for ruining my sexually upbeat mood with *that* reminder." She tugged open the door. "Your payback will be hell, you know. Along the lines of me never telling you a single detail if I do get busy with Will. So there!"

"Hey! That's not fair." Erin stuck out her tongue in response to Cali doing the same thing before closing the door behind her. Erin chuckled. Sex confessions and childish pranks. The peas and carrots of female friendships. And, speaking of friends...

Before returning to what would no doubt be another busy evening, she took a minute to check her e-mail. She hadn't had a chance yet today to see if either one of her Eve's Apple cronies had responded to her wild Man To Do idea.

It took only a minute for the mail chime to ring and but a few seconds for her to scan through her new e-mails and the Eve's Apple mailing list digest to find a response from Samantha. Erin grinned as she dropped into her chair and tucked one foot up beneath her to read.

From: Samantha Tyler
Sent: Thursday
To: Erin Thatcher; Tess Norton
Subject: Re: Magazine Article on Doing Men
Dear Erin: Men To Do! What an idea! I got this total thrill of excitement when I read your note. Could I use an uncomplicated sex-fest? Um...yeah. With the emphasis on uncom-

plicated. I am even sick of the *word* "relationship." Compromise, disappointment, crumbling fantasies... I don't sound *bitter,* do I? Well anyway, count me in.

As for The Scary Guy—I don't know. How scary is scary? I mean is he Hannibal Lecter scary or just scary in how he makes you feel? Truth is, I like odd guys. I was always getting crushes on geeks in high school. They had a lot more personality than those gorgeous swaggering butthead jock types. Ha! Swaggering buttheads. Hey! That's the Man To Do I want. The Swaggering Butthead. Whaddya think?

Well, I say go for it—cautiously. Take pepper spray on your dates and if he ever seems *really* scary and not just intriguing-scary, run like hell. As for how to approach him? Erin, this is a guy we're talking about. Just smile! He'll do the rest. And keep us posted on everything. Love, Samantha.

Erin grinned, reading through the e-mail again. Trust Samantha to be so totally Samantha, even when it came to choosing a man for nothing but sex. The Swaggering Butthead, indeed!

Still, he couldn't be any worse than The Scary Guy. The Swaggering Butthead would certainly be easy enough to find. And he'd definitely be predictable.

That was one thing Samantha, Tess and Erin all agreed on. Men did not change, leaving her to wonder what Man To Do type Tess might have chosen—though Erin was quite sure she'd pegged him in her original note.

Closing Samantha's e-mail and scrolling down the rest of her mail, Erin found the note she'd been expecting from Manhattan's very own Green Thumb Goddess.

From: Tess Norton
Sent: Thursday
To: Erin Thatcher; Samantha Tyler

Subject: Re: Magazine Article on Doing Men

Dear Erin: The Playboy of the Western World? Are you out of your mind? Dash Black is so far out of my league that I'm lucky I get to water his plants. So, okay, I do end up with more than my share of losers, but Brad and I are doing just fine, thank you. He explained about not showing up for our date last night, and hey, that kind of stuff happens, right?

Besides, he's taking me to Robert DeNiro's Tribeca party Christmas Eve. Now all I have to do is find a dress that's priced like Tommy Hilfiger and looks like Versace. Do you think they have Jimmy Choo shoes at the Salvation Army thrift?

As for your Scary Guy? Oh, honey, go for it. Yum. The mind simply reels with the possibilities. The idea is WONDERFUL and you both deserve to let go and have at it. There's a million inappropriate men out there, and they're all just waiting for gorgeous creatures like you to crook your fingers.

Life is short! Eat dessert first! Make it happen. Build yourself some wild memories. Just be careful, okay? Don't go overboard. Think to yourself, "What would Tess do?" Then do the opposite. Love, Tess.

Erin chuckled. Leave it to Tess to shop for Jimmy Choo at the Salvation Army. As if! Erin only wished Tess was here in Houston so the ribbing she deserved could be delivered in person. Sighing, Erin forced herself up from her chair and the e-mail she wanted to answer more than she wanted to return to the bar and all the work she had waiting.

What in the world was wrong with her? She'd lost all her ability to concentrate on Paddington's and too much of her ability to care. At least it seemed that way lately. Maybe a prescription for Prozac was in order.

Or maybe she just needed to get over herself, to suck it

up, to remember all the things Rory taught her about living life to the fullest. About not working oneself to death which, for some reason, had become her stock-in-trade of late. "And that wasn't supposed to have happened," she grumbled, shoving both hands back through her hair.

Well, she sure wouldn't let it continue. She was going to get this funk under control and celebrate the bar's success in style. Her bar. Her concept. Erin Thatcher's very own Paddington's On Main. She had to start thinking of this place as hers, instead of looking back expecting to see Rory frowning his displeasure at what she'd done with his place.

She would also have the recreational time of her life with her Man To Do. No complications, no emotional involvement and, echoing the encouraging sporting wear logo, absolutely No Fear. She'd learned more than a few tricks of survival growing up at the feet of Rory Edwin Thatcher and she was not about to let down her granddad even now.

She would *carry on,* prove herself worthy of wearing the Thatcher name and of the gift of Paddington's On Main.

CALI MADE THE ROUNDS of her tables, chatting with customers, refilling orders, fending off the usual spate of come-ons which, thankfully, were few and far between and innocent at that.

She'd definitely been on the receiving end of worse when working at worse places. Meeting Erin and landing this job had been an intervention Cali's life had desperately needed.

Paddington's On Main attracted primarily a two-tiered clientele. First there were the ones Erin—thanks to Will's smart-mouthed observations—referred to as Rat Pack wannabes, young and slick and confident male professionals who brought to mind Frank Sinatra and Dean Martin and the rest of the original cast of *Ocean's Eleven*.

Cali wouldn't necessarily have made the connection if Will hadn't been a big fan of old movies. But apparently more than a few, uh, professional females hadn't been as slow on the uptake, she mused, watching hips test the limits of too-tight skirts as the night's manhunt began.

Then there were the couples seeking privacy, low lights and an ambience conducive to illicit assignations. The Daring Duo happened to be the most brazen of the regulars who spent long after-work hours indulging in wine and one another. The others managed to keep their romantic affairs private as romantic affairs should be.

Cali and Erin had fun guessing the nature of the relationships, spinning stories of imagined liaisons, both the origin of the initial attraction and the consequences of the covert tête-à-têtes. Pathetic, really. Two attractive, single, twenty-something women carrying on vicarious trysts rather than experiencing sex in the city.

How those television characters managed to balance careers with all the fun they had Cali would never understand. Between work and school and studying and life's little everyday errands and chores, she barely had time to sleep much less find the energy to be witty and clever and all the qualities required of a femme fatale.

Most of the time it was a struggle to feel *femme*. Forget *fatale*. But none of that seemed to deter Will Cooper in the least.

He welcomed and respected her input and ideas as they worked on their collaborative screenplay. And he seemed to enjoy her company for her company's sake. After all, it wasn't like by hanging out at Paddington's he was going to get anything cohesive or coherent out of her to add to their idea.

She did good to get the right order to the right customer, forget discussing their project's plot points or determining the value to be switched in a scene.

Finished clearing a vacated table, she turned toward the bar with her loaded tray...only to catch Will's eye. She pulled in a sharp breath, once again amazed at the intensity of the tenderness that tugged at her heart.

The gold frames of his glasses perfectly blended with the sun-kissed color of his hair and the brandied hue of his eyes. He was absolutely beautiful, a description she didn't normally think appropriate for a man. But it fit Will perfectly.

Cali couldn't resist. It was as if she were caught like a fish by a sparkling lure. Dirty dishes and all, she headed that way, reeled in by his sweet look of boyish mischief. His smile nearly brought her to her knees.

And how clichéd was that? One thing she knew well from her creative writing studies was never to settle for the first thing that came to mind, that originality was worth the struggle and the pain.

None of that mattered. Because this was real life, not fiction. And the way Will Cooper looked at her made putting one foot in front of the other a monumental feat of motor skills. She was a complete wreck, her thoughts of Will having strayed into taboo territory after listening earlier to Erin's plans for seducing a man. A man she didn't even yet know.

And Cali knew Will well.

A light shudder settled at the base of her spine as she set the tray on the bar and leaned her upper arm against it, moving as close to Will as propriety allowed, then moving closer—between his stool and the one beside, when his body heat beckoned.

The look on his face, the pensive expression and slightly

crooked smile, had her longing to crawl straight up into his lap, wrap her arms around his neck and be done with this hands-off business.

"One of these days you are really going to have to re-work your schedule and factor in some time off." Will reached up and tucked an errant curl behind Cali's ear. His hand lingered and then, frowning, he withdrew his touch, a look of uncertain surprise darkening his features—as if he had no idea that his hand had a mind of its own.

Cali did her level best not to scoot even closer and bury her face into the crook where his neck met his shoulder. The temptation of his warmth was hard to ignore. What she did, however, lifting her hand to retrace the path his had taken, was equally revealing. He watched the move-ment of her fingers, the fluttering motions she made try-ing to cover her blunder.

Oh, but she wished she was better at hiding her emo-tions because Will's gaze had snagged on hers and she knew exactly what he was seeing. Her eyes had always been huge and liquid and unable to hide her feelings. And what she was feeling right now was exactly what she didn't want Will to know she felt.

The way her heart tripped through her chest at the thought of his touch, the way her thoughts tripped over one another on the way to her tongue, the way arousal tripped down the length of her spine to settle deep in the core of her belly where she really wished Will would put his hand.

But he was staring and waiting and her hesitation was only making things worse. If only Erin hadn't planted the seed of the idea for seduction. But she had—and now, looking into Will's eyes, standing so close to the stool where he sat, Cali couldn't think of anything else.

She took a step back and strove to appear unaffected.

"I get time off. It's just the same nights I have class. *We* have class."

A corner of Will's mouth quirked with a crooked grin. "So how come if we have three nights a week together in class and I hang out here the nights you work that it seems like we don't have any time together?"

"Because we don't have any time together." Cali shrugged even as expectation increased the rhythm of her heart. Was he wanting them to have time together? "We have class time and work time and we try to squeeze studying and brainstorming into snatches that seem about as long as a commercial break."

"Yeah. I know." He fingered another of her stray curls, this time running the back of his hand and his fingers down the side of her throat. "But I was talking about us. Spending time. Together."

"Us? Together? Not working on the screenplay?" Cali had to be sure of what Will was thinking because what *she* was thinking had to be obvious. Her cheeks felt like two stovetop burners turned up high. Was he really suggesting what she'd hoped now for two months he'd suggest?

"Right." He moved his hand back to his beer mug and winked. "Last I knew it was called dating. Or, at least, hanging out."

He'd added the second part when her breath had hitched at the first. His use of the word *dating* had thrown her for a loop. That was all. She hadn't meant to give him pause when she'd paused. She'd only been making sure she was still breathing and that her feet were still on the ground.

"Hanging out sounds great," she said though it sounded like a crummy silver medal compared to the gold of dating Will. Why the hell had she hesitated?

This was it. Now or never. She had two seconds to

make her decision because a customer had signaled for a refill on his beer. And then she caught sight of Erin chatting with three white-shirt-and-designer-suited hotties at the bar and that was it.

Man To Do time.

Cali picked up her tray. "Hanging out sounds great. But dating? Now that sounds like heaven."

And then she leaned forward and kissed his bristly cheek, feeling the fire of Will's gaze burning into her back as she walked away.

Chapter Three

Chapter 4

Raleigh Slater needed to catch up on his shut-eye. The catnaps and midday siestas he'd been surviving on weren't cuttin' it anymore. He needed eight hours. He needed ten. Hell, combine the two and make it an even eighteen. He was running ragged and it was beginning to show.

Not in his work. That wasn't going to happen. He hadn't busted his ass for the biggest part of his life only to turn around and fuck it up by falling asleep on the job. But it was beginning to show in his face.

He dragged a hand down his jaw, needing a shave, afraid, as dog-tired as he was, that he'd slip and slice through his jugular if he put as much as an electric razor to his skin. He stared at his mirrored reflection, realizing the thought actually held a measure of appeal.

One nice clean slash and it would all be over. His career. His life. And the godforsaken wait for the end he'd seen coming since turning down a devil's

bargain with the prince of darkness himself. A deci-
sion Raleigh was living to regret.

Yep, one good slash and he'd be done with this
nightmare. And wasn't that exactly what HE was
waiting for Raleigh to do. To take himself out. To re-
alize the monumental mistake he'd made when he'd
"just said no."

That was why HE had sent the woman. Raleigh
should've been faster on the uptake. He'd taken way
too long to figure it out.

Every time he turned around she was there, cross-
ing his line of sight while he sat holed up on a stake-
out, distracting him from the subject at hand with her
long-as-the-Mississippi legs and amazingly fair skin—
considering she lived in a city where the sun ate and
burned flesh with abandon—and her copper-colored
hair swinging...

COPPER-COLORED HAIR? Fuck. Had he really just written
copper-colored hair?

Sitting in a booth in a far dark corner of the bar, Sebastian fingered his pencil until it threatened to snap under
the pressure of angry frustration. He stared at the yellow
legal pad, shook his head and snorted.

The female protagonist in this Ryder Falco novel did
not have copper-colored hair. She was a rare white blonde
befitting her angelic nature. Clichéd, perhaps, and he
might change his mind during revisions. But one thing was
certain.

The red hair he was writing about belonged to Erin
Thatcher and not his fictional heroine.

After another night with less than three hours of sleep—
or had it been daylight when he'd finally crawled into
bed?—he'd decided tonight was the night he'd make his

long overdue visit to Paddington's On Main. And this time he'd actually walked through the door.

He'd waited, timing his visit to an hour when he'd known the bar would be busy, wanting to remain undetected as long as he could. The same way he remained undetected when he walked the streets at night—the best way he'd found of getting into Raleigh's skin to move his story forward. So what if Sebastian ended up on the corner across the street from the bar every time, staring through the windows fronting Main Street?

He told himself he needed to observe her in her natural habitat in order to plan his next move. Less of a lion stalking a gazelle and more of a hawk preparing to pluck unsuspecting prey. Though he doubted she was all that oblivious to the sparks biting between them. Not with the way he'd caught her more than once wetting her lips while he watched.

He'd brought pencil and paper to Paddington's and parked his backside in a booth that gave him a full view of the circular bar where she ruled. He liked that about her. That she was a woman in charge of her world.

Confidence was a good thing. Meant she knew what she wanted. Lessened the chances of her being too repressed to answer any questions he asked. Or to reply when he demanded. He wanted to give Erin Thatcher what she wanted. Because making her sweat wasn't going to cut it.

Before he could figure out the source of his obsession, he had to take her to bed.

ERIN COULDN'T BREATHE. She doubted her lungs would ever start working again and, if they did, she still wouldn't be able to breathe. And, no. It wasn't the cigar smoke asphyxia she'd been anticipating for the past year finally doing her in.

She was totally, freaking paralyzed.

Sweat coated her palms, tickled the small of her back, soaked into the underwire bra she wore beneath her black monogrammed polo. The hair growing low on her nape frizzed; her skin buzzed from the static.

Ten minutes ago she'd been fine. Peachy keen fine. Then she'd looked up and seen him. The Scary Guy, her Man To Do, was sitting in the booth behind The Daring Duo. And, of course, he was facing this way, staring at her, unabashedly watching her every move.

What was he doing here? In a million years she wouldn't buy this as a coincidence. He'd never come in to Paddington's before. She would've remembered. And she couldn't believe he'd randomly picked tonight—less than twenty-four hours after she'd brought herself off to the imagined fantasy of his hands—to visit.

This was too weird. Too totally weird.

She'd sent Cali to take his order—but only after explaining the flush of heat to her face in girlfriend-manspeak. Cali had looked at Erin like she'd lost her mind. *He* was The Scary Guy Erin planned to seduce? He looked like a man who had virgins for dessert, tossing them into the volcano for his after-dinner show.

And Erin thought she'd survive sleeping with him? Cali's voice couldn't have screamed, "Are you crazy?" any louder than her expression.

And if Cali didn't get back here in the next thirty seconds, Erin was going to cross the room, strangle—then fire—her best friend. What the hell good did it do for Cali to waitress at Paddington's when it took her this long to find out what the man wanted? This was not good for business. Not in the least.

Count to twenty, Erin. Count to twenty.

She could've counted to twenty-two thousand and it

wouldn't have been enough of a distraction. She needed something, anything, to ease the sensation of having her every move watched, her figure in her black pants and polo scrutinized, her head of burnt straw studied the way one would inspect a ripe peach before plucking it from a branch overhead.

Ripe peach indeed, she mused, even while admitting her juices were stirred. She couldn't help but wonder if he'd actually visited her dreams. Or if he'd been in her room those minutes before she'd fallen asleep, those minutes when she'd imagined his hands to be the ones slipping into her panties and the folds of her sex.

What other reason would compel him to come here? He couldn't have randomly picked Paddington's to visit tonight, not after the fantasies she'd woven of his mouth and his body. She'd psychically summoned him. That was it. He'd come because she'd mentally called.

And nothing had ever frightened her more.

Yet…this wasn't a Hannibal Lecter sort of scary at all. This wasn't a wet-your-pants sort of scary. At least not the wetting usually associated with fear. No, this was more the stirred juices of a plucked peach, wet-your-panties sort of trepidation. The thought had Erin chuckling at herself. And chuckling at herself was a good thing, right?

Oh, God. Please let laughing be good and not the signal of her descent into demented hysteria.

Where the bloody hell was Cali? How long could it take to take the man's order and make the short walk back to the bar? But Erin didn't dare turn around. Not when she knew she'd be unable to pull off anything resembling disinterest. Because her juices were not the only thing stirred. Her interest was spinning as wildly as the bar's blender on frappé.

Finally, Cali's crepe-soled footsteps sounded around the

end of the bar. "Well, well, well." She moved to the cooler and pulled out a bottle of rich amber ale. Rich, imported and expensive amber ale. "I hope you know what you're getting yourself into, girlfriend. You've chosen to do a man with the most excellent taste."

Erin sank into the wide yawn of the floor opening beneath her. Leaning back against the bar, she crossed one arm over her middle and rubbed her forehead with her other hand. "Great. Just great. It's definitely plutonium."

"Say what?"

"Nothing." She waved off Cali's query. "Just trying to decide if I want to back out before it's too late."

"Uh-uh. No backing out." Cali shook her head until her curls heartily bounced. "Not when I've decided to join you in your crazy scheme."

Erin's head came up. "Join me? Now what are *you* talking about?"

"Hold that thought. I've got an order to deliver." Cali inclined her head toward the far side of the bar where the stools were rapidly filling. "And you need to quit slacking off and get back to work."

The rest of the busy weekday evening found Erin and Cali with time to exchange only snippets of conversation, tossing off the verbal shorthand they'd developed during the last year of stepping over and around one another, dodging customers and servers and swinging kitchen doors. The verbal shorthand that helped streamline the bar's operation. The verbal shorthand that was usually enough.

But not tonight. Tonight Erin needed to talk. She counted her lucky stars that it wasn't the weekend or she'd never have managed to find out even the tidbits Cali collected and managed to whisper in passing.

"I'm not sure *what* he's writing," Cali said, exchanging empties for another round of drinks. Erin had noticed his legal pad earlier and sent Cali to snoop. "It looks like an article or a journal. Maybe even a story."

"A story? You're the screenwriter and you can't tell what it is he's writing?" Erin shoved a crate of clean beer mugs beneath the bar. "What am I paying you good money for if you can't even snoop worth a damn?"

"If my salary is your idea of good money, we need to talk," Cali said and scooted out from behind the bar before Erin could get her mouth around a comeback.

She put half her mind back to taking care of the customers clustered around the circular bar. With the hour growing late, the after-work professionals had been joined by the more Bohemian crowd that frequented Paddington's long into the late night hours.

And, why not? Lots of artsy types spent time creating in quiet cafés or corner Starbucks. Even now, Will Cooper sat huddled over his notebook, working to make order from his and Cali's chaotic collaboration, though tonight he seemed more distracted than usual. Interesting that.

So, why shouldn't Erin's Scary Guy find Paddington's to be conducive to his brand of expressive art…if art was indeed what he was writing and not a list of possibilities involving plutonium? Argh, would this night never end?

Getting back to work, she finally talked the Rat Pack wannabes into sharing two pitchers so she didn't have to hover near where they sat refilling one mug after another. Usually she didn't mind the fending off of flirty come-ons that were part and parcel of bartending. But tonight she had too much on her mind. And having her Man To Do in the house wasn't helping her state of mind.

For some reason, she found herself less of the confidante or counselor Rory had always been to his regulars—both here in Houston and in Devon's Paddington's. Rory, being the lovable but landlocked seafarer that he was, had spun many a mean yarn while drawing draft beer or pouring shots, yet had known instinctively when to talk and when to listen.

Erin, on the other hand, sold drinks and served drinks and shot the bull or the breeze without inviting any sort of deeper intimacy from her patrons. A part of her wanted to offer more, to be the proprietor of good drink and better conversation Rory had been.

She wanted her granddad to be proud of what she'd accomplished. Instead, she often felt he wouldn't approve, that she'd *carried on* but at the expense of his vision. And that left her conflicted and more than a little bit blue.

Tonight she had less than her usual cadre of wits, so making chitchat offered zero appeal. Still, welcoming any and all distractions, she allowed herself to be drawn into several of the conversations. Any excuse to stay busy, focused on work, and avoid freaking out over The Scary Guy, wondering why he'd come here, what he wanted from her and why he hadn't yet come to get it.

More carefully this time, she cleared several empty mugs and snifters from the bar and was seriously wiping the finish from the surface when Cali next wedged her way between the cooler and Erin's backside.

"Definitely a story of some sort," Cali said, grabbing a second bottle of ale. "Dialogue markings and short paragraphs. Could be an eyewitness account of The Daring Duo. Though, if it is, I hope they never find out. They don't need any further encouragement, thinking we're actually enjoying their show or anything."

"Good grief. What are they up to now?" Erin's mental gears switched from the first subject to the second but Cali was gone again before she could answer. So, back to The Scary Guy Erin's mind went.

And what if Cali was wrong? What if it wasn't a story at all? What if he was a restaurant critic? Not that she served food worth a critic's time and effort. Her simple fare was just that. Simple. Desserts and appetizers perfectly suited as complements for a bottle of wine. No, what she was selling was the ambience, exactly how she'd learned to do from Rory, though definitely not the ambience he'd sold.

An ambience The Daring Duo was taking *way* too much advantage of, Erin noticed. The two couldn't get their mouths far enough apart to respond to Cali's query about a second bottle of their favorite Pinot Noir. Erin didn't even want to think about what they were doing with their hands.

At the thought of hands, she made the mistake of glancing toward the next table—and found her Scary Guy's focus not on the legal pad in front of him, but on her face, his gaze a bold and steady test of her ability to hold up under a scrutiny that was not the least bit chaste but oh, so, incredibly heady. Her fingers curled into the rag she held and squeezed.

She'd thought him intimidating when they'd passed one another near their building's bank of elevators. She'd thought him threatening when watching in her rearview mirror as his big black muscle car rolled behind her compact Camry into the parking garage.

But the truth of the matter was that on none of those occasions had she felt a fraction, a hint, a trace of the tremors now scuttling down her spine. Tremors that worked their way into the pit of her belly, spreading down between her legs in damp anticipation as she silently accepted his unspoken invitation. Oh, but she was going to die with the waiting.

His eyes were bright, a mad sort of glittering green seeing so many things she worked to hide. Things she hadn't told Cali. Things she would never have told Rory. Things she hated telling herself. But things he so easily divined, capturing and holding her with nothing more than a look.

But, oh, that look. It wasn't hot; it was compelling. It wasn't smoldering or steamy; it was devouring, possessive. Intense in a way that urged her pride to check her hair for flyaway strands, her face for a blemish or a scar. Her psyche for fears she wanted him to explore. She hated, hated, hated the vulnerability. And still she wanted to take off her clothes and give him what access he chose to take.

Suddenly, watching him there as he watched her, her chest felt too small to contain the swell of her fast-beating heart. Her skin burned, as if the touch of his gaze was a physical contact and not the mere suggestion of one. The pits of her arms, the backs of her knees, the valley between her breasts. Perspiration blistered and itched. The creases between hips and thighs grew equally damp. She was literally on fire.

How she survived the rest of the evening she had no idea. But she did, making the requisite bartender chitchat, removing and refilling glasses and mugs, all the while watching the clock over the front door, the huge clock fashioned from the top of the original Paddington's bar, tick its way toward 2:00 a.m.

The Scary Guy she was determined to know better was one of the last patrons to leave the bar for the night.

Will, as usual, hung around waiting for Cali. And Cali always helped Erin close. The three of them had laughed and cut up as usual while wrapping things up and, between Erin's last two trips to the kitchen, *he* had disappeared.

Finally, she'd been able to breathe, lock up the bar for the night and take herself home.

She had no idea if he'd returned to their shared building but a few blocks down Main, or if he had taken himself off to a club that catered to creatures of the night. And that's exactly what he reminded her of, dressed the way he always dressed in dark colors from head-to-toe, and lean in a way that reminded her of an animal on the hunt and always hungry.

He haunted her, and that's why she'd decided to take this bat by the wings and introduce herself the very next time their paths crossed. She'd kick herself forever if she didn't. And, besides. Saying hello was probably the least etiquette required before she and the man embarked on her premeditated fling.

She pulled her Camry into the building's garage and drove up one ramp after another until she reached the fourth level. Paddington's was within walking distance from the loft and the neighborhood was no worse here than in dozens of other parts of the sprawling metropolis.

But the middle of the night was still the middle of the night, whether downtown or in the burbs. And, quite frankly, Erin valued her safety too much to tempt fate, or any lurking criminal element.

She grabbed up her backpack by one strap, slinging it over her shoulder while hitting the auto lock on the Camry's key chain. The locks clicked and she stuffed her keys down into her front pocket. And then she heard it. In the next second. Between her first step toward the garage elevator and the second. She heard the sound she'd been waiting for, the sound she'd been hoping to hear.

A low rumbling purr, a growl that grew louder as the panther-sleek car approached. Dark-as-night black paint. Tinted windows. Shiny wheels and two cylindrical exhaust pipes to match. She remained still, standing where she'd stopped in her tracks seconds before, her hand wrapped in a death grip around the strap of her backpack draped over her shoulder.

The car crept by, a slow-rolling machine built for power, for pursuit, an intimidating shadow stalking every move she made. Foreboding settled into Erin's belly like a heavy weight, grounding her feet to the hard concrete floor. Her gaze remained on the driver's window from which only her reflection stared back.

But she didn't need to see his face to feel the effects of the look she knew he'd directed her way. The electricity remained, the sizzling, popping burn of her overheated imagination and her body that had yet to shake off last night's erotic dreams.

With practiced ease, the car slipped into the parking space at the end of the row. Erin hesitated for several seconds, knowing this was it. The chance she'd been waiting for. The chance she had to take. As soon as he killed the engine and the rumble died and the echo of all that horsepower stopped ringing in her ears, she headed for the elevator.

Once inside, she waited. Her back to the side wall of the elevator car, she waited. Holding down the door-open button, her heart hammering hard on her ribs, she waited. Listening for the approaching footsteps, heavy in the black boots he wore.

Or so she'd assumed they must be.

But she'd assumed wrong because he silently rounded the corner and moved into the elevator's tiny square of remaining space before she had a chance to whip her hand away from the panel. He caught her waiting there. And the only thing she could do in response was smile.

So she smiled, and then she looked down because she'd lost her voice. At least she'd lost the ability to say anything intelligent or coherent. And she didn't think telling him to strip to his skivvies was any way to break the ice—even if she wanted more than her next breath to see him naked.

She didn't know enough about men's clothing to guess his size but his boots were absolutely huge. Deep indigo jeans, nearer black than blue, bunched over the boots around his ankles. And, oh, but his legs were long.

Erin's gaze made a slow climb, lingering for what was probably too long for prudence yet not long enough for prurience on his sweetly thick thighs and the equally compelling bulge behind the crotch of his button-down jeans. If only he'd turn around and complete the picture by giving her a nice close-up view of his backside.

But there was no time.

In seconds they'd reach the ground floor. She had to make her move and make it now. A deep breath did nothing to calm her nerves, only served in fact to rattle her further. She tried again, producing a smile she hoped showed at least a small degree of the sultry sensations giving birth to tremors that ran down her spine to the soles of both feet.

But then the bell dinged and the door opened and she had no choice but to exit and hope he followed. He did. He followed even when she bypassed the main building's elevator and headed for the mailroom in the basement. She felt him behind her like the ethereal kiss of a shadow, a warmth with no substance but that which her wanton imagination bestowed.

A rich hunger stirred to life in her belly, accompanied by the twisting and turning of nerves knotting into a near painful anticipation. The short, dimly lit hallway echoed with their alternating footsteps, hers almost louder than his. The air inside sizzled with blue white waves of electrical pulses. The scent of imminent danger burned with a pungent intensity and caused her nostrils to wildly flare.

Then she caught a second scent. The barest trace of an exotic cologne, an expensive blend of green woods and spice. His scent. And the first time she'd been so aware of his individual, unique, arousing allure. She shuddered then, holding the feeling close as desire blossomed and as she stepped into the mailroom and headed for her box.

He made his way straight to his and Erin could barely concentrate on separating junk mail from bills as desperation grew. Never again would she have a more perfect chance than this one. The hour was late and they were both alone and unattached. Two healthy sexual beings lacking a single reason to say no.

Unless he didn't want her. Didn't find her desirable. Unless she'd imagined the earlier sparks spitting and popping in Paddington's air.

She took a deep determined breath and slammed her mailbox door resoundingly. Then she turned, pausing at the trash bin to toss out flyers and sales papers and the postcard reminder from her gynecologist. The rest of the mail she tucked into her backpack, zipping it closed just as the second mailbox door slammed shut. Three footsteps brought him to the trash bin where he tossed the same junk mail she'd discarded.

The rhythm of her heartbeat was pure rock 'n' roll as she lifted her chin and raised her gaze to meet his.

"Hi," she said, her voice amazingly steady when hunger had her weak at the knees. "I'm Erin. Erin Thatcher. I decided it was time I introduced myself considering we're about as close as neighbors can be, you living above me and all."

His eyes were the clear sort of green of old Coke bottles, a beautiful contrast of light against lashes and brows an indisputably rich gothic black. His upper lip was narrow, his bottom lip full, giving his smile an innately sexy and boyish appeal. Nothing else about him, however, could be mistaken as belonging to anyone but a man.

His gaze that still boldly met and held hers never wavered. Neither did he flirt, or tease, or pretend to sidestep what they both so obviously wanted. Amazing how the want was so obvious. Like sex between them wasn't even a question but was a foregone conclusion, a decision made long before this moment, a reality that neither had any say in defining.

Then, in a voice that sounded as if he rarely had reason to speak, in a voice that reminded her of his car's powerful engine idling at a low RPM, in a timbre that held enough resonance of simmering emotion to reassure her she wasn't out of her mind, he told her his name was, "Sebastian Gallo."

Right before he lowered his head.

It wasn't his kiss she found unexpected. She'd been ready for this since before her fantasies had stripped the both of them bare. What she hadn't anticipated was the hunger he was able to restrain. She felt the tension in the barest brush of his lips to hers, in the distance he kept between them even while standing so close.

Her body came alive and the hands that had been holding the strap of her backpack moved to hold on to him. He was tall and he was solid, his biceps beneath her palms as unyielding as stone. She had to lift her chin, lean back her head, stand on the balls of her feet to reach him. And she was not a short woman.

But the way he settled his hands at her hips—his hands, heavy with warmth and confident possession, his hands that were long-fingered and broad-palmed and were the hands of her fantasy—made her feel tiny and feminine and desired. And then, as if the test was complete and time had come to explore the extent of her willing nature, his kiss deepened, grew hard and hungry and his hands pulled her body flush to his.

She knew she was going to die. Her skin burned with a fever too hot for a body to bear. Her heart thumped with an unimaginably hard rhythm and any moment she expected her ribs to crack. The pressure in her chest was that intense. But neither that pressure nor that burn had anything on the ones clawing and growling deep in her sex.

The moisture she knew to be musky and hot soaked into the crotch of her panties. She wanted more than anything to spread her legs wide open. She wanted Sebastian Gallo to slip his hand between her thighs, to finger flesh damp and swollen both inside and out.

She wanted to feel his mouth, his mouth making wild magic with hers, the very same mouth she wanted more than anything to tease and release the explosive nerves drawn taut.

She wanted all of that. She wanted more. And so far they'd shared no more than a kiss. She wondered how she would ever survive the bump and grind of sex. He took a step into her body, pushing her into the waist-high sorting table that ran the length of the mailroom wall. The sharp edge cut into the center of her back. Cut harder when he pressed harder, pushing his full length against her, grinding a most impressive erection into the soft give of her belly.

Tongues tangled, warm breath mingled. Noses bumped, teeth clashed. Erin slipped her arms beneath his and moved her hands to his back then down to his backside, squeezing and urging him forward, closer. She wanted him closer. But clothing and location stood in her way.

And frustration mounted because there was nothing she could do but stand still beneath his touch and...oh, oh, yes, right there, she silently begged, easing her thighs apart when he wedged his knee between. She couldn't breathe. She couldn't breathe. His mouth was stealing too much of her air. The world tumbled away from beneath her, but his thigh between hers kept her from falling.

How could she have known he would taste like this? Like forbidden fruit, sweet and smooth, addictive. Warm sugar melting like heaven on her tongue. The taste of heat and velvet honey.

Yet this kiss, this press of lips, this open-mouthed exploration of tongues and teeth, nibbling and nipping, was an appetizer leaving her hunger to be sated. Leaving desire to be satisfied. Leaving the ache between her legs to be soothed.

He pulled away, panting, struggling. Choppy breaths, both ragged and raw, blew over the skin of her neck. She shuddered, pulled her arms back between their two bodies and curled her fingers into the material of his shirt. She buried her face against the backs of her hands. She didn't know whether to hold on to him forever or to let him go.

The one thing she did know, the one thing that was not in question, was that she wanted more. And so she lifted her head and she looked into his eyes and she smiled, encouraging him to respond similarly.

But his face remained solemn, even when he lifted a hand and brushed wild strands of hair away from her face. Then he leaned forward slowly, brushed his lips tenderly to the corner of one eye and rested his forehead on hers. "Nice to meet you, Erin Thatcher."

Oh, the sound of her name in his mouth. "The pleasure is all mine," she managed to get out before her voice or her legs collapsed completely.

And then he chuckled, lifting Erin's spirits and saying, "That's good to hear. I was hoping I wasn't the only one getting off on this."

Sebastian take the initiative. Let him take, what a laugh. He'd done exactly as he'd damn well pleased, stepping into the small space behind her and automatically pressing the button to his floor.

She would've loved to sink beneath his weight into her own plush bed, to pull her quilt over their bodies and learn his touch in the private sanctuary of her bedroom. She could imagine the scent of candles burning, the smell of his exotically spiced skin, of his musky warm arousal, the low burning light reflected in his eyes.

Yet, even more than any of those dark desires, she was dying to see his loft, to learn what she could about him from his possessions, his surroundings, the way he lived. She'd wondered for months now about the way he lived. But not half as much as she'd wondered about the way he made love.

The elevator began its slow upward climb and Sebastian took a step forward, and then another. One more brought him within inches of where she stood and she curled her fingers into her fists. Both of his hands moved to the wall above her shoulders, a trap from which she had no desire to escape.

What she had, instead, was a longing for his kiss.

She lifted her chin, parted her lips and his head came down—but only to rub his cheek to hers, bristly skin chafing soft, even as he moved one hand from the wall to her shoulder and squeezed.

The elevator rose higher. Sebastian's hand drifted down, lower, lower still, pressing the flesh above her collarbone before moving to cup her breast. She pulled in a sharp hitch of a breath.

He measured the weight and the fullness, skated the flat of his palm over her pebbled nipple, teasing her with a touch that held incredible promise. She shuddered where she stood, wanting to return the favor, to learn the feel of his body beneath his clothes.

But she stood unmoving. Waiting. Her heart beating. Waiting. His warm breath against her neck sent a sweep of sensation to play over her skin. Shivers raised goose-flesh along her arms, prickling at her nape and her nipples tightened further.

He grinned. She felt the movement of his lips even as he moved forefinger and thumb to lightly pinch and tug. She couldn't help it. Desire rolled up from her belly and she groaned, the sound a murmured hum against his jawline where her mouth rested.

He nuzzled his cheek to her lips as his hand slid lower, measuring her waist. Lower still, to the flat of her belly. And even lower, where his finger found the seam of her pants that ran between her legs and pressed upward, directly against her clit.

She panted and whimpered and barely stopped herself from begging him to get down on his knees. What he did instead caused a missed beat to the rhythm of her heart, even while her blood ran hot and heavy in her veins. He released the button at her waistline, pulled her zipper down, all the while holding her upper body against the wall with the weight of his.

His hand moved into her pants, his skin smooth, his aim sure, as his fingers breached the elastic band of her bikini panties, slipped down to find the plump lips of her sex and her clitoris tight and hard and aching. She nipped at his neck and her fingers gouged into the muscles of his shoulders. She shuffled her feet, opened her legs, allowed him access, lifting upward and...

Oh, yes. Right there. He'd found the one spot, ooh, yes, there. She hitched her hip to the side. Sebastian's finger, one at first, then two, slipped deep, deeper, filling her, withdrawing almost on her next breath, entering again to tease the soft pillow where sensation centered.

He repeated each motion, fingering her like the pleasure was his more than it had ever been hers to enjoy. That thought, that realization that he loved what he was doing hit her hard, a strike on her too-vulnerable female emotions when she'd sworn to keep this encounter emotion free.

Too late, her mind screamed even as her body went over the edge. She shuddered, shook, trembled, shivered, clutching whatever part of him she could find to hold on to. Unbelievable. Oh, oh, she couldn't…oh, his hand, his fingers, big and thick, and she never wanted him to stop. *Don't stop, don't ever stop.* And the spasms continued, rocking her through an orgasm that threatened to buckle her knees and take her to the floor.

Oh…my, she thought, slowly coming back down from a high chemicals could never produce, regaining her physical balance but certain the rest of her equilibrium would never again be so steady. He'd just fingered her to orgasm and they were standing in a bloody elevator, the doors wide open—though when that had happened she hadn't a clue.

Slowly, Sebastian withdrew his hand, his touch still intimately insistent as he pulled away from her sex, lingering along her plump lips, spreading juices to her clitoris as he circled the tiny pearl, wanting her to know what she'd done, what he'd done, that they were nowhere close to being finished.

If anything about him truly scared her—Erin mused, as she adjusted clothing and brushed hair back from her face—it was the way he'd so thoroughly breached any defenses she'd had that she couldn't remember if they'd been there to begin with.

When had another man, any of the men she'd thought herself in love with, ever drawn this physical reaction from her?

She'd certainly had her fair share of sex and probably more than her fair share of orgasms, she thought, accepting Sebastian's hand at the small of her back as he stepped from the elevator and guided her down the hallway.

She'd never been reticent to demand she get hers. And, yes. The drought had been ongoing for quite a long time, but that didn't exactly explain what had just happened, the way she'd let go.

Or why this man—this man with whom she wanted nothing but a physical relationship—had been the one to so boldly blow away any inhibitions she might've had and sweep her up into a wild affair.

She was still working to collect her thoughts and her composure when they reached his front door. He pulled a remote entry key from his pocket, pressed the electronic combination and the lock clicked in response.

Before he pushed the door open, however, he moved his hand from the small of her back, lifted his arm and hooked his elbow around her neck.

He forced her head up, and the first shot of alarm skittered along her hairline, tiny pringles of uncertainty warning her to be on her guard. It wasn't too late to back out. She'd run if she had to. She'd scream. She'd—

"Erin." He caught hold of her gaze, made certain he had her full attention before he said, "We can stop this. It's not too late to stop this."

Wow. That certainly wasn't what she'd expected. She almost didn't know what to say in response, though she did feel an easing of her nerves. "I'm not too sure about that, Sebastian. Neither the mailroom nor the elevator will ever be the same."

He shook his head, his eyes sparkling beneath those dark-as-night lashes. "I'm not talking about the building. I'm talking about you. I don't want you to regret…"

"What we've done?" She wasn't sure why he'd let the thought trail, but she needed him to know she was fine. And that she was fine with what they were doing. "I don't regret a thing we've done."

He shook his head again and this time his hand moved to caress her neck, his finger traveling down her jugular to her neck and into the hollow of her throat. "I'm not talking about what we've done, but what we're going to do."

The way he said it… The way he touched her… Erin couldn't breathe. She couldn't swallow. The look in his eyes wasn't gentle. Neither was it kind, but demanding and predatory, fantastically hungry, wildly hot.

What would happen, she wondered, if he were to lose control? If she told him she'd been waiting for weeks for what they were going to do? If she admitted she'd wondered what had taken him so long?

But since she couldn't find but the barest hint of a voice, she only managed to say, "Let's go inside."

SEX OR NO SEX, bringing Erin Thatcher into his home was not the way to work the woman out of his system. He should've known that. After their kiss in the mailroom—the kiss a mistake he wouldn't make again—he should've had the common sense to see her to her own front door and say good-night.

But he hadn't.

Instead, after her explosive reaction to his touch in the elevator, he'd brought her straight to his front door. A door no one ever entered. And now he stood back and watched as she stepped over his well-guarded threshold and into Ryder Falco's private domain.

Sebastian wondered how long he would manage to keep his identity a secret. Or how long it would take him to lose the rest of his mind. Insanity was his only defense for allowing her to walk through his door and into his life.

Insanity, and his dick that felt as if it would snap in half if he took another step. Then there were his balls that, by now, had to be an unholy shade of blue.

He leaned back against the closed front door and watched as she studied his living space. He didn't have a lot for her to see. A long, black leather sofa. A sound-system-intensive entertainment center. That was about it.

The rest of the main room's walls were lined with shelves that held hundreds, maybe thousands, of hardback volumes. He'd never been a paperback kind of guy. Especially not when he could afford to buy what he wanted whether he needed it or not.

Bestsellers, classics, research books, his entire Ryder Falco backlist. The rolling library ladder currently sat parked beneath a section devoted to paranormal occurrences. Now he wondered if he might've done better studying up on how, when so many before her had tried and failed, one woman had managed to work her way into the core of his psyche. He really was a sick bastard, letting it happen.

She moved into the room slowly, hesitantly, obviously unsure what she'd encounter. After all, she didn't know a thing about him, other than the fact that he knew his way around the female body. He assumed that was the reason she was here. For the sex. He wasn't going to fool himself into thinking she was here for him.

No one had ever been here for him.

"You don't have a television."

Strange that that would be her first observation. "Nope. Not a set in the place."

"I don't have one either. Well, there is one in Paddington's office. I read." She gestured around the room at his never-ending bookshelves. "Obviously not as much as you do," she added with a laugh. "I belong to a reading group online. I love seeing how a handful of readers can hold so many opposing views on a book."

She was nervous. Funny. She hadn't been the least bit jumpy in either the mailroom or the elevator. But now that they were here, now that he'd let her put what space she needed between them, she was nervous.

"Yeah. I like books." It was about all he could think of to say.

The corner of her mouth quirked upward. "I noticed."

She slowly walked toward the closest shelves, scanning the titles, mouthing the words she read, frowning, smiling, enjoying her discoveries which drew the ball in his gut even tighter. Appreciating her silent enthusiasm came a little too close to getting into her mind. And it wasn't her mind into which he wanted to find himself buried an hour from now.

When she reached for a book to pull from the shelf, he pushed away from the door and made his way to her side. To her back, actually, hovering in a way he figured she'd respond to as threatening. His portrait on the back of his book jackets was shadowed and dim, but he didn't want to take a chance on her pulling the copy of *The Demon Takes a Lover* from its slot on the next shelf above.

For a moment she hesitated. Then she slid the book she'd removed back into its place. After that, she waited, her eyes drifting closed as she blew out a long breath that Sebastian took to mean she was ready. He lifted the strap of her backpack from her shoulder and set the heavy canvas tote on the floor. Then he settled his hands on her shoulders, replacing the weight of her backpack with the weight of his touch.

She smiled, a gentle expression he felt in places he wasn't supposed to feel a thing. And her eyes were still closed when she raised her hands to cover his there where they rested. "Are you going to show me the rest of your place?" she asked, turning in his arms as she did.

He took a step away. Instinct told him she'd been but a moment from rising up for his kiss. The kiss in the mailroom had been calculated and of purpose. To gauge her intent and reaction, her willingness of body, her state of mind.

But he'd succeeded on one or two of the levels because he'd been the one caught off guard. So, no more kisses for now. Not until he had a better handle on where she was coming from. "There's not much left to see. Nothing more than the kitchen, the bedroom and the bath. And the cat," he added, as Redrum skulked passed.

Erin's gaze followed the black cat until the arrogant fur ball disappeared into the kitchen. The she looked his direction again, a tiny smile tilting at the corner of her mouth. "I know this is going to sound strange, but I would kill for a hot shower before we, uh, do what you've promised we're going to do." She gave a small shrug. "It's the bar. The smoke. And, yes. I sweat while I'm working."

He'd tasted her sweat there on her neck and caught the scent of smoke in hair that smelled of rich herbs. Both had been noticeable, but neither overpowering, appealing to his enjoyment of Erin as a woman.

But the thought of seeing her naked under his shower appealed even more. She could never know how much.

"That's not a problem," he said, gesturing toward the back of the loft. "And not even any killing involved."

"Well, my bark is really much worse than my bite," she said and fell into step beside him.

They avoided his dump of a kitchen and she didn't say

a word as she took in the state of his bedroom, the way he'd tossed his comforter up over his bottom sheet and called it making his bed. The pile of worn clothing he hadn't yet taken to the laundry. The notebooks and papers and research texts scattered across his workstation that took up more room than the bed.

A quick glance reassured him nothing she could see would reveal his identity. No, she remained silent, pensive, at least until she got her first look at his bathroom.

Then her jaw totally dropped.

It took her at least a full minute of looking around to find her voice, or to decide what it was she wanted to say. Sebastian understood her awe. He'd felt much the same speechless amazement when he'd finally seen the finished design of his dream the first time.

She covered her mouth with both hands, shaking her head as she looked around the room of chrome and etched glass and black-flecked gray marble. The sleek, onyx floor had her toeing off her work shoes to indulge in the coolly sleek surface.

"And I thought my bathroom decadent." She shook her head. "This is amazing. No, hedonistic. I may never want to leave." She ran the tip of one finger over the deep curve of a chrome faucet. "I have a thing about bathrooms, you know."

No. He didn't know. He only knew that he did.

She moved into the shower space and he shut the door behind him. The click of the latch echoed as always in the cavernous room, a sound he associated with solitude and safety. Never before had he chosen to share the ritual of his shower. And he had to push away the sharp clutch of awareness of that fact demanding explanation, why this woman, why here and now.

An easy answer. Sex.

Nothing less than sex. Certainly nothing more than exploring this rabid obsession.

He moved away from the door, through the dressing room and past the vanity counters and into the shower's main space. A sunken hot tub sat unused in one corner. For Sebastian, this room was all about pulsing jets of hot spray beating down from all sides.

And now it was about Erin Thatcher, to see how far he could take her, to see how far she would go. And, once shed of clothes and inhibitions, to see if they could fuck themselves free of the connection they shared—a hot, biting arc of shocking awareness getting in the way of his life.

ERIN TOOK A DEEP BREATH and, hands clenched, turned to face him. She watched while he pulled off boots and socks, tossing the lot halfway across the room. She watched while he reached for the hem of his navy blue Henley pullover and tugged it off. She watched while he freed the button fly of his jeans and skinned the denim down his legs.

Finally, he stood wearing boxer briefs, black, with a pouch that cupped the soft sac of his balls yet barely held the swollen length of his cock.

She wondered how hard a human heart could actually beat in response to arousal. How fast blood could rush to the parts of her body responding to the gorgeous vision of this near naked man standing not four feet away.

His arms were long, roped with tendons and muscles; the round of his shoulders defined their breadth. His legs were those of a runner, his calves firmly developed, his thighs strong, his feet sporting the barest tufts of dark hair. The same dark hair that grew low in soft swirls on his abdomen.

His stomach and chest were smooth, lightly sculpted

and a temptation to touch. She curled her hands into fists and struggled to evenly breathe. And then he moved toward her. That body she'd only seen in head-to-toe dark clothing was now so real and so bare and so incredibly, beautifully hers to explore.

His hands went to the front of her shirt and he pulled the hem from where it had been tucked back into her pants. She let him strip if off, wishing she'd worn lacier underwear, knowing the plain black stretch cups of her bra molded nicely to her curves but weren't particularly sexy. She decided Sebastian didn't care, as he took the weight of her breasts in his hands and tugged the peaks to attention.

She reached for the clasp at her back, wanting to feel his skin and his mouth, his lips, his teeth, his tongue, but he shook his head to stop her. She let him, hating that she had to wait, loving that she had to wait.

He reached for the button at her waistband, his fingers warm against the skin of her torso, his breath even hotter when he leaned down to blow a stream of air across her taut nipples. The distraction failed to pull her attention from his hands moving into her pants.

When her zipper went down and the heat of his skin warmed her bared belly, shivers set in. She held on to his shoulder as he leaned toward her to pull off her pants, one hand working its way over her backside, the other teasing her front while sliding down the boring black gabardine.

She wasn't sure how she was going to survive sex with this man when having him take off her clothes nearly brought her to her knees. And this bathroom. It was as if showering in and of itself was an afterthought. The room was built for sex. She wondered how many women had been here before her. She wondered if she really wanted to know.

And, now that she stood here in her plain black bra and black athletic panties cut high on the thigh, she wondered why she was wasting time wondering anything at all.

Sebastian straightened. Erin dropped her hand from his shoulder and caught a glimpse of their reflection in the mirror behind. A smile touched her mouth and Sebastian turned to follow the direction of her gaze.

The lift of his lips was less appreciative than suggestive and gave him the hungry look belonging to a bird of prey. She couldn't help herself. She stepped back into his body. "What do you think? Perfect as models for Calvin Klein?"

He shook his head, moved his hands to rest on her shoulders. "I don't think we're looking at the same thing."

She was looking at the contrast of black on white, cotton on flesh, the darker skin of his hands on her fair shoulders. Good and bad in a moment worthy of Kodak. Or, better yet, Zalman King's *Red Shoe Diaries*. This was the moment before the thrill.

She shuddered to think of being stared at, even while she couldn't tear her gaze away. "Tell me what you see. Then I'll tell you mine."

"You'll tell me your what? Your fantasies, maybe?" A dark brow arched. "The ones you have of you and me?"

Arrogant beast. "You think you star in my fantasies?"

"Isn't that why you're here?"

She remembered why she was here and wit escaped her. All she could think of was that he had to know that she dreamed of him, that she'd taken him to bed dozens of times in her mind.

"Am I here for the fantasy?" She met his reflected gaze squarely. "This certainly isn't reality, is it?"

"Depends on how real you want it to be."

They were talking in circles. But, fantasy or reality, she

needed ground rules—though better late than never seemed a backward way to work. "Honestly? I want this to be mind-blowing. But I want to know I can walk out of here whenever I'm ready to go. Even if I want to go now."

Sebastian's eyes glittered. His hands slipped over her shoulders and down her arms to her wrists. Then he stepped back and away, leaving her body bereft of his warmth. The upward tilt of his mouth wasn't humorous or cynical, but seemed to signal his acceptance of the reality she'd defined.

Still, she couldn't help but look when he moved his hands to the waistband of his briefs. She caught the barest glimpse of the slitted tip of his erection before he shucked the shorts down his legs and opened her eyes to the amazing dimensions a man's body could take.

Her sex opened and swelled and she had to stop herself from reaching back and copping the feel she so wanted to take. She didn't have time to do more than ogle, however, because he stepped around her, brushing her hip with the edge of his, and pulled the top from a black lacquer box on the vanity.

"I'm going to shower," he said to her reflection in the mirror. "You're welcome to join me."

And that was it. He stepped up into the shower enclosure that wasn't enclosed at all. She counted as, one, two, three, the shower heads blasted on and, in seconds, steam began to rise.

Hot. That's all she could think of. Hot water, hot skin, hot sex. A man hotter than any she'd ever known. This chance was one she'd never have again and was exactly the one she'd been wanting. No ties. No expectations. No regrets.

One deep breath later, she walked to the vanity, peered

into the box and thought wicked thoughts as she reached for a handful of condoms.

Who was the scary one now, she mused, and turned toward the shower.

SEBASTIAN STOOD BENEATH the center showerhead, his forehead pressed against the arm he'd braced on the wall. The water beat down on his back as he waited. He knew she'd come. He'd always known she'd come. They'd played this game now for months and by morning would have gotten what they wanted.

He just had to make sure his twisted mind didn't attempt to take things any further, to imagine an involvement that wasn't there. This wasn't a fictional creation. He didn't need to supply deep motives for either of their choices.

He needed to purge his mind of this distraction, finish up his current Slater contract, then do what he could with the germ of a story idea his muse had planted so he could get the insistent bitch off his back. As motivation, he figured it worked.

And Erin, well, he didn't know what brought her here. Her reasons were her own and unimportant to his plans. But, when he felt her at his back, he forgot about every reason but the one that mattered, the one throbbing like a wild thing between his legs.

Her palms made contact with the center of his back and she stepped into his body. Her breasts were soft and pliant, her belly a sweet curve beneath his backside. He didn't think she could possibly get any closer but, when her cheek came to rest on his spine, she proved him wrong.

He spread his free hand over his abs and then slid his fingers to the base of his cock where he pressed hard to stop the pulse of semen ready to flow. Not yet, not so soon, not when they hadn't yet tasted heaven or one another.

Erin nuzzled her face against him, moved her hands to his shoulders, slid her palms the length of his arms, stopping only when her one hand reached his holding his erection. She worked her fingers underneath his palm and silently demanded he show her the way he liked to be stroked.

If her touch wouldn't have guaranteed an abrupt end to their shared pleasure, he would have gladly spread his legs and let her have her way. Instead, he cupped her hand over the head of his cock, thrust once, oh, damn, into her hand. Then, shaking, he turned.

Her beauty caught him with a sharp sucker punch. Water streamed down her face, through lashes matted together over huge hazel eyes. Her nose was a perky button, her mouth wide and lush and the dream of a man and his dick.

He couldn't wait to see her come again. To see her eyes flash and her nostrils flare and hear sounds she had no reason to hold back. Moving his hands to her shoulders, he backed her across the enclosure until her heels hit the base of the bench built into the wall. He wanted her to sit, to spread her legs and feed his hunger.

He wanted to give her pleasure more than he remembered caring to share with any other woman. And a part of him realized he was feeling that desire in more places than those so obviously physical and that made absolutely no sense. He shoved the thoughts away and bent to taste the skin along her jawline, his hands at her rib cage, his thumbs pressing into the plump sides of her breasts.

Her skin tasted like the sea, and she had the most gorgeous breasts, tipped with hard, dark cherry centers. Leaving tiny nips the length of her neck to her shoulder, he leaned down and sucked a nipple into his mouth. She gasped at first and then she moaned, her fingers digging into his biceps as she held on to him for support.

He slid his hands from her shoulders to her elbows, pinning her arms to her sides and urging her down to the bench built into the wall. She went without question. Sebastian followed, dropping to his knees between her legs. He glanced up and, in the swirling steam, he saw her eyes blaze.

Her expression kicked him in the gut. The heady mix of desire and uncertain anticipation would've been enough to make him rethink what they were doing if he'd been capable of anything resembling thought. As it was, he was nothing but a creature of appetite and a man's most elemental focus. This moment meant nothing but her pleasure. He lifted her legs, draped her knees over his shoulders.

And then he moved his mouth to her sex.

At the first touch from the tip of his tongue, she cried out. And shuddered. He felt her tremors where his hands held her inner thighs, his thumbs pressed to her flesh so soft and firm and giving. He loved a woman's skin. He loved this one's taste. She brought to mind grapefruit, and olives, a salty sweetness warmed by her body's heat and that of the water raining down.

He moved his hands closer to the creases where hips met thighs and slid his thumbs into the folds of her sex, pulling her open to expose her swollen clit and the slick opening to her pussy, a slickness that had nothing to do with the water beating down and everything to do with carnality and lust.

He kissed her, his mouth open on her sex, so plump and ripe and his balls drew up hard, his cock surging up toward his belly. He wanted to wrap his hand around his shaft and watch himself enter her body. That first thrust, the thought of being inside this woman... He shuddered and entered her with his tongue.

She gasped and arched against him, her hands braced

at her hips holding her weight. She pulled her knees to her chest, moved her feet to his shoulders for leverage. Her eager response totally did him in. His tongue circled her clit. He sucked it into his mouth while he fingered her to the same rhythm his other hand used to stroke his cock.

Nothing in his memory, hell, nothing in his imagination had ever been this sharp, this intense, this ball-bustingly hot. He was going to come and that's all there was to it. He had Erin Thatcher in his shower, her legs spread and his body screaming with weeks worth of pent-up want. He wanted to pull her down onto his lap and let her ride him hard. But he was so close and the thought of stopping for a condom was a killer.

It was only when he felt her fingers come to rest on his that he opened his eyes to realize that, some time during his fantasy, he'd abandoned the real Erin for the imagined. He had to be out of his mind. Reaching for the fictional when he had the real thing. Her feet now rested on his thighs and he didn't even remember letting her go.

He looked up, caught off guard by the tongue she held to the bow of her upper lip while she watched him jerk off. Her fingers slid over his to the head of his dick then she pulled her heels up onto the bench and sat, knees up and separated, exposing herself completely.

And then she slipped her own hand between her legs, her own finger into her sex. He couldn't believe what he was seeing. This wasn't at all what he had planned but damn if he could find a reason to stop her. Or to stop himself. Especially when she met his gaze directly and said, "I want to watch you come."

He got to his feet then, a move that put his crotch in her direct line of vision. And then he began to stroke in earnest, rubbing the flat of his palm up and over the head and back down the shaft. He pumped harder, his gaze flicking from her fascinated expression to her own sweet sex that she fingered.

He wanted to be everywhere at once, in her sex, her hands, her mouth, her tight little...oh, fuck. He groaned and let go, shooting semen into the swirl of foggy air, working his cock, pumping, stroking, until he was spent. Spent but still amazingly hard. An anomaly of which Erin took notice.

He sank onto the bench opposite the one where she sat. Though she didn't sit long, pushing up to her feet and crossing the enclosure to stand before him. He expected her to drop to her knees. Instead, she reached above him for a cloth and the bottles of shampoo and bath soap he kept there on a shelf. She set soap and cloth on the bench beneath the center showerhead and set about washing her hair.

Sebastian found himself transfixed. He couldn't tear his gaze away from the picture of Erin's hands in her hair, her eyes closed, her chin up as the spray pelted her face, sending the suds streaming down her spine and over the sweet curve of her backside.

When she reached for the liquid soap and the cloth, he felt the first new stirrings of desire in his gut. He snorted to himself. What a lie. Desire hadn't laid down once since the birth of this obsession. The proof was in his erection that remained at half mast.

And now, with Erin sliding that soapy cloth over her shoulders, down her arms to her elbows to her wrists, and even her fingers, his fixation sharpened.

She moved the cloth to her throat, across her collarbone and down over her breasts, cupping them as she washed the full swells and gumdrop nipples. She stood in profile and suds slid down her limbs, pooling at her feet, her body slick and gleaming.

His hard-on stiffened further, straining toward his belly and begging to be stroked. He refused, and he waited, feeling strangled as he sat unmoving, strangled, tied in knots, grabbed hard by body parts better left unbound.

But when she moved the cloth to soap her inner thighs, bringing the fabric and her hands up between her legs and turning to face him, meeting his gaze directly and putting on a show mortal man had never been meant to resist, Sebastian succumbed to human nature and the call of the wild.

He grabbed up a condom from where the stack Erin had brought into the shower had fallen to the floor and, in three quick strides he was there, and the suds soaping her skin provided an intoxicating friction when he wrapped his arms around her body and backed her into the wall.

Her breath whooshed out from the force of his motion. He told himself to back off, back down and be gentle. But then she dug her fingertips into his shoulders and worked her heels into the backs of his thighs, levering herself up between his body and the wall.

He slid a forearm beneath her for support then tipped his lower body toward her. She released her hold on his shoulder with one hand and reached between their bodies for his cock, guiding him to the opening of her sex and, even after he thrust upward, after he buried himself in her warmth and she gasped, she kept her fingers wrapped around the base of his shaft.

The pressure she applied would've made for a damn good cock ring but it was *her* hand and not a strip of leather or a metal circle and that made all the difference in the feelings surging through him. He shoved hard against her. It was all he could do. He had no room to withdraw, to feel the head of his cock breach her opening the way he wanted. Again and again.

To feel that first pressing thrust, that push of flesh on

flesh, firm into supple, insistent into giving, his hard-as-a-wooden-bat erection buried in the rich complement of her glove soft sex. She ground down against him, squeezing him with inner muscles and that one friggin' hand.

That was it. He grabbed her ass with both hands, pressed his chest into her chest for support as he drove himself into her body and exploded. Erin whimpered, both hands now clutching his shoulders, moving down his back, clawing and scratching as she tried to pull him farther inside to assuage her arousal's itch and ache.

When she came her spasms rocked the both of them. She cried out, and would've fallen if he hadn't braced her up, leaned against her, kept her safe. He felt her contractions grip and pull him farther inside and he shook from the force of her body's response. She shook as well, her head back, her back arched, her hands slapped flat to the wall. Her climax nearly brought him to his knees.

When the force of her completion subsided, when her strength was taxed and her energy spent, he sank to the enclosure's floor, still holding her tight, still buried deep inside. She curled arms and legs around him and he couldn't tell where he started, where she began.

The water continued to beat down. The steam continued to swirl and rise. Sebastian leaned back against the base of the bench, wrapped both arms around Erin where she sat in his lap, and did his best to breathe.

He'd just compromised the entire reason he'd had this shower built. Solitude, personal safety, peace of mind. He'd never step inside again without thinking of Erin in his arms.

And he wasn't at all sure he was comfortable with that.

Chapter Five

CALI GLANCED AT HER WATCH, shook her head, blinked away the grit from her tired eyes—grit left over from work and Thursday's makeup she'd never washed away—and glanced at her watch one more time. Unbelievable. She'd never even made it home from work and now she was due in class in thirty minutes.

Last night after leaving Paddington's, she'd joined Will at IHOP for a middle of the night brainstorming session over Cherry Coke and French fries. Both had been too wound up for sleep and agreed the time would be well spent in working through their screenplay's plot elements.

For hours they'd played "what if," scratching notes as they challenged one another to up the stakes in their collaborative story's twists and turns, to dig for deeper motivation, to breathe life into their characters with added details of personality and goals…and to work on ways to increase the internal conflict between their two main protagonists, not to mention giving the antagonist a better developed back story of his own.

Half the night Cali found herself wondering when Will had become so hardheaded, and if they'd ever come to a meeting of the minds.

Toward that end, they'd stayed until the smell of maple syrup, sausage and hot-buttered pancakes had roused their stomachs for breakfast. Hot coffee had accompanied the meal and given them both a second wind. Had that really been two hours ago? Double unbelievable. She blew out an aggravated breath, shoving a hand back through her hair.

Now she was going to have to skip all the errands she'd planned to run this one free afternoon of the week and catch a nap between class and tonight's shift at work. If not, she'd crash and burn big time. And she *so* did not want to piss off Erin by dragging ass on a Friday night.

Cali gathered her things, shoving pencils, spiral bound and colored index cards, a letter-size legal pad and a textbook into her tote bag, then dug out her wallet to pay for her share of the shared meals.

Will stopped her with a warm hand covering hers. "What're you doing?"

"It's seven-thirty. I have class at eight on Friday." She pointed to her watch. It was now, actually, seven thirty-five. Even worse. "I'm never going to make it."

"You've been late to class before."

"I know, but I hate being late. And skipping is just so not me. I've paid out all this tuition and missing a lecture means I'm not getting my money's worth." Besides, she had to look like crap, being up all night. Baggy raccoon eyes. Splotchy skin. Frizzed out curls from too much tearing out of her hair.

And then there was the little tiny issue of realizing how comfortably intimate the night had been without anything physical going on when she'd actually been thinking of inviting Will to her bed. How could she risk screwing things up for the sake of sex? Sex that she could find elsewhere. Except she didn't want sex elsewhere.

She wanted sex with Will.

"What if I make you a better offer?"

Her head came up from where she'd been looking through her tote for her car keys. Will's eyes were bright, his gaze teasing but issuing a challenge that hit her hard enough to knock the air from her lungs.

She huffed out what breath she had left in response. "What could possibly be better than listening to Professor Smith yammer on about genre fiction?"

"A nap." Will shoved his open legal pad into his satchel, dropped his number two yellow pencil in beside and stuffed his textbook into the remaining space. He wore a distracted look while packing up his things and Cali wondered if he was even aware of what he'd said.

She wondered even more exactly what he'd meant. "You want to take a nap?"

Will looked up, dragged a hand down his face. Then he grinned, a lopsided boyish expression that added a twinkle to his eyes. "That didn't come out exactly the way I'd planned, did it? God, I'm exhausted."

Exactly what she'd been afraid of, she thought, and sighed. Good thing she knew him well enough not to feel slighted that he'd taken back an offer when he really hadn't made one at all. "That's what you get for being a talk, talk, thinker. The worst open-mouth, insert-foot type I've ever seen."

Will grinned widely, crossing forearms and bracing elbows on the table to lean closer toward where she sat in the opposite booth. "I like to speak my mind and, yeah, it gets me in more than a little bit of trouble. But it also ends up getting me what I want."

"Like a nap?" she asked, brows arched. She really did need to get moving. At least the part of her devoted to her degree in creative writing. But the other part of her, the part devoted more to Will—even if it was a borderline schoolgirl devotion—wanted to stay and listen to him worm his way out of the nap he'd offered.

He seemed to ponder the idea, taking his time coming to a decision, the same time she was wasting. One of them had to make a move and, as much as she longed to spend her time enjoying his company, her education called. She hoisted the strap of her tote bag over her shoulder...

...at the same time Will slapped his hands on the table. "Let's do it. Why not. You can read Professor Smith's lecture online this weekend. You know she'll have it uploaded by this afternoon. Her ego will allow for no less."

Cali hesitated. If she left now, she'd miss maybe fifteen minutes of class, barring no run-ins with rush-hour traffic. Who was she kidding? This was Houston, Texas. Have car, will drive everywhere.

She might as well follow Will's example and catch up on her sleep. Sleep, right. She *so* could not believe she was this easy, jumping when he hadn't even snapped his fingers. What had happened to her spine?

"So, we nap. Then what? You want to meet for lunch and see if we can come to an agreement on this third turning point?" She turned her aggravation with herself back to her aggravation with their number one screenplay issue of the moment. She narrowed her gaze and drilled him hard. "Or do you just want to admit now that I'm right and there's no way Jason can go back to the boat dock and risk being caught?"

"You're so far off base, Cali. If Jason doesn't find the knife at the dock, he can't be connected to the fire." Will frowned. "I thought we already settled this."

"No, you settled what *you* think should happen. You're back to thinking plot, not character, and that just won't work in this case. This turning point has to be all about

Jason's need to prove his innocence." Cali got to her feet, tossed down her half of the food bill and an extra large tip. She knew all about working for tips.

Will followed suit, thumbing through his billfold and hesitating longer than Cali had over how much extra to leave. She glanced up, caught the wry twist to his mouth and said, "We've been here all night and poor Dora has been a total doll to take care of us. Don't be a cheapskate."

"Ordinarily, I wouldn't be." He added a handful of bills to the ones on the table and shrugged, stuffing his wallet down in his back pocket. "But as of yesterday I'm unemployed and not likely to find another agency as flexible as Kirkwood's was."

Will had done freelance graphics work for the advertising firm as long as Cali had known him. Shocked wasn't even the word for what she felt. She hardly knew what to say. "They let you go? Just like that? Why didn't you tell me?"

Oh, God, she felt all sorts of caregiver instincts kick in, when more than anything Will would be needing a friend.

"I did tell you. Just now." He put his hand in the small of her back and headed them toward the door. "And, yeah. They let me go. Business is slow. Not much reason to keep me around and pay me for doing nothing but looking good."

"What are you going to do?" And why did she feel the sudden urge to invite him to move in to her place and share expenses? She couldn't even find a response to his comment about looking good.

"Right now I'm going to take a nap." They'd reached their cars parked side by side. The rising sun had Will squinting and replacing his glasses with the prescription sunshades from the case shoved down in the pocket of his baggy khaki Dockers. "You going to follow me? Or you just want to hitch a ride? I can bring you back to get your car later, if you want."

What was he talking about, hitching a ride? Following? Bringing her back to get her car later? Her heart pattered like a thunderstorm on glass. He wanted them to nap together? Oh, great. Now she couldn't breathe. The only safe thing she could think of to say was, "I thought you wanted to meet for lunch later?"

"I'll fix us lunch." He unlocked and opened the door to his sporty black Eclipse. "I'll dig out a pair of sweats and a T-shirt. You can shower then sleep on the futon in the living room."

"The futon. Perfect." Sleeping on his furniture wearing his clothes. Naked in his shower while he...did what? Went about his business as if she wasn't naked in his shower, waiting to put on his clothes and sleep on his furniture? "I'll follow you. I'll need my car later and it'll be out of the way to come back and pick it up here."

"Great. I figure by noon we should be human again. And then you'll see that it only makes sense for Jason to find the knife at the dock." Will dropped down into the driver's seat and slammed the door, giving her a thumbs-up as the engine raced to life.

God, but he was such a guy! Playful and sexy and he made her laugh and caused her tummy to tingle and she loved arguing with him over their screenplay ideas and oh, but she was afraid she was getting close to falling in love.

She stuck out her tongue in a teasing response, and then she tossed her things into her own car's passenger seat, backed out the candy apple red Focus and pulled behind Will into the traffic that wasn't quite as heavy as she'd expected this hour of the morning.

She'd been to his apartment more than once, an apartment that was actually the second floor of an old Victorian house close to downtown, but always to work on their project. He'd cooked dinner a couple of times early in the semester and they'd sat at his kitchen table to hash out their story ideas. True, it didn't happen often because of the very schedules they'd bemoaned last night.

So why was she getting her hopes up that today was going to be any different? He hadn't invited her over as a date—since they weren't *dating,* only hanging out like they'd decided yesterday—but as his study partner. She'd kissed his cheek and that was it. Now they were both going to sleep. So what? They weren't going to be sleeping together. And that pretty much answered her question about the future of their relationship.

Or the nonfuture of our nonrelationship, she grumped to herself, turning up the volume on Alanis Morissette and belting out her irritation under the guise of singing along. And, why not? She sure didn't have a Man To Do to help her work off the frustration. Lucky Erin.

ERIN AND SEBASTIAN NEVER made it out of the shower. Hours later and she still couldn't believe it. She'd been a wrung-out, wrinkled prune by the time she'd dried off and dressed and backed her way through Sebastian's loft—hard to do when he'd followed her, dripping and naked and once again hard—from the bathroom to the front door.

Once there, he'd braced a hand above her shoulder and leaned toward her, smelling of warm clean skin and fresh sex. He'd buried his face in her neck and taken her hand in his, wrapping their joined fingers around his erection and stroking in that rhythm she now knew so well.

He'd opened the door before he'd come. She'd ducked through with a wordless goodbye, stood on the other side and listened to his labored groans, his grunts, the strangled agony of a man in pain—or pleasure. She wondered if he knew she'd waited. She wondered why she had. Even then, as she'd found herself waiting, seeking signs of his movement, his breathing, his heartbeat through the solid wooden door...even then, she'd wondered why she'd stayed. Finally, she'd had to go.

She'd hurried back to her own place, the sounds of Sebastian's struggle still ringing in her ears and her body responding to that need he hadn't shared. During none of the times they'd come together, or the times they'd gotten one another off, had Erin sensed his release to be as rich as the completion he'd found there alone behind his closed door.

If he did know that she'd waited, she wanted to know what he'd thought, how he'd felt about her remaining until he'd finished. She still hadn't decided why she'd stayed. Except that so many things about Sebastian Gallo intrigued her. The size of his library and the opulence of his shower just to name two.

After all that time they'd spent wrapped up in the steam and the spray, she'd known if she'd gone anywhere near his bed she wouldn't have wanted to leave. Neither would she have wanted to sleep and she was desperately exhausted, not to mention achy and sore and more than a little bit raw. Tomorrow she had a meeting with the caterer to finalize the menu for the Halloween anniversary bash. And she needed sleep.

She'd had her pleasure. Hell, in one night she'd had pleasures she'd been without for months, if not all of her life. Now that she was home, it was back to whatever business she could manage before tumbling into bed. At least until the next time Sebastian crooked his finger. And after doing the one thing she had to do before crawling between the sheets.

Call Cali.

A call to her cell produced, "The customer you are try-ing to reach is unavailable," which meant Cali had for-gotten again to turn on her phone. And a call to her home phone got voice mail. Desperate enough to page her, Erin glanced at her bedside clock while kicking off her shoes.

Well, duh. Cali would be on her way to her Friday morn-ing class and wouldn't be home before Erin was asleep. That left one option. E-mail her Men To Do girlfriends. She stripped off her clothes for the second time tonight, and swore she could still smell Sebastian on her skin.

She tugged her nightshirt over her head and settled down into her pillows, settling her laptop on a pillow in her lap.

From: Erin Thatcher
Sent: Friday
To: Samantha Tyler; Tess Norton
Subject: My Scary Guy

I did it! Er, him. I did him! I can't believe it! He was abso-lutely amazing. And, no, not Hannibal Lecter scary at all, though he is definitely frightening in an intimidatingly sexy sort of way.

I had no idea there were actually men who knew how to do the things he did. My body is still reeling. I SO totally picked the right Man To Do! I'd share the juicy details but I'm too exhausted to type, much less figure out how to put thoughts into words.

Which brings me to my problem. I'm not supposed to be thinking about this, am I? This is supposed to be all about sex, right? So, why am I dying to get to know him? Is this that fe-male thing in action? Where we can't separate the physical from the emotional? I don't want the bloody emotional! I don't want anything but the physical. Period. End of story.

But I do want to know why he has a shower that belongs in a locker room. No, not a locker room. More like a hedonistic resort. We're talking three showerheads and staggered levels of built-in benches perfect for, well, yeah, that. And more of that. At least two hours of that. I'm not kidding. I'm a total prune. And I may never walk again!

He also has a virtual library in his living room. The rolling ladder and everything. No television. Just a high-tech sound system like you wouldn't believe and books that go on forever. Classics and bestsellers and psychology texts and…the list goes on.

It's like, if I were looking for a relationship, I'd say he has more potential than any man I've known in ages. I feel like I ought to give it a go, just in case. What if he turned out to be The One? But I'm just not ready. So what do I do? Besides whine!

Oh, and his name is Sebastian Gallo. Love, Erin

She didn't bother to proofread. She was way past exhausted and figured even the most glaring mistakes would get by her foggy, bleary eyes. She hit Send then moved her laptop to the bedside table, leaving the connection open, thinking maybe Tess would check her e-mail before heading out to wave her green-thumb wand over the houseplants of Manhattan.

Or maybe Samantha wouldn't have a client meeting or a court date this early and could whip out a quick reply to help Erin make sense of the night. She felt fuzzy-headed and goofy. And wrung-out and giggly and on the verge of tears. All the symptoms of a classic sex hangover. And what a doozy.

But as appealing as she found the idea of returning upstairs for the hair of the dog that bit her, and bit her, and bit her again, she couldn't think straight about anything without at least a few hours of sleep.

And tomorrow was Friday, ugh, *today* was Friday, one of her busiest weeknights. Figures that she'd start the affair she'd been dying to engage in when she didn't have time to enjoy it. But when *would* she have time to enjoy it? It wasn't like tomorrow was going to be any less stressful than today.

And the day after would be even worse being Sunday— the only day of the week she had time to take care of personal business, though lately the only thing personal she did was go to church and buy tampons. Oh, and catch up on her much needed sleep.

The remainder of her time was devoted to the business of Paddington's. The business of keeping Paddington's alive for her own sake since it was her sole means of income. But also keeping the bar viable for Rory.

Rory who wasn't here, who would never be here again to tuck her under his wing, to encourage her to keep her chin up, or to praise the work she'd done to his place. No. *Her* place, damn it. It was her place. Why was she having so much trouble seeing things that way?

Perhaps because more than anything else, he would never be here to forgive her for getting the hell out of Dodge the minute she'd received her inheritance at age eighteen. For putting her degree on the back burner next to his advice that she not blow the money her parents had intended for her education.

Or for taking such little interest in a place that meant so much to him that, after moving to Texas to raise her, he'd worked the rest of his life duplicating his Devonshire pub only to have her turn it into what she wanted it to be the minute he was gone. She was some piece of work, wasn't she?

Before Erin took that thought beyond her comfort

zone, the chime of her e-mail bell sounded. She leaned over and clicked it open to read.

From: Tess Norton
Sent: Friday
To: Erin Thatcher; Samantha Tyler
Subject: Re: My Scary Guy
You bitch! (Oops, did I say that out loud? I meant, wow, how fabulous for you!!!) I mean it, girl. This is outstanding. I have no good advice, however. I suck at this relationship thing, remember? But I do think the way to approach this whole business is to do what feels right, even if it feels scary. Maybe because it feels scary.

It's all a crap shoot, dear Erin, didn't you know that? And the dice don't give a damn if you think you're ready or not. So you might as well have fun as long as you're already in the game.

Perhaps lots and lots more sex will make things clearer. And if it doesn't, you'll be too tired to care. Love and kisses, Tess

Ha! Tess was just way too upbeat this morning, damn the woman. If sex made things clearer, why this horribly muddled state of mind? She was right about the exhaustion level, however. At least about it existing. Erin felt like she would need the jaws of life to pry her body out of this bed.

Now if she could only get to that place where she was too tired to care. Or at least too tired to think about caring. Too tired to think, period, sounded even better. Though dreaming about Sebastian sounded like an excellent plan. And she was drifting off to do just that when her e-mail chime sounded again. She propped up on one elbow to read.

From: Samantha Tyler
Sent: Friday
To: Erin Thatcher; Tess Norton
Subject: Re: My Scary Guy

Oh, Erin. So many responses! And I'm having a hard time separating all my personal divorce baggage from what a true friend would say so bear with me.

First of all, YUM on the sex. If I wasn't sure I'd freak, I'd be asking if Sebastian (such a cool name!) had any brothers. In the meantime, I'm way happy for you. You deserve every orgasm and bowlegged morning-after you get. Whew! (fanning self)

Second, oh God, be careful. Having sex with a scary guy is scary enough, but feelings? Weren't those entirely outside of the point of Men To Do? They were, you know it.

I guess I'd say follow your instincts. You're not some dopey bimbo, so you know you won't get in deep if he's really no good. But be careful, careful and more careful. Men give their gender a bad name.

Cheers and a victory salute, Samantha

Erin smiled. No, she was not a dopey bimbo, she mused, disconnecting from her ISP. Samantha and Tess were the absolute best. Erin's cyber buddies had provided the perfect sleep tonic to ease her mind, and given her the food for thought she needed to hold her until later tonight.

Then she'd get Cali to talk her back to sanity.

A NIGGLING LITTLE ITCH brought Cali from deep sleep to the edge of wakefulness. She snuggled her face into her pillow, pulling her sheet and thick duvet to her chin.

But this wasn't her pillow, she thought, eyes closed and frowning as consciousness began to return. And this wasn't her duvet or sheet but a worn quilt that felt like the softest cotton on her skin. At least the skin exposed and not covered by the unfamiliar sleepwear...

Will's T-shirt and sweats. Will's quilt and Will's pillow. She smiled, rubbed the fabric to her cheek. If this was his idea of hanging out, she was definitely in for a pound. She couldn't remember the last time she'd been this comfortable sleeping in her own bed.

Which was silly, because she loved her bed. But sleeping here, in Will's place, in his clothes, on his futon, beneath his quilt? She snuggled deeper into the pillow. It was as if she was surrounded by the one thing her life was lacking and she most wanted to find.

Funny, because she truly thought herself happy and fulfilled. And she was happy and fulfilled. Life was great, what with her job and her classes and that disastrous relationship nightmare behind her...

She found herself frowning again and this time opened her eyes, closed them, opened them again and blinked hard. Her heart dropped from her throat, where it beat like a wild butterfly's wings, to her stomach. Will was lying beside her, facing her, his eyes looking straight into hers as she came fully awake.

She curled her body into a tighter ball, keeping the butterfly close. "What're you doing here?"

He grinned his Cheshire cat grin. "I live here."

The purr of his words vibrated the length of her spine. "I know that part. I meant why aren't you in your bed? Couldn't you sleep?"

"I slept. A couple of hours worth." His face was so close she could see new tiny gold whiskers above the scruffy five o'clock shadow he never completely shaved.

She could see the darker flecks in his light brown eyes, and the two or three wild hairs growing straight up out of his eyebrows. He wore glasses most all of the time and she'd never been so close to his eyes. Or to the rest of his body that, oh, God, she hoped wasn't as naked.

Her eyes widened, and she glanced down briefly to see what he was wearing. Not a lot. Nothing but a pair of gray jersey gym shorts. Her heart began to thump harder.

Catching at her bottom lip with her teeth, she moved her gaze back to his, hoping against hope that she sounded calmer than she felt with cocoons bursting open in her belly. "How do you expect to make it through the day on two hours of sleep?"

His arms crossed over his chest, his hands tucked into his armpits, he shrugged the shoulder he wasn't lying on. "I'm young, hale and hearty. I'll live."

He was so blasé. How could he be so blasé when her entire body flinched every time his long lashes blinked? "How long have you been looking at me?"

This time he hesitated before answering, taking his time with the words as if they mattered more than those he'd spoken before. One corner of his mouth lifted and softly he said, "For at least two months now."

"No. I mean…" She stopped, stunned. *Two months?* That meant he'd been looking at her since they'd met at the beginning of the fall semester. He couldn't mean… When all this time… And now he was looking at her… "I mean how long—"

Will shifted up onto his elbows and leaned over her, his face but inches away. "Cali."

Cali rolled onto her back, deciding this wasn't going to be about napping and hanging out after all. She could only manage to whisper her answer. "Will?"

He reached out and twirled one of her wild blond curls around his index finger. "Last night. In Paddington's. We talked about spending time together. Hanging out and having fun. Not messing with the screenplay. Not trying to talk while you work. Do you remember that?"

She nodded. Did he really think she'd forget?

"What happened next?"

She didn't even pretend not to know what he was talking about. "I kissed you."

"Yep." Will pulled his finger from her curl to touch it to the bow of her upper lip. "Did you know I couldn't make a single note that made sense after that?"

No. She didn't know that at all. But she wasn't about to feign disappointment, because that was the moment anticipation struck with a vengeance, sweeping through her belly and down between her legs. "Why?"

"Because you walked away too soon. And I wanted more than anything to kiss you back."

She eased her grip on the quilt and pushed it to her waist. She wanted to be as close to him as she possibly could because she'd been ready for this forever. "Will?"

His fingertips traced the whole of her mouth and moved to her chin. "Cali?"

She lifted a hand to the round of his bare shoulder. "You can kiss me now."

His smile before he lowered his head nearly broke her heart. He brushed his lips oh, so lightly over hers, mouths closed and barely touching as they shared the air they both breathed.

He shifted even closer, his bare chest brushing across her aroused nipples beneath the cotton of his shirt that she wore. The pressure increased, his mouth and his body and the ache buried deep in her core. She wanted him like no man she'd ever wanted. And she told him so when she opened her mouth, asking him to open his in return.

He did and tongues tangled and teethed clashed and hands explored exposed skin and roughly shed clothes to bare more, to bare everything. His body was glorious, smooth and firm where her hands ran over his shoulders and back and buttocks.

He shifted slightly, allowing room for her discovery to move where he most wanted her touch. Sliding her hand down his flat belly, she wrapped her hand around him, so hard, so satiny soft, and she shivered.

He gasped and he groaned. "Cali, you're making me crazy."

Crazy was a good thing, yes? Because, if not, this insanity would bring big fat regrets once they came to their senses. She stroked him again, running her palm up and over the head of his penis, so huge and so swollen. "This is good, then? I don't want to do it wrong."

He gave a strangled laugh. "Nothing you could do would be wrong. Trust me on this."

He thrust into her hand. And this time *she* gasped, imagining that thrust taking him into her body. Yet that gasp became nothing when Will moved down her body and ran the flat of his tongue across the hard peak of her breast. He kiss-nipped the plump flesh before centering his attention on her nipple that begged.

"Oh, Will," was all she could say because now his fingers were slipping between her legs, slipping through the wet folds of her sex, slipping into her body that wept with wanting. She arched her hips into his hand and cried out.

His fingers delved deeper, stroking, rubbing, his thumb teasing her clit that throbbed with the need to come. She didn't want to come without him. Not this first perfect time. This time she wanted to come to the filling drive of his sex and the pressing weight of his body covering hers. "Will, please."

"Please what, Cali?" he asked, sliding back up to kiss

the underside of her jaw, her ear, her neck where it met her shoulder.

She could hardly find the words for what she wanted. And her whisper shook. "Please, please me. I want you to fill me. I want you inside of me. I want—"

"Every damn thing that I want." He braced his weight on his elbows, slid his arms beneath her shoulders and cupped the back of her head. "Cali, honey. You have no idea how much I've wanted to do this and for how long."

When he kissed her this time their mouths came together in a sweet expression of tender feelings, feelings new and unexpected and frightening in that way of a journey into the unknown. When he moved his hand to caress her breast, sensation heightened to a singing pitch of expectation, anticipation, a sharp, fevered want.

When he deftly moved to ensure her protection, when he urged her legs open and settled his weight in her body's cradle, when he guided his sheathed erection to the waiting center of her sex, Cali knew no moment in her life would ever again be this perfect.

At Will's first probing test of her readiness, she caught back a cry of emotion that quickly became a long sigh of nothing but relief at finally, finally, oh, finally he was there, inside her, his first beautiful thrust filling her and she shuddered and he stopped and he groaned, a sound that came from deep in his gut and was so much a part of what she was feeling she barely managed to breathe.

But she didn't want him to stop and she urged him to move with the fingers she gouged into his backside and *oh, yes,* that was where she wanted him, right there where she was so tightly wound up, pressing, grinding, *there, that's it, oh, no, no, not so soon.* She wasn't ready to come, wasn't ready, didn't want, no, this first time, not so fast...as if she could put a halt to what Will had started when she'd first opened her eyes and seen him lying beside her.

"Will, I can't wait. I want to wait." She panted sharply. "I want to wait."

"'s okay, baby." He sounded as out of control as she was. "Next time. We'll do this slow and easy next time."

Next time? He wanted her again. He wanted her again. She didn't even know how she would survive the here and now. "Are you sure?"

He panted to a stop. "The only thing I'm sure about is that this has to happen now."

And then he surged upward, his back bowing as he drove into her body. Cali let go and the thrilling burst that followed took her higher than she'd known she could go. Will's thrusts remained constant and steady, the pressure perfect, the position exactly right and she shivered and trembled until her focus eased away from the sensation between her legs to take in the sensation of Will.

Cali smiled. He'd waited for her. He'd waited, making sure she found heaven in her release. She felt the taut restraint in the muscles of his shoulders and back and moved her hands to his backside that was equally tight. She dug her fingers into his buttocks, her heels into the backs of his thighs and rolled up against him.

He buried his face in the crease where her neck met her shoulder and growled. The tempo of his movements increased at her urging. She met his every downward thrust with a hard upward arch of her lower body until she sensed he was on the verge of losing control.

When he came he would've driven Cali off the end of the futon and into the wall if not for the buttress of pillows. He shook, shuddered, his entire body racked by a completion so powerful Cali found herself fighting back tears—and wondering if he'd been waiting for her as long as she'd been for him.

Chapter Six

WHEN CALI BURST THROUGH the door of the Paddington's office thirty minutes before she was due to clock in for her Friday night shift, Erin looked up from the shuffle of paperwork spread across her desk. The caterer had just left after spending two hours finalizing the menu for the party, yet Erin still wasn't sure the choices she'd made were the best.

She was sure, however, that Cali was about to pop. Erin didn't know if she would do better to come right out and ask, or to let Cali blurt it out when she was ready. What Erin did instead was broach the subject forefront in her mind. "Have you seen the rerun of *Seinfeld* where Jerry eats the black and white cookie then throws up for the first time in years?"

Cali plopped down in the only extra chair in the office, a thrift-store number with crushed velvet gold cushions and freshly varnished arms and legs, and shoved her backpack up underneath. "I think so. Where he and Elaine are in the bakery to pick up a babka and she finds a hair? Why?"

Erin nodded. "That's the one. And I'm only asking because the caterer has black and white cookies on the menu and I wonder if that's what everyone at the party is going to be thinking about. Jerry Seinfeld vomiting."

Cali shrugged and tucked her crossed legs up into the chair. "So what if they are? It'll add some appropriate Halloween gore."

"I don't know." Erin shook her head slowly while she thought. "I just think it has a huge potential ick factor, don't you?"

Cali nodded toward the papers on Erin's desk. "What else is on the menu?"

Erin put the pages of the proposal back into order. "Don't forget, I had to take into consideration a mingling crowd and limited seats, so I did what I could to minimize the need for utensils."

"Finger foods."

"For the most part." The look of concern, no, the look of disgust on Cali's face gave Erin pause. "You don't think that's a problem, do you? I mean, it's not like we're a full service restaurant here to begin with. The caterer is the one putting things together."

A set of blond brows lifted. "Do you have booze?"

"Uh, hello? This is a bar."

Cali waved a dismissive hand. "Then anything works."

"Okay, then," Erin said, deciding Cali's attitude better be about whatever had brought her flying in here or she was going to find herself smacked back to reality. "We have black grapes and white pears. Black bean soup with white rice. Peppered roast beef on white bread. Turkey breast on pumpernickel—"

"So far, so good." Cali held up a finger. "But I'll be heading straight for the chocolate, which you had better have in horrific quantities."

"Trust me. There will be trays of white, milk and dark chocolate truffles everywhere." And she would be the next in line behind Cali. Erin flipped to the second page of the proposed menu.

"Also, toasted marshmallows and chocolate fondue, which works for the fruit, too. Then the obvious devil's food cake and angel food cake. The black and white cookies…maybe. Chocolate mousse brownies and almond blancmange. White and Black Russians. White grape and blackberry punch."

"Spiked?"

"Of course." And that was it. She stacked the pages and waited for Cali's reaction. "So, what do you think?"

Heaving a sigh, Cali slumped down to sit on her spine in the chair. "The only thing I can think about right now is the morning I spent in bed with Will."

Erin blinked, blinked again, shook off her shock and almost shouted, "You did what?"

"I know, can you believe it?"

"No. I can't believe it. You were just whining yesterday about not wanting to screw up your friendship with Will."

"I know. This was just one of those spontaneous things and I didn't have time to think."

"Or maybe this was your subconscious's way of telling you to quit thinking. You've really been obsessing over this way too much, you know."

"I know, I know. Now all I can do is wait and see what happens." Cali blew out a long slow sigh. "I had no idea sex could be so invigorating and exhausting at the same time. Well, I mean I knew about the exhausting part but usually that's more a case of being too tired to even make an effort at orgasm."

Erin chuckled. The old cliché of "Been there, done that" seemed to fit. "And this time?"

Head plopped against the chair back, Cali closed her

eyes. "This time is definitely a case of being exhausted from the orgasms."

"A sex hangover. I know."

One Cali eye opened. "You, too?"

Erin nodded. "Sebastian. His name is Sebastian."

Cali's second eye opened. Her head came up. "Is that his real name or his Scary Guy name?"

"Funny," Erin said, even as she tried not to laugh. "It would be a good Scary Guy name, wouldn't it?"

"What's his last name?"

"Gallo. Sebastian Gallo."

"Oh, that's even better," Cali scoffed. "Gallo? As in, 'Get a rope'?"

"I don't know about the gallows part—" Erin's mouth twisted. She really couldn't help herself. "—but he's certainly hung."

"Eww. Too much information, Erin. Feel free to keep that to yourself." Cali paused, then lost the battle with her own prurient grin. "Though, I must say that Will is certainly not lacking in that, uh, area either."

Frowning, Erin tapped the end of her pencil against the desktop. "Do you think guys really have size issues?"

"Not as much as we do, worrying about our own butts and boobs. Actually, I think once they have us naked and writhing they're more worried they might leave us hanging. And I don't mean that gallows thing you were just bragging about."

Erin sighed. Then Cali sighed. Both slumped back in their respective chairs and took a long, daydreaming moment. Erin had a feeling her best friend was no more in the mood to work than she was. But it was Friday night and only a matter of time before the weekend madness began.

And then Erin wondered what she would do if Sebastian showed up again tonight when she wouldn't have but maybe a minute or two to talk. Not that talk had been a big part of their interaction so far...

"Okay, tell me how bizarre it is that we've been whining about having no man in our lives and we both get lucky within the same twenty-four hours."

Erin looked at Cali who was obviously way on her way to falling in love. While Erin was on her way to...what? Absolutely fabulous sex? Yes, that was it exactly. Exactly what she'd wanted when she'd hatched this Man To Do plan.

"I'm thrilled for you and Will. But I don't think what I'm doing with Sebastian qualifies as having a man in my life. More like having a man in my—" *body?* "—bed."

Cali lifted a brow. "That's what you wanted, though, isn't it?" When Erin hesitated, Cali quickly added, "I didn't have a tape recorder going but I'm quite sure I can quote you verbatim. You're tired, remember? Of double standards and men having all the fun and going to bed alone. Any of that ring a bell?"

What Erin was tired of was being reminded of things she'd said then that she wasn't sure she meant now. "Quite loudly, unfortunately."

"Unfortunately? So, you've changed your mind after one night?"

How could she explain this without going into graphic detail? "I just never expected one night to be..."

"To be what?" Cali scooted to the edge of her chair and leaned forward to prop her elbows on Erin's desk. "I'm all ears here."

It would help a lot if Erin knew what she'd expected from those hours with Sebastian. And why the intensity of what they'd shared had blown her so thoroughly away. "Oh. Like I'm going to share details of my private life when you're over there holding out on me?"

"Hey, I'm an open book. What do you want to know?"

"Last I heard you were afraid sleeping with Will would screw up your friendship, and this was just last night, mind you. Since then, you've spent the better part of today writhing and naked? You mind telling me how you got from Thursday's point A to Friday's point B?"

"Actually we spent the better part of the day sleeping." Cali smiled a beatific smile. "It was the *best* part of the day we spent making love."

Making love.

Those words certainly didn't apply to the acts in which Erin and Sebastian had engaged, did they? Not only hadn't they made love, she wondered if they'd even made like. Or if they'd only been two improper strangers screwing themselves senseless. "What a difference a day makes, huh?"

"Or a night, anyway. I guess in my case it was the difference made by a very innocent kiss that turned things upside down."

"What innocent kiss?"

"It was yesterday, before we closed up last night and left. Will and I were talking and I'd been thinking about your Man To Do plan." Cali shrugged. "I couldn't help it. I leaned over and kissed him on the cheek."

"And then what?"

"Then I walked away and got back to work."

"You tease!"

"I suppose so, but I'd like to think of it more as flirting. It's not like I was going to say no if he asked."

"Which apparently he did."

"Several times. To my complete and utter delight."

"So, now what? Are you actually going to date a good friend? Or are you just going to sleep with him?"

"You mean like you and Sebastian?"

Erin tossed her pencil to the desk and shoved both

hands back through her hair. "We really are pathetic, you know. Just yesterday you weren't sure about seducing Will. And now you're dealing with a possible relationship. All I wanted was sex. Which I got. But now I'm thinking I might want more."

"You want more? Or more with Sebastian? What's he like anyway? You haven't told me a thing about him. Except for that…gallows thing."

"Truthfully?" Erin shrugged. "There's not a lot to tell. We didn't do much talking."

"You just rolled around in bed."

"No. We never made it out of the shower." Erin looked at her hands, front and back. "I'm surprised I'm not still a prune. I also want to know what he pays for hot water."

"So, he has a thing for being clean. Or else he's a fish. What else?"

"He has about a thousand books."

"Books?"

"Books. He has those floor-to-ceiling shelves with a library ladder that rolls. Quite impressive actually."

"Hmm," Cali mumbled. "Literary and intellectual. Maybe even a librarian."

This time Erin pushed to her feet to pace. The more she thought about who Sebastian was and all the things she didn't know, the more frustrated she became. So much for her plan to keep emotions from the equation, to stay uninvolved. She wanted to know everything there was to know about him.

"Not a librarian, no. The intellectual I might give you. He's quiet. Doesn't say a lot though you can tell by his eyes that he never stops thinking. Whatever he does, he makes big bucks. His place is twice the size of mine and built-out like you wouldn't believe."

"Besides his love of books, then. What else did his place tell you?"

"He loves music, which I already knew. And he has a huge computer station. Totally state-of-the art equipment. Makes me wonder if he's a consultant of some type."

"What sort of consulting, do you think?" Cali was once again bright-eyed and curious. "What about the books? What do they tell you? Medical? Technical?"

Erin stopped pacing to think. "Actually, he's a virtual Barnes & Noble. Psychology. Paranormal occurrences. Homer and Shakespeare. Stephen King and Ryder Falco and John Grisham."

"So, the guy's well-read and well-monied. Interesting and intellectual. I guess that leaves you only one option?"

"Which is?"

"Stop thinking so much and get to work."

ERIN WAS STILL WEIGHING the pros and cons of black and white cookies when she glanced up to welcome the customer who'd just settled onto the stool at the bar and found herself looking into the eyes of Sebastian Gallo.

The most intense experience of her life had been spent with this man and she didn't even know what to say.

And so she said, "Hello."

He remained silent, his steady focus launching a fleet of nerves into her veins. She held his gaze and her smile, though the longer he sat there unspeaking, the more wooden her expression became.

Finally, he reached out and took her hand in his, linking their fingers and running his thumb in a caress over the tip of hers. "How're you doing?"

Her heart thumped and thudded. "I'm doing good. You?"

"Still sorta squishy. Leaking. Dripping. But I'll dry out." His lips lifted into a slow sultry smile.

And she laughed, never wanting to let go of his hand but knowing she couldn't draw a draft telepathically. And one of her customers had just flagged her down.

She pulled her fingers from Sebastian's but made sure to keep the visual connection. She needed that much—she needed more—but that would do for now. "Do you want a beer? Glass of wine? It's on the house."

"I was thinking more along the lines of champagne."

A brow went up. She reached for a clean mug and made quick work of the customer's refill. "Celebrating?"

"I am, as a matter of fact," he said and leaned against the back of the stool, hooking his elbows over the railing, his knees spread wide and his feet braced on the lowest rung. "I thought you might join me."

Tonight he wore a wine-colored shirt in rich linen tucked into neat black wool pants. His glossy black hair picked up glints of the bar's lighting and his eyes were clear and attentive and bright.

Erin wanted to gobble him up. "I would. If I wasn't working." Two steps down the bar to deliver the beer. Two steps back. "Can I have a rain check?"

"You can have anything you want," he said and Erin's world went still.

"You might want to be careful what you're offering." Her voice hadn't even wavered once. Amazing when she was shaking all the way to the roots of her hair. "I'm liable to take you up on it."

"I intend for you to."

Whew, but he played the game well. This one was going to keep her on her toes. "You have a preference for your champagne?"

He kept his gaze on her as he considered. "Tell you

what. Give me a beer. The champagne can wait until later."

Later? What did he have in mind for later? And was she included in his plans? "Great. I'll pick out a good one."

"Pick out the best. My treat."

She'd have to see what she could do. If expense was no issue, as he'd seemed to imply... Her interest was definitely piqued. "I'll keep that in mind. I'm sure I can come up with a suitable vintage. Unless you have a preference?"

One that tastes best sipped from bare skin, perhaps?

"Only that it's one you'll enjoy."

"That won't be a problem," she said because she knew that it wouldn't. She had a bit of a champagne fetish. She just wished she had a better handle on where to take this conversation because she found herself searching for wit instead of relaxing and enjoying his company.

She supposed that was what happened when two people skipped several of the natural steps to intimacy and went straight to bed. Might not hurt to read up on Desmond Morris....

"So, other than the fabulous atmosphere and the fabulous drinks and my fabulous company, what brings you here?" There. That ought to do to get things going. She opened the bottle of ale she'd chosen for him and poured.

"I'd say you covered all of it."

Exactly what she'd wanted to hear. Even knowing his response was nothing more than upping the tension strung high-wire taut, it was exactly what she'd wanted to hear. "You don't have the notebook you had with you last night."

"Last night I was working." He reached for the mug of ale, lifting it in a toast before drinking.

Working on what, she wanted to scream because this was like the worst sort of fingernail-pulling torture. Instead, she said, "And now it's Friday and you're done for the week."

He laughed, returning the mug to the bar. "Unfortunately, I'm never done."

He didn't elaborate but Erin seized the opening. "Tell me about it. This entrepreneurial business isn't all it's cracked up to be. Or, actually, it's more. More than I don't remember signing on for."

"You're obviously handling that more pretty damn well." He glanced around the bar, leaning forward and wrapping his hand around the mug. "You've always got a crowd in here."

"I do, yeah, but how would you know that?" He'd been here exactly twice in the year she'd run the bar. Last night and now. If he'd been here before, when Paddington's belonged to Rory, well, she hadn't been here often enough then to have noticed, had she?

Grimacing, she added, "You're not exactly a regular."

"You have windows."

"And you're a Peeping Tom?"

He grinned. "Nope. Just a moth drawn to the flame."

Oh, but she loved the way that sounded. The way tiny wings fluttered in her belly. "How do you figure that?"

He shrugged one shoulder, twisted his mug back and forth on the cork coaster. "I think best when in motion, when on my feet. And I can only pace the loft for so long."

"So you walk the streets."

He nodded, drank again. "A regular creature of the night."

Which brought to mind vampires, not moths. No, not moths at all, but hunger and darkness and needs satisfied only at night. She forced back a shiver as she pictured him striding with purpose in black boots and a long black duster, moving in the shadows, stalking his prey.

Stalking her.

The noise of the bar became nothing but a hum, a background drone swarming around her while Sebastian's gaze compelled her forward. She found herself leaning against the bar and into his personal space, space she wanted to crawl into as desperately as she wanted to pull him into her body.

Thank goodness Cali's timing was what it was because she came to the rescue, sliding to a stop beside Erin and banging her serving tray down on the bar. "I've had it with those two. I've totally had it. I swear, Erin. You're going to have to get another server to cover that table."

The Daring Duo. Erin had been waiting for Cali to boil over about the couple. "I'll send A.J. over to crash their party."

"Yeah, that would work." Cali shoved back her mop of hair and heaved a disgusted sigh. "Except he didn't show up for his shift."

"What?" Erin glanced up at the clock suspended above the center of the circular bar. "He should've been here an hour ago. Where have I been?"

"I have a feeling he won't be showing for any of his future shifts." Cali planted a hand on her hip. "I heard he was looking to get hired on at Courtland's."

The new jazz café opening the next block down was certain to be a competitive thorn in Erin's side. Great. Less than a month to get a replacement hired and trained. As a rule, not that much of a problem.

But with the party coming up... Erin sighed.

"Can I help?" Sebastian reached over and took hold of her hand, which obviously surprised Cali who responded with a questioning, "Uh, Erin?"

Erin glanced up, caught Cali's gaze cutting uncertainly to Sebastian and back. "Oh, I'm sorry. Cali, this is Sebas-

tian Gallo, my upstairs, uh, neighbor. Sebastian, Cali Tippen. The only server here who gets to talk back to me
because she's also my best friend."

"Hi, Cali." Sebastian tipped his head in greeting.

"Uh, Sebastian. Hey. It's nice to meet you." Totally distracted, she rubbed at the obvious headache building behind her forehead. "I'm sorry to bust in on you and Erin
like this but I've reached the end of my rope with two of
our regular customers and having A.J. up and quit without notice means I'm stuck with The Daring Duo."

"I hope he doesn't think he's going to be getting a good
work reference," Erin grumbled, tossing Sebastian's empty
bottle into the trash.

"I wouldn't even give him a character reference,"
Cali added.

But Sebastian turned the conversation an entirely different direction when he asked, "The Daring Duo?"

Cali rolled her eyes, shook her head, raised one stop-
sign hand. "Don't even ask."

Though Erin chuckled, she did feel Cali's pain. "It's
simply a term of endearment for the couple sitting in the
far booth behind you on the right. They're not as discreet
as Cali—and as I—obviously wish they would be in their
displays of affection."

"Wrong, Erin," Cali interrupted. "Affection is a light
brush of her lips to his cheek, or his arm wrapped around
her shoulder. Maybe even their hands on the table with
fingers entwined. I'll even give them hands under the table
with fingers entwined."

Cali's gaze brushed over Sebastian's hand still resting on
Erin's before glancing back out into the room. "But we're
talking about things going on under that table that might
require the intervention of a good vice cop."

At that, Sebastian laughed, releasing Erin's hand to lean

back in his stool. Immediately she felt—and hated—the loss of warmth, not only from the contact of his hand but from his nearness. That personal space he'd abandoned when he'd shifted to sit back in his chair. Oh, she was going to have to watch out for this one.

"They're regulars then?" he asked of Cali.

"Regular pains-in-the-ass." She turned to Erin for backup, brow furrowing as she thought. "What? At least three or four nights a week, right?"

Erin went about wiping down the bar where the bottle of ale had been sitting. She nodded. "Three or four nights a week for six weeks or so. Same table. Same wine. Same R-rated behavior."

"And when it borders on X-rated, I'm the one stuck having to crash their party. I do have to admit that it's not as bad as a porno flick. But, still." Cali shuddered and, thinking further, shuddered again. "All that tongue-sucking business and the way she's always breathing hard. And then there's his belt that seems to always be unbuckled…it's just too close to voyeurism for this girl."

Sebastian seemed to consider the information then asked, "So, this is a fairly new relationship?"

"For us or for them?" Erin replied, answering his question with a question.

He smiled at that. "For you, of course. But I'm thinking for them as well."

"Why do you think that?" Cali asked.

"First blush of passion. Can't keep their hands off each other."

The idea made sense to Erin since keeping busy was the only way she'd managed so far to keep her hands off Sebastian. She glanced from him to Cali. "Newlyweds maybe?"

Cali shook her head. "I don't think so. Neither one of

them is wearing a ring and, yes, I know that doesn't prove anything. But the idea of those two being married doesn't gel. Besides, if they were married, they'd be home in bed. Not in the bar."

"Not necessarily." Both Erin and Cali turned when Sebastian spoke. He shrugged one shoulder, the burgundy-colored fabric molding to the muscles beneath. "Exhibitionism might have been part of their initial attraction. They enjoy the thrill of seeing what they can get away with. It's part of the high of arousal."

"So, saying they are married, and I'm not saying any such thing," Cali quickly added. "Then why no rings?"

"Part of their game. Wanting others to see." He leaned forward, his sharp green gaze snagging Erin's. "Wanting others to wonder."

"Just like we're doing now," she managed, though her voice resonated with no more sound than that of a whisper. And he wasn't even touching her. Only looking. Watching. Knowing she was remembering all the things they'd done.

"Exactly." He glanced up, taking in the placement of the track lighting. Then glanced back at Erin. "You might think about adjusting the lighting. Spotlight their table. See if that deters them."

"I'm afraid that might encourage them further." Oh, but this conversation would be so much easier if her gaze wasn't constantly drawn to his mouth as he talked. She was too well-versed in the things he could do with his lips and his mouth and her nerves buzzed with arousal's first stirrings.

"Yeah," Cali cut in. "Before we do anything to encourage them further, can we please reassign that table to another server?"

Erin laughed. "Yeah. I can do that."

"And hire someone to replace A.J.?" Cali begged.

Erin glanced at a pleading Cali. "Let me pull the applications I have on file. I'll put them on my desk. If you get a chance, maybe you can glance through them and see if you recognize any of the names. If you've worked with any of them or heard anything. Bad or good. Save me the grief down the road."

"Actually…" Cali tugged nervously on a lock of her hair. "I know someone who needs a job and would be perfect."

"Who?"

"Could we talk in the office for a minute. Nothing personal," Cali added for Sebastian's sake.

He waved off her apology. "Not a problem."

"Sure," Erin said. "I'll be right there. Let me check with the bunch at the end of the bar and get Robin to cover me. So, give me five minutes?"

"Yeah, that'll give me time to make a quick round through my tables. Hopefully I'll return without having my eyes singed out of their sockets." Cali picked up her tray and headed back onto the battlefield.

Erin chuckled, watched her best friend walk off, then turned her attention to Sebastian. "Can I get you anything else?"

He shook his head. "I'm set."

"Great." She wanted to ask if he'd be there when she got back, if he planned to wait for her, to hang out the rest of the night then strip her naked and take her with reckless abandon there on top of the bar.

Instead, she said, "I'll check back with you in a few."

He lifted his mug. "I'll be here."

His words made walking away only marginally easier to bear.

TEN MINUTES LATER, Erin walked into the office to find her best friend pacing the small space, serving tray gripped at her side and bouncing off her hip as she walked.

Erin wondered what was going on, why it was Cali who seemed nervous when it was Sebastian sitting at the bar and totally destroying Erin's concentration.

She pulled open the file drawer where she kept the employment applications and pulled out the folder that had grown admittedly slim. Most of the servers she'd originally hired had stayed on.

A few had left after opening, lured away by the newer establishments promising bigger crowds, mega-tips and a level of energy with which Paddington's had never tried to compete.

Erin had purposefully redesigned the wine and tobacco bar with intimacy in mind. Rory's pub had been a lot like that, a second home for his regular customers, a place where men were able to raise a pint and blow off steam at the end of a long working day.

The pint and steam concept hadn't changed. She'd just made a few adjustments to the ambience, keeping her fingers crossed that Rory wouldn't mind, yet still looking over her shoulder expecting his growling censure. A strange reaction since he'd never once growled.

Not even when she'd ditched any steady dedication to her studies and had, instead, used a chunk of the inheritance from her parents to finance a backpacking trek through Europe, where she'd played and feasted and made mad love from Rome to Lisbon with the first of her life's true loves.

True love. Ha!

She dropped the applications folder onto the desk and, when Cali jumped, crossed her arms over her chest and lifted an inquiring brow. "What's up with you?"

"Only about a million things. Most of them named

Will Cooper." Cali stopped, turned, shook her head and waved off the question hanging on Erin's tongue. "But never mind Will. What is Sebastian doing here?"

Erin hadn't yet answered that question to her own satisfaction. She certainly didn't have an answer for Cali. "Besides making me extremely nervous? I have no idea. So forget Sebastian for the moment and tell me about Will. What's going on? You were all glowing when you talked about him earlier."

"I was not glowing. And he's not here yet, that's the problem. Which means he thinks sleeping with me was a mistake and I should've listened to my head instead of my heart." Cali snorted. "Or I guess it wasn't exactly my heart I was listening to, was it?"

Oh, poor baby. Erin braced both hands on her desk and leaned forward into Cali's space. "Yes, Dork. It was your heart. Otherwise you'd've been boinking Will a long time ago. You know that."

"I don't know anything."

"Well, I do. And I know he'll show up. I've watched you two together, Cali. Will's not the type to hit-and-run, if you know what I mean."

"Okay. You're right. I know he's not like that. I wouldn't want to be with him if he was." Cali buried her face in her hands. "Why does sex have to suck?"

"Because orgasms are really good that way?"

Cali chuckled, then laughed, then totally broke up into hysterical cackles and collapsed into Erin's chair to catch her breath. "That's not funny."

"Yes, it is. Now, who do you know that's looking for a job and can I get a decent night's work out of him or her?" Erin propped a hip on the corner of her desk. "Or is the lure of all that jazz at Courtland's going to be hard to resist?"

Cali flipped through the short stack of applications. "I doubt this would be long term, but I know it would get you out of the bind you're in for the party."

"So, speak woman."

"It's Will. The ad agency where he's been freelancing let him go."

Erin wished all her business decisions were this easy. "He can start tomorrow. Hell, he can start tonight the minute he gets here."

"*If* he gets here, you mean."

"Stop it already or I'm going to have to hurt you." Erin backed up toward the office entrance. "Now, if he's out there when I open the door, you're going to owe me for putting up with all this ridiculous grief of yours."

"If he's out there, I'll give you half of tonight's tip money."

Erin knew what Cali made in tips. Half of the money would pay for more than a few black and white cookies. But the wager was hardly fair. She'd seen Will walk through the front door while on her way to the office.

Still...

"You're on, sister. But I'll stash the money in a safe place and add it to your honeymoon fund. I'm thinking Tahiti or Fiji. Sand and surf and sun and very little clothing. You could get by with a carry-on bag as long as it would hold all your condoms."

"Oh, very funny," Cali said but her smile was firmly settled in place and the idea one Erin knew wouldn't be easily dislodged.

And wasn't that what best friends were for.

Chapter Seven

ERIN SET TWO FLUTES AND the ice bucket into which, thirty minutes ago, she'd placed a bottle of Perrier-Jouet on the table—the very table—occupied by The Daring Duo earlier tonight. Paddington's was closed, the room dark but for two brass lanterns that remained burning night and day, flanking the bar's heavy oak door and glinting off the stained glass inset.

She'd hurried the staff through the routine of close, keeping Robin and Laurie both longer than usual to help Cali set the bar room to rights. Will had helped as well, having been more than happy to accept Erin's offer of employment. He really was a good guy. Cali was a very lucky girl. Erin was thrilled the two had finally gotten together.

She herself had rushed through the register tapes and the cash drawers, the deposit of the evening's take and the accounting she had to make each night of stock to be re-ordered and the labor percentage costs versus the total receipts. The analysis of those numbers, however, would have to wait until tomorrow.

Whether or not she rushed or lingered now, she'd have to go over the books again in the morning. Because, no matter how much time she took tonight, her mind was elsewhere and even Rory looking over her shoulder couldn't guilt her into forgetting about the man waiting for her in the bar.

Forget about Sebastian Gallo. As if.

Tonight, in fact, she'd gone so far as to bring to work a change of clothes, a washcloth and a bottle of her favorite chamomile shower gel. Once she'd finished with the books, she'd taken full advantage of the private office bathroom to pull off her monogrammed polo and gabardine pants. She'd washed away the sweat of the last few hours then changed into the sexy lace bra she wished she'd been wearing yesterday.

Donning her long black skirt and soft cashmere sweater, she did what she could to check herself out using the warped dressing room mirror hanging on the back of the door. After twisting and turning in the restrictive space, she decided that, as long as she didn't really look as distorted as her funhouse reflection, the emerald green was a very good choice judging by the sparkle in her eyes.

So, by the time she locked up after the others, made with the quick sponge bath and retrieved the champagne, she was frantic Sebastian would've given up on her and left.

Finding him should've set her mind at ease.

What it did was make her wet.

She slid into the small circular booth, sitting beside him though she left several inches of space between their bodies. She wanted to share the champagne and the celebration. She wanted to be far enough from him to be able to look into his eyes. She wanted the distance because she wanted the temptation of closing it.

Never before had she known a sweeter taboo than Sebastian Gallo. A taboo because he should've been off-limits and out of her reach, physically, emotionally, definitely sexually. Yet a taboo she couldn't resist because he fit so perfectly into her plans. Yes. That was the reason. He was her Man To Do. That was the source of this incredible fascination. It was all about the forbidden, the unexpected, the thrill of the unknown.

Or so she repeatedly told herself.

"So, this is The Daring Duo's table?" He opened the champagne, smoothly managing the pop of the cork, equally smoothly filling both flutes.

Tiny bubbles danced in the cold, tempting Erin to drink and savor the crisp tingle. "The very one. But it should be safe. Will wiped down all the benches, Laurie mopped, and Robin replaced the tablecloth."

The dark indigo and wine fabric brushed Erin's knees when she crossed her legs, legs left bare beneath the long skirt. As bare as her bottom *sans* panties or thong. She wanted to be ready for whatever Sebastian had in mind and had dressed appropriately—or undressed, as it were.

Besides, she had her own mind wrapped around a few fantasies where clothing would only be in the way. "Do you really think they're married? Putting on a show for our benefit?"

Sebastian sipped, paused, sipped again then downed nearly half the contents of his flute. He didn't answer Erin's question directly, but poured himself another drink, turning on one hip to better face her.

"Their show isn't for our benefit, Erin." He ran his finger around the flute's fragile rim. Around and around, hypnotically. "It's for their own. It's what turns them on, knowing people are watching. It gets him hard. It makes her wet. They use the knowledge of being watched the same way you might use a vibrator." He looked up then, his gaze heated and compelling. "Or the same way I might use a hot shower."

Erin didn't even know what to say. She wasn't sure she

could breathe. She remembered too well his hot shower and the memory of the way she'd watched, the way he'd taken himself in his hand and stroked to completion, the way she'd wanted to wrap her mouth around the plum-ripe and plump head and enjoy his taste as much as give him pleasure.

But she wasn't going to talk about her vibrator because more often than not her fantasies were lived with only her hands. And, lately, she'd imagined her hands to be his. But she did want to understand about his shower. The decadence of space and design, the potential for hedonistic indulgence, had not been lost on her. Had, in fact, been demonstrated quite clearly.

So…why?

"Tell me about your hot showers. About that space. The benches. The showerheads. That's not…" She fluttered one hand, reaching for her flute. "That's not the bathroom of a man who only showers to wash his body. It intrigues me." She lifted the flute to her lips and, before she sipped she added, "You intrigue me."

She watched as emotion flickered through his eyes, truth battling fiction, real involvement fighting the tempting attraction of a casual affair.

And she knew whatever he told her, if he told her anything at all, that she would never know with any certainty if he'd chosen to let honesty win the war with the fantasy of a provocatively spun yarn.

Or if he'd only told her what he wanted her to believe in order to keep them wrapped up in this sensual spell.

He inched his way closer, his thigh and hip brushing hers. He draped an arm on the curve of the seat back and toyed with strands of her hair. His gaze was wickedly sharp as it snagged hers and held. "I shower to think."

Erin's pulse jumped at the contact. If he moved any

closer, if his touch grew more intimate... She might as well give up now on any sort of coherent thought. "You told me you walked to think."

"I do both."

"Depending on what you need to think about?" she asked and sipped at her champagne.

He nodded, fingering the fragile stem of his own half-filled flute. "Depending on what I need to work out in my mind. Walking is about fresh thinking. Getting the blood to flow to my brain."

"And the hot showers? That amazing piece of real estate you call a bathroom?" She *would* get to the bottom of this if it killed her. Or if it took her all night—even though she was quite certain all that heat and water was about blood flowing to other parts of his body.

He took the flute from her hand and set it on the table. "The showers should be obvious. The steam straightens out the wrinkles the walking puts in my brain."

That caught her off guard and she chuckled, then reached for her flute again but he took hold of her hand and stopped her. She stared at his much larger hand covering hers that was so much smaller. "I never realized certain thinking was done better under certain conditions."

"But you do it all the same." He laced their fingers together, studied her short, practical nails.

"No. I don't have that luxury." Though even as she refuted his claim she realized she thought more about her issues with Paddington's while at the bar, thought more about the missing needs of her personal life while at home.

"It's not a luxury. It's what I do." He reached for her other hand, holding both of hers in both of his, and she shifted on the bench to better face him. "You do it more than you realize. I'm just more conscious of where I need to be, what I need to be doing in order to get my head on straight."

Her head would never be on straight. Not when he was making love to her hands, massaging her fingers and the base of her thumbs, her palms, her knuckles, the pads at the tips of her fingers. His touch seduced her and made concentrating on this strange conversation more than difficult.

Nearer to impossible. As was any cognizant reply. "You think too much about thinking."

"Thinking's what I do."

That was the second time he'd said that and she knew the remark was worth pursuing. But, at the moment, she wasn't able to pursue anything at all. She was relaxed and hypnotized by what he was doing to her hands.

Maybe he was a street magician, a magic man like David Blaine, the legal pad filled with notes on the tricks of the trade, all that thinking he did part of the process of working out the subtleties of deception.

It all made sense, she supposed, except she wasn't supposed to be wondering about who he was and what he did because she was only here for his body, not his mind. Or so she continually worked to convince herself wondering if she'd ever succeed.

So when he took her hands he was holding, cupped her palms and covered her breasts with their joined hands, she forgot all about his shower and his thinking because the lantern light had turned his eyes to a compelling contrast of light green and dark desire from which she couldn't pull her gaze.

He pressed his forefingers and thumbs to her forefingers and thumbs and worked her hands over her nipples. She gasped, unable to hold back her response because it was the response of her fantasy. This was her fantasy. Her hands that were his hands arousing her darkest desire.

"When I was a boy," he began, his hands leaving hers

and moving to the tiny pearl buttons of her sweater, "I lived on the streets. I never knew anything about my father. All I remember of my mother could be called select-ive. Only the things I want to recall."

"Is this true?" she asked, her hands growing still on her breasts as her focus switched from his touch on her body to the touch of his words on her mind.

"Don't ask questions. Just listen."

He continued to release her buttons, each tiny seed pearl slipping easily through the grosgrain ribbon facing the cashmere placket. One button, then another, air kiss-ing her skin as the two sides began to part.

Yet, she remained silent, wanting to hear and to feel. Her hands fell to her lap as she concentrated her focus on his voice and his hands.

"I had a toy truck. One wheel was missing, but I didn't care. I sort of liked that it had to fight against the odds, bumping along the way it did." He reached the bottom of the unending row of buttons, his knuckles brushing the fabric of her skirt where it covered her belly.

"I rolled it across every inch of the concrete floor in the building where I lived. A building with no glass in the windows. Cardboard didn't do much against the wind, but that's all that was left with the plywood hav-ing been burned for heat. The ashes made for a great con-struction site."

Erin listened to his story, wishing he was doing no more than entertaining her, lulling her with the magic of his words, seducing her with the magic of his hands. But she knew that wasn't the case, that he was doing much more than that. That what he was telling her wasn't any sort of tale at all, but the truth she'd been hoping to find.

His timing totally sucked, she grumbled, because how

was she supposed to concentrate on what he was saying when he had opened the front of her sweater and was, even now, pushing it back off her shoulders?

His gaze devoured the ecru lace that made up the cups of her bra, lace through which her nipples strained and pouted. He reached for her champagne flute and sipped, then rubbed the wet rim beneath her nipple, over and around before he poured champagne over her breast and leaned his head down to drink.

The sensation caught her struggling to breathe. The air on the damp lace was cool, his mouth was hot, his tongue swirling and circling, his lips sucking the peak into an unbearable tightness rivaling that in her chest, making it hard for her to catch her breath.

Harder still for her trembling heart to beat.

When he finally lifted his head, Erin wondered, what next? What now? How would she ever get enough of what he did to her body? And how long was she going to manage to keep her emotions uninvolved when he told her stories of little boys and their trucks?

"I don't know how old I was when I was finally picked up. My mother had long been gone. When I wanted to try and get a handle on the timing of things, I remembered the birthday cupcake she must have begged from a bakery. I used that and counted forward. She told me we were celebrating the first day of spring and making it through the last five years. So, I must've been eleven—or close to it—when the authorities managed to get their hands on me."

All the while he'd been speaking, he'd worked the straps of her bra off her shoulders, trapping her in sleeves of cashmere and the bra's ecru lace. Yet it was the bondage of his gaze that kept her still.

He studied her quandary then reached around to free

her arms and release the clasp holding her bra in place. The sweater dropped to the seat behind her. The bra fell to her lap, baring her full breasts that ached for his attention.

"Come here," he ordered and pulled her onto his lap.

The edge of the table gouged into her back but she hardly noticed. She was too aware of his erection solidly pressed between her thighs and his hands and mouth that were everywhere at once. Kneading flesh so incredibly sensitive and dying for his touch.

She held on to his shoulders because it was all she could do, and tossed her head back, feeling like the wanton she knew she had to look. She spread her legs wider, her skirt bunching around her thighs as she ground against him, wanting him there where she was so incredibly wet and ready and open.

He blew a long breath onto her skin between her breasts where his face was buried. And then he moved a hand between his own legs and stroked his erection before reaching deeper and pressing hard to halt what he could of the surging sensation.

He shuddered, and his hand found its way up between *her* legs, to the very spot where she was naked and waiting. His second breath heated her skin and a string of raw curses followed. In the next moment she found herself filled by the thick length of two fingers.

She arched toward his lower body but all he did was widen the V of his spread legs, forcing her thighs farther open there where she sat on his lap. His thumb circled her clit; his tongue circled her nipple.

She braced her hands on his shoulders and rode his thrusting fingers hard, wanting more, wanting to wait, wanting him now even while wanting to draw out the anticipation until both of them were ready to burst.

And just when she was ready to come, he pulled his

hand away, moved his mouth away and sat back, his chest heaving beneath raw and ragged breaths.

"Why did you stop?" she panted.

"I'm not ready for you to come."

To hell with what he was ready for. She was ready enough to take matters into her own hands, to get herself off to the fantasy she'd grown practiced to using, and groaned when he stopped the downward reach of her fingers.

"Not yet," he bit off.

"You're making me crazy."

"I want you wetter."

Wetter? Moisture seeped from her sex to run into the crevice of her thigh. She smelled her own musk and saw his nostrils flare. She doubted it was possible to be any wetter. She wasn't sure she'd ever been this wet.

"I swear, Sebastian. You're out of your mind. You don't think this is wet enough?"

"Trust me," he said moving his hands to her waist and boosting her to sit onto the edge of the table. She pushed herself upward with the heels of her palms. Then he slid his hands up her calves to her knees beneath her skirt. "Lean back."

She hesitated, but did as he asked, knowing she was putting herself in an incredibly vulnerable position, yet unable to stop the thrilling, edgy flutter of nerves.

Sebastian pulled his hands from under her skirt and settled his palms on her thighs, inching the soft black fabric upward until her skirt rode high. The thought that she was so close to being spread across the table, a feast for his consumption, ripe fruit for his hedonistic indulgence...

She tossed back her head, stopped short of releasing the bubbling laughter, uncertain whether what she was feeling was nervousness, wickedness or total disbelief that she was actually so incredibly bold.

He shimmied her skirt up farther until his thumbs found the skin of her inner thighs. He rubbed there, small circles, inching closer to the crease where leg met hip. If nothing else, he'd certainly mastered a very effective method of torture. She was panting, in pain, and ready to scream.

He leaned forward, kissed her thigh, blew a stream of breath against her skin, ran his tongue along the patch he'd just heated. He repeated the action on the opposite side, only this time he moved closer to her sex. He shifted forward, returned to the leg where he'd started, repeated the process and proved her earlier assumption totally wrong.

She was wetter, more ready, more aroused than she'd been minutes before when he'd made love to her with his fingers. She could not believe the intensity of her own incredible response. The way flames licked through her body's center. The way her skin sizzled from the inside out.

This time, when he moved closer, he pushed her skirt up over her hips to her belly, completely exposing her nakedness, and leaned in to blow a stream of hot breath from her clitoris down between her legs, blowing directly into the mouth of her sex and then blowing lower still.

The waiting, the Tantric sense of anticipation and denial would've been fun if she didn't ache quite so badly, didn't yearn quite so wildly to find her completion. She didn't think she'd ever been so desperate to come. And Sebastian's obsession with arousing her further, the concentrated sensation of his hands and his mouth…five minutes more and she'd be out of her mind.

And then he returned to his tale. "I spent six years living off the State. We had a locker room set up where we showered. A dorm's worth of teenage boys all at one time, looking over our shoulders, watching our backs, hoping to make it through those quick fifteen minutes without the need for stitches and our virginity intact."

Erin pulled in a sharp breath. His shocking words hit her at the same time he gently pressed the knuckle of his thumb into the crevice between her legs and dragged it down. She wanted to think about what he was saying, tried to think about what he was saying, but couldn't get beyond what he was doing and doing so incredibly, amazingly well.

"I showered like that four times a week for six or seven years. I did okay. I made it out. And I swore whenever I finally got on my feet and could afford a place of my own, I would never again worry about hot water or how long I spent taking a bath."

All the while he'd been talking, he'd been watching the play of his fingers in and around her sex. Erin could easily have gotten off twice now. But she'd gritted her teeth and listened to his story. Still braced back on her elbows, she'd tucked her chin to her chest and kept her gaze trained on Sebastian's face.

Never once had he hesitated in the telling of his story and never once had he looked up to see if she was listening or if she'd dissolved into a mass of writhing sexuality which so aptly described the sensations in her belly and below. Twisting, twining, kinky knots and ropes of enflamed nerves.

When at last he sat back, she knew he was ready. Or so she thought until he picked up the champagne bottle and used it to stroke along both her inner thighs. He moved the bottle higher, rubbing the mouth over the lips of her sex and between, circling her clit, slipping the cool glass along her folds, down one side, up the other, teasing her unmercifully before finally lifting the bottle to drink.

Yet, even as he swallowed, even as Erin waited breathlessly for him to return the bottle to the table, pull a condom from his pocket and set himself free, he drizzled champagne there above her strip of trimmed hair and leaned forward, drinking both the wine and her moisture from between the folds of her sex.

Erin couldn't take it any longer. She cried out, her body rigid beneath the shattering sensations of orgasm, the rush of pleasure sending her arching upward toward his mouth. Her flesh tingled and burned and throbbed, and still she came because this wasn't enough. She needed to have him inside her.

She pushed up from her elbows, pushed Sebastian away and against the back of the booth. She reached for the waistband of his pants. He reached into his pocket. She longed to stroke him, to watch his eyes glaze, to draw forth that first bead of moisture telling her he was ready to come.

But she doubted they'd ever be able to take their time coming together because of this combustible fire between them. He tore into the condom packet and rolled the sheath the length of his erection. Erin didn't even ask. She slid off the table and into his lap, her hand between their bodies to guide him to her center.

He filled her, and it was like finding a part of herself that had been missing. The fit was snug and perfect. She gripped him with muscles still sore from last night. With her hands braced on his shoulders, his hands on her waist, she rode him hard. Her breasts swayed and he pressed his forehead against her chest, panting hot ragged breaths there in the valley between.

Her thigh muscles burned from exertion. Her pulse raced, the blood in her veins fairly sang. She was raw from the friction of his late evening beard, raw from the flat of his tongue, raw from the thick scraping slide of his cock and she didn't even care. This was what she'd wanted. This aching, bursting, joyous connection of bodies in need.

Sebastian spread his legs wider, slumped down onto his spine and drove himself upward, his head pressed back into the padded booth, the tendons in his neck drawn taut. She wanted to ease his torture, his agony, but the strain on his gorgeous face only incited her further.

She came again, his thrusts wild and urgent, spurring her over the edge. Guttural groans of release ripped from his throat as he joined her. She collapsed against his chest, tremors shuddering through her. She missed the feel of his bare skin against hers. But urgency hadn't given him time to undress beyond exposing his sharply cut abs when he'd shoved his pants down his hips.

His heart thudded with hers in a matching beat. Her heated breath condensed on his neck where she'd rested her head and she inhaled the scent of his skin the way she inhaled the aroma of coffee in the morning. A necessity to her very existence. She doubted she could ever get enough of breathing him in.

Or a more fulfilling sense of her world being right as she rested against him, his arms around her back holding her close, his body buried in hers still pulsing in response to her last lingering quakes.

This was the high she'd been physically craving, this sated sense of exhaustion on the heels of mind-blowing sex. She didn't think she'd ever known such satisfaction of body.

It was the satisfaction of soul that she wasn't sure she could bear.

CALI CROSSED HER LEGS AND scooted closer to the coffee table. She sat on the floor in front of Will's futon, digging into the huge banana split they shared. Will sat similarly on the other side. Their knees bumped beneath the low table.

They both wore white T-shirts, gray sweatpants and thick athletic socks, compliments of Will's wardrobe. The ice cream was a middle of the night feast celebrating his new job at Paddington's and the last two hours they'd spent in bed.

Cali wasn't sure she'd ever spent a more perfect Friday night in her life.

He'd been such a great sport and so much fun to work with while they'd helped Erin close up for the night. When he'd suggested they eat a late dinner and had even volunteered to cook, she'd jumped at the chance. This girl wasn't no fool. By the time they reached his apartment, of course, neither one of them was in the mood for food.

She figured the ice cream would sate the hunger in her empty tummy until they got around to something more substantial after sleeping off the sugar and the sex. Ah, yes. And what sex it was. Her body sang with satisfaction, thanking her for the dual indulgence. So what if she got up off the floor having gained five pounds?

Will didn't seem to care that she was curvy rather than willowy and gaunt. Seemed, in fact, to totally enjoy the fact that she didn't gouge him with fashionably protruding hipbones. A good thing, too, because she really liked the way his body felt cradled on top of hers. And she loved that he wanted to be there…though maybe *love* wasn't the best word to use.

Sighing, she turned her spoon over onto her tongue and licked it clean of caramel and chocolate sauce then used the bowled end as a pointer. "You know I'm going to have to totally cram tomorrow to catch up before Monday's class."

"You mean you're going to totally have to cram *today*." Will scooped up a huge bite of mostly whipped cream and maraschino cherry bits.

Cali groaned. "It is today, isn't it? Saturday already. How come when I'm with you I totally lose track of time?"

Will pulled his spoon from his mouth, slowly shoveled it into the mountain of Blue Bell Homemade vanilla ice cream, Hershey's chocolate syrup and about a dozen other toppings from M&M's to chopped pecans.

He left the spoon standing upright, braced his elbows on the table and leaned forward into Cali's space. His eyes twinkled like snifters of brandy in firelight. "Do you really want me to answer that?"

She considered for only half a minute or so whether she'd consumed enough energy-laden carbs to have another go in the bedroom, or if the sugar would knock her out before she could get his clothes off, not to mention her own.

Then she decided she'd been far too easy every time they'd been naked and this time, if there was going to be a this time here in the middle of their ice cream feast, she was going to make Will work a little bit harder.

Even with the extra five pounds added onto her original extra fifteen, she was worth the effort. She really wasn't as easy as the last two days made her out to be. And she didn't want him to think she'd desperately been waiting around for him to take an interest and notice her. Or to find out he'd taken pity on her after seeing her heart on her sleeve—an accusation Erin leveled way too often.

Cali pulled up the boot straps of her self-esteem, aware that she'd picked a strange time to get prickly over her sexuality and desire for Will. Especially coming on the tail end of her reminiscing. "No, I don't need to hear your man-sex answer. I can answer perfectly well for myself."

Chuckling under his breath, Will shook his head and retrieved his spoon and a mouthful of banana. "This I gotta hear."

Deep breath, Cali. Take a deep breath. This was not the time to get all teary-eyed and emotional which, for an inexplicably hormonal reason, she felt ready to do. That meant she needed to turn the conversation in a new direction. And she knew exactly where to go. "The time we're together passes quickly because all you want to do is argue down every one of my ideas for Jason's role in the screenplay."

Will's easy smile vanished, replaced by stoicism and that stubborn male need to always be right. "That's bull, Cali. I'm not arguing down anything. I know as well as you do that without Jason we don't have a screenplay. It's his story."

At least they agreed on that one unarguable point. Now to get Will to understand how and where the rest of his story logic didn't hold water. "Exactly. Which is why our obsession with the external action is diluting the focus."

"This isn't some trendy art house idea." He attacked the ice cream with a vengeance, jabbing his spoon repeatedly into the same crevice. "Didn't we agree on that early on? That we're writing for the big screen? Which means, duh, we need action?"

Cali really hated to pull out the big guns but it was the discussion they'd had the first day of their screenwriting class that had gotten them here in the first place.

Each class member had been asked by the professor to name the one screenwriter or screenplay that most impacted his or her decision to study the craft. The discussion that followed had sealed the fate she now shared with Will.

And so she prodded him with a gentle reminder. "Christopher McQuarrie. *The Usual Suspects.* Nineteen-ninety-five Academy Award for Best Writing of a Screenplay Written Directly for the Screen."

Will shook his head, glanced up at her from beneath his long lashes, unable to hold back a twist of a smile. "The sucker was brilliant. Totally brilliant."

Yes! Now they were getting somewhere. "The movie or the writer?"

"Both. Same thing. And you know that's what I want to do," he said, abandoning the spoon he'd been stabbing hard down into the bowl.

"Well it's not going to happen if you don't do for our Jason Coker what Christopher McQuarrie did with Keyser Soze."

Will's smile froze, then faded. "And you don't think that's what I'm doing."

"I *know* that's not what you're doing," she said quickly before she stopped to think about Will's feelings, or anything but the honesty of her answer.

A look of defeat clouded his expression. "So, what do I do? Start at the beginning? Analyze this beast one element at a time and see what I'm missing?"

Cali spoke hurriedly again, same reason, same possible regrets. Hoping he didn't come totally unglued when he heard her off-the-wall proposal, one that had started as a niggling itch last night. "You know, I have an idea. I really can't say why I think this makes sense, just that it does."

"Well, what? Speak up, woman."

She placed her hands palms down against the table on either side of the huge crystal bowl, wishing she had a better surface into which she could wrap her fingers and hold on. "This is totally out of left field, I know, but why don't we give a rundown of our idea to Sebastian and see what he has to say."

Will blinked, frowned, frowned harder. "Sebastian? Gallo? Why do you think he'd have any valuable input?"

"Something." She shrugged, toying with her spoon, pulling it slowly through the ice cream mountain in an effort to dig a deep enough trench to use for her grave. She had a feeling she was going to need it. "I'm not sure. I don't know."

"Well, yeah, then. I can see how that would make sense," Will huffed, pushing up from his crossed feet to stand. He began to pace in short jagged turns.

Cali pulled her knees to her chest, wrapped her arms around them in a tight hug and leaned back against the futon. "Before you got to Paddington's tonight? Erin and I were telling Sebastian about The Daring Duo. You know, the couple in *that* booth?"

"Yeah." Will snorted, shoving an agitated hand back over his hair. "The ones you and Erin are always talking about."

Cali frowned at that. "Actually, they're not the only ones we talk about and, no, it's not a stellar quality we share. More like a big fat personality flaw. But there are just some people who tend to rev up the ol' curiosity, ya know? And so we make up stories."

"I see," he said with a roll of his eyes to go with the rest of his high-handedness.

Uh-uh. She wasn't going to put up with this crap. Not from him. Not ever from him. "Oh, get over yourself already, Will. I've heard what you've said about more than a few of our fellow students, not to mention a professor or two."

"Yeah, yeah, whatever." He remained frowning but it was almost an expression of being taken aback. And his tone had softened. "So, what's this deal about Sebastian. What do you know about him anyway?"

Deep breath in. Deep breath out. Okay, she'd yelled and he hadn't run off—or anything worse. This was a good thing. "Not much, really. Erin's only been seeing him a few days, though he's lived in her building since she moved in."

"Hmm. I wondered what the connection was," he said and finally stopped pacing.

"She didn't pick him up in the bar or off the street if that's what you're asking." Though, Cali decided, choosing Sebastian as a Man To Do made it nothing but a matter of semantics. "It just wasn't the right time for them to get together. Not until recently."

She held her breath, waiting for Will to comment on the coincidence that the two of them had finally gotten together at the very same time. The very same day, in fact, though no way was she going to tell him about the Man To Do article, or how Erin's decision to go after Sebastian had impacted Cali's determination to explore her chemistry with Will.

But he didn't say anything so she continued to fill the silence. "I'm not sure I know what else to say. He picked right up where we stalled out, making up a story about who they might be and how they got together. It was so cool."

Hands at his hips, Will stood on the other side of the table and stared down. "And because of that you want him to advise us on our idea? Don't you think that's stretching it a bit, Cali?"

Her idea had merit; she knew it did. She was not going to let his ego knock it down. "You know, Will, just because he's not in our class or an expert doesn't mean he wouldn't have good instincts about the story."

"*I* have good instincts about the story. And *I'm* your study and project partner. Not Sebastian Gallo."

Argh! Save her from hardheaded men. This one in particular. "I know who you are, Will. And I know Sebastian has nothing to do with our project. It's just that we've been so wrapped up in what we're doing I'm afraid tunnel vision is setting in. And I don't see how a fresh pair of eyes could hurt anything. It's not taking away from any of the work you've done, or we've done, it's just…"

"It's just that forest for the trees thing, isn't it?" he asked, circling around to drop onto the futon. He lay back, one knee up, a forearm thrown over his forehead even while he stared wide-eyed at the ceiling.

Cali swiveled around where she sat on the braided rug covering the hardwood floor. She leaned an elbow on the futon mattress and propped her head in her hand. He looked so exhausted, and it had to be about more than the screenplay. He had just lost his job, after all.

She had no idea if he was worried about money but she suspected the blow had hit him harder than he intended to let her know, even if the strike was more to his ego than his wallet. She wished she could kiss it and make it all better. Instead she did the next best thing, resting her hand on his chest and rubbing tiny circles with her fingertips.

He moved his hand to cover hers and sighed. "You're probably right. We've been working on this without a break for two months and I'm getting ragged." He turned his head and looked, really looked, into her eyes. "How are you?"

Now that you're here? I don't think I've ever been so good. She smiled. "Exhaustion is my life. But I'll live."

He toyed with one of her curls. "I didn't thank you for putting in a good word with Erin."

Cali beamed. "I hardly put in a word at all. She jumped on you like…well, like I've been jumping on you the last couple of days." *Like I could jump on you now,* she thought, even though all she wanted to do was jump into his arms and wrap him up tight.

"And what's stopping you now?" he asked, his tender smile negating the lecherous waggle of both brows.

And that was all it took. She climbed up next to him and snuggled into his body. When he wrapped himself around her and pulled her close, breathing deeply as he drifted off to sleep, she knew she was exactly where she was meant to be.

Chapter Eight

Chapter 5

She'd found him.

He hadn't been clever enough or quick enough; he hadn't even been aware enough of where he was to duck. He had, in fact, seen her coming and all he'd done was sit behind the wheel of his car and watch as she'd walked his way.

The night had been pitch-black. The hour as late as it got. He'd been parked down the block from the building he'd seen her enter. Not the building his partner still covered from the other side. Not the building where they'd find the dealer scum they'd been after for weeks.

Raleigh couldn't believe it but he was so incredibly fucked right now. His career, his life, hell, even his mind. And it was too late to see if he couldn't get this right the second time around.

There wasn't going to be a second time.

This was it.

She walked toward him.

What the hell had he been thinking, blowing off

the job he was paid to do? And all because of a distraction that he should have seen coming. That he was trained to see coming. That was coming right toward him.

Now it was too late.

She was here and he was done for. Fried up like battered frog legs to taste just like chicken. Yum, yum...

CRAP. Pure and total crap.

Sebastian shoved away from his desk and headed for his bedroom window. His chair rolled backward across the room to bounce off his highboy dresser, sending Redrum skittering and scratching across the hardwood floor.

What in the hell was wrong with him? He couldn't even string together a sentence that didn't sound like...pulp. Garbage. Bird-cage liner. Camp-fire fuel.

Raleigh wasn't the only one with a career in the toilet. Sebastian might as well pay back his advance and stake out a prime street corner, a successful panhandler's first plan of action. One he knew well.

It was early Saturday morning, not yet dawn. The city was silent without the workday noise to which he usually climbed into bed. The air was cool, crisp and clean but for the bite of diesel from the trucks down the street in the *Houston Chronicle* loading dock. He stared at the police cruiser rolling by seven stories below.

What the hell had he been thinking, telling Erin the things he had about his life in lockup. He could only hope she hadn't believed a word he'd said, that she'd blown it all off as bunk he'd made up for her entertainment. A safety net of sorts so she could pretend she hadn't let a virtual stranger go down on her in the middle of the bar.

He sure as hell didn't want her coming to the ridiculous conclusion that he'd purposely pointed out the one and only chink in his armor, enabling her in finding a way in. He didn't want her to find a way in. No matter that, in too many ways, she was already there, working to dismantle his tightly held independence. Working to convince him that he didn't have the grasp he claimed on his gentler emotions.

He figured she'd feel better about herself if he fed her a story to chew on. He sure didn't want her feeling bad about any of what they'd done. He wanted her to feel good. Damn good. As good as he was feeling. And that was saying a lot because he was supposed to be an expert at turning a cold shoulder and walking away. From involvement. From caring. From concern for another's emotions as well as from his own.

Those were the tenets that had gotten him through his teenage years and had carried him into adulthood. Why would he be so asinine as to open himself up, to invite a woman into his private life after all this time? Yet, in ways and levels he couldn't put into words, he had. And she'd accepted, both the invitation and the man he was.

He'd deny it all—the invitation, the emotional lapse— if she asked. He'd go on to tell her he'd been exercising his right to dramatic license. The story definitely fell into the realm of far-fetched. *That* much he figured she'd buy.

Shifting a hip onto the window, he swung his legs through to stand on the tiny fire escape ledge. The sky was awash in the first strokes of indigo and soon, very soon he'd need to turn in. The hour he now went to bed was the same hour he'd been rousted out for longer than he cared to remember.

Before spilling his guts to Erin, he'd never told another person about those years. Hell, the only person he'd even talked to at any length during that nonexistent time in his life had been Richie Kira. Richie, who'd been the closest thing Sebastian had ever had to a friend.

The sixty-year-old inmate had worked in the detention center's library, helping the kids confined to the facility with research and reading and any other information their instructor assigned them to find. Richie had sensed Sebastian's innate curiosity, a young boy's thirst for knowledge dying to be quenched.

The older man had introduced him to the vastly amazing worlds found on the shelves, between the pages of the books Richie had tended like a gardener would tend a prizewinning rose bed. Or like a farmer would tend the fields of corn and wheat that provided his livelihood. The comparison wasn't that far off the mark.

Books were Richie's connection with a life outside prison he hadn't seen in over forty years. But he read, and he remembered, and he told it all to Sebastian. Stories of war and women. Of football games and fights with neighborhood gangs. Of fast cars and loud music and how to kiss a girl so she never forgot your name.

He'd been the father Sebastian had never had, the mentor he'd needed, one who had advised him on the ways of the world without couching his words from a parent's perspective. He hadn't couched his words at all, but had instead let fly with advice straight off the street.

Advice from the prison yard, too.

Sebastian had gotten real good at watching his back and cutting his losses. He'd just never expected to have to watch his front.

Richie might've taught lessons in female anatomy and birth control but never in dealing with the female mind. Or explained the way a woman's eyes had of sparkling like a beckoning finger right before landing a gut-slamming punch.

Three hours ago Sebastian had walked Erin to her door. She'd wanted him to come in. He'd wanted to do just that, to walk into her loft and drag her off to bed. And so he'd told her goodbye there in the hallway and walked back to the elevator, feeling both the heat and the uncertainty of her gaze on his back all the way.

He'd come home and poured his energy into his work in progress, well aware of his looming deadline but still unable to concentrate long enough to put more than a few words down on the page. Words that stank like week-old shit.

No matter how hard he tried to concentrate on Raleigh Slater, to get into the character's head, to slip into his skin and feel the terror gnawing at the detective's insides, Sebastian found his muse flirting with that *other* idea.

The one he'd been putting off until the right time. A story that didn't belong to Raleigh at all. That obviously didn't belong to Sebastian either since his muse had taken total control. The idea frightened him half to death, as did the implicit demand that he'd have to devote all his time and attention to the social order of his fictional world.

He wouldn't have time for Erin. And that caused a strange sort of jolt to the rhythm of his heart.

He stepped back into his bedroom, his foot skating over Redrum's back as the cat skulked toward the bed. Sebastian nearly broke an ankle, tripping across the floor, and the damn cat did nothing but jump into the center of his bed. Typical female. Sneaking up to blindside him.

Sebastian grabbed his chair and hauled it back to his desk, rolling up to his keyboard. The distraction of Erin Thatcher was beginning to make more sense. He wasn't focused. He wasn't concentrating. He was letting his muse have her way, giving in to her temptation, embracing the flow of creative juices and the energizing high.

That left enough of a gap in his absorption with his work for disruptions to pull him away. Now he needed to get both Erin and his non-Raleigh story idea out of his way. Erin he'd think about later.

Right now he was in the mood to write.

ERIN WOKE EARLY SATURDAY morning, earlier than usual and extremely early for not having gotten to bed until dawn. One thing was for certain. She would never look at The Daring Duo's table the same way again.

She was afraid, in fact, that every time she saw them sitting there she'd be tempted to pull them by the hair out of what she now considered *her* table. Hers and Sebastian's.

Dealing with what they'd done last night was going to take longer than four fairly sleepless hours. She certainly hadn't had the time or the energy to put anything into perspective once she'd arrived home. Having walked from the loft to the bar earlier in the evening, he'd accepted her offer of a lift since she was going his way.

She'd almost thought he'd decline, that he'd disappear into the city's shadows. But the ride up in the elevator was nothing like the one they'd shared the previous night. This time he'd said goodbye to her when the doors had opened on the sixth floor. Not with a kiss or any such intimate gesture, but with nothing more than one raised hand while he leaned against the back wall of the car.

She didn't know why she'd expected more; so what that they'd spent the past two hours engaged in mind-blowing sex? Having a Man To Do wasn't about sharing anything but their bodies. Sebastian seemed to have a better handle on that than she'd managed to grab thus far.

The four hours she had slept seemed to have been all the recharging time her brain needed. Her body still ached and craved another eight but her mind was racing, demanding she get her butt in gear. Still, before getting out of bed to brush her teeth or take care of the rest of her bathroom business, even before stumbling to the kitchen for the coffee, she did the one thing she had to do before she did anything else.

Unload on Tess and Samantha.

She dragged her laptop into her lap and began to type.

From: Erin Thatcher
Sent: Saturday
To: Samantha Tyler; Tess Norton
Subject: Screw Me Once? Shame On Me?

Okay, girls. I'm totally screwed. (Well, I've been totally screwed but that's another subject for another letter!)

You know all my talk of keeping emotions out of this affair with Sebastian? Uh-uh. Not happening. Too late. I won't say I'm in love...but I'm definitely way over my head in like. So, what now?

He told me things last night. Things I'm still not certain are true. Things about his past that almost seemed to be a story made up for my benefit. To appease my curiosity, as it were, perhaps even to frighten me a bit so I'd quit wondering all the things I've been wondering and keep my mind and my heart from getting as involved as my body.

But the bone he threw me (ha!) totally backfired because he made me even more curious. And I couldn't exactly ask him to stop talking so I could find out if he was bullshitting me considering I was in a rather compromising position at the time. (How compromising, your nosy selves ask? <g> Let's just say there's a certain table in the bar I'll never again be able to look at with a straight face.)

And so my dilemma. Do I press him for the truth about what he told me? (I really do want to know!) Or do I just go with it, forget trying to figure out who he is and enjoy his company and his, uh, tongue? <g> I mean, right now, this moment, I could call this whole thing off and be able to look back with fond memories (she says, wondering as she does so if she's lying to herself). Yes, I'd miss the incredible sex.

But I'm afraid I'd miss Sebastian even more.

I guess I never did figure on wanting to get to know my Man To Do. (Stupid me!) There's even a part of me that has thought about ditching the sexual fling and seeing if we'd work out as friends. I think he'd really be interesting to know. More interesting to know even than fun to...well, you get the idea.

What do I do? ::whine, whine:: Erin

Not that she necessarily expected Tess or Samantha to have the perfect solution, but even a hint of what tack to take would help. As it was, Erin's mind might've been wound up into high gear, but it was a total wasteland when it came to any sort of cognizant decision-making.

Coffee. Then shower. Before anything else.

She headed to the kitchen, ground the last of her Sumatra beans, poured filtered water from the refrigerated jug into the coffeemaker and waited for the caffeine to brew. Double-size mug filled to the brim with the addition of sweetener and cream and she was on her way to being human.

She was also on her way to the shower, mug in one hand, towels in another, when her e-mail chime sounded, requiring a quick detour back to the bedroom. First things first. Waking up completely would have to wait another minute or two while she checked to see who had come through with much needed advice. Or the swift kick to the backside she deserved.

From: Tess Norton
Sent: Saturday

To: Erin Thatcher; Samantha Tyler
Subject: Re: Screw Me Once? Shame On Me?
Dear Erin:
Do exactly as I say. Do not deviate from this plan. Do this now:
1. Go to the nearest Starbucks
2. Order the Caramel Mocha Frappuccino
3. Also order the biggest chocolate brownie in the case
4. Sit down in a comfy chair to drink/eat
5. Ask yourself what's the worst that can happen with Sebastian?
6. Ask yourself what's the best that can happen with Sebastian?
7. Realize that NEITHER OF THOSE TWO THINGS ARE GOING TO HAPPEN! What will really happen is something you can neither anticipate nor prepare for.
THEREFORE:
1. Enjoy your coffee and brownie
2. Enjoy your time with Sebastian
3. Be true to your inner voice
4. Honor your libido
5. Don't play games—if you have a question, ask it
My, my, don't I sound wise? Sort of like Dr. Phill on estrogen. All kidding aside, I think the above is true. I think the key is the voice inside, and listening to it instead of making rationalizations for the things we want to listen to instead.
Not that I do that, mind you. I'm a moron and should be watched 24/7 by a team of psychiatrists. But that's another e-mail. I gotta run!
Love and kisses, Tess

Well, thought Erin, Tess was certainly on a roll this morning. She'd obviously been sniffing too much plant fertilizer if she thought she needed a psychiatrist. Tess had to be one of the most levelheaded women Erin had ever met—even if they'd only met in cyberspace.

She carried her mug to the shower, setting it on the ledge above the showerhead where she kept her shampoo and gel. Between the hot water and the hot coffee, she'd eventually get her body going. Curling back up in bed for another couple of hours sounded like a lot more fun than going to work. Curling back up in bed with Sebastian sounded even better.

But she had a party to plan. And no matter how much she'd rather do a half-dozen other things, including doing her Man To Do, she owed this one to Rory.

"I'VE BEEN TRYING TO GET Will to understand how Sebastian made up the story of The Daring Duo. Will thinks I'm exaggerating." Cali pouted. "I mean, I know I didn't hear all of what Sebastian was saying since I was working. But Will just doesn't believe that what I did hear was as cool as it was and it's totally pissing me off."

Cali's interruption of Erin's distracted musings was not the least bit unwelcome. She'd been wishing she'd followed Tess's advice and taken time for the Caramel Mocha Frappuccino and the brownie before coming to work, but she'd been thinking more about the party and less about her mental health.

All these hours later she was paying the price for that particular lapse in priorities. And the price tag kept getting higher. She'd think about the best thing that could happen with Sebastian then she'd think about the worst thing before starting the cycle all over again. For some reason she never could get to that place of nirvana halfway in between.

Yep. Two brownies would've been even better. A girl could never have too much chocolate. Whether or not she could have too much sex, or an adverse reaction to the sex she'd been having was something else altogether. Either Erin's long dormant hormones were bubbling against the lid of a pressure cooker—or else she was on the verge of succumbing to love at first sight. In this case, love at first sex.

"Exaggerating how?" Erin glanced from Cali to Will who was loading down his tray with frosted mugs and a pitcher of beer. Will's mouth was drawn into a tight grim line instead of into his usual boyish smile. Obviously Cali telling tales of their lover's spat did not sit well. For once Erin was on his side, the side of the one done wrong.

"Cali seems to think Sebastian has some sort of magical storytelling gift." Will hoisted up his tray. "I've been trying to convince her that there's nothing magic about telling a story. It's all about the elements and the way the author puts them together."

Erin's loyalties swung back to Cali. "Well, I don't know about an author's elements but I do know my granddad Rory could've given Hemingway a go. And Rory never put a word on paper. It was all in the way he told the tale."

Cali looked triumphant. Will looked just plain mad before walking away. Erin shrugged, not really wanting to get into the middle of what she was afraid was a personal problem between Cali and Will and their screenplay and not at all about Sebastian's storytelling skills.

Of course, they didn't know about the tale he'd woven last night while he'd had her spread open across The Daring Duo's table. The story that was giving Erin bloody hell today as she'd tried—unsuccessfully and all day long—to put what he'd said into any sort of perspective.

Or even into a context around which she could wrap either side of her brain. But logic wasn't working. Neither was her imagination. It was too far out there, the story he'd told. Little boys and little trucks and a cupcake begged from a bakery's back door.

"That's exactly what I'm talking about." Cali tossed a tray full of empties into the trash can designated for glass recycling. The bottles clattered loudly and Cali flinched before screwing up her face in apology. "Sorry."

Erin arched a brow. "You didn't learn anything from me taking out my frustration on the mugs the other night?"

With Will gone, Cali had room to speak freely. "Men are *so* aggravating. Everything has to be their way or the highway."

"Sometimes their way isn't such a bad thing." Erin glanced across the bar to the table where earlier she'd seated three female single twenty-somethings-seeking, unable to bear the thought of The Daring Duo defiling the table where she'd experienced Sebastian's firsthand knowledge of heaven.

"If you're being cheap and sleazy and talking about sex, then I agree. Having a man who knows what to do once he's got your clothes off is a beautiful thing." Before Erin could agree, Cali added, "But I hate it when they try to be an expert on everything and turn up their nose at even the hint—" she held forefinger and thumb a fraction of a millimeter apart "—the tiniest hint of a suggestion that they might be wrong. Or that another man might have the answer when they don't."

Erin turned her attention to wiping down the bar. "And this has to do with Sebastian how, exactly?"

Cali scrunched up both shoulders. "Just that I told Will it might be kind of cool to see what Sebastian thought about our screenplay."

Erin shook her head. "I don't know, Cali. I'm not an expert on men, obviously," *what an understatement* that *was* "but I can see where that might piss Will off. You wanting to get another man's input rather than trusting Will's intuition, especially when you two have just gotten started on what might really be a good relationship for the both of you."

"Well, yeah. I can appreciate that." Smiling, Cali waved at a customer on his way out the door. "I was just trying to find a way to save the screenplay for Will. This isn't about me or my grade or anything. This doesn't mean half as much to me as it does to Will. And I thought if he heard what I've been trying to tell him, but heard it from another guy instead of me, well, maybe he would listen."

"Do what you have to do then, I guess." Erin's heart began to thump harder.

"Oh, thanks." Frowning, Cali grabbed two bottles from the cooler and sluiced ice from the labels with one hand. "What kind of advice is that?"

"The only advice I can think of at the moment," Erin said because Sebastian had just walked through the door.

She was totally unprepared for the overwhelming emotion that hit her. She felt like *then,* before Sebastian, she'd only existed, and *now* she'd finally started to live. No matter how exciting her Man To Do adventure, that suggestion of having idly cruised through so many years didn't sit well. Especially coming on the heels of the plaguing doubts she'd been dodging here recently—doubts that had finally caught up with her.

If she were to be blunt, the entire situation sucked. The idea that she had only been drifting through life made a total mockery of the years spent learning the ropes with Rory, of the time she'd trekked across Europe on foot with the boy who'd been her first love, of the university credits she'd earned toward a degree she'd never declared.

Had she really spent her life in limbo? Waiting? For a man? The thought sent a wave of panic crashing like cymbals over her ears. This was just stress rearing its ugly head the way it did when she least needed the crushing reminder of all the things she had on her plate.

Oh, no. No way. This was getting ridiculous. A man was not the answer to her problems or her prayers. Certainly not Sebastian Gallo. That wasn't why he was here. She wiped her hands on her apron and turned to Cali. "I need to run to the little girls' room. Get Sebastian a beer and tell him I'll be right back, will you?"

"Sure, but don't you..."

Erin didn't hear the rest of what Cali had to say because the slamming of the office door drowned out her voice.

Count to thirty, Erin. Count to thirty.

Yes, she'd always known there was the possibility of involving her emotions, no matter how often she told herself not to let it happen. She was totally female, after all, and subject to all those niggling female anomalies like thinking on the heels of sex came love.

Grr and *grr* again. She banged her head back against the door on which she was leaning, then pushed off and finished the count to thirty while she crossed the small room. She dropped into her desk chair and, in desperate need of a distraction, pulled up her e-mail program, hoping Samantha had gotten around to answering this morning's pitiful cry for help.

And she had, bless her always timely heart. Willing her heart to calm its thundering pace, her blood pressure back to normal, her head to stop the pounding that was now echoing in her ears, Erin sat back to read.

From: Samantha Tyler
Sent: Saturday

To: Erin Thatcher; Tess Norton
Subject: Screw Me Once? Shame On Me?

Oh, Erin. Be careful. You don't really know all that much about Sebastian except that he's...ahem...talented. Make sure you're not mixing up "I love sex" with "I love you." A chick cliché!

Offhand I'd say forget being friends. If you guys have that much chemistry, there's no way you can back off from it and have that stick for more than...generous estimate? Twenty, thirty minutes.

I mean, think about it. Doesn't just looking into his eyes make you horny? I remember when I was falling in love with my ex, even his dandruff made me horny. (Okay, that was over the top, but you know what I mean.) And you think you can be his buddy?

(Samantha shakes her head vigorously and makes that tsk-tsk noise that is *so* annoying.)

Friendship plus sex equals love. If you think there's potential for a future together, then stick it out. If not, run like hell. That kind of heartbreak no one needs, and the longer you wait, the deeper you get in, the worse it hurts.

The middle ground? Keep your mouth shut unless it's giving pleasure, your ears closed to any of his human side, and leave your heart at home? Nice idea, but no. Never works. If you're falling in love, that's not going to stop the slide, no matter how much you tell yourself it will.

I hate to sound negative. And remember, my divorce is probably making me a bitter, cynical hag before my time. I would love, love, *love* you to have a happy ending with this guy, but what are the odds?

Remember, you picked him out because he's so wrong for you! I wish Tess and I could meet the guy! Samantha

P.S. So what the hell *is* all this stuff you're finding out about his past that you're hinting at and driving us crazy by not telling? What was he, a mafia hit man? Drug lord? CIA? Salad prep at the Chew and Chat?

The Chew and Chat? Oh, good grief. Erin chuckled, then sighed, then shook her head. That Samantha was a piece of work—not to mention the perfect diversion. She'd also made more than a few points that gave Erin pause. *Friendship plus sex equals love.* The sentiment made so much sense, as did the rest of what Samantha had said.

So where into her equation did Erin's feelings for Sebastian fall? Serious like. Definite infatuation. A truly consuming lust. All things that fit with a relationship's adrenaline beginnings. But this was not a relationship. Or even the beginning of one. She didn't even know if anything she'd learned about Sebastian was real.

She'd gone into this affair looking for relief—from work stress and her worries about disappointing Rory, not to mention her horny hormones. All she'd accomplished was a temporary appeasing of the latter. Because every time she saw him she wanted him more than the time before.

She rubbed at the thundering, pounding, blood pressure headache. It was so simple really. All she needed was a light at the end of the tunnel, the tiniest ray of sunshine filtering down through the murky water of her mind. That wasn't asking too much, was it? To know she wouldn't spend the rest of her life feeling so decidedly out of sorts?

A sharp rap sounded on her door and, before she could decide whether or not to answer, Sebastian walked into the room. She swallowed hard, wishing for an analgesic. Better yet, a margarita, hold the salt. Hold the lime. Hell, hold everything but the tequila.

His gaze on hers, he shut the door behind him. And even from where she sat on the other side of the desk, Erin felt the reverberation.

Chapter Nine

"ARE YOU AVOIDING ME?"

Not in the way he was implying. She hadn't run because she didn't want to see him again. Quite the contrary. But, yes. For the moment she thought it best to work out her emotional conflict alone. "What? Can't a girl take a bathroom break without coming under suspicion?"

One darkly arched brow went up but his mouth remained...not grim, but certainly unsmiling. He crossed his arms over his chest and leaned back against the door. "Is that what you're doing?"

She gave a one-shouldered shrug, inclined her head toward the private office bathroom. Nonchalance came at a huge price to her stomach that burned as if she'd picked up a six-pack of ulcers. "I haven't made it yet. I stopped to check on an e-mail I was expecting."

"And now you're thinking about how to respond?"

How did he manage to remain so coolly detached when she was on a razor's edge of coming undone? "Actually, I'm thinking about what I read, trying to decide if it helped my current dilemma."

"You have a dilemma?"

"A bit of one," she admitted, striving for the objectivity she'd never find as long as he stood in the room, her night creature who should've been uncomfortable in the confining space of her office but managed to look totally at ease while she simmered and stewed.

And then it hit her, that this was all wrong. He should've been the one pacing while she sat back calmly and watched. This was her turf, her place to work while he walked the streets, doing the thinking that apparently kept him up all hours for whatever reason he hadn't bothered to share. He was the source of her agitation, his seeming unflappability in the face of an involvement making her insane.

She wanted to see if she could rile him up, scare him away, make him pay for part of what she was feeling. Elbows propped on the arms of her chair, she laced her hands over her midsection and lifted her chin. "You're my dilemma."

"You don't say."

"I do say. It's quite inconvenient actually, you see, because every time I'm near you I want to take off my clothes. No wait." She held up a hand when he started to speak. "That's not exactly right. Every time I see you, I want *you* to take off my clothes."

"And that's a bad thing?"

She had to give him credit. He'd actually managed to keep a straight face. "You tell me."

"C'mon, Erin. I'm a guy." His gaze grew piercing, intense, finally revealing that he was not unaffected. "What do you think I'm going to say?"

I want you to say what you're feeling, not what you're thinking, and not some obvious male cliché. "I guess I just want you to be honest."

"You want me to be honest." Lips pressed tight, he nodded while he thought it over, then lifted a brow and asked,

"You want me to tell you that when I see your eyes light up I get hard?"

She blinked, tried to remember how to breathe. Why, oh, why did he have to say things like that? It was all she could do to keep her gaze from dropping from his face to his groin. "If that's your honesty. Then, yeah. Feel free."

"It is honest. And it is real. And, yeah." He huffed out a breath of self-directed ire, looked away, looked back. "It's been that way for more than a few months."

A *few months*? So...the initial sense of mutual attraction hadn't been her imagination? And this affair wasn't as out of the blue, as crazy as she'd thought? But it was an affair, wasn't it? No matter who had been the one to make the first move, what they were doing here now was all about the chemistry of bodies—not that existing between souls.

It wasn't even friendship. She had no idea what he did for a living, where he ate his favorite food, what the hell his favorite food might be. He liked champagne and books and showers and got hard when he looked into her eyes.

"A few months ago, huh? That's when I moved into the lofts." She waited for him to answer the question she hadn't really asked. To admit that she was his distraction. That he shared even a fraction of her fixation and fascination that they'd come together the way they had.

All he did was push away from the door and walk toward her. "I know exactly when you moved in. And I'd really gotten used to living alone."

He circled her desk and Erin's heart pitter-pattered as he moved to block the only path from her chair to the door. She swiveled to face him—and face her fears—head-on. She wanted the truth. What did she have to do with the reality that he *did* live alone?

He leaned his backside against the edge of the credenza

that turned her L-shaped desk into a horseshoe. Wrapping his hands over the edge of the dark wood on either side of his hips, he stretched out his legs. His gaze held hers with no effort at all. She was right; he was a magician. And she was totally under his spell.

He wore black denim and biker boots, and crossed his ankles at the ends of his very long legs. His V-neck sweater was rich chocolate brown and tonight the growth of beard on his face was later than a five o'clock shadow and added to an aura just this side of menacing.

She refused to allow the intimidation. "You still live alone."

He shook his head. "No. You live there. Not physically, but you're there. And I have hell going to sleep. Forget what you've done to my ability to concentrate on work. Or now what you've done to my showers."

"Showers you take alone." It hit her then, what he was saying. His fantasies had been on a par with hers...yet they'd been different. They'd been more.

Slowly, she pushed out of her chair, braced her body against her desk, facing him in a mirror to his pose, the toes of her shoes touching the soles of his boots. He left his feet where they were, giving her the encouragement to continue. "You do more than shower alone, don't you?"

He didn't shrug off her comment, which meant she'd hit a bull's-eye of sorts, a target she wasn't sure he was aware of giving her with his admission that he couldn't shake her off as easily as he might have wanted to do.

She waited patiently, as patiently as she could manage with curiosity eating her up, and was finally rewarded when he blew out a breath of surrender, telling her almost as much with that sigh as he did with the words that followed.

"Well, I don't have family. I work at home. My business contacts are long-distance for the most part. No close friends, or at least none living here. So, yeah. I eat alone. Sleep alone." A corner of his mouth lifted. "Walk the streets alone."

"And you have sex alone."

She waited for the denial, the resentful response to the implied insult she'd cast upon his masculinity. The "how dare she suggest" he made do with his own right hand because he couldn't get a woman into bed. Funny how quickly she forgot who she was dealing with.

None of his reactions to the things she'd said or done had ever been remotely similar to the responses of other men she'd known. Why did she think this time would be any different? Whoever Sebastian Gallo was, he was secure in himself, in the way he lived his life, in the choices he made defining his existence.

The air in the room grew heavy and still, thick with the tension left uncut between them. Neither one of them moved; both remained standing, staring, cross-purposes like an invisible web of motion sensors keeping them apart. The whir of the computer's fan hummed in the background, and Erin swore she could hear the tic of the vein in his temple.

The face-off continued, the strain more about untold revelations, about Sebastian giving up a part of himself he wasn't ready to share, than it was about anything sexual. Yet, the picture of Sebastian in his shower, alone and in the throes of self-satisfaction stirred Erin beyond belief.

"Having sex alone has been known to happen."

"As can be said of most men. But you're not most men." A fact of which she'd be eternally grateful, no matter how much further they took this affair.

For now, however, she was more interested in taking this conversation to a place where she could find her answers. "You said you don't have any family. Have you ever been married?"

He shook his head. "Never."

"Relationships?" She arched a brow and added, "Old girlfriends who keep you company when you get the urge?"

"The urge to do what?" He moved, but only to cross his arms over his chest. "Have sex that doesn't involve the shower, the soap and my right hand?"

She did her best not to smile. "It's been known to happen."

"Not with old girlfriends, though."

"With who, then?" she asked, pressing forward.

"With girls—" He stopped, corrected his misstep. "With women, who happen to be friendly when I stop by."

"When's the last time you stopped?" She didn't know why this was important, only that curiosity demanded she ask.

"I don't know," he answered without missing a beat.

"You don't know the last time you slept with a woman?" He had to be bullshitting her. "Isn't that something most guys notch on their bedpost?"

"I'm not most guys."

Okay. She knew that. She also knew most guys would lie through their teeth before opening themselves up with that sort of admission. And if he was being truthful about the sex he hadn't been having before having it with her...

"So, the story you told me last night? About living in the abandoned building? That was the truth?"

One, two, three heartbeats passed before he nodded once and said, "As raw as it gets."

Her heart shattered into pieces she was sure she'd never put together again. She buried her face in her hands. "You can't do this to me. You can't tell me that you don't have family or friends. That you live alone and work alone. That you have sex alone."

"Why not, Erin? It's my life. Not yours. I don't dwell on any of that. It's who I am."

She waved her hands frantically. "No, no, no. You told me that you can't sleep because I'm there. How am I supposed to respond to that when I know that you're so truly alone?"

How terribly he must've been hurt as a child. A hurt he denied, a hurt she couldn't even imagine resulting from a truth so horrible she almost wished he'd told her his words were a lie.

"Alone, Erin. Not lonely. And I never said I didn't want you there."

Erin waited, looking into his eyes, knowing that couldn't possibly be all of what he had to say. But his mouth had drawn into a thinly pressed line...his mouth that she'd only kissed that night in the mailroom. How could she not have realized that they'd never kissed again?

Why had he never kissed her again?

The office door burst open. Sebastian's head came up. Erin jumped to her feet and whirled around. Cali stood in the doorway and wore the panicked look of a gunshot victim waiting to fall.

Erin's pulse raced. "What is it? What's going on?"

Cali's eyes grew even wider. "Erin you are not going to believe what Will just found out about Courtland's."

CREWE COURTLAND, THE NEW jazz café down the street from Paddington's, had announced their mid-November grand opening date weeks ago. What they hadn't made public until tonight, or until last night since it was now the wee hours of Sunday morning, was their pre-grand opening.

On Halloween night.

Paddington's anniversary night.

Erin's night.

Sebastian felt the urge to drive his fist into the mouth of the nearest trumpet or sax.

He couldn't put his finger on the reason why, but he had a feeling word of Erin's party plans had leaked—in which case his fist would make more of an impact connecting with the jaw of the suspect ex-employee. But he kept his suspicions—and his thoughts of violence—to himself. He needed to consider Erin's needs, not his own. Though, lately, he'd found it difficult to differentiate between the two.

Strange, but coming to grips with that reality hadn't been as hard as he'd thought.

Along with Cali and Will, Sebastian had come home with Erin after the bar had closed. The late hours didn't bother him and he knew Erin was used to being up half the night. How the other two managed he had no idea. But he was glad the couple had been there for Erin.

After the intensity of the encounter earlier in her office where, having finally come to accept the truth of the past that he'd lived, she'd nearly fallen apart, Sebastian had a feeling he and Erin wouldn't have made much headway toward a reasonable resolution to her problem.

But with Cali and Will as buffers, the four of them together had come up with a workable list of options to make sure Erin's anniversary party didn't put her in the red. Not that a single option on the list would have the impact of what Sebastian was going to do.

What he had to do—and would do for the reasons and the feelings he'd been fighting since the day they'd met. Reasons he'd refused to give credence because it shouldn't have mattered that a woman he hardly knew was on the verge of losing her business. Feelings he'd refused to give life because loving her increased the risk to the only way he knew to survive.

Yet, Erin losing her business did matter, and tied into the primal response of a man's need to protect his woman. If only they'd met at a different time, a different place. Too many obstacles remained for him to voice his true feelings—obstacles he saw no way to overcome. His entire career depended on maintaining his solitary existence. Yet Erin was about to lose the career she'd worked her entire life to build.

Even counting the personal cost, the loss to his anonymity, how could he not intervene?

For some reason during the foursome's brainstorming session, Erin's concerns about Paddington's had returned over and again to her grandfather. Sebastian hadn't yet figured that out. He hoped to get some kind of answer here shortly. Which was why he was sitting in her window seat, one leg stretched the length of the padded cushion, one foot dragging the floor.

Will had left earlier claiming the need for sleep. Cali, whose wistful gaze had followed him out the door, was still in the kitchen with Erin helping to wash up the group's wineglasses and ashtrays. None of them smoked, but tonight it had seemed like the thing to do. Erin especially. Her stress level had finally mellowed.

Though Sebastian pitched in an idea or two here and there, he'd been a lot more interested in people watching. The dynamics of these three people in particular and especially how Cali and Will had both rallied around Erin as if they shared in the fate of Paddington's.

What they shared in was the fate of Erin. The same trap Sebastian had unwittingly fallen into.

Interesting concept, friendship. He didn't write about

it a lot because Raleigh didn't have friends. He had co-workers and informants the same way Sebastian had an agent, an editor and a publicist, as well as an attorney and financial planner. These were the associates with whom he "did lunch."

He didn't have anyone to help him pull a party or a plot out of the toilet. Richie had died ten years ago, but he'd never quit harping on Sebastian's insistence on remaining a recluse. The aging inmate had badgered Sebastian every time he'd visited. Richie never had liked the way Sebastian kept to himself. Seeing him get involved with Erin and the others would've had the old man cackling.

It rather had Sebastian laughing at the irony. Richie had always said a woman would be the one to take Sebastian down in the end. He'd never believed it, of course. Nothing to do with his mother abandoning him in the first place and having any sort of impenetrable heart. It was just that vow he'd taken all those years ago to never rely on another human being for safety, sustenance or support.

For the most part he'd included sex in the equation and had made do with his shower. For the most part, because once in a while he'd allowed himself the need of women. He'd admitted as much to Erin, but hadn't been totally honest. Had, in fact, evaded answering her direct question about the last time he'd had sex.

He didn't plan to give her an answer because, quite frankly, it wasn't any of her business. But that was the short meaningless response. The truth was that he didn't want to think about sex that hadn't meant anything when it was beginning to mean a lot with Erin.

He pushed open her window, listening to the silence of the city, realizing this was exactly where she sat when he was thinking of her from one floor above. That this room was where she slept when he restlessly paced upstairs.

His pacing of late was even beginning to get on his own nerves because it meant his concentration level was shot. And he really doubted fantasies of Erin would cut any mustard with his publisher's legal department when he turned in this manuscript late.

Even if it felt like the best work he'd ever done. And even if he knew he had to take the chance on the new direction his writing seemed to be headed these days thanks to his muse.

Damn the bitch for making a mess of his life.

And damn himself for seeing no way out.

CALI PULLED HER Focus out of Erin's parking garage at 4:00 a.m. and headed home. Considering the hour and the last four nights' combined lack of sleep, logic said she should be exhausted. She was anything but. In fact, she was totally jazzed.

After Will had left the emergency brainstorming session earlier, Cali had managed to snag a bit of Sebastian's time while Erin dozed. Leaving with Will would've been Cali's preference, but she couldn't go until she'd helped Erin wash up the few dishes they'd used. Or without making sure Erin was going to be okay.

Besides, Will hadn't asked.

At first, Cali had pouted. Then she realized Will's being gone meant she and the screenplay were alone with Sebastian. She couldn't have planned it better. While Erin had fitfully napped, Cali had tucked her feet up on the sofa and pitched her idea to Sebastian sitting at the opposite end. He'd listened, but he'd kept one eye on Erin curled up on the love seat at his side. And that was okay. In fact, Cali found his divided attention endearingly cute.

In hushed tones, Cali had explained to Sebastian the version of the screenplay she and Will had on paper, and had then gone on to share her personal vision of the story idea. Sebastian had agreed with all but one of the possibilities she'd tossed out. And then he'd given her more input on crafting a plot than she'd ever expected. In fact, she'd walked out of Erin's building with her brain reeling.

Never in her life had she wished for a mini-tape recorder more than she did during the drive home. As it was, she'd headed out of downtown with the light over her rearview mirror trained down on the passenger seat where, one eagle eye on the near-empty road, she'd jotted notes on her ever-present, letter-size, legal pad.

An amazing night's work, she thought, finally turning into the narrow driveway separating the two squat buildings that made up her tiny apartment complex in midtown. A dozen efficiencies for like-minded cheapskates and starving student waitresses. One of these days, with the right screenplay in hand...oh, yeah. She'd be moving uptown. And she could hardly wait.

She cut the car's engine, keeping the light on while she scribbled down several thoughts still fresh in her mind. A sharp rap on the passenger glass sent thoughts, pencil and pad skittering. Her hand flew to her throat, then to her heart. Nerves fired from eyes to brain and she finally registered Will's face. A deep breath later, she hit the door locks and Will dropped into the passenger seat.

She backhanded his upper arm, once, twice, a third time for good measure. "You scared the crap outta me."

"I figured you saw my car. You parked right beside me." He rubbed at his newly bruised shoulder.

"Well, I didn't. It's dark and my mind was...elsewhere." She reached back for her tote bag in the floorboard behind her seat, hoping to stash the legal pad before Will noticed exactly where her mind had been. "What're you doing here anyway? I thought you were tired."

"I was. I am." He shrugged and then he smiled. "I couldn't sleep. I've gotten too used to you tucking me in."

Cali wanted to revel in the sweet feelings inspired by his admission; it had been so long since a man had cared the way Will cared, accepting her, wanting her. Loving her with his body even if he hadn't put the feelings into words.

But her bag was caught up beneath her seat and she feared his discovery of her betrayal. At least what he would consider a betrayal. She considered what she was doing exactly what a good student would do.

"Grr. Stupid bag," she muttered and tugged harder.

Will leaned toward her, reached back and freed the tote. Handing it to her with one hand, he reached up and tucked a curl behind her ear with the other. "That's okay. You don't have to tuck me in if you're not in the mood."

"It's not that." His touch made this that much harder. She glanced furtively at the pad before stuffing it down in her tote, knowing as she did that she'd just given herself away.

Will followed the direction of her gaze, frowned and slid the pad back out. He scanned her hastily made notes. "What's all this?"

"Nothing really." She shrugged. "A few ideas I was thinking about on the way home."

"Hmm." He continued to read, frowning, snorting, shaking his head. "I don't think this is nothing, Cali. I think this is you going behind my back." Another couple of minutes of study and he handed her back the legal pad, as if daring her to deny what was so plainly scribbled in blue ink on yellow.

So, she faced the charge. "You left. Erin was half-asleep on the sofa. So, Sebastian and I got to talking."

Will nodded as if he didn't believe a word she said. "And the subject of the screenplay just happened to come up?"

Cali shifted in her seat to better face him. "No, I brought it up. I told you I was thinking of running the idea by Sebastian. I don't know why you're so surprised."

"I guess I shouldn't be." He slouched defensively in the corner of the seat, his back against the door. "Nothing I've had to say has mattered so far."

"Bullshit," Cali blurted, shocking even herself. "This is a joint project and has been since the beginning. That doesn't mean it's perfect."

"I never said it was perfect." He jerked his glasses from his face and rubbed at his eyes. "What I said was that I didn't see any reason to ask Sebastian's opinion."

"And I told you that I did. That I thought his input might be worthwhile. Or interesting at least." Cali took a deep breath, working to dispel her aggravation before it turned into anger. "I haven't known too many people able to tell a story off the cuff the way he can."

"This is so friggin' ridiculous." Will shoved his glasses back in place and hooked his fingers over the door handle. "I can't believe I'm having to put up with this crap."

She wanted to say "ditto" because Will was dishing out crap based on nothing more than hurt feelings. At least her "crap" came from a desire to do right by the screenplay. "Do you want to find a new study partner then?"

"What good will that do this late in the semester? Like we can split the screenplay?" He bit off a curse and instead added a terse, "Right. I can see that happening."

Which meant if he could find a way to do just that, he would. Cali knew well how to listen to what he wasn't saying as clearly as she heard what he did.

She finished shoving the legal pad into her tote bag. "So, if we're this diametrically opposed to our story approach, where do we go from here?"

He faced her then, his brown-gold eyes glittering in the

car's bright interior light. A tic jerked at his jawline beneath the stubble that added to his look of weary indignation. "I don't know. Why don't you tell me?"

She was not giving up on this. She was not. "I don't know about you, but I'm going inside. I'm going to sleep. And, when I get up, I'm going to work on incorporating what I can of my notes into the screenplay."

She wondered if he remembered that, yesterday, she'd brought home his laptop. If he took the computer back, he'd make her effort that much harder. Right now, she wouldn't put it past him. "I just want to see if these ideas work before I toss them off as fodder."

"What? You mean there's a chance the great Sebastian Gallo doesn't know his head from a hole in the ground?"

Cali frowned. "Are you jealous? Of Sebastian?"

"Jealous?" Will sputtered. "Try again."

Cali shrugged, hoisted her tote strap over her shoulder. "I can't. I'm clueless."

"You're right. You are clueless." He pushed open the door and climbed from the car. Cali followed suit, hitting the automatic locks and staring at Will across the car's roof. She did her best to ignore what he'd said, to put it into context, but the hurt lingered.

The interior light faded, leaving them in darkness but for the streetlamp at the driveway's entrance. Will shoved a hand back over his already mussed hair. "No, Cali. I'm not jealous. I'm angry. I'm pissed in a very big way. I don't see this as the way a partnership works. That one half does what she wants over the objections of the other."

"I know how a partnership works, Will." And even as she said it, she knew she was adding a deeper subtext to their own personal plot. "It's a hashing out of joint ideas and, yes, the exploration of individual ones. This doesn't mean any changes I make will end up in the finished project. But I have to do this. For me. I have to know if my intuition is right."

"Sebastian's intuition you mean."

"No. My intuition. My ideas. Sebastian was nothing but a sounding board. He was open-minded. And he listened." Cali paused and, before fully thinking her comment through, she added, "That's the least I expect in a partnership."

Will remained silent, his fingertips drumming on the roof of her car. His mouth thinned into a grim line. His eyes went flat. Cali felt the first stirrings of big-mouth regret deep in the pit of her stomach.

"Fine," Will finally said. "Whatever. You do what you have to do. I'll do the same." He turned and headed for his car, calling back over his shoulder, "Bring my laptop to class on Monday. I'm going to need it."

Chapter Ten

AT THE SOUND OF THE bedroom door closing, Sebastian looked up. Erin, exhausted, leaned back against it, still wearing the head-to-toe black Paddington's uniform that looked like no uniform he'd ever seen when she wore it. Her complexion was more pale than usual, the circles under her eyes darker than he thought he'd ever seen.

But she was still an incredibly gorgeous creature and his groin tightened in response. The sensation was one he'd grown to expect and embrace. But the same sort of tightening that clutched at his chest was new, not particularly welcome, and a feeling he had no intent to explore.

At least not now, tonight, this morning. Not when his current agenda involved more closely examining what was going on with Erin, not with himself. He'd done way too much of that already the last few days. And he was more than uncomfortable with the conclusions he'd reached.

He shut the window and got to his feet, crossing the room and silently taking Erin by the hand. He led her to the foot of the bed where he faced her, tugged her polo shirt from the waistband of her pants and off over her head.

She didn't say a word, didn't object by expression or

body language, even when he released the clasp of her bra and freed her breasts. All she did in return was lift the hem of his sweater and pull it over his head.

Her hands found their way to his shoulders and she slowly dragged her palms down his chest, circling her fingertips over his nipples then pushing into his armpits and laying her head gently on his chest.

He wasn't about to deny his arousal but right now it meant next to nothing compared to Erin's needs. Leaving the briefest kiss on his sternum, she moved her hands to the fastenings of his pants. He reciprocated and both pulled off shoes and socks and skinned pants down legs until wearing nothing but practical black cotton underwear of the same cut they'd been wearing the first time they'd shared this intimacy.

But this time their bare skin was more about baring souls than bodies and that realization hit Sebastian hard. So hard he wondered for a moment where and how he'd been so weak as to let her get to him as she obviously had. Erin backed away and moved to douse all the room's light but for the single bedside lamp. She pulled back the quilt and crawled beneath, pleading with her gaze for him to follow.

And so he did, stretching out his much longer legs and tucking the quilt around her shoulders, tucking her weary body spoon-fashion back into his. They lay that way for at least five minutes, sinking into the pillows and mattress, bodies adjusting to being together in bed, hands here, feet there, legs working in and out of one another until their breathing settled into a matching rhythm, their chests rising as one.

"I can't believe I'm this exhausted," Erin said, her voice barely above a whisper.

"You've had a lot going on lately. Work, planning your party." He hesitated, added, "Me."

She didn't say anything and he wasn't sure if she wasn't listening, if she agreed, or if she was weighing options for easing her stress load. He would be the easiest to get rid of and the first to go. As well he should be.

And being long ago done with any abandonment issues he'd once battled, he wasn't quite sure why the thought of her kicking him out left him ill at ease.

"I've put so much effort into this celebration. How the hell is Paddington's supposed to compete when Courtland's is bringing in the jazz talent most fans have to pay big bucks to hear?" She sighed but her body had already grown tense. "Half the time I don't even know why I bother."

He didn't know her well but what he did know assured him she wasn't a defeatist. "It's not a bother. It's your life."

She shook her head against the pillow and against his chest. "It was my granddad's life. My life is…"

She let the sentence trail and he wondered if she really didn't know or have an answer. He placed his hand on her hip and she moved closer to his body, if closer were truly possible considering he could already feel her bones where the curve of her spine pressed his torso.

"I grew up with Rory, my granddad. He raised me after my parents died. I was eleven and Rory gave up his entire life in Devon and moved here so I wouldn't have to be uprooted."

Sebastian rubbed her hip, up and down in a soothing motion to work out what tightness he could from her muscles. He adjusted his other arm beneath his head on the pillow and nuzzled his chin on the top of Erin's head.

She exhaled a bone deep sigh. "Rory did so much for me and you would think the least I could do for him would be to carry on with what was the joy of his life."

Strange thing to say. "Isn't that what you're doing?"

"I suppose so, but in case you haven't noticed there isn't a lot of joy involved for me."

Actually, he hadn't noticed that at all. What he'd seen he had chalked up to the normal stress of running a business, not dissatisfaction at feeling stuck in the life. He gave a small shrug, wondering exactly whether she considered the bar hers at all, or whether she still thought of it as Rory's. "So, sell the bar. Do what you want to do with your life."

"I don't know what I want to do with my life," was all she said.

But it was the way she said it, the exhaustion that went beyond the need for sleep, a tiredness that spoke of a weary soul that clutched hard in the region of Sebastian's heart. He didn't want to feel the need to set things right, or the urge to soothe whatever he could of her emotional ache. A few things, however, he couldn't control.

Funny how they both seemed to be at a crisis point. His had been a nagging pain in the ass now for several months, rearing her annoying little head every time he sat down with Raleigh to write. He wondered… "You've been running Paddington's for a year?"

She nodded again. "Rory died three years ago. Once his estate was settled, I worked with a designer on the remodeling of the bar. We reopened last October."

He continued to rub her hip, over the cotton of her panties to the smooth skin of her thigh. "Before he died. What were you doing then?"

She snorted. "Nothing. Everything. I traveled. I took university classes. I have way too many credits for someone with no degree. I thought about declaring business as my major because Rory was always asking my advice, which was a totally ridiculous ploy to get me involved in the running of the bar. He'd been in business longer than I'd been alive."

"You had money from your parents, then."

"Oodles. Ridiculous, really. All the money to do what I wanted and I never knew what I wanted to do."

He thought about that for several minutes, his hand moving to Erin's waist and rubbing there and down over her belly. He'd known for as long as he could remember what he wanted to do. Hell, he'd made up stories when pushing that little yellow truck through the ashes of dead fires.

Richie had been the one to help prep Sebastian for college when the visiting counselor had shot him down, telling him he'd be wasting his time to aim beyond trade school. He'd aimed way, way beyond and had put himself through the five years it had taken to earn his four-year degree.

Five more years and his first book was in the publication pipeline. He'd found his niche, but he still wasn't satisfied, greedy bastard that he was, wanting more.

Erin rolled over onto her stomach and propped up on her elbows. The plump side of one breast pressed against his ribs. Her eyes glittered and her gaze probed. "What are you thinking?"

He couldn't tell her. Writing was a part of his life he didn't share. Even being here with her now, this way, talking about life and dreams. He was growing too complacent, too comfortable, and he stiffened rather than answer.

Erin grew pensive, obviously sensing his backing away. "Do I frighten you somehow? Are you afraid I'm going to tie you up and torture you free of your secrets?"

Sebastian rolled over onto his back, crossed his arms behind his head. "Torture away. I don't have any secrets."

Erin's grin said give-me-a-break with more sarcasm than her voice. "What're you talking about? Everything about you is a secret. You haven't told me anything about who you are or what you do or things you've done in your life."

He stared into her eyes, watching the low-burning lamplight draw silver flecks from pure hazel. Her nose was long and straight, her mouth lush, her lips plump in the way a man enjoyed. He felt an urge to cup the back of her head and pull her mouth to his.

An urge he forced himself to resist even while forcing a retreat from the intimacy she sought. Safety, sustenance and support. He needed no one to give him any of those things. What Erin looked ready to offer went totally off his radar and he had no choice but to push her away.

"Is that what I'm here for? That's what you want? To know everything about me?" When she didn't answer, when she continued to meet his gaze without blinking, he added, "I didn't think what we were doing required more than what we already know."

Her expression remained unchanged though the softness paled and what he could only imagine was hope faded away.

"You're right," she finally said. "There's not a thing you could tell me that would make any difference to why we're here."

He waited, tensed, expecting any minute for her to ask him to leave. So, when instead, a minute later, she moved closer and climbed up to straddle his lower body, all he could do was close his eyes, let her have her way and play the part of the convenient dick.

Not that doing so required much effort. Certainly not the same effort required to ignore how right this felt because this was Erin sliding down his body and not some nameless female or even one who'd mentioned her name before rolling on his condom.

He tensed further, told himself to relax. Impossible, because Erin brushed her lips down the center of his torso and dipped her tongue in and out of his navel. She nipped at the surrounding skin, tiny bites with the edges of her teeth followed by a soothing bath from her tongue.

Blood pooled heavily in his groin and he held himself still when he wanted more than anything to surge upward. Her bare breasts plumped against the tops of his thighs and her hands at his hips held fast.

She moved lower, her teeth, lips and tongue toying with the waistband of his boxer briefs where it rode low on his abs and behind which his erection strained. When she drew one finger from the head of his dick to the base, Sebastian gave up all attempts to stay aloof and groaned from the center of his gut.

He spread his legs, knowing if this was going to go where he wanted her to take it, his shorts had to go. He lifted his hips; Erin shoved him back down, keeping a hand flat on his stomach. *A woman in charge.* He liked the concept, liked it a lot. He'd let her be the boss as long as she didn't stop what she was doing, blowing hot air through her open mouth down the same trail her finger had followed.

Her fingertips slipped beneath the elastic—finally—and she eased down the band, but only far enough to expose the head of his dick which she summarily took into her mouth to suck. He huffed out several short breaths and this time it was Erin who pulled off his shorts when he lifted his hips and begged.

She took him fully into her mouth. He hit the back of her throat and felt her lips wrap around the base of his shaft. *Unbelievable.* He hated to move, to dilute the sensation, but when she pressed her most intimate kiss around him and pulled upward, he followed, thrusting because she made it impossible to do anything less.

She wrapped her hand around his erection and held him still. Her mouth moved up and down, her tongue swirled over the head, her lips caught the ridge where sensation centered. Her hold tightened, the pressure and the rhythm of her mouth increased.

And then she slid her other hand between his legs, stroking behind his balls and finding the source of his building pressure. She pushed hard, pushed harder. He groaned and she took her exploration lower, fingering him in places he most wanted her touch.

But he was going to come and this wasn't what he wanted. He wanted to be buried as deep in her body as size and position allowed. "Erin," he grunted, his voice hoarse and ragged.

She released him, her hands and her mouth moving back up his torso, tickling and teasing until, still wearing her panties, she straddled him. Her smiling face hovered inches over his.

"Damn you, woman. Tell me you have a condom."

Her smile widened and she reached into the drawer of her bedside table and handed him the packet. She worked herself out of her panties while he worked himself into the latex. And then she positioned her body above his and lowered herself completely.

He couldn't stand it. He couldn't handle anything else that was slow and easy. He wanted her now and he flipped her over, driving his body deeply into hers. Fingernails scraped down his back. Heels urged him forward, digging into his backside, her long legs moving up to wrap around his waist. She cried out. It hadn't even been a minute and she came. He continued thrusting, driving, pumping into her.

His orgasm consumed him. There was no other word for the overpowering sensation of being ripped in half, burned alive, torn apart from everything safe he'd ever known. He couldn't wait to come down, to finish, to be free of her hold. He pulled out, rolled up to sit on the edge of the bed.

For a moment all he had the strength to do was sit, elbows on his knees, face buried in his hands. Sit and breathe and do what he could to pull himself back together. He felt Erin turn toward him, felt the touch of her hand to his back and, before she had the chance to call out his name, he left the bed.

Once in the bathroom, he pulled off the condom and flushed. And then he looked into the mirror. And he didn't like anything about the man looking back. The man who lived alone for a reason and had known the first time he'd crushed his mouth to Erin's that he was making a huge mistake.

He'd abandoned every one of life's lessons for what he'd tried to tell himself was nothing but a great piece of ass, when the reality was that he was in over his head, far beneath his comfort zone of emotion with no possibility of ever surfacing for air. Taking her down with him only furthered his sensation of strangling. Which was why he would save her.

But then he would destroy her.

There was nothing else he could do.

ERIN NEVER WENT TO THE bar on Sunday. Never, because Sunday was her one and only completely free personal day of the week. She'd promised herself never to do more than attend church and buy groceries. The rest of the day was for shopping or the movies or anything else she deemed fun.

But here she was, unlocking the back door into the bar having walked the several blocks from the loft. She'd woken with an insane headache and spent too long in the shower trying to steam it away. The shower, in fact, only doubled the pain's intensity because the ache spread down her neck, over her shoulders, and wove a web around her heart.

The resulting nausea had convinced her to skip buying groceries—who could eat when on the verge of vomiting? And, since she'd already missed church, she figured she might as well use the time to catch up on Paddington's accounting, having slacked off the last three nights.

She turned on the lights and the ceiling fan low to stir the still air. Dropping into her desk chair, she wondered if Tess and Samantha were tired of her yet. She opened her e-mail program but hesitated before starting a new message, waiting while the usual spam mail and Eve's Apple digests filled her inbox.

Erin groaned. She was *so* behind on reading Anaïs Nin. No doubt the group had already discussed *Little Birds*—which she hadn't picked up since reading those few pages after work on Wednesday night—and moved on to *Delta of Venus*. If she didn't get busy and participate, she'd lose her spot in the queue for choosing the next author, and she was determined to introduce the group to Emma Holly's erotica.

Neither Tess nor Sam had said a word about the goings-on with Eve's Apple, but she hadn't thought to ask, being so caught up sending them her Man To Do missives. She hated whining to her cyber-girlfriends as much as she hated whining to Cali. Besides, Tess and Sam would both be well within their rights to give her a big fat, "I told you so."

Not only had Erin *not* gone to Starbucks for a brownie and a Frappuccino à la Tess, she'd also stupidly done all the things Samantha had warned her not to do. Especially the worst offender. The infamous chick cliché. Mixing up *I love sex* with *I love you*.

Erin had known Sebastian Gallo now for two and a half days. If anything, she was a victim of sex at first sight. More than that would've been a true stretch of her credibility as a savvy, independent woman, assuming that's what she was. And she was. She knew she was. She just hadn't been terribly savvy about opening up her emotions to a man she only wanted to screw.

She should've kept her opening up to her girlfriends. But she knew Tess and Samantha had to be rolling their eyes that she'd managed to botch things so quickly. And then there was Cali who had her own issues with Will and didn't need to be hit first thing this morning with a blow-by-blow of Erin's night.

Erin's morning would be going a lot better if she could understand why Sebastian had left her bed so suddenly. For the first time this week she'd felt as if they were on the verge of making love. No, she *had* been making love. And she had a feeling that was exactly what had driven Sebastian away.

Because he was right. If all they were doing was sleeping together, she didn't need to know more of who he was than the little bit she'd learned. And the very fact that she'd asked meant...what?

"Yes, Samantha. I know. I know. I'm in love with the sex, not with the man," she grumbled to herself while pulling up her accounting software. But for some untold reason, Erin didn't believe a single word she said.

She went back to close down her inbox, stopping when the subject line *Anniversary Party—Paddington's On Main* caught her eye. The sender's name wasn't familiar, doubling her curiosity.

She opened it up, read through, read through a second time while her heart pounded wildly in her throat. The note was from the publicist who represented Ryder Falco.

The Ryder Falco, the bestselling horror novelist dogging Stephen King's heels.

Falco was to be in Houston the weekend of Halloween and his publicist understood she was hosting a good versus-evil themed party. Would she be interested in having Falco sign advance copies of his newest Raleigh Slater release, *The Demon Begs to Differ?* After all, was there a single pop culture figure to better embody good-versus-evil than Ryder Falco?

Erin rocked back in her chair, shoved all ten fingers into her hair. This was totally insane! Unbelievable and wholly unreal! The post-party results of implementing every single one of last night's *Save Paddington's* brainstorming ideas wouldn't have half the impact of a Ryder Falco signing.

But how? No one knew of the recent conflict with Crewe Courtland's pre-grand opening event but Cali and Will and Sebastian...

Of course! This was Sebastian's doing. Erin hadn't a single doubt that this man about whom she knew next to nothing was responsible. Tied into his reticence to reveal personal information and the incredible library of books he owned, this made perfect sense. The business associates he'd mentioned had to be in publishing.

Surely he'd realize she'd put two and two together? Had he planned to tell her about making this amazing contact on her behalf? The very fact that he had made it...

She rocked her chair forward again, propped elbows on her desk, chin in her hands and stared at her electronic salvation. How would she ever be able to thank Sebastian for the invaluable gift when the very fact that he'd given it had her struggling for words?

HALLOWEEN NIGHT ARRIVED, finally, only to find Erin pacing madly through the bar, checking on the caterer's serving tables and fretting over decorations. The black and white, good-versus-evil theme had been played out from glittering snowflakes falling through shadowy spiderwebs to the jailhouse black and whites worn by the caterer's staff to the incredible array of visually contrasted food and drink.

Never in a million years would she have believed in the neutral color scheme's sensory appeal. But she had to admit the bar had never looked better. Even the black and white cookies worked, she realized, thinking about scarfing down a quick dozen. Nerves had kept her from eating for days and she suddenly found herself famished.

Yes, all the work she'd poured into the party had paid off—at least in presentation. She wouldn't change a thing. And her ace in the hole, Ryder Falco, virtually guaranteed she'd pull in the crowd she needed. She laughed, amused by the ridiculous understatement.

Ryder Falco guaranteed more of a crowd than she could ever fit into Paddington's and remain within code. Which was why she'd put two bouncers at the front door to man the line of Falco fans here for the autographing only. She realized she was dealing with a logistical nightmare and prayed for cool tempers and a zero percent chance of rain.

Once the bar hit capacity and hopefully stayed that way, the success of the night would be out of her hands and solely contingent on the work that had gone before. All she could do would be to cross her fingers that the party paid off at the cash bar and in returning customers.

She'd been a total wreck for the past three weeks, working to pull everything together and thinking this night would never arrive. The anniversary had loomed like an execution date when it should've been an exciting celebration marking the past year of her dedication on top of the dozens of years Rory had spent behind the bar. She hated that she still felt so bound to Paddington's instead of reveling in her success.

She and Sebastian had continued to see each other, their affair losing none of the initial intensity, settling into an intimately comfortable accord. She'd been grateful beyond reason for their shared schedule. More than once she'd stepped into her building's elevator at 3:00 a.m. and pushed "7", not bothering to stop on her floor before heading for his.

He was always awake as she'd known he would be. And he was always waiting, never surprised that she'd been drawn to his door. What had surprised her, however, was the way she'd so quickly grown secure enough in their involvement to invite herself into his shower instead of cleaning up in her own.

Sebastian's shower did come with one benefit hers didn't offer. Sebastian. She'd come to think of him as Poseidon, king of his water-filled domain. And, yes. Serving at Sebastian's feet had become one of her life's greatest pleasures—even if they'd yet to have sex in his bed. They'd slept there together but, the mornings she'd come awake in his place, she'd hurriedly dressed and left.

She'd never forgotten his first hasty flight from her bedroom almost a month ago. He'd never explained; she'd never asked. But she hadn't again made the mistake of thinking their coming together was about making love. They were here for the beauty of joined bodies. Love was the antithesis of having a Man To Do.

Her Man To Do had dodged her inquiries into his connection to Ryder Falco and the Halloween night signing, admitting to nothing more than calling in a few favors. After that, she hadn't asked him anything else personal. He seemed to prefer to talk about her, or to not talk at all.

She wouldn't be surprised to learn she was the first person he'd ever told about his showers. Or about the little toy truck, the ashes of burned-out fires, and a five-year-old's crushed birthday cupcake. And an intuitive female part of her doubted her knowing those crucial parts of his past sat well with the way he now lived his life.

More than once on the nights she did go straight home, she arrived to find him sitting outside her front door, waiting, wordlessly watching as she walked down the hall. Her heart blipped each and every time, and it was all she could do to rein in her emotions before she reached him. Harder still was the struggle to keep her feelings hermetically sealed while he stripped off her clothes and covered her with his bare body.

Tonight her emotions clashed in a virtual riot of ups and downs, sky highs and barrel bottoms. When deciding on her costume earlier in the month, she'd wavered between good and bad, uncertain whether or not embracing the dark side would reflect negatively at all on her position as hostess and as Paddington's owner.

Next she'd considered coming as the opposite of Sebastian, except that he'd never mentioned a costume or even his intent to attend. She'd tried not to be hurt, though it was difficult to maintain the detachment when she had started thinking of them as a couple of sorts.

Once this party was put to bed, she'd make the decision she knew she had to make about continuing their arrangement of seeking out one another for sex. Yes, it had been her idea to pursue Sebastian as a Man To Do, but it was also her female prerogative to change her mind. Continuing to deny her emotions was bound to blow up in her face. She loved him. Not that it did her a bit of good...

In the end she'd decided to dress as the epitome of good and had donned flowing white scarves over a cat suit of ecru-hued lace and presented herself as the mythical virgin sacrifice Cali had once accused Sebastian of looking ready to consume. Totally apropos, Erin thought, since he consumed her on a regular basis.

The setup for the Ryder Falco signing was absolutely perfect. Erin had paid the caterer extra to work with Falco's publicist and create an ambience suited to both the party theme and the author's notoriety as a mysterious recluse. She'd read his first novel, *The Demon Inside,* and had decided she'd stick with Nora Roberts for her fiction.

Falco's work was too sinister for Erin's tastes—exactly the reason the grotto of stones and live plants in the bar's darkest corner, lit with black lights casting a red-tinted ultraviolet glow, fit so well with the ambience of both the room and the man's reputation.

She circled through the room one more time then headed to her office to dress. When she returned thirty minutes later, Cali was already behind the bar, checking the crates of mugs and racks of wineglasses as well as the stock of hard liquor. She looked up as Erin joined her, twirling in a pirouette that sent her scarves floating.

Cali's eyes grew extra wide. "Oh, my God! You look totally awesome. Sebastian is so going to jump your bones."

Ignoring Cali's prediction, Erin raked her gaze over the other woman's costume of white shorts and a ribbed white tank that showed off her gorgeous curves. Cali also wore a halo atop her mop of blond curls and a huge set of iridescent angels wings flapped on her back.

"You look pretty damn cute yourself." Erin felt her mouth twist into a wry grin. "Are you the angel of Will's salvation?"

"Something like that," Cali said with a bit of a prurient expression. "I couldn't decide on being good or bad and finally went for a combo."

Erin gave her friend another once-over. "Well, you succeeded in a big way. He's not going to know what hit him."

Cali's smile begin to fade. "If he even notices."

"Why wouldn't he? How could he not notice?" Erin glanced toward the door as a party of four vampires came in.

"Oh, he'll notice, but he won't care." Cali pushed the crate of mugs back beneath the bar. "You know how guys get when they're pissed off. Whatever they're mad about is the only thing they can think of. They couldn't care less that someone went out of her way to make sure she looked good enough to eat."

"Wait a minute." Erin waved a scolding finger. "You know we're supposed to dress for ourselves, not for men."

"Puh-lease," Cali said with a huff. "What kind of *Cosmo* girl are you anyway? You can't tell me you dressed like that and never thought of Sebastian." A teasing light dawned in Cali's eyes. "Unless maybe you were thinking of seducing Ryder Falco."

Erin frowned and snorted. "Right. I dressed to seduce a man I don't even know."

"You didn't know Sebastian when you seduced him," Cali countered.

"That was different." Erin *had* known Sebastian. She'd been making love to him for months in her mind. They just hadn't yet met—a horse of an entirely different color. "And I dressed this way for me. I don't even know if Sebastian is going to be here."

Cali's hands went to her hips. "What're you talking about? Why wouldn't he come?"

A trio of goth females—pale white complexions, dark lips and eyes, spiky black hair...oh, wait. One was a guy, Erin realized, shaking off the illusion. She turned back to Cali. "I imagine he will. He just never committed to coming."

"Maybe he assumed he didn't have to commit. Like he knew you knew he'd be here." Cali hesitated. "Y'all are still together, right? I mean, now I'm the one doing the assuming but you haven't said that y'all weren't still dating."

"C'mon, Cali. When have Sebastian and I ever *dated?* You know what our involvement is all about." It was exactly what it had been intended to be about from the get-go, Erin admitted, logic nicely stepping in to remind her of the facts.

"I know. I just thought…" Cali sighed, waved off the rest of her comment with one hand. "I don't know what I thought. I obviously have no business analyzing relationships since I don't even have a handle on my own."

"You never told me what's going on with Will. What's he being a grump about?"

"The screenplay. What else?" Cali picked up her serving tray to make a round through the bar. "He's not too happy that I discussed it with Sebastian."

"Hmm. Where is Will anyway?" Erin glanced up at the clock above the bar. "It's almost eight. Oh, God. It's almost eight." And Ryder Falco was due at nine. "Can you tell me about Will later? I've got to make sure Robin knows Falco is her number one priority tonight."

"Relax, Erin. Robin's been working for you as long as I have. She knows her stuff. Everything'll be cool," Cali added before heading out into the crowd to circulate.

All Erin could do was take a deep breath and trust that Cali was right.

Chapter Eleven

WALKING THROUGH Paddington's back door without first giving Erin full disclosure wasn't going to be fair. Sebastian knew that. Had for the last three weeks, in fact, recognized the building ache in his gut as guilt over what he was going to do. During tonight's short limo ride from his publicist's hotel to the bar, he sat expecting to physically implode.

Revealing his identity any earlier would've rendered the admission worthless. He knew that as well. Erin would've gone and canceled the signing and told him to get the hell out of her life. He'd be doing that soon enough. Tonight, as a matter of fact. But he didn't want to go without showing her that he'd never taken their involvement lightly.

He cared about her in ways he didn't know it was possible to care for another human being, ways he'd never once experienced throughout his thirty-four years. Except for the time spent learning what he had from Richie, Sebastian had been on his own from day one—and had followed his personal creed to the letter.

He never relied on anyone but himself. He never looked to another for what he couldn't beg, borrow or steal using his wits, his street smarts or the education he'd received in lockup, compliments of the State of Texas.

At least he'd never looked elsewhere before now.

Until lately, when he'd been looking to Erin for things he couldn't name, things indefinable yet significant, that had doubled his creative energy, spurred his enthusiasm toward the bitch of a project he'd been warily circling for months.

He didn't know what exactly was going on with her in regards to Paddington's and her grandfather. She hadn't been particularly up-front, had been damned evasive in fact, when he'd asked her those questions a few weeks ago while lying in bed at her side, holding her close, pulling her back into his body, content to do nothing but touch.

Okay, so he'd only been a temporary fix and not a permanent part of her life. She didn't owe him any answers. That said, he still wanted to know. His interest was real and true and drawn from that place where he felt too much and too strongly for this woman he was going to have to let go.

Slumped in the limo's back seat, he stared out the tinted window at the taillights on his left, shoving away the encroaching emotion he couldn't afford to feel. Not tonight. Tonight was going to be tough enough, worrying about her reaction to his deception, unable to talk to her, to explain until the signing's end.

Dealing with his own strange sense of loss on top was too much of a distraction to his focus. Later, maybe. After gaining the distance he needed. Then he'd be in a better position to look back objectively, to appreciate the time she'd allowed him into her life. For now, however, he would be the bastard he played so well.

Since Paddington's was spitting distance from his loft, his only caveat to the signing was going in costume. His publicist was used to his covert way of doing what little promotion he agreed to do and wasn't concerned by the subterfuge, just thrilled to have the reclusive Ryder Falco making a personal appearance.

Sebastian didn't want to be recognized in his own neighborhood after tonight. It might happen, but he was taking what precaution he could. Funny how tonight's chance for exposure registered lower on his personal radar than it had in the past. He added that inconsistency to his list of "laters" growing longer the more he sat and stewed.

The costume had worked. No one had looked at him twice on leaving his publicist's hotel where he'd dressed. Erin, of course, would recognize him immediately. Like he'd said, totally unfair. But it was either do it this way and give her the boost Paddington's needed, or never say a word about who he was and watch her suffer while Courtland's pulled in the landslide business that should've been hers.

He figured this way was the lesser of two evils. And, yeah. The signing went a long way toward assuaging a conscience he shouldn't have had. A self-reproach tied into the fact that he wouldn't be seeing Erin again after tonight. If he expected to string together one hundred thousand words that made sense and prove he had more in his creative repository than detectives and demons, he needed to shake off the sweetest distraction in which he'd ever indulged.

The mess he'd made with his newest Raleigh Slater story proved even recreational involvement with Erin was out of the question. She had too much impact on his state of mind when he needed complete clarity of thought. He couldn't afford the risk to his career. A career that was his entire life, his safety, sustenance and support.

His agent had been only marginally more tolerant of Sebastian's new project idea than had his editor. And understandably so. They both liked the guaranteed gravy of his Raleigh Slater series. Hell, he was partial to the stuff himself. His muse was another matter. She'd demanded he take up her gauntlet and give this new project his undivided attention—the very reason he had to cut himself off from Erin. From the little interaction he had with Cali and Will as well.

His success had come at a high price, but relying on self and self alone had taken him to the top. He hit the *New York Times* bestseller list with every new hardback release, and then again with the mass market printing a year or so later. He'd done it all on his own. And taking his career in a new and risky direction doubled the necessity of cutting off contact with the world outside the one in his mind.

He didn't expect Erin to understand. And the explanation he'd have to give her wouldn't satisfy her right to know or excuse his actions. But he had to do what he had to do without worrying about Erin being hurt.

He was having a hard enough time dealing with the strangling ache near his heart.

"OH MY GOD. OH MY GOD. Oh, Erin. Oh, God."

Erin hurriedly swiped the half-melted ice cube from the bar into her free hand and tossed both the ice and the rag into the bin beneath the bar. Ryder Falco. He was here. He was here. Oh, God. He was here. She sounded as hysterical as Cali.

She smoothed down her flowing scarves, a ridiculous effort that defeated the costume's entire purpose. "Do I look okay? First impressions are everything, you know." Cali worked so hard at swallowing, Erin worried her friend would choke. "Cali? What's wrong? Are you all right?"

Having scooted behind the bar and up to Erin's side, Cali grabbed Erin's upper arms and held tight. "Forget the first impressions. Just promise me one thing."

Erin frowned down at her friend's viselike hold. "Uh, Cali? Can this wait for a better time?"

Cali shook her head. "No. It can't. Now, promise me that, well, that…just promise me that you won't flip out or anything."

"Why would I flip out or anything?" Erin asked.

"Promise?" Cali's eyes both went wide. "I mean, this is important, Erin. This party is going to go a long way toward making sure you don't lose the bar. That's all that matters here, okay? You have to remember that."

Okay. This was getting weird. "What is it? The cops? The alcoholic beverage commission? Little green men?" When Cali didn't even crack a smile, Erin began to get nervous. She pried her arms free and said, "No flipping out. Or anything. I promise."

"If you do, I'm dragging you out of here. I swear." Cali made a spinning motion with one finger.

"No flipping out. I promise," Erin said then turned to face the grotto—and immediately forgot how to breathe.

Ryder Falco stood behind the grotto table, hands at his hips, the long tails of his black duster caught back like flared batwings. His black bad-guy hat was pulled low on his forehead; his black bad-guy bandanna was pulled high on the bridge of his nose. Only his eyes remained visible.

His eyes were all Erin needed to see to know who he really was. To remember the way he'd looked at her from across the bar the first night he'd come into Paddington's. To relive the moments he'd watched her only hours later as she'd walked into his home and shared his shower. Except suddenly his eyes seemed to be that of a stranger. She felt as if she didn't know him, had never known him, at all.

A man she assumed was his publicist stood at Sebastian's side, talking to the member of the caterer's staff responsible for the Falco book display. Yet, for all Sebastian's appearance of listening, Erin knew he wasn't. His attention was on her and no place else. They could easily have been the only two people in the room.

She loved a man who had lied to her, she realized, even as another painful truth struck. She had been equally dishonest with him—about the truth of her feelings, about the shallow and selfish reasons she'd invited him into her life. Still, her sin of omission hovered in the realm of petty. And, according to the weighted fist crushing her heart, Sebastian's ranked above the seven deadly.

And, now that she'd finally begun breathing again, she wanted to kill him almost as much as she wanted to do herself in. When had she become so blind? So gullible? And where could she get her hands on a weapon to slash his heart into shreds resembling hers? How in the hell did he plan to justify his deception? Anger quickly followed denial. This she could not wait to hear.

Erin took a deep breath and the first long step toward the grotto. Sebastian's gaze followed her the entire way. She kept her head up, her mouth set, her eyes focused straight ahead. Let him wonder. Let him squirm. She refused to give away an inkling of what she felt and held tightly to the power of that advantage.

Once she reached him, she pasted on a smile and extended her hand. "Mr. Falco? I'm Erin Thatcher. It's an honor to meet you. I owe you an amazing debt of gratitude and I'm not sure I'll ever be able to properly thank you."

Sebastian held on to her hand longer than required of a simple handshake. His eyes sparked and the bandanna barely muffled his voice. "No additional thanks are necessary, Ms. Thatcher. And the pleasure is all mine." Propriety finally demanded he release her. "This is my publicist, Calvin Shaw."

"Mr. Shaw. My thanks to you, as well." She shook the other man's hand, giving him her full attention while feeling Sebastian's devouring gaze. "I have no idea how you managed to convince Mr. Falco to leave his lair, but I'm incredibly glad that you did. You may have just saved the day."

Calvin Shaw crossed his arms over his chest and inclined his head toward Sebastian. "I'm the one glad to see Ryder here in the flesh. We get together so rarely that I've started to wonder if he's the fictional character instead of Raleigh Slater."

Erin forced an appreciative laugh when truly she felt like she might vomit. "Well, he looks like the real thing to me. Living, breathing. Totally three-dimensional. Not a work of fiction at all."

She returned her gaze to Sebastian, watched his eyes express all the things he was unable to say. She imagined the vein pulsing at his temple, the hard grinding tic in his jaw, the fullness of his lower lip pressed tight to his upper, all hidden behind his bandanna.

It was a small victory, but it was enough to know he couldn't say a word without giving away the whole gig. "I hope you didn't have any trouble finding us. I know the construction has been terrible and we're not exactly one of the city's better known hot spots."

"No. No trouble at all," Calvin said, slapping a palm to Sebastian's back. "Ryder knew exactly where to find you."

"Really? That surprises me." She narrowed an eye in speculation. "Unless, of course, you've been here before. You should've introduced yourself. Your secret would've been safe with me."

"He claims the risk to his anonymity is too great. Or at

least that's the excuse he gives me every time I try to book him a signing," Calvin said.

Erin was still waiting for Sebastian to answer. She wasn't leaving the grotto until he did, until he gave her a hint of an explanation for what felt like an unforgivable deception. If he thought she was putting him on the spot, all the better. Look what he was doing to her!

He pulled the brim of his hat even lower. "I have a couple of friends who live here in town. They love this place and wanted to help you out of your jam. Plus I knew it would get Cal off my back for a while."

"So a little bit of the goodness of your heart and a little bit of a peace offering?" Her grin grew brittle. "Your friends are lucky to have you. You've been extremely generous."

"I try to be. At least when it comes to the people I care about." He was good, way too good.

She wanted him to hurt like she did and resented his effortless cool. "Your friends are lucky to have you."

"I think I'm more lucky to have them." He offered a one-shouldered shrug—one almost apologetic, self-deprecating even. "Helps keep me sane in my isolation, knowing they're out there."

Erin fought back what felt too much like sympathy. He had done this to himself. She was not about to offer him her open arms. "Well, maybe now that you've seen how friendly we are, and that we're not out to devour hapless authors, you'll stop back by whenever you're in town."

Calvin rearranged a stack of books for maximum impact. "I'm hoping he'll see that getting out does not mean an automatic invasion of his privacy."

Sebastian might've smiled beneath the bandanna, but the emotion failed to reach his eyes. "Cal makes it sound like I never leave home."

"Do you?" she asked, willing Calvin to walk away and leave her to get the answers she wasn't getting.

"Sure," Sebastian said. "I walk through my neighborhood a lot. There's a great bar I frequent. Under the right circumstances, I can be downright sociable."

"Don't let him fool you." The table arrangement to his liking, Calvin pulled out Sebastian's chair. "He can be downright intimidating."

"Let's see." Erin gave Sebastian—The Scary Guy—a once-over. "Big guy. Head-to-toe black. Menacing eyes. Hmm. It's not hard to imagine that he might cause a ripple of fear." What *was* hard was standing here making small talk with a celebrity who had buried himself in her body as fully and completely as Sebastian had.

She supposed she should be starstruck. She wasn't. She was angry and hurt and beginning to shake from the emotional rush. She didn't know how she'd managed to pull off her role of hostess this long. She needed to get out of here—and now.

"Let me get you gentlemen a drink and then your fans can have at you. Again, thank you and enjoy the evening." She turned without waiting for Sebastian to respond and she never once looked back.

"DID YOU KNOW ABOUT THIS? That Sebastian was...that Sebastian *is* Ryder Falco?" Wearing black cape, mask, and gaucho-style Zorro hat, Will stood with a serving tray rather than a sword tucked beneath his arm, his gaze following the ebb and flow of the crowd while he questioned Cali.

She might've been more inclined to answer had he been talking to her and not to the room. Yes, he was busy doing his job. No, he was not ignoring her. But the last few weeks had been rather tense, what with their screenplay issues, and she found herself reading too much into everything he said. And everything he didn't say.

Especially when what he said had no basis. Like now. "Why would you think I would be privy to something even Erin didn't know?"

This time he did look at her, casting her a sideways glance from beneath his black mask, a glance that was just this side of a smirk. "Oh, I don't know. Something to do with the way *you* wanted *his* input on *our* screenplay? No, wait. How about the way you *went* to him for his input? Even though you knew I didn't give a damn what he thought?"

The heat of anger rose in a flush. Why was Will so intent on ruining her night? He knew every reason for what she had done. Knew, as well, the validity of the arguments she had made for the changes. He was just being a hardheaded egotistical man. And she wasn't sure she possessed the patience to put up with his crap no matter how she felt.

"Yes. I asked him, okay?" She stopped, took a calming breath, knowing she shouldn't have made the changes without telling Will.

But she'd wanted him to see the alterations once they were done—not while the story structure was in a state of flux. "I had no idea who he was when I did but, now that I know? His insights make a ton of sense. He was so intuitive about what would make the idea work."

Will went back to checking out the crowd, turning more than a cold shoulder Cali's way. "The changes you made might be your idea of what it needed but they sure weren't mine. I thought and I still think that it worked just fine as it was."

"You haven't even given it a chance. You haven't even read the story through since I tweaked it. You've just nitpicked certain scenes. That's hardly fair." Cali had known that having Sebastian look over the screenplay wasn't going to sit well with Will once he found out.

But she'd really wanted an outside opinion, one that would confirm her instincts if possible—exactly what Sebastian's input had done. She'd since gone through and made small and subtle changes where possible, keeping intact what she could of Will's skeleton. No matter that his feelings were hurt, she knew the story was stronger.

Now if she could only get him to agree. Then get him to understand why his major plot point wasn't going to work. But when he bodily turned to face her, banged his tray on the bar top and pulled off his mask, she didn't think much about his mood was agreeable.

"Me not reading the changes isn't fair but you making them without telling me is?" Without the obstruction of his glasses, Will's eyes glittered with sparks the likes of which Cali had never seen—

—and wasn't sure she found the least bit attractive. Her heart pounded painfully. "Please read it, Will. That's all I'm asking."

"I'm not sure I want to read it. Or work on it." His expression closed down. "It's not the story I wanted to tell anymore."

Cali wanted to stomp her foot in frustration, but she'd sworn tonight to be on her best angelic behavior for Erin's sake, and because she'd never make her point with Will by throwing a childish hissy.

"I did what I felt had to do, Will. I'm sorry you don't trust my motives or my instincts." Probably not a fair response but she'd be damned before she backed down on this—even though she had no idea how to correct the inevitable outcome of their current collision course.

The decibel level of the party crowd and party music

rose higher, giving Will the option of shouting or of moving closer to be heard. He moved closer, offering Cali so many intimate reminders of having him near. The fight between her heart and her head and her warm and willing body grew fierce.

Will's expression grew fiercer. "And what exactly are your motives, Cali? To have it your way? To prove my way wrong by bringing in a celebrity author to vet your ideas?"

Pulling her gaze from Will's, Cali swept empty mugs into a dirty dish tub with no respect for their fragility. "You know I had no idea who Sebastian was until tonight. Erin didn't even know. She picked him to do because of their mutual attraction, not because of any fame and fortune."

Will shook his head as if trying to settle a thought that didn't sit well. Or dodge a buzzing mosquito. "Wait a minute. What do you mean, Erin picked Sebastian *to do?*"

Uh-oh. *Way to open mouth, insert foot.* The dish tub went under the counter. Cali got busy wiping condensation from the bar with the first rag she found, wishing she could wipe away the past few minutes of speaking without first gathering her thoughts. *Oh, why the hell not.* Honesty never killed a girl.

She shrugged out of her angel wings and shoved them beneath the bar. "Erin went after what she wanted. An involvement with a man she found attractive. The very same thing men do all the time with women."

She waited for a male denial, ready to go to the mat on this one, but Will kept his mouth shut, damn it, when she was finally itching for a fight. So she tried again. "What Erin did was nothing but reversing a centuries-old dating practice. A woman picking up a man. Being gutsy enough to go against convention."

"Man the torpedoes, full steam ahead?"

"Exactly." *And so there!*

Will took a minute to consider his reply, then came back with, "Is that the same reason you came home with me?"

"What're you talking about?" Cali asked, recognizing that she was about to be in really big trouble. "I've come home with you more than a few times this semester."

Leaving his tray on the counter, Will walked around behind, leaning an elbow onto the bar and forcing himself into Cali's personal space. His voice dropped to a volume meant only for her ears. "But you haven't come into my bed until recently. Kinda convenient that we started sleeping together about the same time Erin was doing Sebastian."

"I'm not sure I know what you're implying," Cali went back to wiping the bar. "Or even that I want to know."

"I'd think it's pretty obvious in context, Cali. Picking out a man you want to do? But, then again. It doesn't really matter, does it?" He spun his hat Frisbee-style down the bar and shrugged off his cape to go.

Cali grabbed at his elbow before he'd gotten completely out of her reach. "It matters to me. And, okay. I'll admit it. Yes, knowing Erin's plans did impact my decision to come home with you. But I'd wanted to come home with you for a very long time. I borrowed what I could of her guts and did it. I guess I shouldn't have."

The crowed milled noisily in the background while the world became nothing but the two of them and the tension of lovers at odds. Will stood still, the overhead track lighting casting over his hair a nimbus of light that was brighter than the one Cali wore. "If you wanted to be with me, Cali, it should've been about you and me. Not about what Erin decided to do."

He sounded too rational, too right. So much so that doubts burst rather than blossomed from recently sown seeds. "Does it really matter how we got together?"

"Does the end justify the means? Is that what you're asking?" He didn't give her time to say anything else before adding, "I think it does, yeah. Sex shouldn't be about a bet or a dare. And it sure shouldn't be some sort of twisted group seduction project."

Cali balled her fist around the rag she still held, afraid Will was about to wash his hands of her. "I can't believe you're being this way about the reason why I finally decided to come home with you. Or because of a lousy class project."

Will's brows went up. "Lousy? So now the screenplay is lousy?"

Cali pulled off her halo and flung it into the trash. "No, it's not lousy. I wish you'd quit mucking up everything I say."

Will shook his head, gave a laugh that was more about frustration and disbelief than about anything he might've found humorous. "I'll tell you what's mucked up. That's the way you can take Sebastian's word about making changes without talking to me first. That you don't have that much respect for me. Or that much faith that I might eventually 'get it' if you drum it into my head often enough.

"I really might, you know." He paused then, studying her face with eyes that reflected a sad disappointment. "But you didn't give me that chance. You went to Sebastian because he immediately told you what you wanted to hear. And, yeah. That is totally mucked up."

. He reached back and pulled out the copy of Sebastian's book he'd tucked into his waistband. He tossed the hardback volume onto the bar where it skidded to a hard stop against Cali's forearm. By the time she'd found a steady enough hand to pick up the book from the counter, Will had disappeared.

She opened the cover and read the inscription. Then she turned her back to the room and cried, while the words glared up at her. *It's a rare woman who is able to let a man be a man. You, Cali Tippen, are one of the best. I know it. And Will knows it, too. Friends always, Sebastian.*

ERIN COLLAPSED INTO THE gold velvet chair in her office because her desk chair wasn't big enough to contain her crushing despair. If despair was even the right word for the cloying fog that had wound itself in and around the flowing scarves of her costume until her feet felt too heavy to lift, her body too sluggish to move.

Her heart too brutally battered to ever beat again.

Ridiculous, really. So what if Sebastian hadn't breathed a word about his alter ego? They'd never agreed to any sort of full disclosure. What they were doing here was all about sex. He'd found an easy lay. She'd tumbled him as a lark. No one said their involvement meant anything more.

But it did. For both of them. Because, no matter what bullshit he'd given her weeks ago about calling in favors, there was absolutely no reason for him to have revealed his identity to save Paddington's. Not unless he had feelings for her. He could've had any woman he wanted. But he'd wanted her.

And she knew she'd fallen in love with him that first night in his shower.

After welcoming Sebastian and his publicist and feigning excitement when her giddiness had been more about hysterical misery, she'd spent the last two hours avoiding the grotto and circulating through the crowd as befitting her position as hostess. She'd laughed and refilled drinks and flirted and danced when hijacked onto the dance floor—until she couldn't fake the light-hearted charade any longer.

She'd had to get away. And now she sat rubbing at the headache building behind the bridge of her nose.

God, she needed to talk to Cali. But Cali was busy running the show Erin should've been out there handling. She wasn't about to add to her best friend's stress load, so she pushed up from the comfy velvet chair and dropped into the one in front of her keyboard instead.

From: Erin Thatcher
Sent: Saturday
To: Samantha Tyler; Tess Norton
Subject: The Secrets That Men Keep

Y'all were wondering if the things Sebastian told me were true? The secretive things I hinted at earlier? Well, they are. And it's worse—or better—depending on your viewpoint.

I'm sleeping with Ryder Falco. No, I'm not kidding. Ryder Falco is my Man To Do. I guess that wouldn't be so bad if I hadn't fallen in love...

Erin,
who can't even think of anything else to say

She hit Send and collapsed back in her chair. Not only couldn't she put together another cognizant sentence, she also couldn't get beyond the dimensions of the sacrifice Sebastian had made. For her. What he'd done said so much about the man he was. And that, more than anything, made loving him impossible.

Already she suffered enormous guilt at the thought of letting down the grandfather whom she'd dearly adored. Now she had Sebastian's sacrifice to come to grips with. And then there was all the work Cali had done. And Will. Not just in the bar and cohosting the party, but in their amazing concern and effort to bail her out of the Courtland's debacle.

And the worst part was that, after all of this, ungrateful cow that she was, she wasn't even sure she wanted to save Paddington's.

Before she could flagellate herself further, or wrap one of her flowing scarves around her neck and pull it tight, the e-mail chime sounded. Good grief. What were either of her cyber-girlfriends doing up at this ungodly hour?

From: Samantha Tyler
Sent: Saturday
To: Erin Thatcher; Tess Norton
Subject: Re: The Secrets That Men Keep
Erin! I don't know which is freakier, that this guy turns out to be a mega-celebrity or that you are in love with him!

But I sure as hell want to hear more. There's a whole, whole lot you're not telling us. Judging by the tone of your e-mail, I'd say you aren't overjoyed either about who he is or the fact that you're in love with him. Or maybe you're just exhausted and overwhelmed? I hope that's all it is.

In any case, you owe us one whole cartload of details, so give! I won't rest easy until I hear.

Wondering and worrying and crossing my fingers hard that it works out for you, honey.

Samantha

Too bad there wasn't going to be anything to work out, Erin mused, closing out the e-mail. Samantha couldn't know that, of course. Couldn't know that Erin had managed to screw up the life of the man she loved.

Chapter Twelve

SEBASTIAN KNEW HE'D FIND Erin in the office.

He'd seen her disappear behind the safety of the door an hour ago, but he'd been stuck in the shadows of the grotto, developing carpal tunnel from repeatedly signing his name. His own fault, he reminded himself, scratching out *Ryder Falco* another fifty times.

He wasn't worried that she'd been in there all this time falling apart. She was too strong to let that happen. She had no reason to let that happen. During their time together, he'd been more than careful to make sure he did nothing to encourage her emotional involvement. Not that he'd succeeded. He'd seen too much hope, too much longing in her eyes.

Unless what he'd seen was his own damn reflection—a highly likely possibility.

Never had he been so close to abandoning every principle by which he'd lived since he'd taken back his life. And all because of what Erin Thatcher made him feel about her—and about himself. The hope was the worst, the sense that she'd be there any time he extended his hand when he knew better than to reach out in the first place. Yeah, the hope was the main reason he wouldn't be seeing her after tonight. If he ever finished up this damn signing...

Ninety minutes later, he'd depleted the books supplied by the distributor and finished with the fans who'd brought copies of his earlier titles. As Ryder Falco, he escaped through the back door, climbing into his publicist's limo rather than taking the chance of being followed on foot. Three blocks later he was out of his costume and demanding the driver pull over.

Wearing biker boots and jeans and the black T-shirt he'd had on beneath his Aztec print western shirt and long black duster, and having ditched both the bandanna and broad-brimmed black Stetson, he headed back to Paddington's and, as Sebastian Gallo, walked in through the open front door.

He ignored the lingering party-goers, ignored servers clearing tables, ignored the caterer's crew dismantling the grotto, pulling down spiderwebs and snowflakes, even ignored Cali Tippen as she tried to flag him down. Unless he found Erin's office door locked, he wasn't stopping for anyone.

He didn't stop, in fact, until he'd shut the door behind him. This time he made sure to turn the lock. He had too many things to say and no patience to deal with interruptions. Erin sat at her desk, her head down on crossed arms, those sheer scarves draped over her body that drove him wild. A fall of red hair covered her face. He steeled himself as she raised her head.

At least she hadn't been crying. That much he was desperately glad to see. It was the blanch of white skin, however, and the purple boxerlike bruises underneath her eyes that told him discovering his identity had not been one of the better moments of her life. She was beaten up and badly so.

"Why didn't you tell me?" she asked, her voice a steady whisper, her brows drawn together in a frown of frustrated confusion and loss.

The loss is what got to him the most when it should've made what he had to do that much easier. He wasn't always big on honesty being the best policy, but tonight he owed her no less. And he'd get there. Eventually. "I never tell anyone."

"You told half of Houston tonight," she accused.

"Not really." He moved away from the door and sank into the cushy crushed velvet chair opposite her desk. "Thanks for accommodating me the way you did. The cave was great."

"It was a grotto."

"It was perfect," he repeated.

She sat up straighter, straight enough to lean back in her chair, brace her elbows on the chair arms and protectively lace her hands over her midsection. "Well, your publicist did say you weren't much for exposure. I mentioned that I'd heard that. Had I known we shared experience with one and the same person, I could've given him my personal insight."

Sebastian shrugged, though none of what he felt registered on the scale labeled nonchalance. "Like I said, I don't tell anyone. Ever."

She met his gaze directly, her eyes taking on a life that hadn't been there when he'd first walked into the room. And a fiery life at that. "Why *did* you tell me?"

"It was time." That was honest enough. "I could hardly pull off the signing without you knowing who I was." Another bite of indisputable truth.

"That's what I mean." She put her chair into a side-to-side swivel. "Why would you go to so much trouble to keep your identity secret and then blow it like that?

Paddington's is such small potatoes in the scheme of your career."

"You're not small potatoes." And that was as honest as it got. Nothing else he said would ring with a louder sincerity.

"Compared to Ryder Falco?" She swiveled faster, color returning to her cheeks. "Oh, I think that I am."

"We're not talking about what you think."

"That's patently obvious. If I had known what you were going to do…" Bringing her chair to a complete stop, she shook her head and let the sentence trail, though they both knew what she was thinking.

Frankly, he hadn't expected her to so easily make his argument for him. "And that's exactly the reason I didn't tell you before."

"I suppose I should be grateful that you've come to explain it to me now, after the fact, instead of disappearing out into the night." She huffed. "It all makes sense now. The walking, the thinking, the steaming the wrinkles out of your brain."

One ankle squared over the opposite knee, Sebastian slumped down to sit on his tailbone, shoved both hands back over his hair and laced his fingers there on top of his head. "I've never lied to you, Erin. You know that. I was vague. Ambiguous. Elusive, even. But I never said a word that wasn't the truth."

She crossed one long leg over the other. Filmy scarves fluttered with the movement then settled to expose thighs near enough to nude to toss a blip into the rhythm of his pulse. Her chin jutted forward—her spirited nature warning him he wasn't in for an easy time of it.

"Then what the hell is this truth?" she asked. "You get to call all the shots in this arrangement, is that it? I don't have any say in how we play things out?"

"This was my shot to call, Erin."

"No. It wasn't. Not when you did it because of—"

"Because of you?" he asked, cutting her off as frustration mounted. "Why else would I do it?"

"I don't know, Sebastian." The skin over the knuckles of her laced fingers tightened. "I'm too tired to deal with this cryptic conversation. Why don't you just tell me why and save me the trouble of sorting out the puzzle pieces?"

She was neither dense nor naive. What she was was wracked with some misplaced guilt over a decision *he* had made. A telling realization that he knew her that well, when he'd worked hard to convince himself none of his knowledge about her went that deep.

"I've watched you drive yourself insane the past few weeks, working to pull this party together. And then Courtland's comes along with an advertising budget you don't have and, what?" He dropped his hands to the chair arms and held tight. "You expect me to sit back and let you be steamrolled when I can stop it from happening? I don't think so."

"Allow me to be skeptical about your altruism. For whatever reason, you've made it a point to avoid involvement with the city, with your fans, even with your neighbors," she said and waved an encompassing hand. "Except for me. And I really don't buy that you'd break your long time seclusion for the sake of good sex."

Sebastian ground his jaw. "I didn't do it because of the sex."

"Then that leaves you doing it because you feel you owe me for something, which you don't." Her spine straightened further. "You haven't taken advantage of me. You haven't demanded anything I haven't wanted to give. And this is not the sort of sacrifice one lover makes for another...not when being lovers has nothing to do with being in love."

His jaw remained tight, making it hard to maintain a level tone of voice. "Can you find a place for friendship in your conspiracy theory?"

She considered his explanation for no longer than it took her to blink it away. "This seems to go beyond the bounds of friendship."

Talk about hardheaded women. "Wouldn't you do the same for Cali?"

"Sure, but Cali and I have been best friends for three years. You and I have been intimately acquainted for only a month. I just can't make the same leap. It's way too much of a sacrifice." She pressed her lips together as if holding back the rest of what she had to say. And then she let it go. "I can't decide which is stronger. The need to thank you, or the urge to tell you to take a flying leap."

Sebastian's irritation began a slow upward climb, approaching that place where he was afraid he was going to regret his words—and very possibly his actions. "Why are we even having this conversation, Erin? What's done is done. It can't be changed. All we can do is go on from here."

Erin tossed up both hands. "Sure. Let's go on from here. Where exactly are we going to go?"

Take it slow, bonehead. Nice and slow and easy. If he could manage to find the right words—and how hard could that be for a writer—they might emerge from tonight with at least their friendship intact. "Your party was a hit so, if anything, I'd say you're headed into your second year of business in a very big way."

For an extended heartbeat she maintained eye contact, allowing him to see the flurry of thoughts as her mind processed the implication of his suggestion. But the longer he watched, the longer she remained silent, the clearer it became that a second year of business failed to offer any appeal.

He shifted in the chair and leaned forward, bracing both forearms on his side of her desk. "I don't get it, Erin. Isn't this what you wanted?"

She raised a questioning brow. "Which part? Yes, I wanted the party to succeed. I can't stand the idea of blowing all that effort. Or all that money."

She might as well have added the "but" because Sebastian heard it loud and clear. "And the second year of business? After the amazing first year you just celebrated?"

Again she paused, taking a long moment to reflect before asking, "Was it really that amazing?"

Was she looking for validation? Surely she recognized the height of her success. "Your granddad would've loved what you've done."

"You think so?" she asked, a tiny quirk lifting one corner of her mouth. She pushed up from her chair, crossed to the corner file cabinet above which hung an eight-by-ten photo of Rory behind the bar of the original Devon Paddington's.

She stared at the framed snapshot, then turned to lean against the file cabinet, her hands behind her and the scarves of her costume floating like ethereal ghosts in the air. "I'm not so sure I agree."

"Why wouldn't he?" he asked, then quickly changed his approach. "Don't forget. I've lived here awhile. I've watched what you've done from the beginning."

She was too far away. Sebastian rose, walked to the end of her desk and propped a hip on the corner. "In one year you've turned this place from beer hall to a slick urban bar."

She gave a delicate little snort, stared down at the toes of her clear glass-looking shoes. "And now I'm bringing in authors. Next thing I'll be having poetry readings and performance art and who the hell knows what else."

"And what's wrong with that?"

She rolled her eyes, dropped her head back against the wooden drawers. "Only that Rory is probably turning over in his grave."

Amazing. Totally frigging amazing. "You know, Erin. You've just had a kick-ass party. The crowd was capacity all night. Yes, I know. A lot of them came when they heard about the signing."

Erin huffed. "A lot? Try seventy-five percent."

"That's bullshit and you know it. They came for me, but they stayed for you. Because of what you've accomplished here with what your granddad left you." He crossed his arms over his chest so he wouldn't choke her into admitting the error of her ways. "And you can't even enjoy your own success because you're worried what Rory might think."

The fire returned to her eyes; her chin came up higher, her shoulders straighter than before. "Rory gave up everything, Sebastian. Everything. He came here to take care of me when I was eleven years old. He never had a life of his own except for this place. So, yeah. Forgive me if I'm a little bit concerned that I'm not taking care of it the way he'd want."

How could this same woman who'd been unbelievably intuitive in her dealings with him not be equally perceptive about the man who'd raised her? "Your granddad loved being his own boss. The independence made him incredibly happy. Here or in Devon, it didn't matter. And you know that, the same way you know he'd want the same for you."

For the first time since he'd known her, tears shimmered in her eyes. Her lower lip quivered and her entire presence grew vulnerable and small. He couldn't stand the distance between them any longer.

He went to her, pulled her into his arms, pressed her

cheek to his chest, his chin to the top of her head and inhaled the fragrance of her hair that reminded him of green fields and sunshine.

He was so far gone he wondered how he'd survive walking away. "Be true to yourself. That's the best way to honor his memory."

"What if being true to myself means dumping the bar?"

"The only way you can disappoint anyone is by not doing what's right for you. Even if it means selling the bar." Her hands slipped around his waist, making it harder to ready himself to back away. "We all have to do what's right for us. That's the only thing that matters in the end."

For a moment it seemed like she'd forgotten to breathe and then she stiffened and asked, "And what's right for you?"

You can do this. You can let her down easy. Yeah, he could let her go and drop his heart in the trash can on his way out the door. "A book I've wanted to write for a while. It's different, not my usual Slater stuff. First I had to convince my agent I wasn't going to crash his gravy train. Then I had to work out a schedule with my demon contracts."

He gave a small shrug before stepping away. "Basically, the time had to be right."

Erin threaded fingers through her hair, pushing it out of her face. She stepped around him and moved to the far side of her visitor's chair, as if needing both the barrier and the distance. "So, now the time is right?"

He nodded, and he followed, even though he knew what he had to say would be best said with the cushion of space she'd given him instead of from where her subtle scent enticed him. "I haven't been this excited about a project in a very long time."

He wanted to add more, to tell her this last month spent

in her company had renewed his creative energy. He wanted to explain how he'd fed off her enthusiasm for her party, off her drive to save a business she considered more burden than blessing.

He wanted her to know that with her, in her, he'd found the part of himself missing since he left to fend for himself at eleven years of age. And that he'd finally learned his soul had never been stronger than since finding its mate.

But those weren't the things to say when the truth was he didn't know any other way to live than on his own.

"That means you're leaving, doesn't it?"

"I'll still live above you."

"But you're leaving. You won't be around."

He nodded because she'd put into words the number one truth he couldn't bring himself to admit. "No. I won't."

And then he went to her, took her face in his hands, cradling her gently as he lowered his head and brushed his lips to hers. She was so incredibly sweet when she trembled. And she tasted like so many good things he hadn't yet had time to explore.

He moved his hands into her hair and pulled her lower lip between his until she closed her eyes and shuddered, her hands moving to his back where she pulled his T-shirt free from his jeans and caressed the skin beneath.

She held him tenderly, telling him with tiny flicks of her tongue to his of her feelings. Of the wonder of what they'd found together. Of the regret bound in the impossibilities of their lives. He hated that he'd caused her to suffer and soothed what he could of her sorrow by ending the kiss to hold her close.

She sighed into his T-shirt, the warmth of her breath heating the fabric damp from her tears. When he finally set her away, he found it difficult to speak, difficult to swallow. So he squeezed her hand once, his fingers trailing over hers as he let her go and headed for the door.

ERIN DOUBTED THERE would be another Halloween night in history to rival the gore of this one. She couldn't think about Sebastian or Paddington's or anything right now. Right now, all she had the will to do was climb into her car and go home.

First she had to close up the office so she could close up the bar and the kitchen. She was definitely going to have to pay Cali double-time for taking care of things the last half hour. Yet, before Erin could make the short walk to shut down her computer, another e-mail arrived.

From: Tess Norton
Sent: Saturday
To: Erin Thatcher; Samantha Tyler
Subject: Re: The Secrets That Men Keep
Ryder EFFING Falco? You have got to be kidding. Oh, my God, you know how much I love his books. I've read every one. Some twice! Holy shit, girl!

Actually that expletive was more about that, uh, little bomb you dropped. Love? Did I read this correctly? LOVE as in LOVE?

My, my. Not exactly the goal of the Men To Do project, but then, who cares? You're in love. What you didn't mention is if he is in love back. How could he not be, but still. Men are a strange species, and I've found it's best if I don't try to anthropomorphize them. <g> Seriously, I need to hear the details about this, and I need to hear your voice, and I need to be much wiser than I am, which is going to be hard to do in the next 24 hours, so don't do anything drastic. Chocolate. My best (and seemingly only) advice. Love, Tess

Well, one thing was certain, thought Erin, shutting down her computer. Sebastian did not love her in return. He liked her well enough. He lusted after her without a doubt. His investment had to be more than physical or he would never have revealed his identity. But love? Ha! Love was not part of his emotional capacity.

Or, if it was, he refused himself the pleasure, burying his head in make-believe worlds where life was simply black and white. She wanted to hate him for it, but all she could think of was that little toy truck.

A knock on the door brought Erin's head around expecting Cali. But it was Robin, one of the other servers to work the party tonight. "Where's Cali?"

"Said she was feeling like crap. I told her to beat it and I'd finish up. Which I have, so…" She pulled off the tail of her cat-woman costume. "I'm heading out. The caterer will be back Monday afternoon with a truck to pick up the fountain and rocks."

"Thanks for handling the cleanup." Robin, Laurie, Cali and Will had all gone above and beyond the call of duty. "I think the fact that we actually pulled this off wiped me out. I hadn't realized how exhausted I was."

"You deserved the downtime. You just missed a hell of a party. Oh, there's a guy out here who's been waiting to talk to you. We told him you were busy but he insisted," Robin said, adding air apostrophes around the last word.

"I need to come out and lock up anyway." Erin crossed the room, cut off the light and locked the office door. She hoped her visitor was made of strong stuff because she had a swift kick ready for anyone with a penis. "I'll show him out, if you'll hang around for a minute?"

"Not a problem." Cat tail now draped around her neck,

Robin grabbed her purse from beneath the bar. "He's at the front door. I'll leave that way."

"Thanks, Robin. And for all your help tonight, too."

"Sure. I'll wait here till you're done." She slid into the nearest booth while Erin headed toward the front door.

Her visitor leaned one shoulder on the brick wall and wore nothing remotely resembling a Halloween costume—unless his costume was the epitome of *dressed for success.*

His hair was fashionably short, grayed at the temples. He wore a long black wool coat over a pair of designer pants and Italian loafers worth more than her black and white cookie bill.

Intriguing, she thought, and approached. "May I help you?"

"Ms. Thatcher?" he asked and she nodded. "My name is Nolan Ford."

Erin took his offered hand and shook. A firm business-like shake. "What can I do for you Mr. Ford?"

"I wonder if you've ever considered selling this place because I'd like very much to talk to you about buying it."

THANK GOODNESS FOR twenty-four hour Kinko's, Cali thought, ruining yet another page of the screenplay. She'd had the sense to make five sets at the copy center earlier, anticipating that she'd never get the changes reversed the first time out.

Having the disk would've made this whole groveling process easier. But her disk was in Will's laptop where she'd left it after making the initial revisions based on Sebastian's suggestions. She didn't have a computer of her own, using Will's or renting time at Kinko's.

Since she'd saved her edits over the original file without making a backup, it was six in one hand, a half dozen in the other whether she did this on the screen or by hand. She supposed Will might have a printed copy of the original since he was so emotionally attached to the beast. But knowing his version would never pass a credibility test, she'd tossed all the copies she'd had.

Yes, she'd learned her lesson. Always make a backup file. She'd learned another lesson as well. *Men sucked.* She wadded the paper and tossed the crumpled ball across the room. No, that wasn't exactly the truth. Not all men sucked and men didn't suck all of the time. But right now neither scenario fit her mood.

Especially since she was rapidly compromising her own self-respect. She was giving in because she didn't want to lose the one man who meant more to her than any single man before. Her rationalization that this was only a project for a grade and not any sort of life-altering decision didn't do much to keep the situation from rubbing against her personal grain.

She was getting close to hating herself as much as she hated Will. Hating Will made perfect sense, after all, since she loved him so desperately. And this last week of working together and taking classes together hadn't gone particularly smoothly since they hadn't said a single civil word.

A knock on the door of her efficiency apartment sent her pencil scrabbling off the end of the page. *Finally.* Erin and the damn bottle of wine she'd promised to drop by with when she'd phoned earlier this afternoon. Cali tossed her paperwork to the love seat and hopped up to get the door.

Only it wasn't Erin. It was Will, looking like his Sunday off hadn't been very relaxing either. He hadn't shaved and his glasses didn't do much to hide the circles under his eyes. She supposed she didn't look much better. She was wearing ragged denim shorts and the stubble on her legs matched that on his face. She'd been sleeping alone this last week. Shaving had hardly seemed to matter.

Oh, well. She was human. If she hadn't been she wouldn't be tearing her heart out over what she had done and what she was now doing with the screenplay. She would've cared less about Will's feelings and more about the grade. Cared more as well about getting him to admit he was wrong. Suddenly, that didn't seem to matter.

Wearing a distressed leather bomber jacket and gray athletic T-shirt, he leaned against the doorjamb, shoulders shrugged up against the cold, hands stuffed in the pockets of his baggy black cords. "Hi."

It was all he said. Cali gave a little wave, an even smaller smile.

Will inclined his head. "Do you mind if I come in?"

She pulled the door farther open and ushered him inside. She still didn't trust her voice. She pushed the door closed and turned the lock out of habit—not because she planned to never let him go.

And then she remembered the screenplay. The pages tossed willy-nilly over the love seat. She remembered at the same time Will spied her work.

"What're you doing?" His gaze cut sharply back to hers.

She crossed her arms over her chest. Her faded pink sweatshirt hiked up to expose her middle. "Trying to fix a big mistake."

He dropped into the seat probably still warm from her body and picked up the pages, shuffling them into order, flipping through them one at a time. Cali could only cringe at her very raw, very rough, way too often sarcastically noted corrections.

And then there was that note on the fourth page...

Her face flamed and she jumped forward to snatch the

pages from his hands. Too late, of course, because he held them high, reached out and pulled her into his lap.

She tumbled there like the biggest buffoon. Her heart on her sleeve wasn't even an issue. Not when it was right there in a sketch of Cupid shooting his arrow and a tree-carving caption that read C.T. + W.C. 4-EVER.

"Don't be so grabby," he said. "I want to see what you've done."

"I haven't done much," she said, hoping to dissuade him from looking beyond the first page or two. "I was trying to remember as much as I could of your original version."

"*My* original version, huh?" Will settled back to get comfortable, spreading his knees and shifting Cali into the corner of the love seat and onto one thigh, her legs draped across his lap.

He had one arm around her back so that she rested in the curve of his shoulder. His other hand was busy flipping through the pages. She wasn't sure whether she dreaded more his discovery of her leg stubble or her childish scrawl.

He got to the fourth page and stopped, glancing the length of the page before canting his head around to look her in the eye. "What happened to this being a joint project?"

"I think it's obvious that we've jointly gone about as far as we can go. We might share the same idea for the end, but we'll never agree on the means to get us there." She looked at him, and it was all she could do not to lean forward and nuzzle his cheek.

She knew his scent and his warmth and his texture and it was so hard not to wrap her arms around him. Especially with the way he was looking at her, with an expression she couldn't quite decipher but raised her hopes nonetheless. "Why did you come here, Will?"

His eyes grew glassy and bright. He heaved an enormous sigh as if blowing out the last of his pent-up anger. And then he grinned his Cheshire cat grin. "To tell you that you were right. That I was wrong. That I don't have half the talent you do and absolutely no confidence that I'll ever learn enough to 'get it.'"

"What are you talking about? Your instincts are great. And we all need a little fine-tuning now and again. I'm certainly not perfect. If I were, the changes would've been my idea, not Sebastian's." She stopped talking then, realizing she'd lifted her hand to cup his cheek and remembering nothing about deciding he needed her touch.

Her feelings for him were that natural, that right, and that awareness made it easy to make the admission she'd been holding back. "I only did it because I love you."

Will dropped the pages he was holding and reached up, covering her fingers where she still caressed his face. He squeezed, then moved her hand to his mouth and kissed her palm.

With his gaze locked on hers, he softly said, "Then love me by making me be my best."

Six Months Later…

GOODBYE, PADDINGTON'S. Hello, rest of my life.

Erin would never have believed she could walk away from the sale of the bar with such a light heart. Especially after the months of angst and worry over doing the right thing for herself and for Rory.

Now those days and nights seemed as if they'd never happened. She owed such a debt of gratitude to Cali and Will, to Tess and Samantha, and to Sebastian for making her face all the truths she needed to face.

She owed a debt of a different nature to Nolan Ford,

for his timely toss of a life preserver into the middle of her personal storm.

She and Sebastian had spoken a few times over the last several months but had never shared more than could be said in a six-floor elevator ride, a trek through the parking garage, or while standing and sorting mail in the basement mailroom.

His book was going well, he'd told her. Practically writing itself; he hoped to finish before summer. She was glad, she'd told him. Because that meant by summer they'd both be free of the pressing obligations wedged between their friendship.

He hadn't had much to say in response, but that was okay. Erin had learned how to hear what he didn't say by looking into his eyes. His eyes had given her hope. Every time they'd run into one another, his eyes had given her hope.

She'd sold the bar and gotten her act together. This fall she would be starting back to school to finish her degree, though in truth she'd be starting over. The study of business had never truly held any appeal. And after the publicity generated by the Paddington's On Main Halloween party, she was much more interested in marketing.

But right now it was summer.

She didn't know if Sebastian had finished his book, but he hadn't turned her away when she'd called earlier and told him she was on her way up. She took that as a good sign that he wasn't averse to seeing her. She never had really thought he'd be averse. She just wasn't sure how welcoming he might be.

She couldn't let doubts of his reaction deter her. This is what she had to do. The same way she'd sold Paddington's and, working with her advisor, put together a plan to return to school.

It had taken her a while to come to grips with the truth of what Sebastian had said that night he'd walked out of her life. But he had been right. Rory had given her the means to pursue her dream. He'd loved her and would never have wanted her to run the bar unless it meant as much to her as it had always meant to him. What she'd been doing, she'd been doing for Rory out of a misplaced sense of guilt and obligation.

And she'd finally looked beyond the tangible assets of Rory's gift to the intent. The same way she'd finally come to accept the intent behind Sebastian's sacrifice. And that was the reason she was here. His exposure as Ryder Falco had not been about saving the bar, but about showing her the worth and the depth of a man's love.

A love she returned beyond reason.

She knocked; he didn't answer. She turned the knob, found the door open, let herself in. The front room was dark, blues playing on the stereo. She'd never been up on her artists but she was pretty damn sure this was B.B. King. He was singing "Hold On! I'm Comin'."

She wanted to laugh out loud at the fluke. Especially since she knew Sebastian would be in the shower listening to the music pour through the bathroom's speakers built into the ceiling above the steamy enclosure. She couldn't wait to join him.

She found him exactly where she'd known he would be. She'd opened the door to the bathroom to the sound of the blues and running water and Sebastian was there, sitting beneath the center showerhead, legs spread wide, his palms on his thighs, the whole of his sex heavy from the heat.

For a very long moment she could do nothing but stare.

He made such a picture of male beauty that breathing no longer seemed to matter as much as filling her senses with the memories of making love. And it had been love. Maybe not that very first time here in this shower. She hadn't even known him then. And still she didn't know all she wanted to know. What she hoped she'd have a lifetime to learn.

She slipped out of her clothes and stepped into his arms, knowing no decision she'd ever made had been so right. He felt glorious. All male and head-to-toe hard and slick and wet. She loved the bunch of muscles at his shoulders and running along either side of his spine.

She loved the strength in his neck, the tendons and veins there as well as those in his forearms. There wasn't a thing about him she didn't find perfectly gorgeous. *Especially that*, she thought, grinning as his erection came to life against her belly.

Lifting her head, she leaned back far enough to look into his eyes. His expression epitomized tenderness. And love. And the pain of a man caught in an unbearable loss. So silly. He'd never lost her. She'd always been here.

"Do you remember when you kissed me Halloween night in my office?" He nodded and she continued. "I couldn't tell you then that I love you. So I'm telling you now."

"I love you, too." And his mouth came down hard to take possession of hers. His lips devoured, his tongue swept over hers like a tidal wave from which she had no way to escape.

As if escape was any more of an option than telling him no when he backed her into the wall and urged her legs around his waist. He pressed forward, upward, filling her body with one smooth thrust, then another, another, another still until he'd set a rhythm from which there was no return.

His mouth never left hers, not for a second, not even when he came and took her with him, tumbling her into an incredible abyss and catching her when she reached the end of her completion.

Only then, when she'd finished, when he'd seen to the last of her tremors, grinding there where she needed the friction one last shuddering time, only then did he lower her to her feet and relinquish possession of her mouth.

Thank goodness because she could hardly catch her breath by breathing through her nose. Water cascaded and she held him tight, feeling his heartbeat thunder beneath her cheek resting on his chest. She didn't think she'd ever in her life been this happy, this complete.

Or this amazingly tired. "Tell me a story."

He chuckled, stroked a hand down the back of her hair. "Once upon a time—"

"No." She shook her head, his skin sweetly salty when she stuck out her tongue and lapped. "Get to the good part."

This time when he spoke, he did so on a quivering comet tail of emotion. "And they lived happily ever after."

Epilogue

THE SECRETS OF AN INNOCENCE
By Sebastian Gallo

Chapter 1

It came to him later that the defining moment of his life had occurred when he wasn't even looking. The beauty of the memory caught him off guard as had the event at the time. He'd never imagined he'd need one single woman in his life more than he'd feel the need to breathe. But he had.

She'd been his sustenance for all the long years of his life, the safety net catching him at every fall, the support that kept him upright when the world around him came tumbling down. He loved her more than he'd ever known a man could love a woman. And, most amazing of all, she loved him back.

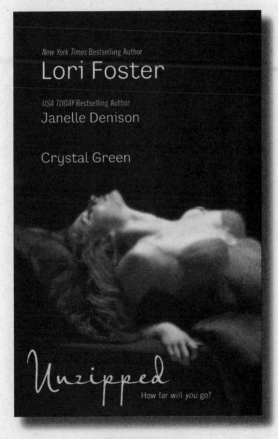

Blaze™

Red-Hot Reads—
look out for more sizzling stories!